Also by Alysa Wishingrad

The Verdigris Pawn

BETWEEN MONSTERS AND MARVELS

ALYSA WISHINGRAD

HARPER
An Imprint of HarperCollinsPublishers

Between Monsters and Marvels
Copyright © 2023 by Alysa Wishingrad
All rights reserved. Printed in the United States of America.
No part of this book may be used or reproduced in any manner
whatsoever without written permission except in the case of
brief quotations embodied in critical articles and reviews. For
information address HarperCollins Children's Books, a division of
HarperCollins Publishers, 195 Broadway, New York, NY 10007.
www.harpercollinschildrens.com

Library of Congress Control Number: 2023932840
ISBN 978-0-06-324487-0

Typography by Laura Mock
23 24 25 26 27 LBC 5 4 3 2 1
First Edition

For all my Beasties.

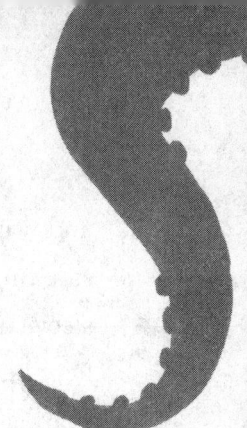

CHAPTER ONE
An Awful Girl

Dare Coates was an awful girl.

Everyone on Barrow's Bay said so. The adults, hiding behind satin-gloved hands, whispered it through tight-lipped sneers. But the children said it out loud, every chance they got. On the streets, in class, and they were saying it now as Dare stalked out of the schoolhouse.

She didn't even want to be in that pathetic Founder's Day pageant, let alone play the monster. But then she'd be condemned to repeating the entire year's lessons under the schoolmarm's tutelage. There was awful, and then there was the unbearable.

Dare tried to lose Frances Cooper and the rest of the class as they trailed after her, slinging taunts and teases all the way through the center of town. She wound past the shops, around the gazebo on the village green, and even into the middle of the street, hoping to ditch them among the passing carriages and wagons. And still she made no effort to conceal that her stockings were torn, her hair a tangle of knots, and the left sleeve of her favorite dress was ripped wide open. Instead, she kept her gaze pegged dead ahead and her upper lip fixed in a snarl, a warning to passersby to steer clear.

It'd always been easy enough to ignore them when they teased her that her hair wasn't done in the latest style, for rescuing a spider from certain death at the hands of one of the boys, or for having no shame about speaking her mind. In fact, she went out of her way to be a walking affront to everything the *GOOD* people of Barrow's Bay valued—beauty, conformity, and the sparkle of wealth. She was happy to be a thornbush among the lilies, for even the sharpest thorns serve a purpose. They're a warning, protection. A defense. And Dare was more than content to shine every one of her points and angles until they gleamed.

But they crossed a line when they talked about her father. Her kind, mild-mannered father who served them so dutifully deserved more. Respect, gratitude. Just because the last monsters were said to have been killed off while he was still an apprentice didn't mean his position as Captain of the Guard was useless. How could everyone be so certain that none of the monsters had survived, that they weren't just hiding out waiting to reclaim their island? What would the *GOOD* people do then, if Captain Coates wasn't on duty?

No. They could say what they liked about Dare, but clever slights and cutting barbs weren't nearly as effective as a balled-up fist when they said those awful things about her father.

Frances Cooper got what she deserved, and Dare would never apologize.

"Watch out!" Gavin Lord, the self-appointed head boy, shouted back to his band of followers. "There's a monster stalking the streets!"

"You know there are no more monsters," Melody Day called back. "Dare just smells like one."

"I heard she has a tail, and toenails like talons!" Talbott Redmond snorted. That idiot always laughed at his own jokes.

Dare kept walking, holding her awful at bay.

But then, just like Frances had during the pageant rehearsal, Gavin went too far. "At least her father can finally earn his salary by catching her."

That broke it.

Dare let loose a howl fit to curdle milk and spun on that gaggle of twits. She rushed at them, yelling and gnashing her teeth, ready to knock them all to the ground if she had to.

That was enough to send them scrambling back, leaving Dare room to cut through the gardens surrounding Founder's Hall and head to the narrow lane that led out to the salt marsh.

Not even Gavin would follow her out there. Like everyone

else on the Island, he might pretend to know there were absolutely no more monsters, but he wasn't brave enough to put that theory to the test.

Once she was safely outside the town limits, sand and dune grass crunching underfoot, Dare began to uncoil. The relentless loop replaying the events of the day was replaced now with the promise of checking on the turtles' nesting grounds. This was the Barrow's Bay she loved. The wild, untamed shoreline of the back bay. The great oak trees, dripping with moss, bowing to one another on either side of the lane. A wilderness that had been thriving long before the *Paragon*, with its sole survivor, had washed up on these shores three generations ago.

Sometimes when she was out here alone like this, Dare would pretend it was she, not that milksop Louise, who had survived the shipwreck and landed here all alone on this island filled with monsters. Stronger and far braver than Louise, Dare would have fought the beasts off herself. And when Bascombe Barrow and his crew landed, looking for survivors from the wreck of the *Paragon*, she would have welcomed them to *her* island—Dare's Bay—then told them to shove off. No fussy mansions, no shops, no schoolhouses, and, most especially, no other people allowed!

Well, there was *one* other person Dare would have allowed on her island. Father. She couldn't imagine a life without him, so she always included him in her game. Everything she knew about monsters came from him—their names, what they looked like, which ones had terrible claws, fangs, and poisonous spikes—all of which made this imagined world of hers that much richer.

But she was in no mood for playing today. The schoolmarm casting her as the garbinol in the pageant was cruel, especially with Frances playing the part of Louise. The monster's attack on Louise was known to be vicious. Dare was only playing her part; Frances was the one who had changed the script and added all those thinly veiled insults. And yet Dare was the one who had gotten in trouble. Again.

Word of the fight had probably already reached Mother. While the balmy weather on Barrow's Bay might be its greatest asset, gossip was its most precious commodity. Dare couldn't risk going home yet, not until she was certain Father had returned from his rounds. He had a way of smoothing Mother's anxiety and softening all of Dare's edges and angles.

Dare followed the lane all the way around the salt marsh, past the dunes, and down to the beach, where she stopped to take off her boots. She liked to feel the sand underneath her stockinged feet, and she posed less of a danger to the turtles this way. Should she happen to step on a nest by accident, she was less likely to harm any of the buried eggs.

She made her way down the beach, gingerly hopping from one foot to the other all the way to the turtles' traditional laying grounds. The eggs should be hatching any day now.

She'd only been lucky enough to see the march of the hatchlings once, for as soon as the baby turtles broke through their shells, they took off at a waddling run into the sea. It was the funniest and most miraculous sight she'd ever seen, and she'd been hoping ever since to witness it again.

But as the laying grounds came into view, Dare stopped, the hairs on her arms bristling.

The entire nesting area had been laid to waste.

The sand was littered with large holes and knee-high mounds, and all those soft, precious eggs had been scattered in every direction.

Thinking, and yet not thinking, Dare hurried to collect as many eggs as she could, to rebury them before it was too late. But it was no use—she couldn't find any that hadn't been cracked, or exposed to the hot sun for too long and drained of their treasured cargo.

The entire clutch of hatchlings had been demolished.

Dare's awful began to rise. Whoever did this would pay! She'd get her boots on, then race straight back to town, up the front stairs of Founder's Hall, and into Governor Kingston's office, demanding an inquest.

Then she saw them. Long claw marks carved deep into the sand. Dare wanted to believe it was a common coyote, or a greedy racoon. But there was only one thing she knew of that possessed claws as long, as thick, and as capable of moving such great amounts of sand as these.

Yet it was what she spotted mixed in with the sand that fixed it for certain. Clumps of hair.

No, fur.

Long, curly fur, dusty orange with dark green spots.

Fingers of fear wrapped around Dare's neck, making it hard to catch a full breath as she flipped through the catalog of monsters in her mind. Which ones had curly coats with this coloring? Front claws that long?

But it was too hard to think, so her legs took over.

Dare raced across the sand, barely remembering to grab her boots, and then all the way back to the safety of her own home and her father's protection.

Dare slammed the door shut and was headed for her father's den when her mother stepped out of the parlor. "You look a fright. And no boots on? What have you gotten into this time?"

There was no answer Dare could give that wouldn't send Mother off into one of her worried flaps. So instead Dare made to push past her. But Mother reached out then to try to smooth Dare's hair, and the prongs of her wedding ring got caught in Dare's tangled locks. "Oh, Dare. Why must you be this way?"

Dare bit her cheeks, trying to conceal the urgency roiling her blood while Mother worked to get them untangled. She finally managed to slip her finger out, although the ring remained ensnarled. "If you'd let me style your hair in a proper fashion, this wouldn't have happened."

No, this wouldn't have happened if Mother had kept her hands and opinions to herself and just let Dare go. But there was no point in saying so and starting a row, not now, not when Dare had far more important things to do.

"We're going to have to cut it out. Then how will you look? And what's this? What happened to your dress? Ripped straight up the seam. Ruthann has enough work around here without constantly having to repair your clothes...." Mother's face fell, the pink fading from her cheeks as understanding dawned.

"It's fine. I'll sew it myself." Dare tried to wave her worry away.

But Mother wasn't going to be waved off. "Did you get in another fight? Please, I've begged you. Your father's position exists by the good graces of the governor. Do you want us sent off island, back to the mainland? We'll wind up penniless, in the Must with the rest of the unfortunates. Is that what you want?" Mother didn't yell, or even take a scolding tone. She never did. Still, the grievous weight of her disappointment and fear could be measured in tons, not pounds.

"You worry too much about the wrong things." Dare pulled away and continued toward the door at the end of the hall.

"Don't bother him." Mother twisted at the place on her finger where her ring should be. "He only got in at sunrise."

Dare stopped. This was the third time this week.

Her fear of monsters paled when compared to her fear for her father's well-being.

Like the snap of a twig underfoot, the mood shifted. That Dare and her mother were too often at odds no longer mattered now that they were both standing on the same side of a gulch of worry.

Dare smoothed her hair. "I'll see if he needs tea."

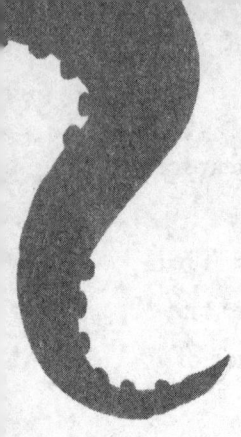

CHAPTER TWO
Torn Stitches

On the surface everything looked as it should in Father's office. He was, as usual, at his desk surrounded by a mountain of paperwork. Pretty, the small bird he'd rescued while out on patrol a few years back, was perched on his shoulder, also as usual. Father looked up and greeted Dare with a smile as he always did, but his cheeks were sunken, and dark circles filled the hollows below his eyes. Even Pretty's brilliant blue and green feathers were dulled. The air in the office had changed; it was heavy now, not with the usual scent of clean soap and beard oil, but with an aura of worry and anxiety.

Could he already know about what Dare had seen?

"You look like you've had an adventurous day so far." Father set Pretty on her perch and rose to envelop Dare in a hug.

"So do you." Dare never shied from being frank with her father, but he was wearing his weariness like a shroud. She'd proceed carefully, test the ground first. "I was out by the salt marsh."

Father winced as if he'd been bitten by a large bug. "You saw the nest."

Dare nodded.

"I was going to tell you." His voice was thin and reedy.

"So it's true, then." Dare let the face of a new reality wash over her. "The monsters are back."

"Of course not," Father chirped, some of his usual lightness returning. "It was an accident. Surveyors out testing the ground. They didn't know they'd chosen to dig in the middle of the turtles' laying grounds until it was too late."

"No. I saw claw marks in the sand, and a tuft of orange fur with—"

"Marks from their tools, is all. And a piece of fabric. Nothing more, I'm sure."

"It wasn't fabric, it was fur. I felt it. Come back there with me, I'll show you."

"You've got a wild and wonderful imagination. Of course, you'd want to make sense of the loss of all those eggs." Father kissed Dare's forehead, then ever so gently extricated Mother's ring from her hair. "See that your mother gets this back quickly. She'll be worried about it."

He was tucking the ring into Dare's hand when his eyes landed on her ruined sleeve.

Dare pulled away and folded her arms behind her back;

the last thing he needed was to think about how he would afford new clothes for her.

"Don't worry about it," she said, even though she was certain the very fibers of the fabric were too shredded to repair.

"There's nothing we can't fix, dear Dare." Father settled her into his leather-backed chair and reached into a wooden box he kept in a drawer of his cramped desk.

That wondrous box somehow always produced the perfect solution for Dare's troubles. It could be something as simple as a drawing of Pretty, a newly sharpened pencil, or a piece of chocolate. This time, it was a needle threaded with a length of green thread, a perfect match for her dress.

Stitch by stitch, Dare began to feel whole again.

"You and I are cut from a different kind of cloth than the rest of the Island, Dare," Father said as he worked. "The coarseness of our weave scratches their more refined sensibilities, but our thicker fibers make us more durable."

"And tougher," Dare added with a toss of her head. "The worst I got was a ripped sleeve. She barely grazed me."

"Frances Cooper again? I thought we agreed, no more fights."

"I tried. I did. But . . ."

There really was no "But." Both Father and Dare knew that.

Ever since she'd started at that school, the other children had delighted in taunting Dare, winding her up, then watching as she twisted and stormed. She'd begged her parents to let her study at home like she had when she was younger, but Father's position entitled her to a place at school alongside the Island's elite. Having Dare enrolled there was a privilege Mother wore like a badge of belonging.

Mother wasn't the one who had to pull spitballs out of her hair or write lines on the chalkboard every time she stood up for herself.

"I told the schoolmarm I didn't want to be in that tedious pageant. Then she went and made me the garbinol and put that smelly costume on me."

"That's a wonderful part to play. You get to growl and stomp. And eat Louise."

Father showed his teeth and snarled, slashed the air with his hands crooked like claws.

But Dare didn't laugh as she usually did when Father tried to cheer her up. "She'd be as sour as bog berries."

"I see." Father turned serious, concerned now. "I assume Frances is playing the part of Louise. Were you hoping for that role?"

"No!" Dare might as well have sucked a lemon. "All she does is cry and faint. I don't understand how she supposedly survived on her own for an entire month among the monsters, only to suddenly get weak and die just as help arrived. I don't care that's what happened, it's an insipid story and I don't know why we tell it every single year."

"Louise's story is the story of Barrow's Bay. We are fortunate to live here on this paradise. We have much to celebrate on Founder's Day."

Even though he and Dare shared the same intolerance for people who had nothing better to do with their days than tear others down, Father never said a word against anyone or anything.

"Frances said you were useless, that the governor was wasting good money paying your salary and we should be shipped off to the mainland where we belong. I had to make her stop."

"So you believed her?"

Dare wanted to say "Never!" but there was a corner of her heart that worried Frances was right. If it was true that all the monsters were gone, then what purpose did he serve? Yet Dare would never say that to him; instead, she tried to just shrug it off.

"They're only words, Dare. Remember, we're durable." Father pounded his chest, a sly smile peeking out through his tired eyes. "Some people talk to convince themselves they believe what others have told them to. Hold fast to what you know."

Father called to Pretty, summoning her with the whistle he'd trained her by: three rapid repetitions of the same sound—*Tweeewooo tweeewooo tweeewooo!*—followed by a nod of his head toward Dare, and the bird hopped from her perch onto Dare's shoulder, trilling her sweet song.

She was a petite thing with a twisted beak and eyes set too close together. Her wings were bent, and her tail was broken off to a nub. She'd never have survived in the wild had Father not found her that night a few years back. But her blue and green feathers were as soft as down, her song a soothing lullaby, and when she nuzzled Dare's ear, as she was now, Dare was instantly cheered.

"Go back to school tomorrow. Head high, rehearse for the pageant, then, on Founder's Day, play that garbinol with all you have," Father continued. "You've got performing in your veins, just like Madam. Go on, make her proud."

"Your aunt is a star. I doubt she was ever made to play the monster."

"The best of us have all been made to play the monster at some point or another."

There in his warm office, with Pretty perched on her shoulder and her father working at stitching her back together, it was easy for Dare to view the world and her place in it the way he did. She could see herself through his eyes and like what she saw. She could envision herself being as calm and placid as he was. After all, they had the same sense of humor (dark), the same nose (angular), and the same hair color (ashy brown).

Yet there was a difference between them. Captain Coates knew how to keep to himself; he was rarely seen anywhere on the Island except when on his rounds, which made him practically invisible. If you couldn't be rich on Barrow's Bay, the least you could do was be inconspicuous.

Dare was anything but inconspicuous.

She promised herself that she would try harder to be more like him and less like herself. And though this wasn't the first time she'd made that vow, this time, it would stick. It had to.

Once he'd finished with the repair, Dare's father knotted off the thread and snipped it with a tiny pair of scissors.

"Stronger than ever."

As he put the sewing supplies away, he told her he'd make things right with her teacher and explain it all to Mother. He had a talent for presenting Dare's dustups in a way that both laid out the facts and smoothed the road ahead for his daughter.

He set Pretty back on her perch, kissed Dare on the top of her head, then sent her off as he always did, saying, "Remember always: you are loved."

Dare worked hard to believe him, to be more like him, until the next day, when she stepped back into the world as she knew it, a world where girls who said horrid things and ripped her sleeve wide open were praised and comforted by the teacher while Dare was shamed and punished.

As the week continued, Father's patrols lasted longer and longer each day. He'd return more bedraggled, his uniform caked with mud, his cuffs soaking wet. He'd spend what little time he was at home holed up in his study, where Dare could hear him through the door, scratching out notes, wearing down quill after quill. He barely slept, insisting the curtains throughout the house remain drawn, and he refused to eat, subsisting instead on the endless pots of tea Ruthann set outside the door of his den.

There was no more tucking her in at bedtime. No stories filled with tales of the garbinol, caltungs, bandicots, or any of the other beastly monsters that once roamed the Island. No assurances of any kind.

After several more days of this, Mother's calm veneer cracked. She pushed Dare through the door, saying that if anyone could get through to him, it would be her. But Father barely looked up from the desk, littered with papers and dirty teacups.

"It's the monsters, isn't it?" She was certain this time. "I was right, they are back, aren't they?"

"Hush, now. I told you, it's nothing," he promised. "I'm tired, is all."

Dare went to let Pretty out of her cage, but her father waved her off as he dropped the cover over the birdcage. On her way back around the desk she stole a glance at the papers in front of him. She expected reports, lines of notes, not the series of aimless loops and lines he was drawing with his pen.

"What's that?" she asked.

"Just trying to find a direction, is all. Go on your way now, Dare." There was no cruelty in his voice, only resignation, as he hustled her out of his dusty burrow. "There's work to be done that only I can do."

Dare tried to convince herself that he was right about the fur and the claw marks. It was only some careless surveyors, not a monster. Yet just as the citizens of Barrow's Bay knew that every day would be balmy and bright, Dare knew a lie when she told herself one.

She took to finding a star every night to wish upon, promising to try even harder to be less awful, to try to fit in, if only Father would go back to his old self. But her wishes only pushed the promise of hope further away, until finally, the night before Founder's Day, Father returned from patrol in time to tuck Dare in.

He looked better, closer to his old self, all smiles and warm hugs.

The storm had passed. He was right: the only monsters had been the ones in her thoughts.

"Will you tell me a story tonight? One about the whiskwolf, maybe, or what about the jacklers? They're the ones that look like foxes, right? Or the garbinol and how it uses the spines on its forearms to slash and kill. It'll help me get ready for the pageant tomorrow." Dare growled and made her hands into claws.

Father only shook his head and said, "We'll not speak of monsters anymore."

Then he rose from his seat next to her bed and turned to

leave her room. Perhaps it was a slip of the tongue caused by exhaustion, but instead of saying "Remember always: you are loved" as he usually did, Father paused to look back at Dare and said, "Remember always: you were loved."

The storm returned.

There should have been some consolation in knowing that her fears weren't a product of her imagination. Dare knew what she knew. But that, by definition, begged another, far scarier truth: monsters were still lurking somewhere on the Island.

CHAPTER THREE
A Funeral

The day Dare's father was killed was as fine as any other on Barrow's Bay. Founder's Day dawned with crisp morning air giving way to balmy sunshine and the slightest hint of a breeze. The trade winds guaranteed that clouds never lingered for very long and just enough rain fell to keep the land verdant and thriving.

Dare had been out back in the garden staring down her garbinol costume, trying to decide if she should hide out or see the rotten pageant through, when the news arrived. The sounds of the carriage pulling up to the front of the house were too clean, the creak of highly polished boots on the walkway too crisp to be anything other than an official visitor.

Dare understood what had happened even before the sound of Mother's wails floated out the kitchen window. She'd fought back the creep of fear all night after Father left her room.

Voices dripping with sympathy and care filtered into the garden. One had the well-practiced tone of someone trained to deliver bad news. That had to be the Comfort Officer, the poor fool who'd landed the job of telling people their loved ones had died. The other voice had the commanding edge of someone accustomed to being listened to and respected.

Governor Randolph Kingston.

That he'd come to the house to deliver the news meant that Father wasn't only dead, but that his death was either terribly heroic, or incredibly tragic.

Dare knew she should run inside to be with her mother. But she didn't want to move. She *couldn't* move. Light, sound, air, even time, they all disappeared as she slowly sank into a bottomless chasm of grief.

She remained there, on the bench—sinking, thinking, silently weeping—until Ruthann came out into the yard.

"Oh, Dare," the maid said, choking on her words. "Your father, he's gone. Taken from us too soon. What will we do?"

Dare looked at Ruthann, saw her tears, the pain in her eyes. The fear for her future.

But the loss of Father was not something Dare was willing to share. Others might be sad, they weren't broken like she was. Mother and Ruthann had other people who had loved them, understood them, who knew them as they wanted to be known. Dare had only ever had Father.

Dare wouldn't remember later how she got from the garden into the kitchen—no doubt Ruthann had led her by the hand—where words like *inquest*, *investigation*, and *tragedy* floated overhead like thunderclouds on the edge of bursting. Mother's hugs, the governor's stiff-fingered hand patting her on the head, even a weak smile offered by the Comfort Officer. None of it meant anything. Nothing meant anything anymore.

It was in that moment, standing in the kitchen surrounded by people who could only pretend to understand what she was feeling, that Dare began to build a bridge of anger and stone over that chasm of despair, thick enough to protect her poor shattered heart from every last shred of daylight.

Dare remained shuttered in her own thoughts for the next two days, going through the motions of life, only peeking out from underneath that bridge when Ruthann insisted she eat or change her clothes. When Mother said they'd be opening the house for mourning calls, Dare assumed it would be like every other time people were invited in. Mother would eagerly have Ruthann set out the best china, send for a tray of pastries they could barely afford, and style her hair in what she hoped was the very latest fashion. Then she'd sit perched on the settee in the parlor for hours, waiting, hoping, daring not to be disappointed. Dare wanted to shake her, make her understand that there was no reason to expect anything of other people, that they would always let you down.

But at the stroke of noon, the *GOOD* citizens of Barrow's

Bay and several dignitaries who'd come from the mainland for Founder's Day began filing into the house. They crowded into the parlor, drinking and eating enough to drain the stores in the pantry and the cellar. And all those tears—manufactured for the occasion, no doubt—left stains on the arms of Father's favorite armchair, the red velvet wingback that belonged in front of the fire but was now perched in the center of the room like some kind of ceremonial pyre.

Dare had been sure the visits, which were only for show, would be brief. Yet an hour later, the sound of other people's mourning was still ringing in her ears. So many sighs, so much emotion.

Confined inside with too many of those *GOOD* citizens made Dare chafe.

What did they know of her father? These were the very same people who had never missed a chance to declare his salary a waste of their money since no one had seen a monster in Barrow's Bay in over twenty years, who constantly snubbed Mother—turning down her every invitation, excluding her from their teas, dinners, and balls—after she'd married a man they deemed below her station. The very same people who laughed when their own children shouted nasty names at Dare in the streets.

Dare tried repeatedly to make a run for her bedroom and the comfort of Pretty's company, but each time another doleful gasbag draped in silks and furs stopped her to tell her how incredibly, completely gutted they were.

"He was the kindest of men, so good, so gentle. How will we ever go on without him? He couldn't have left any money behind for you and your mother, could he?"

"However will your poor mother go on? His pension couldn't possibly be enough to support her."

And even "Such a terrible tragedy, and on Founder's Day, no less!"

Dare wanted to scream "GET OUT, YOU GHASTLY COWS!" But Mother looked so comforted to have the company and to be the center of attention. Let her have this moment, for the gasbags were finally right—she and Mother had been left with nothing and soon would be living in squalor in the Must.

Dare pushed through the crowd to once again attempt an escape, but the logjam of bodies in the hallway left her wedged between two men smoking cigars at the foot of the stairs.

"I thought he'd be here by now," one said, smoke billowing from the side of his mouth.

"Any minute," the other chimney replied. "He knows we'll stay and wait for the autopsy results and the conclusion of the investigation no matter how long it takes. There's nothing Kingston likes more than a captive audience."

There it was. These so-called mourners hadn't come to remember her father or comfort her mother. They hadn't even come to see and be seen—they'd only come to hear the results of the investigation into the first murder on the Island in twenty years, to make sure they were still as safe from monsters as they'd wanted to believe themselves to be.

Liars and snakes!

A ball of awful welled up inside Dare and was about to explode when Governor Kingston, trailed by four or five other men, entered the house.

His entrance seemed to absorb every bit of light in the room. Tall and thin, he was all angles and edges, and wore his ceremonial sash draped across the front of his black mourning suit, which glittered almost as if lit from within. Dare didn't recognize the men accompanying him, who were also sharply dressed, not a stitch out of place or a wrinkle in sight.

The governor greeted Mother with a solicitous bow of his head before bidding everyone to gather in the parlor, where he planted himself in the middle of the room, his hands resting on the back of Father's favorite chair.

And just like that, the mood shifted. Gone were the sympathetic nods, the doe eyes directed at Dare and Mother, replaced now with a kind of eager hope focused on the governor.

The governor waited until the room was silent, then cleared his throat. "As you all know, our fair Island has been safe from monsters for these many years now. You need only look to our thriving population for proof that there has never been a time of greater peace, safety, and prosperity on Barrow's

Bay. And soon our numbers will double again, once Villum Village is finished. And through it all, Captain Virgil Coates stood ever vigilant, ready to protect us should the need ever arise. Then came the fatal morning when our good Captain ventured out on his rounds."

Dare clenched her fists as the governor paused for dramatic effect, checking that all eyes in the packed room were still glued to him. Like everyone else, Dare stood on pins waiting to hear the full and awful truth of how exactly her dear father had lost his life. But unlike everyone else, Dare needed to know so she could try to begin to heal. If that were even possible.

"I am here to assure you that while the beast who killed our Captain Coates was indeed a monster, they were as human as you and I." The governor paused again, allowing the collective sigh of relief that erupted at the news to subside. "A common thief traveled to our shores with the explicit purpose to prey on us. A person so cold-blooded and low, he valued stealing a handful of coins over a man's life, and in so doing took from us a father, husband, friend. Hero."

Dare looked around the room at the blur of faces all relaxing. Even Mother's tearstained cheeks softened, leaving her looking somehow clearer, reassured.

There was no such relief for Dare; her insides itched as if the rough cloth from which she was made had finally sunk in beneath her skin.

The governor continued. "Our poor Captain was determined to try to live up to the legacy of Bascombe Barrow even as he came to the job too late. By the time he became Captain, his predecessors had done all the real work, the hard work. Yet who can blame him for striving to be half as brave as the man who, on a mission to rescue poor, lost Louise, faced down the monsters and founded our island home?"

The room replied with echoes of "For Barrow!"

"Indeed." The governor surveyed his rapt audience and offered a benevolent smile. "Many of us here—nay, most of us—are descended from the crew that fought alongside Barrow. Those who lived to tell the tale carried high the banner for those who lost their lives. And whether our ancestors survived or perished in that first fight, they, the valiant Barrow Twenty, gifted us a legacy of bravery, leadership, and responsibility. Our good Captain was simply hoping to continue to carry that banner. Yet in so doing, he worked himself sick. His focus flagged, his nerves frayed, leaving him weak and vulnerable to the designs of a common thief."

The itch became unbearable. "That's a lie!" Dare shouted. "He wasn't weak or vulnerable!"

She knew she should leave it there, but once loosened, her tongue refused to be tamed. "Where's your proof it was a thief and not a monster? I know how he died, and where. Only a monster could have killed him like that!"

The room erupted into a cacophony of confusion. Ladies

fanned themselves and gentlemen grew pale, reaching to loosen their ties, until the governor calmly restored order.

"Now, now. The girl isn't wrong." Governor Kingston adjusted his cuff links as he continued. "As I've already said, Captain Coates's killer is the worst kind of monster: the human kind. As for proof, we found him trying to stow away on a ship leaving for City-on-the-Pike. He gave a full confession and has been safely locked up. He'll never again see the light of day."

"That's not proof it wasn't monsters! You know how he was killed, you saw the wou—"

"That's enough!" Mother's voice broke over Dare's, issuing like a viper's hiss.

In an instant, Ruthann had Dare by the wrist and was whisking her away up the stairs. But before they had reached the top, Dare wrenched free and planted herself on a step halfway down. She didn't try to go back into the parlor to defend herself or convince anyone to believe her. She knew that would never work. And then, too, there was the look that had flashed across Governor Kingston's face when she'd shouted "monsters!" It'd been just a small wince, a tiny pull of the upper lip. It lasted no more than a moment, yet it told her all she needed to know—he had a secret.

"The poor girl is clearly upset!" The governor shook his head, his voice dripping with sympathy and care. "Grief has a way of heightening our most awful instincts. Let us leave the

Captain's family to their mourning."

His poorly veiled insult bounced off Dare. The truth had already seeped deep into her bones: there was a lie here somewhere, and Dare was going to find it.

As quickly as they'd descended on the Coates's tidy little house, the cream of Barrow's Bay society lined up to bid their most heartfelt adieus to Mother. Dare remained on her perch on the stairs watching as double-handed handshakes punctuated with sighs and the promise of invitations to dinner, the club, or tea were exchanged for fur wraps and hats adorned with colorful feathers. Dare would have swept them out like mud from the bottom of her boots, yet through it all, Mother remained ever gracious, smiling. Beautiful.

And there, perched at her elbow like a hawk on the hunt, was the governor.

He was still standing by Mother's side two weeks later, his hold on her arm more familiar, the angle of his gaze more direct. He was there three weeks later when the new Captain of the Guard took possession of the house and Mother informed Dare that rather than being sent to make their own way on the mainland, they were to stay in an apartment in the governor's mansion—a gesture of great generosity. He was there at Mother's side every morning after breakfast, on the way out the door to dinners and seasonal balls, and nearly every waking hour in between. He was always there.

Comforting, offering, preening with the Island's most beautiful woman on his arm.

Six months after Dare's father was found with his gentle, kind head cleanly severed from his neck, the governor's place by Mother's side was to be sanctified.

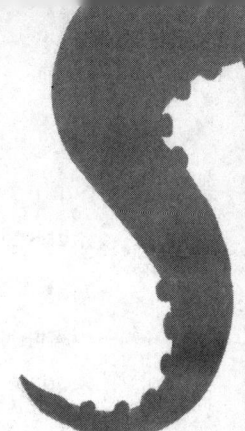

CHAPTER FOUR
A Wedding

"Awful, just awful!" Mrs. Malcolm snarled through gritted teeth. "If today were any other day, I'd lop this all off and leave you as bald as the fish man!"

To hear the governor's housekeeper complain, one would think it was her hair being yanked with a fine-tooth comb, not Dare's. "I can't for the life of me understand how you get so tangled up every night."

Terror takes a toll.

But there was no point in saying that now, for no one—not Dare's mother, not Mrs. Malcolm, and certainly not the governor—believed anything Dare said about the monsters, neither those she was convinced still lived nor the ones she dreamt about.

They laughed at her conviction that there were still monsters roaming. And of her dreams, they told her that she ought to think of more pleasant things before going to sleep, that she needed to control her imagination.

Yet the dreams felt like so much more than any nightmare Dare had ever had. While she could barely make out one monster from the next, she could feel them there, crowding her, hovering overhead, slithering over her skin. And then, too, there was the stink. It wasn't an odor, exactly, more of a vapor, as if she'd been visited by a surfeit of spectral skunks.

The first night it happened, Dare had run to Mother's room terrified, the guttural shriek they'd let loose lingering in her ears.

"They're here!" She had hardly been able to get the words out. Mother rubbed her back for a solid ten minutes before Dare was able to catch her breath and explain.

"Monsters. They are alive. They were in my room!" Saying the words out loud took so much yet gave her such relief. Speaking truth to make it true. "I saw them. They killed Father and they're coming for me!"

That first night, Mother had comforted her, told her there was nothing to worry about. "We're safe and sound here at the governor's. No monsters. Only dreams." But after a week of the same scene playing out every night, the tenderness and worry were replaced with a sour look and the stench of disappointment.

"I've been patient. Gave you time to accept your father's death. Made excuses for your ramblings about monsters, your constant search for clues that simply do not exist. It's time you accept the circumstances of your father's death. Now back to bed." Mother rolled onto her side. "And have a wash first. What have you gotten into?"

From that point on, Dare learned to keep the dreams—like everything else she thought and felt—to herself. Besides, Mrs. Malcolm clearly thrived on battling Dare's countless imperfections. From the moment Dare and her mother had arrived at the governor's mansion, the housekeeper took it upon herself to see to Dare's day-to-day care and upkeep so that Mother could attend to more *important* business. But Mrs. Malcolm's idea of upkeep was complete renovation.

In her attempt to turn Dare into a *proper* girl, the housekeeper had frills, feathers, and ornate buttons added to all of Dare's dresses. Dare hated them and would only wear her plain gray frock. But today was to be different, and Dare had already agreed to wear a horrendous green velvet dress done up with lace and bows, as long as she didn't have to put it on until later.

"The entire staff is busy getting ready for this afternoon. I trust I can rely on you to stay out of trouble?" Mrs. Malcolm emphasized the word *trust* as she inspected the ornate plait she'd tortured Dare's hair into. "It will have to do. The governor is expecting you for breakfast in thirty minutes, after which you may have some time to yourself before getting changed. I advise you to rest up for later—it's going to be a very special day."

Not in Dare's book, it wasn't. But she'd given up on trying to change her mother's mind about marrying the governor. No amount of calmly reasoned arguments, fits, or tears had managed to convince her otherwise.

"I loved your father deeply," Mother had said. "Now that he's gone, the governor offers us a chance at something new. Better. We'd be penniless and living in City-on-the-Pike in a crumbling tenement in the Must by now without him. Please don't begrudge me happiness."

Father would never have held a grudge, not even about Mother's ridiculous new wardrobe, or her new-found (and long-hoped-for) ascent into high society. And so, Dare tried not to either, although she didn't have to be happy about it.

At least she had most of the day to herself to do the only thing that really mattered.

She waited until the sound of Mrs. Malcolm's footfalls disappeared before leaving her room and heading down the back stairs to the servants' hall.

On this morning, the kitchen was busier than usual, the stoves were working overtime, and the scent of burning wood filtered in from the kitchen yard where three fatted calves were being roasted for the wedding supper.

Dare had just reached the door to her destination when a kitchen maid, all fluffed up like a broody hen, stepped up and blocked her way forward.

"You shouldn't be down here. Go back where you belong."

"If only I could," Dare muttered as she pushed past into Ruthann's workroom.

Tiny and cramped, this room was the only place Dare felt at home. It was where Mother had consigned Pretty (she didn't think the governor would approve of them keeping a pet) and where Father's last few possessions had been stored—his bird and papers the last tangible connections Dare had to him.

For the first several months after he died, Dare tried to hold on to her every memory of him, as if to keep him alive somehow. She promised herself she'd never forget the sound of his voice, the tone of his whistle. Their weekly walks to the edge of the salt marsh on the western edge of the Island, the sweep of his beard as he bent down to kiss her good night, or the way he'd carry in the scent of the evening fog on his clothes after making his rounds. But soon the memories began to collect like barnacles on a boat, adding to the weight she was already pulling along behind her.

Going through his papers was different.

She wasn't wallowing; she was investigating.

It took a few days after the funeral for Dare to understand why the governor's story about a thief murdering her father for a few coins had made her itch so badly: Father rarely carried money while on patrol; he said it only weighed him down. Still, it was that look the governor had gotten at the mention of monsters that had sealed it for Dare. The governor was hiding something and she'd been digging to find it ever since.

Mother had been taken to the place where Father had died, but she refused to tell Dare where it was, saying it was not the kind of information Dare should have to carry with her.

Dare did not agree.

So in those early days after the funeral, she scoured the Island, searching for clues. She was convinced it had happened out past the marshlands, near the devasted turtle laying grounds but the sand had been smoothed over by the tides, and it was as pristine as ever. Then, once they'd moved to the governor's, Dare was forbidden from leaving the mansion grounds. Of course, that didn't stop her, although the members of the watch stationed at every possible way in or out did. Her every attempt to escape—day or night—was thwarted. So instead, Dare devoted her time to poring through her father's daily logs, looking for the slightest hint that he knew monsters still lurked on the Island. That he'd met his end bravely.

But so far, all she'd found were accounts of lost dogs, rogue alligators, and migrating birds blown off course by the trade winds.

Still, she returned every single day, certain that if she looked hard enough, she'd find a clue, something to lead her to the real murderer. And when she did, she'd take its head as it had taken her father's.

Dare firmly shuttered the workroom door and whistled for Pretty: three rapid repetitions of the same sound, the same whistle her father had used to call the bird.

It usually took no more than one call for Pretty to fly to Dare's shoulder. Yet Dare whistled once, twice, five times, and still there was no sign of the bird.

Dare threw open the tall wooden cabinet where Father's boxes were stored. "Where are you, you silly bird? Did you get yourself locked in here?"

Pretty wasn't in there.

And neither were her father's boxes.

The cupboard was bare.

Panic exploded in Dare's chest and sent her racing out of the room and through the kitchen, leaving a flock of flustered kitchen maids in her wake. She headed for Mother's rooms—wedding or not, she'd have her answers right now. Halfway up the stairs to the first floor, Dare nearly slammed into a footman carrying a tray full of champagne glasses. The crystal teetered and threatened to fall, a thin imitation of Dare's own instability.

She'd just emerged into the first-floor hall when she spotted Ruthann, her arms loaded with yards of lace.

"Saints and snakes, girl!" Ruthann declared as she spotted Dare. "You'll not disturb your mother today, not in one of your moods. It can wait."

"No, it can't." Dare set her teeth. "Where is she? Where are they?"

"What are you talking about?"

"Pretty, and Father's boxes."

Ruthann shifted her load of lace as if suddenly the weight was too much to bear.

Dare's stomach churned, her lip twitching as a thin bead of sweat bloomed on Ruthann's upper lip. "They came for the boxes this morning."

Dare promised herself she wouldn't explode until she'd wrung every detail out of Ruthann. "Who is 'they'? And where did they take the boxes?"

"Just some men who work outside here at the mansion. They took the boxes out back to the kitchen garden, I assumed to store them elsewhere."

"And Pretty? Please tell me you moved her to Mother's room, or mine?"

Ruthann could barely manage to shake her head. "They must have left the door ajar when they were moving things, and Pretty must have flown away. I didn't think they'd—"

Outside. Behind the kitchen.

Dare tore away from Ruthann and blindly ran toward the kitchen yard, the world a blur, the only sound the buzzing in her head.

Until she landed outside.

Then everything changed.

What had been blurred snapped into sharp focus. The buzzing in Dare's head switched off and became instead a tinny silence. The air turned thick, making it hard to move, to believe her own eyes. But the heat and the smoke were real. As were the sparks popping and dancing out of the pyre over which the calves slowly roasted.

Dare felt herself begin to crumble, her heart cleaved in half as she watched two workmen feed the last of her father's things into the fire.

A howl born of pain started to unfurl from deep inside her when she spotted him. A boy with a shock of unruly dark hair, not much older than her, standing off to the side. He had the look of someone who spent their days out on the water, a fisherman's son or dock boy. It wasn't strange to see someone like him in the governor's kitchen yard—it was the single blue feather in his hand that stopped her. Pretty?

"You!" Dare shouted. "Did you see her? Do you have her?"

Buoyed by a single stitch of hope, Dare started running across the yard toward the boy, but the sunlight was too bright, and she couldn't keep him in her sights. As she stopped to shade her eyes one of the men stepped forward, grabbed the last of Father's boxes, and tossed it into the fire, the papers inside igniting in a puff of smoke.

The stitch popped and something in Dare broke. "THAT'S MINE!" she screamed. She raced toward the fire, ready to go in after the crate, to save what she could, when one of the men picked her up.

"Stupid girl," he scolded as he hauled her inside. "You could 'ave been burned."

"Let go!" she howled, and sank her teeth into his hand.

A plume of unrepeatable words filled the air as he dropped her, leaving her free to run back to the fire.

But by the time she got back outside, the boy with the feather was gone, as was Pretty, and the last of her father's boxes had turned to ash.

"I thought we'd made better progress with your behavior," the governor said between sips of his coffee. "Yet this display, and in front of the servants too, was completely unacceptable, Darvlah."

He refused to call her Dare, pointedly using only her given name. In turn, Dare refused to use any name whatsoever to address him—not his given name, not his title, and especially not "sir."

"Good thing your mother is taking her breakfast in her room this morning," he continued. "I'd hate to worry her with this outburst of yours, today of all days. Especially since all has already been decided."

Dare's stomach lurched. "What's been decided?"

The governor didn't reply; instead, he reached under the breakfast table and pulled out a wrapped box tied with grosgrain ribbon. It reeked of the new perfume Mother had taken to wearing—a ghastly mix of tuberose, lime, and something else that made Dare want to heave. Pepper? Patchouli?

Pretension.

"This is for you." The governor set the box on the table and pushed it toward Dare. "A little bon voyage gift from your mother. Something to ease your travels."

"My travels? You're the ones leaving."

Less honeymoon than work, the governor and Mother were to spend two months at his newly built cottage out past the marshlands in Villum Village so the governor could more directly oversee plans for new houses to go up there. Mother had gotten him to promise to preserve the turtles' laying grounds, a fact Dare would only believe when she saw it.

"There's been a change of plans." The governor set his coffee cup down, then straightened his cuff links, first one, then the other. "Your mother is worried about you. And we both find your unwillingness to accept the facts as they are troubling. It's time you stopped roaming around the past. A change will give you a chance to understand all that's been given to you. Besides, Mrs. Malcolm will be too busy while we're gone to be burdened with caring for you."

"I don't need anyone to care for me."

"On the contrary—it's abundantly clear you need constant supervision. Running through a fire, for what? To catch some bird, save some old papers? Ridiculous."

"It's not ridiculous." Dare matched his caustic tone with one of her own. "She was my pet. Mine. Not yours. Just like my father's papers that you had burned weren't yours."

"The papers served no purpose and were taking up valuable

storage room. As for the bird, had I known you were keeping it, I'd have insisted it be released long ago. Wild creatures belong in the wild. You, young lady, must be tamed. I suggested we send you off island to a school properly prepared to set you straight. Mother insisted instead that we send you to the city."

"The city?" The words stuck to Dare's teeth like stale brittle.

"She thought it would be nice for you to spend time with your father's dear aunt Emily," the governor continued. "She raised him, she's all that remains of his family; you should know each other. And she has a large home where you'll be safe from the worst City-on-the-Pike has to offer. With her theatrical career having concluded in the past few years, your great-aunt will have the time to watch over you."

Dare's ears rang and her fingertips went numb.

She was to be shipped off, an inconvenient child sent to live with a distant relative she'd never met before in a place as gloomy and awful as Dare. Overcrowded, cold, rainy, and riddled with smog, City-on-the-Pike was home to the Must, and the factories that were the engines of industry feeding the bank accounts of the citizens of Barrow's Bay. The only ones who ever ventured to those shores anymore—unless they were going to check on their factories—were those unlucky enough to lose their fortunes.

Dare bit back the impulse to snap, to scream, to rip that smug mustache from the governor's thin upper lip. But without Pretty or any other lingering connection to Father, maybe Frances Cooper had been right for once in her rotten life. That cold and dark place was exactly where Dare belonged—along with the rest of the unfortunates.

And so she simply said, "When I am to leave?"

"We thought it would be next week," the governor replied. "But it turns out there's a ship bound for the mainland setting sail this evening. Fortunate timing, don't you think?"

For him? Most definitely.

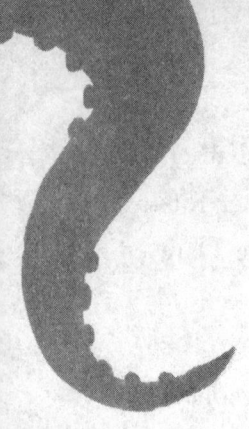

CHAPTER FIVE
Boat Bound

The rest of the day passed by Dare in a blur of flowers, tulle, and pageantry. She had no fight left to do anything except stand where she was told to stand and say the words they wanted to hear from her at the wedding. Every last drop of clever had disappeared with Pretty, all hope burned with her father's papers.

And once the wedding ceremony was over, it was time for Dare to leave.

Mother had said at least seven times that she had every intention of seeing Dare off herself.

"We've timed everything perfectly between the end of the ceremony and the beginning of the reception. I wouldn't miss sending you off on your grand adventure!"

Dare knew she meant it. Mother might have had some less than admirable qualities—she was willfully helpless, and terribly vain—yet she never said anything she didn't mean. She'd truly convinced herself (or more likely allowed Governor Kingston to convince her) that sending her only daughter away was something other than a punishment.

"I will always love your father," Mother said as she prepared to walk down the aisle. "But loving him can't provide for us. As the governor says, we ought to leave the dead to themselves."

As if that were possible.

Then the ceremony started late, and the receiving line wound up being longer than they'd anticipated. "Who knew we'd have so many well-wishers come out to see us married?" Mother had exclaimed.

Probably anyone who'd stopped to think about it for even half a minute. Of course, the entire year-round population of Barrow's Bay would come to shake their governor's hand and get a close-up look at his new wife.

The governor leaned in to his new bride. "I think it would be best if Mrs. Malcolm takes Darvlah to the dock. The captain sent word that they must depart no later than four o'clock."

"I promised I'd be the one to see her off," Mother cooed.

"You're a wonderful mother," he replied. "She understands, don't you, Darvlah?"

If that had been a real question, Dare would have said, "No. I don't understand anything anymore." But she understood it wasn't.

"Be brave," Mother said as she kissed Dare on the top of the head. "Be sure to ride in one of those new horseless carriages for me. Automobiles, they call them. Why, you'll be like a modern-day Louise, an intrepid traveler to unchartered lands!"

A modern-day Louise.

What a perfectly fitting fate for Dare—to be like the girl who, stranded alone on this very island, had managed to fight off monsters on her own for weeks, only to die just as her rescuers arrived.

Mrs. Malcolm barely said a word to Dare the entire way to the dock, which was strange, because she rarely missed a chance to deliver long lectures on manners and extol the virtues of virtue.

Oddly enough, though, Dare wished the housekeeper would unleash one of her lectures now. At least then she'd have something else to think about besides the unbearable weight of so much loss, or how ever-sunny Barrow's Bay—with its rows of brightly painted houses lined up like peacocks on display in the sun—suddenly felt more like home than it ever had before.

But as soon as their carriage reached the dock, Dare realized why Mrs. Malcolm had been so quiet. Not even a world-class scold could feel good about packing a twelve-year-old girl off on a ship like the one waiting in the harbor.

To call a vessel that scrubby a "ship" was an exaggeration at best; "boat" might have been a passable description, but "death trap" was the most accurate.

Rigged with three tattered sails and a hull covered in barnacles, the *Golden Slipper* was neither golden nor very slipper-y looking. The main mast was held together by rope and tar, and the figurehead was so disfigured, one couldn't tell if it had once been a woman or a gargoyle. All of this to say nothing of the oddly oversize crow's nest perched atop the mizzenmast, upon which two large vultures sat perched.

"It's not quite what I was expecting. It's rather rough around the edges, but the governor always knows what he's doing." It was hard to tell who Mrs. Malcolm was working hard to convince, herself or Dare. "He paid extra for you to have a private cabin. I'm sure you'll find your quarters comfortable. Here, this is for you." Mrs. Malcolm handed Dare a small picnic hamper. "I packed you a taste of the wedding supper, including some of the cake."

"You cut into the cake before the reception?" Dare didn't care about the cake, but was shocked Mrs. Malcolm had it in her to break the convention.

"Goodness, no!" Mrs. Malcolm batted the thought away. "I had the kitchen make a small cake to send along with you. I thought it might make the journey more pleasant."

"That was very . . . nice of you," Dare said, surprised to be using that word for the housekeeper.

"I'm a very nice person." Mrs. Malcolm handed Dare her hat. "Now put this on and be on your way."

"I despise this hat," Dare grumbled. "It makes me look like a freshly sprouted mushroom."

"It's the height of fashion, and it'll keep the sun off your face, preserve what's left of your complexion."

It wasn't worth the argument; nothing was anymore. She'd take the hat off and toss it into the sea as soon as they left shore, leaving Mrs. Malcolm none the wiser.

Dare allowed Mrs. Malcolm to pin the awful hat in place, then followed her out of the carriage and onto the dock. They'd just passed the monument dedicated to poor, dead, and oh-so-noble Louise when an old sailor accosted them from behind. "That Darblha Cates?" Every word was punctuated with a fresh spray of spittle.

"This is Miss *Coates*," Mrs. Malcolm corrected. "Who's asking?"

The sailor stood barely a head above Dare upon legs that looked too thin and bowed by time to be up to the task of carrying his weight; yet there was nothing weak or aged about his imperious sneer. "I am."

Dare thought she saw a moment of regret pass over Mrs. Malcolm's expression, as if suddenly the idea of watching Dare while the governor and Mother were gone wasn't as tiresome as she'd first thought. "I meant who are you to be asking?"

"I'm the poor dupe who has to watch her on the crossing." The sailor adjusted a dirty bandage wrapped around his hand, grabbed Dare's suitcase from the housekeeper, and started for the gangway.

"That can't be right!" Mrs. Malcolm snatched the suitcase back. "The governor paid for the best accommodations for the girl. Surely that includes a worthy escort on a solid boat."

The sailor turned and slowly leveled his gaze on Mrs. Malcolm. "This bucket is the only one that can slip the winds at this time of year and make it in one piece to the other side. That worthy enough for you?"

Mrs. Malcolm winced, then stretched out a rubbery smile to try to cover it up. "I see, I didn't realize that."

She then turned to Dare, the edges of her smile grown brittle. "Behave yourself, Darvlah. Keep yourself tidy, no ripped seams or broken buttons. And watch your tongue and those moods of yours. I expect fame made a proper lady of your great-aunt Emily. She'll have traveled in the best circles and will expect you to meet her mark."

For the first time ever, Dare heard a tremor in Mrs. Malcolm's voice, noticed a crack in her shiny veneer. Dare's carefully constructed bridge swayed a bit, and she moved to hug the housekeeper. Until she remembered herself.

Mrs. Malcolm cleared her throat, as if to expel her own sentimental impulse, and straightened Dare's hat. "Now go. I'm sure you'll be sent for after your mother and the governor have had some time to settle into married life."

"How long will that be?" Dare asked.

"As long as the governor says it ought to be."

For once Dare was glad she'd stomped on an impulse. Hugging Mrs. Malcolm would be like kissing the executioner before they leveled the axe.

Dare took her first steps onto the *Golden Slipper*, certain the boards would buckle under her weight. But the deck was sturdy. The vultures had disappeared—a good sign—and even that poorly mended mast didn't look quite as rickety up close.

"You got time to stand around staring later," the old sailor grumbled, leading the way toward the hatch. "Now we work."

"I'm a paying passenger," Dare snapped, sounding more like Frances Cooper than herself.

"Who paid for the privilege of arriving alive on the mainland, which means you've gotta do your share."

Arriving alive was Dare's intention, although perhaps it wasn't the governor's when he booked her passage on this rotting excuse for a ship.

The old sailor led Dare down a narrow stairway into the dank, cavernous hold. The stink of too many bodies living too close together was cut by the scent of oranges and marsh grass. The bright tang of orange was easy enough to trace: crates filled with the only export of Barrow's Bay stood piled at one end of the hold. But since when did grass grow on ships?

"This'll be your place." The sailor nodded toward a narrow door tucked into a back corner.

Dare opened the door, expecting to find an empty coal bin or a small cupboard at best, not a proper cabin lined with mahogany paneling and bright gas lamps. There was even a full-size bedstead made up with crisp linen and fluffy pillows.

The sailor opened a built-in cabinet.

"Use them straps on the wall to hold your things in place. Undo them only when I say so."

Dare tightened her grip on the picnic basket. "What if I need something?"

"You can follow my words, or don't. If I was you, I'd do." The sailor pushed past her and out of the cabin.

He was a nasty, dirty old creature, and Dare wanted to hate him for how he was speaking to her. Yet unlike the *GOOD* people of Barrow's Bay, his disdain wasn't hidden behind so-called social graces; it was clear and honest and fully on display. She almost liked him for that.

Dare secured her bag and the basket of food in the cabinet, deciding she might even share her cake with him. A reward for his candor. She tossed the ridiculous hat on the bed, unraveled Mrs. Malcolm's tight plait, and followed the sailor out. At least she tried to—finding her balance as the still-docked ship pitched back and forth was a challenge she'd not expected.

It's not like she hadn't been out on the open water before. Father used to take her out on the bay in a dinghy to fish, though they rarely tried to catch anything. Mostly they'd bask in the sun, letting their fingers and toes run ripples through the water. But she'd never had to find her balance while standing still before. At least not on a ship.

Dare's ornery guide led the way across the ship's deck, weaving in and around other sailors as they rushed about, preparing to set sail. "You're gonna meet Captain Fortune now," he warned. "And you're gonna speak only when he says so. He don't like passengers and he especially don't like children passengers."

"Why not?" Dare said. "We don't smell bad enough to blend in?"

"'Cause the last time he ferried one of you across, it nearly cost him his ship, his crew, and his life."

Dare wasn't sure if she should believe him. "Why?" she tested. "What did they do?"

"Left something loose in their cabin," he replied as he started up the stairs to the upper deck, where the captain stood at the helm reviewing a map.

"And that nearly sunk the ship?" Dare laughed as she followed him.

"Not sunk—ripped it in two."

CHAPTER SIX
Slipping the Winds

Dare didn't so much meet Captain Fortune as endure several minutes of him silently glaring down at her from under a pair of thick brows gone gray and wiry with time. She couldn't quite tell if he was the tallest man she'd ever seen or just had the posture of a flagpole. Whatever it was, he loomed large as he stood five steps above her and her surly escort on the bridge, his long fingers wrapped loosely around the helm of the ship. She'd been stupid to leave that awful hat in the cabin. While it might have made her look like a mushroom, it would've shielded her from the dueling glares of the sun and the captain.

"You're Coates's daughter," Fortune said at last.

"Was," Dare corrected.

"He was a good man. A type rarely seen in this port."

This ship was full of surprises.

"You do as Tupper says and all will be fine." The captain

dismissed them with the slightest nod before taking up his spyglass to survey the seas ahead.

"Tupper?" Dare said, trailing the old sailor. "That's your name? I figured you'd have a proper sailor's name like Snuffy or Crooked-Neck Jim."

Tupper continued his march across the deck, her insults slipping off his back like water over a shoal.

"Where are we going?" Dare asked. "You going to make me scrub floors, or peel potatoes?"

Tupper stopped at the bottom of the mizzenmast and grabbed hold of the flimsy rope ladder. "Climb."

"Very funny," Dare drawled.

"Climb," Tupper repeated.

Dare looked up the tall mast at the crow's nest perched way up at the top. "I am *not* climbing up there!"

"Then I guess you'll be swimming back to shore." Tupper sucked his teeth.

"Are you threatening me?" Dare challenged.

"If you call truth-telling a threat, then I guess I am."

Maybe he wasn't that big a fool. It was frighteningly high, but there was no way Dare was going to let him know she was scared. Then he'd have something on her, and that would never do.

Dare bit back her nerves and grabbed hold of the ladder. "If this is a test, I'll pass it. And if I fall, it's your funeral."

"Noted." Tupper held the ladder steady as she took her

first tentative steps upward.

At first, the sway of the rope ladder was kind of exhilarating, every rung higher a triumph over fear—until Dare could see over the side of the boat. They were so far above the blue waters of the bay that one slip, and she'd be done. Her exhilaration washed away in a wave of nausea.

"This is far enough." Dare couldn't stop the dread from leaking out between her words now.

"Keep going." Tupper was unmoved.

"I can't." Dare cast aside the last vestiges of her false bravado and started to climb back down, but Tupper was behind her now, hanging from the ladder with one hand, the other ready to push her up if need be.

"Pin your gaze on your hands and keep climbing."

That was the worst advice Dare had ever heard, and if she wasn't so scared, she would've said so. Still, with him blocking her way down, up was her only choice.

She focused on her whitened knuckles until they were the only thing she could see. Though she'd never tell him, Tupper was right—she could almost believe there was no swaying ladder, no terrible heights, no open sea ahead waiting to swallow her whole. Just one hand reaching above the next.

When she finally reached the crow's nest, Dare collapsed inside. Tupper swung in behind her, pulled at a pair of heavy waxed ropes bolted to the mast, and reached to wrap them about Dare's middle.

"Get away from me with that!" She kicked her legs, connecting her boot with Tupper's shin. It was a hard blow, but Tupper didn't even wince.

"You are a nasty one, aren't you?" Tupper drawled. "Can see why they're shipping you off."

"No one is shipping me off! You're too old to know anything."

It was a weak insult, but Dare's heart wasn't in it to dig for anything stronger. Of course they were shipping her off.

"Stop moving!" Tupper growled. "You want to be safe or not?"

"Getting strapped into a crow's nest is what you call safe? I'll die up here!"

"No. You. Won't," Tupper grunted, emphasizing each word as he tightened the straps, finally managing to tie her to the mast.

"I'll tell the governor!" Dare shouted and kicked. "He'll see you and your whole crew in jail!"

Tupper gave a kind of snorting chuckle. "Only if he's in there with us."

Dare stopped, the truth landing with a thud.

"He knew you were going to do this to me." She already detested the governor, but now her loathing hardened into a rock-solid heap of hatred. "What better way to get rid of an inconvenient child than murder?"

"If they wanted you dead, you'd never have made it on

board." Tupper gave the straps another tug for good measure before leaning back against the mast and winding a second set of straps across his own shoulders.

"Ha! Very funny. At least tell me why you're tying us up here as bird bait." Dare paused before adding a very reluctant "... please."

Tupper squinted at her. "You at least know about the trade winds, right?"

"*I've* been to school, have you?"

Tupper yawned at the insult, then said, "The winds sit about fifteen nautical miles from shore on all sides. They ring the Island like a curtain hung on a round rod. Time was, they'd keep all the bad weather from coming in, and the fair weather from going out. It was the winds what made it so hard for Bascombe Barrow to find the Island afore he found Louise stranded there."

"I already said I know all this."

"Either I tell my story, or you won't hear it."

The ship had cleared the harbor and was picking up speed as it headed for the open sea. The wind sent Dare's hair spiking into her eyes.

"Lately the trade winds been getting unstable, and especially nasty in the winter months. That's why all of them fancy people who don't live on the Island year-round leave at the end of the season now. Only fools try to cross the winds this time of year."

Dare tried to swallow back the alarm drying out her throat. "Then I guess that makes us fools."

"Nah, this ship'll slip them better than anyone. There, look up."

The waves had calmed, and the ship sliced smoothly through the water, allowing Dare to look at the horizon without getting nauseated. There was something about the quality of the light, though slanted and grayer than it was on the Island, that left Dare feeling calmer, less on display—even while trussed to the mast like one of those calves on the spit.

Then she spotted something out on the horizon, hovering above the water, reaching midway up to the heavens. The winds curved along in a large, luxurious arc, extending in either direction as far as Dare could see. Golden light played throughout, sparkling and bubbling, like a crystal lit by candlelight.

"Guess they didn't tell you about this part in that school, did they?" Tupper was clearly enjoying himself.

"*That's* the trade winds?" Dare was trying to match the idea in her head with the vision before her.

"Told you they're like a curtain."

They truly were—if a curtain could be sewn of clouds, air, and light.

"They're beautiful."

"From here they are." Tupper leaned back and closed his eyes. "Up close, they're tempestuous. Black clouds, fierce gales, rainstorms that whip up out of nothing and last for days or weeks. Ship this size tries to sail straight through the winds, you're gonna be smashed to pieces. You've got to find a place to slip through."

While Tupper spoke, the sounds of rigging and chains being unwound carried over the crow's nest and out to sea. Down on the deck, sailors were rushing about, shouting back and forth to each other, but it was when the captain bellowed some indecipherable command from his post at the helm that Tupper sat up at attention, every muscle tensed and ready for action.

"We're getting ready to cross," he said. "If we're lucky, we'll catch that bugger lingering on the edge of the winds."

"Why would you want to catch a storm?"

"Not a storm." Tupper sneered. "An agicole."

"An agicole? What's that?"

"One of the few seabound beasts. They prefer staying close to shore, until *events* lead them farther out to sea. Then they'll hide out by the winds."

Dare balked. She should have known better. "You're making this up! My father told me about all the monsters, he never once mentioned your *agicole*."

"Well, I guess he didn't tell you about them all, then, did he?" Tupper sucked his teeth.

Dare was fit to spit, but then it clicked. "I know what this is. The governor put you up to this, didn't he? Teach me a lesson, finally get me to say, like everyone else does, that there are no more monsters!"

"They do say that, don't they?" Tupper rolled up his right sleeve, exposing a veritable canvas of finely drawn monsters tattooed on his arm. "I got a temper, don't have a penny to my name, and I once cut a man who kicked a dog, but I don't lie, especially not about monsters."

Dare snorted. "Everyone lies."

"Think what you want. I'll tell you some things that are true. Monsters still abound, no matter what people say. You shouldn't believe every story you hear, whether it's written in books or etched in stone. And something else you wanna know? Your daddy wasn't killed by some common thief."

Tupper's list of truths hit Dare like a tidal surge. It was everything she'd been hoping to hear from someone, anyone. But there was no relief now, only a whirlpool of confusion threatening to swallow her whole.

"How do you know that?" Her challenge came out like a dart aimed to land in the bull's-eye.

"I know lots of things I suspect you'll want to know, too. Or maybe I don't, since I'm just an old, bent-up sailor, aren't I?" Tupper nailed Dare with a look; he wasn't going to give up anything for free.

But neither would she. "How do I know you're not just saying all this? Why should I believe you?"

"You shouldn't," Tupper replied. "Better question is, do you believe it yourself?"

"Of course, I do! I—" The sailors down below began shouting in unison, a singsong round of "*Heave! Ho! Heave!*" before the mast supporting the crow's nest began to bend and bow.

"What's happening?" Dare cried, helpless to try to stop herself from falling face-first into the sea.

"Hold tight, girl." Tupper smiled. "We're going for a ride."

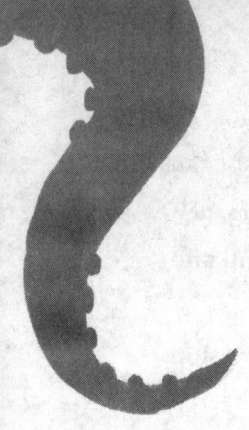

CHAPTER SEVEN
Monsters Abound

"You said I wasn't going to die up here!" Dare screamed. She did not want it to end this way! Without a fight. Weak and cowering, like Louise.

"Come on, now." Tupper snorted as the mast slowly keeled toward the sea. "You're not scared, are you?"

He was right, she wasn't scared. She was terrified.

As sky, sun, and sea rushed past, Dare thought of her parents. Poor Mother would be sad, devastated, even. But she'd live on, pull out her memories of Dare daily, polish them like silver until they shone and gleamed. A mirror image of the truth, not the truth itself.

At least Father hadn't lived to lose her; it would have crushed him.

Dare squeezed her eyes shut, bracing for impact into the cold hard sea. Would she feel the water fill her lungs, or might there be some mercy and the shock would knock her out first?

She didn't care—just let it end fast!

But as quickly as it had begun to fall, the mast jarred to a sudden halt.

There was no pain, no biting cold devouring her whole. Nothing but a far-off crackle and whoosh, like a candle at the moment of snuffing.

Was this what death felt like?

Dare swallowed back the bile gathered in her throat and slowly peeled her eyes open.

Her hands, her feet, her heart were all still intact, and the world was as it was before, except in the wrong order. Up was out, and down was sideways, for while the crow's nest was still attached to the mast, it now lay jutting out over the water at a neat 90-degree angle.

Tupper released his straps and fell from the mast.

"Are you out of your—" Dare began, until she realized the old sea dog had landed on his feet on what had been a side wall of the crow's nest and was now effectively the floor.

"Come on down. You're missing the view." Tupper pulled at Dare's restraints.

"Don't you dare!" She tried to bat him away, but she was too late. The ropes fell free and she tumbled out, landing at his feet.

Fear was one thing, humiliation another.

She tried to get up, but between the bobbing of the ship and the remaining ripples of fear it was impossible to find balance.

Yet there was Tupper, placidly standing next to her, a gap-toothed grin reddening his cheeks. "You want a hand?"

"Not from you." She'd find her balance on her own if she died trying.

After several shaky attempts, Dare finally managed to stand. Feet set wide apart and one hand gripping the edge of the crow's nest, she pushed the hair out of her eyes. "You couldn't tell me the falling mast was intentional?"

"You wanna hunt, you got to get close." Tupper opened a hatch in the center of what once was the floor of the crow's nest, producing two lengths of rope, a long grappling hook, a burlap bag, and several smaller sacks each about the size of a melon.

To watch the old sailor was like seeing a shadow of her father before he set out for a tour on the bay—he kept the very same kind of kit in the shed.

It's a funny thing when you know something deep inside that everyone tells you is wrong. Part of you is convinced they must be right, while the other part sinks down deeper into the knowing. Dare was accustomed to feeling that way. It would be easiest to think Tupper was some punchy old man with dreams of battles left to fight. That her mother and the governor were right—the nightmares that felt so real were figments of her imagination born of mourning.

It was like Tupper said: she had to listen to the truth that lived deep in the marrow of her bones.

"You really *are* hunting monsters. They do still exist."

"Well, just one right now. There's not too many agicoles left, though that acrid muck they spew out of their blowholes makes 'em some of the hardest to catch. And the buggers can live for, what? One, two hundred years, they say. That's a long time to swim around. Now come stand here. Don't want you to fall in." Tupper pulled Dare over to the end of the platform, just above the water's edge, then quickly began to tie the straps around her ankles.

"Why would I fall—" Dare stopped cold, realizing what was happening. She tried to scramble back, but she was already fixed in place, nowhere to go. "You're using me as bait to catch it, you filthy—"

She'd have lunged at him if she could have.

"You make it sound like it's a bad thing." Tupper laughed off her anger as he picked up the grappling hook and stationed himself next to Dare. "And besides, we call it droving. It's a talent, not everyone can do it. Your daddy thought you had the knack. Time to see if he was right."

Dare stopped fighting the straps at the mention of her father. "He said that? To you? When?"

"Lots of times. But don't think it's for free. Talent's a burden, it takes as much as it gives, and . . ." Tupper's words drifted off as he tipped his chin toward the open water. "Now, that's a sight, ain't it?"

Dare didn't want him to stop speaking, she wanted her

answer, to know how he knew her father. To know all of it. Then she saw it, and for the first time in her life, she understood what it was to be dumbfounded.

The view of the winds up close was . . . well, she had no words. What from afar had looked like one solid curtain proved up close to be a series of overlapping layers bristling and sparking against each other. Those champagne bubbles and fairy lights revealed themselves to be flashes of lightning and patches of boiling seawater.

"Will it hurt?" Dare asked, staring out into the winds.

"If captain rides them right, which he usually does, it feels like flying through a cloud."

"And if he doesn't?" Dare wasn't entirely certain she wanted an answer.

"Then the way it feels is the least of your worries. First, we got work." Tupper handed Dare two of the smaller sacks, his gaze never once shifting from the open water. "Let's go fishing."

Dare was waffling between being certain this was all a grand scheme to humiliate her, and something even worse. Then he started whistling a repeating pattern of *Tweeewooo tweeewooo tweeewooo!*—the same call her Father had used with Pretty. The sacks turned to stone in Dare's hands.

"How do you know that whistle?"

Tupper shook his head and sucked his teeth. "I won't speak poorly of the dead, but your pa should have taught you a thing or two, so you wouldn't have to be learning it all on your own now."

"I seriously doubt he ever thought I'd be shipped off the Island and used as monster bait. Tell me why you know that whistle!" she demanded.

Tupper ignored her as he crouched at the edge of the crow's nest, inches from the open sea. "Keep your eyes looking. If the sea swine does pop out, you fling them sacks of marsh salt out there. You're not aiming to hit it; you only need to land it in the beast's vicinity."

Dare nearly lost her footing, though this time it was the waves cresting inside her, not the ones buffeting the boat about, that threatened to knock her down.

The salt from the marshlands on Barrow's Bay is calming to the seabound monster. Imbued with peat from the land, it disarms and soothes them, she remembered her father explaining one night during his bedtime tale. *You've got to stun them first, or they'll stun you worse.*

"Why did you say my father knew I'd be here one day? Did he know what was going to happen to him?"

"No one ever knows what's going to happen to them. And I didn't mean *here* exactly. But bloodline has a way of sending family members down the same roads," Tupper replied. "Like me and my grandda. He was the first drover, the first to figure out how to bag monsters. Wouldn't be no Barrow's Bay without him."

"Your grandfather was Bascombe Barrow?"

"Thank the stars he wasn't. He was a member of the crew. He—" A clap of thunder shook the very timbers of the ship as they neared the edge of the trade winds. Tupper started working faster now, wrapping a section of rope around his waist and securing the free end to the strap latches. Then he gathered the second length of rope, which he'd tied into a lasso, and laid it out in evenly spaced coils by his side.

The ship slowed and began nosing into the bank of silvery-gray clouds. The light softened into a bluish hush—brightness diffused as if it had been split into an infinitesimal number of pieces, then flung far and wide. As for the air, it was neither warm nor cold. There seemed, impossibly, to be almost an absence of temperature.

And then there was the silence. Gone was the wind and the thunder. It was a quiet so complete, it swallowed everything else—the rasp of Tupper's breath, the creak of the ship, even Dare's pounding heart. She wasn't even entirely certain that if she opened her mouth to speak, words would come out. Not that she wanted to test the theory—breaking the silence felt like a sin against nature.

Tupper leaned forward, straining to see through the fog. But Dare didn't need to strain. She saw it straight off.

Or did she? It wasn't something she could really describe, it was more something she sensed. Tupper smiled, then slowly reached his right hand toward the rope coiled next to him, stopping short of grabbing hold of it.

"You smell it too, don't you?" His voice cracked the air like ice hitting hot water.

How could she not? It was pervasive. Like the vapors that accompanied her dreams, and yet somehow riper, more pungent.

"The smell of fear," Tupper said. "Ours, not theirs. They know how to use our weakness against us. How to hunt the hunters—" Tupper stopped mid-thought, grasped the lasso, and effortlessly threw it out into the void.

A sound like glass shattering mixed with terrified high-pitched squealing washed over the ship.

"Toss the salt," Tupper said as he slowly stood back up and began pulling the rope in hand over hand.

Dare swallowed back the fear threatening to numb her and threw the sacks of salt into the gray mist, even though she was certain salt to the sea could do no good. But no sooner had she heard them land with a splash than the waters began to boil up. Hot bubbles of seawater biting at her face and hands sent Dare scuttling back into the safety of the crow's nest.

"Nicely done," Tupper crooned.

He stood relaxed, all tension drained from his arms and shoulders as he reeled in their catch, pulling it closer to the ship.

And then, as if he were out fishing on a sunny day, that crooked old sailor landed the nastiest, smelliest, ugliest thing Dare had ever seen.

CHAPTER EIGHT
The Most Hated Hat

Dare always liked the ugly and the broken, the things no one else wanted. Once when they were assigned to raise a plant for class, Dare chose a spindly, nonblooming cactus. When she'd been allowed to choose the fabric for a new dress, she'd picked a dull green cotton with a skewed windowpane pattern. And when her father came home one day with an abandoned baby bird with a twisted beak and broken wing, her mother recoiled, calling it unsightly. But Dare immediately fell in love, and named her Pretty.

She didn't do it to be contrary (unlike much of her behavior at school and out in town)—she truly thought odd and misshapen things the most beautiful.

But this thing Tupper fished out of the water was not so much ugly as tragic. Made up of an entangled series of spirals, it looked like a large conch shell with short finlike legs. It was the size of a newborn baby, and its surface was riddled with countless gnarls, short spikes, and jagged holes. While it was definitely grotesque, it didn't look like any of the monsters she'd ever heard of.

"You lied." Dare pegged him with a glare. "You think I'm stupid. That's not a monster. It has no claws, no fangs, no spines. It doesn't even have a beak. Throw the poor thing back and let it, and me, be."

"If you knew anything, you'd know agicoles don't need any of those to kill, and asides, danger ain't always something you can see," Tupper grumbled as he fought to drop the flailing agicole into the burlap sack.

Convinced that she'd been taken for an elaborate ride, Dare was about to let loose on him when he dropped two salt sacks in with the beast. The thrashing stopped immediately, leaving only the echo of water lapping against the ship's hull, and the memory of her father's story about seabound monsters and salt from the marshlands.

"Only a monster would do that." She hadn't meant to say it out loud, to admit that so readily to him, but truth will always push to get aired.

"Now you're using your eyes." Tupper untied Dare's ankles, then shouted, "Got 'em!" to which a chorus of sailors replied in unison, "Hurrah, huzzah!"

"Grab hold of the ropes," Tupper advised as the mast started levering up. "The ride back up is easier than down."

Dare hardly cared about the moving mast now; she'd already been thrown fully off-balance.

"Is this the one that did it?" she asked quietly. "Did the agicole kill my father?"

Tupper looked at Dare long and hard, his mouth puckering as if to speak before pulling back into a tight thin line again. Finally, as the crow's nest stopped moving, he shook his head. "Doubt it."

Knowing it had been a monster should have been enough, but a little knowledge is never satisfying. "Do you know which one it was? What kind? Where? How many are even left?"

"Can't say I know."

"Well, will you help me figure out which one it was?" she pressed. "To catch it? Kill it?"

"Don't know. We'll see." Tupper patted Dare on the shoulder then threw the burlap sack over his back and started down to the ladder. "For now, we've got to get below before the winds hit."

"Before they hit?" she asked. "What were they doing before?"

"Warming up for the big show."

As soon as Dare and Tupper were back on deck, the winds picked up and the sky grew gray and heavy with clouds. Tupper resettled the sack on his shoulder and made for the hold as the rain began.

Only this wasn't like any rain Dare had ever seen. Unlike the Island's refreshing summer showers and light spring mists, it arrived with a crash of thunder and an ice-cold torrent that immediately began pooling at her feet. Dare had to fight to keep from slipping and sliding as she followed Tupper belowdeck, past her cabin and on through narrow corridors. Swinging from handhold to handhold, trying not to lose her footing, she fought to keep up with him until he finally stopped midships and unburdened himself of the sack.

With one foot planted on the neck of the bag, he lit a lantern and handed it to Dare. "Hold this," he directed, pulling open a trapdoor built into the floor.

Dare peered down into the open hatch. The space below was empty except for piles of browning marsh grass. "This is where you're putting it?"

"The marsh grass keeps 'em from banging around, and helps keep them calm," Tupper explained.

"Why keep it alive at all? Kill it now!"

Tupper held the sack over the hatch, leaving the beast to fall into the hold. "We're only in the business of capturing, not killing."

"Who's in that business, then? That's who I want to know."

"No, you don't." Tupper grabbed a large pail of water that was stationed nearby and tossed it on top of the beast before stepping back. "Go on, close it up."

Dare started to close the trapdoor, but stopped.

Had the creature just shivered?

She leaned in closer. Under the lamplight, its twists and knobs somehow began to resemble a face, or at least animal-like features splattered around in all the wrong places. What had looked like a gaping hole now more closely resembled a mouth on the thing's neck. Two of the small holes situated on the pointed tip could've been ears or eyes, and the spike could have been a single beaklike mandible.

Dare reached a hand in, the need to touch the shell oddly overpowering, when Tupper pulled her back.

"I told you, watch out for them blowholes." He kicked the hatch shut, then turned and stalked back to her cabin, flung open the door, and waited for her to go through. "That's enough for now where this beast is concerned. You'll ride out the storm in here. We'll make port at City-on-the-Pike come morning and I'll fetch you then."

Dare planted herself firmly outside her cabin. "What'll happen to the agicole then?"

"Nothing more means nothing more." Tupper tried to give Dare a small shove inside, but she grabbed hold of the doorjamb.

"What are you lying about?"

"You *are* your daddy's daughter, aren't you?" Tupper snorted. "Don't know when to take a no, to stop digging and quit pushing."

Dare didn't recognize that part of her father, not that she'd let Tupper know that. She folded her arms and gave him her best dead-eyed stare. "Teach me to hunt, help me find the beast that killed him."

Tupper shifted his jaw from side to side, the sound of his teeth grating filling the hold, until finally he blew a sigh of capitulation. "We'll talk about it when we're back on land. For now, the sea has plans for us. So get in there and make sure everything is tied down."

Dare bit back a smile. She couldn't let him think she was satisfied by such a measly promise, even if it was worlds better than she thought she'd ever get when she woke up this morning.

She went into the cabin with every intention to do as Tupper had asked, but she couldn't settle in. All she could think about was the agicole.

She should have despised the monster on sight, yet curiosity outstripped hatred, leaving her with an urge that was too strong to quell.

The crew was up top, shouting and running as they steered the ship through the winds and rain. No one would be coming down this way until they'd reached calmer waters.

Lamp in hand, Dare crept out of her cabin, working with the pitching of the boat as she made her way back to the trapdoor and eased it open.

The beast still lay in the hold, listless.

Revulsion, fear, and fascination fought for first place in her thoughts. Her hand wanted nothing more than to touch it even as her legs twitched to run.

As always, her more awful impulse won out.

Dare lay down on her belly and inched up to the edge, letting her arm reach deep into the hold, tentatively touching the beast. It was dormant, knocked out by the salt. What she assumed would be a cold hard shell was warm, almost spongy, pulsing with a slow rhythm like the heartbeat knocking at her own wrist.

"Are you really a monster?" she whispered as she let her fingers trail along the agicole's back.

The beast let out an almost imperceptible noise in response. Low and rumbling, it was an otherworldly sound, unlike anything she'd ever heard. It was the kind of noise that filled her father's stories of monsters, a sound that rippled under your skin, roiled your blood, yet never quite reached your ears.

A monstrous noise.

Dare's mouth went dry as she backed away from the hold. She'd just gotten to her feet when the ship was tossed up by a wave. She managed to stay upright as the ship crested, until the hull crashed back down. She was batted against one wall, then the opposite before she went stumbling into the pit, landing hard on the agicole.

They howled in unison. The pain, shock, and fury of a girl and a monster trumpeting as one. Then the agicole bucked up, heaving her to the side as its four short finlike legs sprouted steely sharp claws. With a hiss and a shriek, it scrabbled up and out of the grass-lined hold.

Fueled by pure impulse, Dare launched herself at the wall of the pit, barely managing to get a hand on the edge. Boots scrambling for purchase, she heaved herself back onto the deck and raced after the beast as it headed straight for the open door to her cabin.

Luck! All she had to do was trap it and toss a sack of salt inside. The beast would be easily subdued. She'd have it back in the pit before Tupper or the crew ever found out what happened.

But before Dare could reach the door, the monster grabbed her hat in its beaklike mandible and was back out the door, spewing a trail of brown slime out of its many blowholes, coating the floor with the oily sludge. Dare lunged and grabbed for the monster, but she slid and slipped as the agicole raced toward the upper deck.

The beast reached the stairs and slowed to a crawl. As it was trying to maneuver up the steps, Tupper and two crewmen armed with sacks of salt came racing down. Tupper held a burlap sack open with one hand and waved another bag of salt in the air with the other. The monster immediately began to falter and sway as the two other sailors closed in, waving their bags of salt, herding it closer to Tupper.

Then one of the sailors slipped on the slime and the sacks of salt went sailing out of his grip.

The monster lurched away and sent Dare's hat flying straight for Tupper. The old sailor caught it handily, then threw it across the hold, but in that moment when his attention was turned, the agicole blew its rancid muck into his face.

Tupper howled as blood began flowing from his nose and mouth, turning his shirt crimson. Dare screamed and ran to his side, all thoughts of the monster gone. At the same moment, the captain and several more sailors burst in, exploding into a blur of bodies grabbing, slipping, and lurching to catch the beast. Amid the blood and shouts, Dare fought to stay by Tupper's side, but between the rocking of the boat and the scuffle to contain the monster, she kept getting cast aside.

When at last the beast was subdued and packed off by two sailors in one direction, four others gently picked up Tupper to carry him off in another. Dare scrambled to follow, but someone picked her up and threw her into her cabin. She lunged for the door but was too late to stop it before it was slammed shut in her face. She heard someone issuing a string of curses laced through with her name from the other side, followed by the sound of the bolt sliding into position.

And then, at last, there was silence.

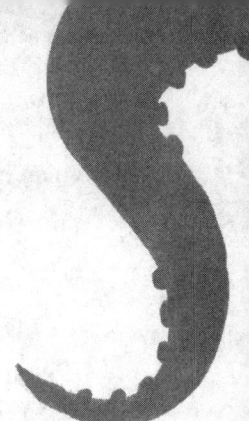

CHAPTER NINE
City-on-the-Pike

Overwhelmed by guilt and the certainty that Tupper hadn't survived the attack, Dare spent the night pacing. By the time morning arrived, she'd exhausted herself and was close to numb. It was a familiar sensation by now, feeling too much easily spilled over into feeling nothing. She went to splash some cold water on her face, an attempt to force herself awake, when she realized she didn't have to fight for balance—the water outside had calmed, and the ship sat at a standstill.

Either they'd dropped anchor to hold a funeral at sea, or they'd moored on the mainland.

Dare tried the door. Finding it still bolted from the outside, she pushed open the cabin's small window and was trying to look outside when voices floated in from the deck above.

"I got word by wire from the Island to come and fetch her," a man said, the edges of restraint beginning to fray.

"I don't care how or from where you got word," another

voice replied, a shrug implicit in his tone. This was the captain—that low-timbred growl hard to mistake for anyone else. "I'll deliver the girl myself."

There was a pause, and though neither man spoke, Dare could practically hear the scowls they were casting at each other.

"You're making a mistake, Captain," the man replied at last. "You might want to reconsider going against this request."

"And you might consider never setting foot on my ship again." The captain was not trying a new tactic.

A loud huff followed by the indignant tread of shoe leather crossing the ship's deck was the only reply to the captain's rebuff.

After what she'd done to Tupper, Dare expected the ship's captain would be happy to be rid of her. Unless he was saving that chore for himself.

She didn't have very long to wonder what he was planning, for a moment later, the door was unbolted and the captain was in her cabin.

"Let's go." He collected her bag and thrust the food hamper at her, nearly knocking her over.

"If you have such little regard for me, why didn't you send me with that man?" she asked, trying to hold her composure.

"Only person who's taking you to the safety of your great-aunt's is me. Now let's move."

Dare didn't. "Who sent him, then? Who was he?"

"Who doesn't matter as much as what."

"And that is . . . ?"

The captain took off his hat and ran a hand through what few gray hairs he had left. Without the cap, Dare could see the map of wrinkles creasing his forehead, hollow cheeks, and heavy brow for the first time. "Best avoided."

"Why?"

"Do you always ask so many questions?"

"No." Dare shook her head. "I usually ask more."

He looked Dare over, his eyes finally settling on the hem of her dress.

"You didn't change?" It was hard to tell if it was pity or disgust in his voice.

Dare looked down at her dress: it was covered in dark splotches.

Blood.

She dropped the food hamper and began furiously batting at the dress, as if to wipe away the entire, awful episode along with the blood.

"Ease up. It'll wash out," the captain said as he headed out the door. "Besides, he's still got plenty left."

"Left?" Dare repeated. "So Tupper's alive, then?"

"It'll take more than a lousy agicole to kill him," the captain muttered.

For the first time since boarding the boat, Dare felt steady on her feet. Relief. Now lightened by the news, she picked up the food hamper and followed the captain back up to the deck.

"I want to see him before we go."

"I already told you, he'll not die from this," the captain

replied without looking back. "Now move, we got to get you where you're going."

Dare dropped anchor. "I'm not leaving until I see him."

The captain's face reddened, the furrow between his brows grown deeper. "We'll be back in port in ten days. You can see him then."

"Ten days is too long. The monster that killed my father is still out there somewhere. What makes you think you won't be next!"

That was enough for the captain to drop her bag and set his nose inches from hers. "Unless you want to see the bottom of the harbor for yourself, you'll watch your every word, especially *that one*."

Undaunted, Dare leaned closer. "People need to know monsters still roam. My father would have—"

"Expected you to be smart." The captain's low-pitched grumble became a growl. "Expected you to watch what you say, and who you trust."

"Oh, so then I'm right to not trust you," Dare challenged.

"Exactly."

Hemmed in by towering brick factories all spewing thick smog, the port of City-on-the-Pike teemed with volume, vice, and industry. Unlike tidy and bright Barrow's Bay, the city harbor was churning with sludge and grime and packed with vessels of every imaginable size. Sailors, laborers, and hawkers swarmed the docks as tall cranes shuttled nets loaded with cargo about with nary a thought for any nearby heads. The air, choked with smoke, raw sewage, and fish, hit Dare like a damp towel across the face. The mainland was exactly the cesspit she'd always been told it was.

Dare trailed the captain as he pushed through the swarm of people shouting, hawking, and hustling. He sliced through the melee with no problem, until they passed three uniformed officials dressed in crisp blue uniforms with the words *Member of the Watch* stitched in yellow across their caps. That was the only moment Captain Fortune looked like he was trying to make himself smaller, invisible, even.

As they were nearing a gateway out to the street beyond the port, a young boy—no more than seven or eight years old—sidled up to Fortune's side. Assuming the boy must be lost or afraid, Dare was surprised when the captain stopped his course and pushed the boy back with a stiff arm. It was a gesture of callous indifference, devoid of compassion. "Looking for something?"

"Your purse." The boy's face was caked with dirt and his coat reeked of mold, yet he held himself as if he were a king among men. Not even Dare would have had the courage to speak as he did when caught so red-handed.

"You've misjudged, boy," the captain said. "Go find another carcass to pick over before I use you for bait."

"You and your crew are closer to being bait than me." The boy grinned. "They're coming for you. Pay me and I'll tell you what I know."

"They're always coming for me, boy. I don't need to pay to know that."

The captain shoved the boy back, picked up Dare's baggage, and continued on his way.

"How are you so cruel?" Dare demanded, trailing Fortune. "You could practically see his ribs through those rags on his back."

"A boy like that never starves." Fortune doubled his pace, forcing Dare to run to keep up.

"Define 'starves.'"

The captain stopped. "You've been on this shore for all of five minutes. Things work differently here. If I gave a coin to every gnat who tried to rob or blackmail me, I'd soon be joining them on the streets. Poverty is big business here. Never get in the way of commerce."

"What does that mean?"

"I hope you never find out." The captain barreled through the gates and out to the street, affording Dare her first glimpse of City-on-the-Pike.

A jungle of redbrick, smokestacks, and narrow winding streets lay before her, as if vomited out the mouth of the gateway. Towering factories, their windows blackened with soot, loomed above sagging two-story wooden buildings jammed so close together, it was hard to tell where one started and another ended. And on the street, pure chaos reigned. Horse-drawn carts, buggies, and even, occasionally, those shiny new horseless carriages they were calling automobiles competed for the narrow roadway, leaving pedestrians running for their lives. Two members of the watch stood smack in the middle of the chaos, whistles seemingly glued to their lips, their hands and arms performing an elaborate dance directing traffic.

"Welcome to City-on-the-Pike." The captain swept his arm up to hail a hansom cab.

If there was some sense of control at work here, it was nothing Dare recognized. Then again, she hadn't recognized anything since the day her father was killed. The unknowable was all she now knew.

In a place as brutal at City-on-the-Pike, that might be a blessing.

Responding to a sharp whistle from the captain, a two-seated cab pulled by a chestnut mare cut hard to the right, sending other carriages veering and scrambling to avoid a collision as it stopped in front of Captain Fortune. Dare jumped back, fearing a crash, but the captain didn't even flinch as he impatiently motioned for Dare to climb on board. "The Nesbitt Grand," he called up to the driver.

"Aww, come on," the driver clucked. "You wanna show your daughter theater, take her to the Madison or, if you're a real sport, Padgett's Palace."

"The Nesbitt," the captain insisted as he threw Dare's bag into the cab and climbed in.

As they rode in stony silence, the carriage bouncing hard over cobbles and potholes, Dare caught the first whiffs. It was hard to detect at first amid the stink of the City—rotting garbage, sulfurous smog, streets littered with horse dung—but she knew that pungent vapor all too well. It was the stink she sensed in her dreams. That funk Tupper had called the smell of fear.

Monsters.

Dare's hands went numb.

There were monsters here? How?

She moved to lean forward to look out, to try to spot them, but the captain pulled the shade.

"You've got no business in this part of the city. Only thing out there are factories and the poor folk who got no choice to work them."

"I just want to look." She reached for the shade, but he beat her there and held fast.

"You're a lousy liar."

"No worse than you, trying to tell me there's no such thing as monsters, after what I saw." She peeled his hand from her arm and sat back. "You can't scare me into thinking what you want any more than the governor could. I don't scare."

The captain rubbed his temples with his thumbs. "You'd be better off if you did."

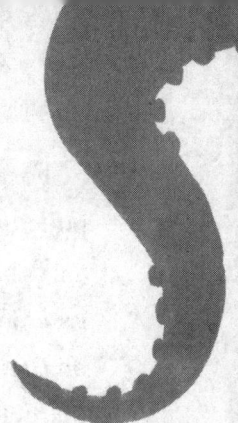

CHAPTER TEN
A Home in the Theater

The hansom cab lurched to a final stop in front of a small, drab theater. The soot-covered white-brick facade was made even gloomier by the fog of an approaching storm, not that bright sunshine would've enhanced the place.

"Why are we stopping here?" Dare asked.

"Why wouldn't we?"

"My father's aunt was a grande dame of the theater. This place is . . ." Dare searched for the word.

"Her theater, and that"—the captain gestured at a shabby three-story house—"is her home." Though the gabled house had likely been grand in its day, the green paint was peeling, the banisters were rickety, and the roof looked ready to slide off.

Of course this was where the governor would think to send Dare. It was bleak, unsightly, and, like her, wholly disagreeable.

Fortune set Dare's suitcase down at the front door and pulled the call bell.

While they waited, Dare eyed the theater next door, with its empty box office and weathered playbills flapping in the breeze. It wasn't that the theater was small, or even that the marquee was dilapidated; what struck her was the sadness of the place, a melancholy so thick you could practically taste it. With only a few other buildings scattered along the street, it was as if City-on-the-Pike were a teapot and this block was the last drop to fall from the spout.

The captain pulled the bell again as two boys came racing up the street. One of them, taller and older-looking than the other, skidded to a halt in front of the captain while his companion took up a position a few feet behind him.

"You're the cap of the *Golden Slipper*, right?" the tall one said. "Got a message for you."

Fortune looked ready to spit. "I already told your friend at the docks, I'm not the sucker for you."

"They said to tell you they paid me already." The boy pulled a letter from his pocket. "Said it was the only way you'd take it, that you're too cheap to pay."

"Now that's not a nice thing to say," the other boy laughed.

Dare couldn't see his face, but the way his thick hair stood up in uneven shocks gave him the look of someone who'd touched the live end of one of those new electrical lines.

Was that . . . ? Could that be the feather boy?

"Hey, you!" Dare shouted. She moved to step in his direction but the captain pulled her back, then snatched the message from the taller boy and sent him off.

As the captain read the letter, Dare strained to catch a better glimpse of the second boy, but he was already gone. "Where'd the other one go?" she asked. "Was he on the ship with us?"

"Huh?" the captain muttered, lost in reading.

"The boy." Dare pointed down the street. "The one with the hair."

"No, I said ignore them all." The captain shoved the note into his pocket and knocked on the door. Hard. His agitation was so thick, it seeped into Dare's bones, feeding her own worst doubts.

"What did it say?" Dare pressed. "Is it Tupper? Did he die?"

"I told you, he'll survive fine." Fortune yanked the call bell harder still, until finally, a bespectacled woman opened the door.

She wasn't old, but she wasn't young, either. Nor was she either pretty or unsightly. She was completely ordinary. Not exactly the image of a grande dame of the theater.

"Captain!" A smile that could not be contained broke over her face, and one hand rushed to do better by her upswept hair. "What a surprise! What brings you to us today?"

"The girl." Fortune barely lifted his gaze. "I brought her."

"Yourself?"

He shifted his weight. "You were expecting someone else to do it?"

"Oh, I assumed it would be a member of your crew, not the busy captain himself." The woman straightened her glasses and squinted at Dare. "Are you sure she's the right one? So skinny for someone from Barrow's Bay!"

Dare swallowed her own opinions, knowing it best not to show her true colors so early on. "Hello, Aunt."

The woman turned three shades of red and broke into a nervous laugh.

"Oh, me?" She fanned herself with her hand. "Can you imagine? Mistaking plain Mary for Madam Emily Nesbitt? I'm just the housekeeper. Well, don't stand there, come in, come in!"

Fortune set the suitcase down just inside the door, then tipped his hat. "I've got business. You'll tell Madam I said to keep close tabs on this one, she won't know the ways of the city."

"Of course." Mary's smile vanished into the embarrassment pleating the corners of her eyes. "I believe there's meant to be something else that came with the girl. A letter, or a package perhaps?"

"None that I know of."

"I see." Mary's disappointment was tangible, but she quickly covered it over with more pleasantries. "I hope you'll come back to see us again soon."

"I'll try." The captain started to go, but Dare grabbed him by the sleeve.

"Not try," she challenged. "Ten days. You promised."

The captain curled his lip and muttered something fit only to be heard out at sea before adding, "Right. Ten days."

This time, he made it halfway out the door before Dare intercepted him again.

"Wait." She removed the cake box from the food hamper and offered it to him. "Bring this to Tupper. Tell him it's from me. Please."

The captain eyed the cake box as if it were a live grenade. But after a deep sigh and a shake of his head, he left, cake box in hand.

"What a lovely man." Mary sighed, watching him disappear.

"That's not the word I would've chosen."

"You're right," Mary agreed. "'Magnificent' is much more fitting."

People like to say looks can be deceiving. Dare knew they unequivocally are.

On Barrow's Bay, it was always the adults with the broadest smiles and the brightest expressions who were the most viperous. The fanciest houses were bound to be the coldest and most impersonal—the governor's mansion being the perfect example.

That's why Dare liked the ugly and decaying: she could trust them to be honest.

Yet Nesbitt House challenged that rule. That dowdy and downcast exterior gave way to a surprisingly handsome interior. Warm parquet floors, walls upholstered in cream-colored silks, and thick carpets greeted Dare as she followed Mary inside, all accented with a hint of lilac hanging in the air.

A second glance, however, revealed carpets worn thin, mirrors gone spotty, and the slightest hint of must lingering behind the lilac. Just enough decay to inspire Dare's trust.

"Come along, now, but leave that food hamper here. I'll put whatever food you brought away myself." Mary headed for the long, sweeping stairway at the end of the foyer, leaving Dare to manage the heavy suitcase. "Your room will be up this way. I'll need you to be quiet, so as not to disturb Madam. She's a very busy woman."

"Oh." Dare sagged under the burden of her baggage. She was no more wanted here than she'd been on Barrow's Bay.

Mary started up the stairway, the walls of which were lined with portraits of Emily Nesbitt. Her pose in every painting the same: left hand on left hip, right hand cradling an object, which varied according to the theme of the painting. The expression on her face was constant as well—a three-quarter view highlighting the commanding sweep of her nose, cut of her cheekbones, and hooded green eyes casting the slightest hint of a smile. She wore a different costume in each painting, her hair color and style varying in accordance with the role. She was featured as everything from a poor peasant girl holding a cup of matches to a socialite dripping in jewels and gripping a sheath of legal documents.

"These are the overflow from the theater's gallery." Mary cast a loving, almost forlorn look at each of the portraits as they passed.

Dare stopped in front of a portrait in which her aunt was dressed in green tights, a green jerkin, and a jaunty hat, a small animal perched on her shoulder—a short-eared rabbit maybe, or a large squirrel, perhaps; it was hard to tell.

"How many plays has she been in?" Dare asked.

"All of them!" Mary declared, as if there were any question otherwise. "All that are worthy of her talent. Come along, you can admire them later. You'll address her as Madam, everyone does. And perhaps you'll even meet her this evening or maybe tomorrow, might be the next day, I can't say, she's—"

"Right here!" Tall, lean, and draped in a flowing silken dressing gown, Emily Nesbitt stood at the top of the stairs, beckoning Dare forward. "Dear Dare, I'm so happy to meet you, at long last!"

No sooner had Dare landed on the top step than her great-aunt gathered her into her arms. Dare's first impulse was to pull back, escape the hold, but Emily Nesbitt smelled like honeysuckle and warm sheets. It was hard to resist.

"She was delivered by Captain Fortune himself," Mary noted.

"How kind of him." Emily Nesbitt released the hug only to gently cup Dare's face in her warm hands.

"You are a vision for these weary eyes, my dear. I am so sorry I wasn't there for your father's funeral. I . . . well, I couldn't make the trip. But you're here now with me." She pulled Dare in for a second hug, swaddling her with a kind of tenderness Dare hadn't known since losing her father.

That bridge of stone and ice Dare had erected inside herself wobbled, and Dare didn't entirely hate it.

"Come, let's go see your room, shall we? Mary, take that heavy case from her."

Mary smiled and took the suitcase from Dare as if she'd meant to all along.

Relieved of the burden, Dare followed her great-aunt down a hall that gave way to three doors. The first two they passed were shut, though the third lay open, affording a view into a sitting room overfilled with plants and white wicker furniture.

"It's like an indoor garden," Dare said.

"It *is* an indoor garden," Madam corrected. "I had it built for . . . well, for someone I cared for very much."

A cloud descended over Madam's eyes for a moment before she changed direction and headed up a second, far less grand staircase, which led into a hall with three doors, one on either side and one at the end. Emily Nesbitt stopped at the door on the right and swept it open.

"This will be your room."

When Dare and her mother had first arrived at the governor's mansion, Mrs. Malcolm led Dare to her new room there in much the same fashion. Dripping with anticipation, she'd opened the door as if it were a portal to heaven itself. It was the first time Dare had electric lights, running water in the bathroom, and sheets spun from silk.

How she'd hated it all. Like the rest of the governor's mansion, it was overwrought and stuffy, even with all the windows open.

But this room was different.

It was clean, quiet, and as lovely as could be, with a nice large bed, a dressing table, a reading chair, and a large sunny window. The floors sloped unevenly and the wallpaper, faded in spots where the sun hit, had seen better days; even the eiderdown covering the bed was a bit ragged at the edges.

It was perfectly imperfect.

"You must be exhausted after your journey, dear." Madam took Dare's coat from her and handed it to Mary. "Have a rest, I'll see you for supper."

"No, I'm fine," Dare insisted, too eager to spend more time in Madam's presence. But a yawn quickly betrayed her.

"There will be plenty of time for that later." Madam took Dare's hand in hers and gave it a tiny squeeze. It was a small gesture, but filled with such warmth that Dare's shoulders couldn't help but to unwind, her bridge to sway.

There weren't any monsters here, real or imagined, her great-aunt seemed to say. Just the promise of rest, comfort, and relief.

And because she truly needed to, Dare believed it.

CHAPTER ELEVEN
A Parade

For the first time in as long as she could remember, Dare slept through the night. No nightmares tangling the bedsheets, no monster dreams waking her up. The webs of sleep only began to slowly dissolve when Mary arrived with a basin of warm water and fresh towels.

"I've never seen a girl sleep so hard." Mary opened the curtains. "Tried to wake you for supper last night. You wouldn't move. I had to take a mirror to your face to make sure you were still breathing. I'll confess, I wasn't looking forward to calling the coroner back in. He never wipes his feet and always leaves behind a stink of formaldehyde. It takes me days to clear it from the air. Madam had a faint from the smell the last time he was here."

Mary pulled a clean dress out of the wardrobe. "I'm washing the one you arrived in. This one suit you for today?"

Dare nodded, not so much out of agreement as shock.

"The last time? How many people have died here?"

"Including Madam's husbands?" Mary silently counted out numbers on her fingers. "I think . . . four. No! Five. Yes, five, because there was that lovely theater critic who collapsed in the foyer. A shame, too—he never wrote a single unkind word of our Madam."

Mary spun Dare around to undo the buttons of her dress with surprising dexterity. In fact, if Dare had been paying attention to anything other than the knowledge that no fewer than five people had died in this house, she would've noticed how nimbly Mary worked the tiny buttons. Even Mrs. Malcolm fumbled them.

"People are fragile," Mary said, whipping off Dare's dress and landing the clean one on her in one fell swoop. "Then again, you can't tell who'll drop just by looking at them. Fate has its own ways of doing things. You never know when you might meet a runaway carriage or catch a flu."

As Mary cheerfully adjusted Dare's collar, Dare felt her bones slowly melting. What circle of hell had the governor banished her to?

"You look like Saint Joan at the beginning of Act III. With a full head of hair, though." Mary laughed as she straightened the shoulder seams. "You have nothing to worry about. You're young and healthy. Aren't you? Now, downstairs with you, breakfast will only get colder."

As long as the food wasn't nearly as chilled as the cold comfort Mary offered, Dare would be happy to eat anything.

***

Down in the kitchen, warm biscuits, coddled eggs, hot oatmeal, and a pot of fresh raspberry jam were laid out on the table. Mary's food was simple and delicious, the opposite of meals at the governor's—which were all about presentation over taste. Dare had become so used to denying herself any kind of happiness at the governor's that it was nice to enjoy something as simple as a well-jammed biscuit.

"Unless Madam is entertaining, you have the run of the house, with the exception of the second floor. None of those doors are for you to use." Mary was busy cleaning the kitchen with the focus and determination of a bee gathering pollen before a storm. "Second floor is Madam's sanctuary, you leave that to her. You can play in the alley between here and the theater, or out front. Mind you take care before you ever step off the curb out on the streets, and don't ever bring anyone or anything into this house without my permission. And always be back inside before dark. The members of the watch don't take kindly to having to ferry children home when they should be tucked into their houses. Flu and carriages aren't the only thing that can get you in City-on-the-Pike, if you understand my meaning."

Dare wasn't entirely sure she did.

"We've got unsavory criminal elements here, desperate people, people with no means," Mary continued. "Your Island had its monsters—we have our own kind here. So, you mind your purse when you're out. Understood?"

Now Dare understood. Mary's dangers weren't Dare's. The vapors she'd caught on the ride to the house were like her dreams, figments looking for meaning in the real world.

"What time should I be here for lunch with Madam?" Dare asked.

"You're a funny one, aren't you?" Mary clutched her collar as if she suddenly felt overexposed. "You'll eat with me. Madam's guests don't eat with children, and truth be told, children shouldn't eat with them, either. Now, out with you."

Before Dare could even try to resist, Mary trundled her out of the kitchen, shutting the door in her wake.

Deadly carriages, dying critics, and disreputable luncheon guests. Nesbitt House would absolutely horrify Mrs. Malcolm. That was enough reason for Dare to decide she was going to like it here, that this might be the perfect place to make herself over. The time spent waiting to see Tupper again would be tedious, and ten days was a long time to sit on a secret. But if it meant learning to hunt monsters, and finally getting to the full truth of her father's death, she'd find the patience.

Dare spent most of the morning wandering through the rambling town house, looking for clues left behind from her father's childhood (though finding none), memorizing the layout of the house, marveling at the portraits of her great-aunt, and imagining what it must feel like to play at being someone else. Before she knew it, Mary was calling her down for lunch.

Back in the kitchen, Mary served Dare a plate of creamed chicken with peas.

"When you're done eating, put your dish in the sink. I've got Madam's lunch to serve now." Mary left the kitchen bearing a silver tray laden with dome-covered plates.

Dare tucked into her food, intending to get back to exploring the house as soon as possible. But then she heard the music—horns and the distant strains of a melody—filtering in from the street.

What plans can't be derailed by a passing parade?

Dare put her plate away and headed to the front door. She disengaged the locks—of which there were several—and quietly slipped out of the perfumed air of Nesbitt House and onto the street.

The sidewalk, which had been deserted yesterday, was now occupied with a healthy sprinkling of people watching the parade pass by. Dare claimed a spot for herself at the edge of the curb and watched in wonder as a platform pulled by a team of four white horses passed by, bedecked overhead with a large banner that read

Padgett's Palace of
Wonders and Delights
Home to Boundless Amusements
Endless Entertainments

A bare-chested man juggling torches was featured in the center of the platform. His quick movements left circles of fire hanging in the air as a trio of contortionists twisted themselves into ever more complex configurations around him. It was an amazing sight to see, though not nearly as amazing as the gilded carriage that came next.

Carved with an intricate design, the carriage pulled a small stage behind it, upon which a woman clad in a gown of shimmering gold stood singing an aria. Her voice dripped with sentimentality and emotion and was reaching notes so high, the empty wineglass perched on a stand next to her quivered. And then, right as the float was about to pass Nesbitt House, the singer hit a note so high, it shattered the glass.

The crowd cheered, and so did Dare; she couldn't have stopped herself if she'd tried. The only entertainments she'd ever seen—aside from that awful yearly Founder's Day pageant play about Louise—were the endlessly boring weekly recitals at the governor's.

But this, *this* was exciting.

The rest of the parade included a procession of horses ridden by trained acrobatic dogs, a woman dressed in a very daring costume riding an emu, and a strong man carrying a giant barbell over his head. Three clowns shouting into megaphones brought up the rear.

"Come one, come all! We've got wonders, we've got spectacles, we've got adventure!"

Whatever this place was, Dare wanted to see more.

Want quickly turned to need as the clowns shouted more enticements from down the street: "We've got brawn, beauties, and monsters galore!"

A chill tripped up Dare's spine. Had she heard what she thought she'd heard? She turned to a woman with a baby carriage who was standing nearby. "Excuse me," she asked as politely as she could, "did they say they have monsters?"

"They've got entertainments, is what they've got," the woman replied. "Ask your mother to take you and go see for yourself."

While she might not have a mother handy, Dare did have Mary and Madam.

She was starting back to the house to ask Mary for some money to go see these monsters—if that's what they were—when someone caught her eye.

The boy with the shock of hair, the one she'd seen at the governor's, and then yesterday, here by the front door, was ducking into the alley between Nesbitt House and the Nesbitt Grand. Unless the world was filled with boys sporting ridiculous cowlicks and guilty expressions, it was the feather boy. Dare was certain.

As much as she wanted to go find this Padgett's Palace and its monsters straightaway, the whine of rusted door hinges assured her this was her chance to corner the boy at last!

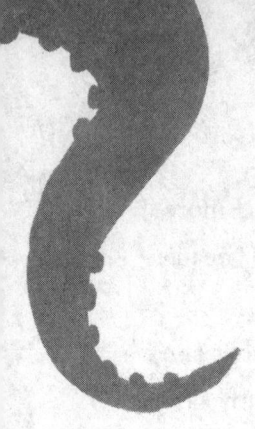

CHAPTER TWELVE
Ghost Light

The exterior of Nesbitt House might have been deceiving, but the Nesbitt Grand's tattered and worn exterior gave way to an interior made to match. Dark, dim, and dusty, the backstage entrance looked more like the gateway to a warehouse than to a grand theater.

"Where'd you go, feather boy?" Dare shouted to the rafters. "I saw you come in here. You can't hide from me. And don't even think about trying to scare me."

There was no answer.

Dare gathered her courage and made her way toward a dim yellow light emanating from somewhere deep inside the theater. Kicking up layers of dust that had settled into place long ago, she followed the glow past a heavy fringe of velvet curtains and onto the stage, where she found the source—a single electric lamp burning bright enough to illuminate the first several rows of the empty auditorium.

The sight of those high-backed red velvet seats lined up like so many soldiers awaiting orders swept Dare with the urge to tidy her skirt. Check the corners of her mouth. Take a grand sweeping bow before collecting imaginary flowers from offstage admirers, wondering what it might feel like to have an entire theater looking at her, hanging on her every word. Loving her.

Then she caught herself. That would never happen.

Dare continued across the stage, headed for the opposite side when the rasp of aged boards creaked behind her.

"Where are you? Are you watching me?" Dare spun around as she shouted to the dusty air. "I know you're in here! I saw you come in, and I can hear you. Show yourself!"

No answer came.

"Fine!" Dare declared to the void. "I'm turning out this light and locking the door. That'll teach you to sneak in where you don't belong!"

She was charging over to switch the lamp off when she spotted a small white bundle peeking out from underneath the dusty red velvet curtain. Her first thought was that it was a discarded rag, but it was so bright, so clean, it couldn't have been there very long.

Hoping it was a clue left by the feather boy, Dare was reaching down to scoop it up when it moved.

Spooked, she jumped back, only to have to laugh at herself

as the bundle revealed itself to be a small white animal.

She assumed it would scurry away, run for cover, yet it sat there, watching her, its short, fuzzy tail lazily wagging side to side.

What a funny little thing—it showed no fear of her at all.

Dare slowly moved to a crouch to get a better look, trying to decide what kind of animal it was. It was too large to be a mouse or a rat, and while its long ears drooped like a rabbit's, its front and hind legs were the same length. Besides, what would a rabbit be doing inside? Its large green eyes and piglike pug nose made it hard to place. And then Dare remembered the day Frances Cooper arrived at school with a pet her father had gifted her. Dare had only gotten the quickest glimpse of it—Frances made some nasty comment about Dare scaring it—but she saw enough to know it was small and furry, with large, bright eyes. Frances had called it a chinchilla and said it didn't make her sneeze the way her cook's cat did.

Could this also be a chinchilla? It was puzzling that Frances would favor a pet this funny-looking; then again, she had seemed most interested in the fact that it was the only chinchilla on the Island, and that she alone had one.

Dare decided in that moment that if she managed to catch the animal, she'd keep it for her own.

She slowly lowered herself to her knees, careful not to make any abrupt movements, whispering, soothingly, "It's all right, you're safe with me."

But the animal never once seemed frightened. In fact, as soon as Dare's knees touched the boards of the stage, it crept away from the curtain and up to her outstretched hand. Unlike the wounded turtle she once tried to rescue on the beach who'd fled from her shadow, this little critter fairly invited her to scoop it up.

Dare knew she ought to ask Mary or Madam first, but she knew a lot of things she had no trouble ignoring. She deserved something, the smallest of comforts, a friend. A pet as off-putting as she seemed only fitting.

Back outside, Dare found the street once again empty and desolate. The spectators were all gone, no one out sweeping up after the parade, not even a stray dog or hungry pigeon looking for crumbs. It was almost as if all those people had appeared out of nowhere for the parade, then melted back into the ether once it had passed by.

Free of watchful eyes, Dare cupped the chinchilla in her hands and looked it over as she walked. Its white coat almost shimmered and, from the right angle, looked more like feathers than fur. The eyes seemed to flash between green and red, depending on how the light hit them, and its tiny claws sparkled as if they were shrouded in glistening cobwebs. And all the while Dare inspected the creature, it too seemed to be sizing her up.

The poor little thing. Lucky that she'd rescued it.

"I'll make a nice little bed and put you somewhere Mary won't find you," Dare promised. The critter gave up a kind of coo in response. "You're a smart little one, aren't—"

The force of a larger body slamming into her shoulder sent Dare stumbling back as a man in dirty work coveralls scolded, "Watch where you're going!"

"You watch where *you're* going!" she shouted back. "You nearly killed me!"

The man shrugged and continued down the street. "You're lucky you didn't get hurt."

"Says you!" Dare grimaced as if in terrible pain. "I'm going to call the watch on you! Who do you think they'll believe? Some brute, or the twelve-year-old stepdaughter of Governor Kingston?"

Dare would never, ever consider herself his stepdaughter, but this creep didn't need to know that. Although clearly he didn't care, for all he did was shout "Good luck with that, girl!" as he continued down the street.

Her awful fully ignited, Dare searched for some horse dung to fling at him. It had been too long since she had a proper row with anyone, but the touch of a cold, damp nose at her ankle sent a wave of cool water to temper her. It was the little beastie.

"Oh no!" Dare scooped it up, searching for any evidence of harm. "I'm sorry, I forgot about you. Are you hurt?"

The little critter gave a contented snort in reply.

"I hope that's a no." Dare stroked its back, marveling at how soft its coat was. No wonder Frances Cooper bragged so mightily about the one her father had given her.

"Let's go inside before someone else comes along to push us around. Mary was right, it is dangerous out here."

Dare put her new pet in her pocket and was about to head back inside when a round of slow and severely sarcastic clapping pulled her up short. She followed the sound of fake adulation to the front entrance of the Nesbitt Grand, where she spotted the feather boy leaning against the shuttered box office.

"Now *that* was a performance worthy of the great actress herself." He tipped his head at the marquee above him. "You could be Madam Nesbitt's understudy."

Dare tried to wither the boy with a look. He didn't shrink. In fact, his smile only grew brighter, an expression that highlighted the divot-like scar on his chin. "You okay now? You going to survive?" he asked.

"What do you know about it?" Dare shot back. "And who are you, anyway? Why were you at the governor's house with one of Pretty's feathers? What did you do to her? Did you kill her or steal her?"

"Who's Pretty?"

"She was my father's bird, and she went missing. . . . Why I am I telling you anything? I'm the one asking the questions!"

"I've never killed anything, and I don't know who Pretty

is. I was at the governor's looking for something, but the only thing I found was that feather."

Dare narrowed her eyes. "What were you looking for? Something to steal, maybe?"

"I'm no thief. And besides, you can't steal what's yours."

Dare was simultaneously intrigued and irritated; he was almost as cagey as she. "What would the governor have of yours?"

"My . . . my future," the boy replied. "Or so I thought."

Dare narrowed her gaze, trying to spot his game. "So you went there for a job?"

He raised a brow—a kind of nod.

"What kind of job?"

"It doesn't matter." The feather boy shrugged it off. "It didn't work out in the end the way I hoped it would."

"That doesn't explain why you had one of Pretty's feathers."

"I found it, is all."

"And you take whatever you find?"

"Sometimes. Kind of like you did in the theater."

"I didn't take anything." Even as Dare batted away the accusation—true as it might have been—she had to fight the temptation to place a protective hand over her pocket.

"Course not." The boy cocked his head. "After all, why would the beloved stepdaughter of a governor ever have reason to lie?"

Most of the barbs slung at Dare back on Barrow's Bay

weren't particularly clever, or insightful. They stung, but they never cut. This boy, whoever he was, saw through Dare too easily.

"Go back to whatever hole you crawl into at night," she shot back. "You don't know anything about me, or what I can or cannot—"

"There you are!" Mary exclaimed as she rushed out of the house, Dare's coat in hand. "I've been looking all over for you. Madam has come down with a terrible headache, and I've just given her the last of our powder. I need you to go to Crosby's and fetch more." Mary threw Dare's coat on and buttoned it up with the speed of a hummingbird, then handed her a slip of paper. "Here's the address. You tell the chemist to put it on our tab, and that I will settle with him next week. Understand? You tell him next week."

Dare understood Mary's instructions fine—it was the address that was completely meaningless to her.

"I . . . how do I . . . where is this?"

"Goodness' sakes, child! Turn the paper over." Mary swept a stray tendril of hair back under her cap. "I've drawn you a map. See? It's very simple. Now, go! Watch your pockets, and be back as quickly as you can. Cool compresses will only keep my poor Madam comfortable for so long!"

Dare looked at the map—it was little more than a serious of lines going off in different directions ending at a circle marked *Crosby's*. "Wait! Mary, this makes no sense!" But the only answer Dare got was the slamming of the front door.

"I know where Crosby's is," the boy said. "I can take you there faster than that map can."

"Like I'd trust you to take me anywhere," Dare scoffed.

"Your choice." The boy threw up his hands and started down the street before doubling back again. "By the way, that line about calling the watch might play on your island, but not here. A member of the watch is just as likely to rob you as to catch a thief. So good luck to you out there."

Then, finally, with a cynical salute, he left.

Dare was usually the one to get the last word in, but he'd left her with no good comeback. Her fingers twitched, and her awful was starting to boil when the little critter in her pocket began to scrabble around, tiny nails hooking into her skin.

"You don't like him, either, do you?" Dare soothed as she pulled him out of her pocket. "We'll find our own way there, won't we? And we can go look for Padgett's Palace while we're out, too."

The chinchilla curled itself into a ball and sighed as Dare traced the curve of its back with one finger. Its coat was as soft as mink and gave off the slightest hint of chamomile.

"I like your confidence." Dare carefully tucked her new friend into her coat pocket and set off, oddly feeling for the first time in a long time as if she knew where she was going.

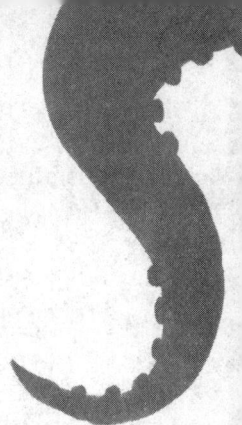

CHAPTER THIRTEEN
Into the Must

As it turned out, Dare's confidence only got her so far, and Mary's map got her good and truly lost.

The turns Mary had indicated weren't marked with street names and Dare soon realized—after passing the same row of stout brick houses for the second time—that she was going in a circle. It wasn't only Mary's map's fault; the streets in the city twisted about in unexpected ways, winding here, dead-ending there, or widening out and narrowing as neighborhoods seesawed from quiet and refined to crowded and coarse. It was almost enough to make Dare pine for the neat uniformity of Barrow's Bay.

When at last she was certain she was well and truly lost, she looked for the friendliest face to stop and ask for directions. Only no one looked very friendly or approachable, so Dare opted for the first woman she saw—an older lady in a stained apron, carrying a large basket of washing.

"Crosby's is three blocks that way." The woman nodded back in the direction Dare had come from.

"That can't be right," Dare said.

"I wouldn't have said it if it wasn't." The woman walked off, muttering something about rude children.

"I can show you rude," Dare called after her.

"She's not entirely wrong," a voice remarked from over Dare's shoulder.

Dare spun, ready to combat yet another boorish city dweller, only to find the feather boy grinning at her.

"Oh, it's you." She let her irritation drip like honey from the comb. "Why are you following me?"

"I think it's you who's following me," he corrected. "And I'm the only one of us who knows how to get to the chemist's shop."

Dare considered her options. She could run him off and keep wandering in circles, or she could use him to get where she needed to go, then ditch him.

"Fine. Take me there," she ordered. "But I have no money and nothing worth stealing."

"That's not really true," the boy said. "Though I'm not the one you should worry about, anyway."

"What's that supposed to mean?"

"You can't ever know what other people consider valuable, is all. Take your coat, for example—lots of people in this city would kill for something that warm."

Dare gathered her coat collar tight around her. "Anyone tries to steal my coat, and I'll scream loud enough to melt glass."

"I'm sure you would," the boy laughed. "Come on, Crosby's is this way."

Dare slipped her hand into her pocket and felt the little critter nudge her hand with its nose. Even though that small ball of fluff was hardly protection, it was comforting to know she had someone on her side.

Dare followed the boy for three twisting and turning blocks. He tried to make small talk along the way, but Dare vowed to keep silent—the less he knew about her, the better—until they arrived at *Crosby & Sons: City-on-the-Pike's Largest and Finest Chemists*.

Occupying nearly half the block, the shop looked less like a chemist's shop than a holiday fair. Decked out with large electric lights and colorful banners, the shop beckoned the eye as if to tempt even the tightest purse to open.

"Want me to come in with you?" the boy asked. "Make sure you get what you need?"

"I'm perfectly capable of doing this on my own," Dare replied. "And I could have found my way here myself."

"I'm sure you would have," he agreed. "Eventually."

Dare tossed her head in a rather convincing imitation of Frances Cooper, then marched into the shop and straight to the counter to order the headache powder.

"That will be twelve cents," the clerk replied to Dare's request.

"Put it on Madam Nesbitt's account, please."

The clerk cleared his throat and straightened his bow tie, which was in no need of straightening. "I'm afraid that's not possible."

"Mary said she will come next week to settle," Dare explained.

The clerk pushed his spectacles farther up his nose. "Either you pay now, or you take your business elsewhere."

"I have no money," Dare said. "And my aunt needs the powder."

"That is a problem." The clerk shifted his gaze over Dare's shoulder and called, "Next, please."

"I'm not done yet!" Dare protested. "I told you, Mary said she'd come pay you next week."

"I'm sure she did." The clerk flashed as fake a smile as Dare had ever seen, then added, "Please step aside for *paying* customers."

Dare's upper lip twitched with the temptation to throw a fit, but all that would do was forestall purchasing the powder Madam needed. She stalked out of the shop and back onto the street.

"No luck?" It was the feather boy again, and he didn't even wait for an answer before setting off down the street alongside her. "There's other chemists you can try. One not too far."

While she'd never admit it out loud, Dare was a bit grateful he hadn't left.

"Why are you bothering to help me?" she demanded.

"Because you need help."

"What kind of person does that? That's weird!"

"You're saying that helping others is weird?"

"People you don't know, yes, it is. There must be something you want. Or you're trying to make up for something you did. Like you feel guilty." That was it—she had hit on it. "You're the one who let Pretty out of her cage! You've been lying."

"I did not, and I have not. But since you can't really know whether someone's lying or not, you might never believe that." He looked ready to leave it at that, then added, "I did see a man, big fella, carrying a birdcage out to a wagon back at the governor's."

"Why didn't you tell me that before!"

"You didn't ask. Besides, the cage was empty."

Another brick landed on that bridge inside Dare.

Poor Pretty.

After Father died, the bird had reverted to the state in which he'd found her: thin and sickly. She was molting, and she needed coaxing to eat. Dare tried to see her every day, but she'd missed the day before the wedding. There was no way Pretty was strong enough to survive on her own.

Dare was beginning to spiral down the hole of regrets when the boy cleared his throat to get her attention.

"Here we are." He'd stopped in front of a shop with dirty windows and a faded sign that read *CLARKE'S CHEMISTS, EST. 1874.*

"Strange," he said, more to himself than to Dare, as she tried the door. "I was here not too long ago and it was open, thriving."

Dare peered in through the windows. "Looks like it's been closed up for years to me."

"Tough times can hit fast." The news seemed to land harder on him than it should have.

"Isn't there another shop? I can't go home without the powder."

Or let Madam see her awful.

"There are more, plenty."

He wasn't wrong: there were plenty more chemist's shops in City-on-the-Pike, and not one of them would extend Dare the credit.

After five more shops rudely refused her, Dare's irritation turned to anger. "I thought the people of Barrow's Bay were the depths of cruelty, but how can anyone deprive a person of medicine?"

"They'll deprive you of a lot more than that," the boy said. "Look around at how all too many people live in this city."

Dare had been stewing in her own darkening thoughts

and hadn't bothered to take in where they were. Until now. The roughly cobbled street bulged with shabby one- and two-story buildings crammed between ramshackle shacks made of rotting wood and tar paper. Lines filled with drying clothes crisscrossed overhead, casting shadows on the already gloomy street. Children with hungry eyes and dirty faces, some covered in tell-tale bites of fleas, sat on stoops or played amid the trash lining streets.

"Is this the Must?"

"The edge of it. The worst of it is that way." The boy pointed down the street toward a line of factories towering overhead, their great chimneys spewing curling plumes of black smoke and grime into the air.

"This is as awful as I've heard it was," Dare said. "There's nothing like this on Barrow's Bay."

"It's here so it doesn't have to be there."

Dare had always known that the denizens of Barrow's Bay were factory owners and industry magnates. One couldn't spend even an hour on the Island and not be reminded who exactly the *GOOD* people were, although even among the wealthy, there were levels of *GOODNESS*. Much of Founder's Day was dedicated to celebrating the most powerful, their enterprising natures lauded and applauded. As with the rest of that ridiculous day, Dare hardly paid attention to what was said, but it had never occurred to her to ask at whose expense all that progress was being made.

The boy led Dare through ever narrower streets, crowded by the push of people leading carts and dray horses around potholes and vendors hawking their wares, until they reached a small shop tucked into an alleyway.

"Here we are," the boy said. "I hope they give you what you need—it's one of the last shops I know of."

Dare eyed the storefront. There was no sign other than the building number, 528, framed by a faded design, no window display, and no other customers waiting to be served—only the thin desperation of a sparsely stocked shop. She was about to surrender her pride and ask the boy to come in with her when the critter in her pocket stirred—a reminder that it was there. The warmth emanating from her pocket and the steady rise and fall of its breath were reassurance that hope was still possible.

A small, wiry woman with thinning hair and sunken cheeks greeted Dare with a wary look and a harshly toned "Whatever you're looking for, I don't have any." But as soon as Dare told her what she was after, and for whom, the shopkeeper's manner changed. It was as if the cloudy kerosene lamps had been suddenly replaced by new electric lighting.

"It'll be my pleasure to provide whatever Madam needs," the shopkeeper said. "I saw her once on the street and I couldn't help to stop to thank her for the free show she'd done in these parts some many years ago. I mostly expected her to dodge me, but she thanked me as nice as one could hope. She can have as much credit here as she needs."

A few minutes later, Dare fairly danced back out onto the street, a parcel of headache powder clutched in her hand like a hard-won prize.

"Good timing, too," the boy said. "Sky is about to open up."

In the short time Dare had been in the shop, the day had grown darker, danker, wetter. It wasn't exactly raining—it was more of a piddle, a damp curtain to be pushed through.

"If we hurry, you'll get home before the worst of it starts."

He seemed so concerned, so invested in keeping Dare safe. It didn't make sense.

"Why do you care if I get rained on or not? I got the powder for Madam, so why still help me?" It was an honest question, one she didn't intend to come out as harshly as it did.

But if his feelings were hurt, he didn't show it. "Because you need help."

"And . . . ?" Dare waited for the rest of it. "What do you want in return?"

"Nothin—" The boy paused. "Wait, there is something."

"I knew it!" Dare crossed her arms over her chest. "I still don't have any money."

"I don't need any of that. All I want is your name."

Dare recoiled—that wasn't what she'd expected. "That's all?"

"And for you to know mine," the boy added, as thunder rumbled off in the distance.

Ha! She had him. "That's two things."

"You're right," he confessed. "Fine, then, I'll owe you."

Savoring her small victory, Dare considered her terms. "I'll tell you, and agree to hear your name, if you show me where that entertainment palace is, Padgett's I think it's called."

The boy kicked at the cobbles in the street, suddenly less sure of himself. "I don't know that I know where that is."

Dare crossed her arms. "Then I don't know my name."

The boy groaned in frustration and relented. "I guess we can find it, if you pay your debt first."

Now it was Dare's turn to relent. "Fine. It's Dare."

"Nice to meet you, Dare. I'm Gil. Now let's hurry before the sky falls."

CHAPTER FOURTEEN
A View of the Palace

Under normal circumstances, the streets of City-on-the-Pike were a disorderly tangle. But the approaching storm pushed it to a new level of havoc as Dare and Gil wound their way through the Must. Wagons filled with teetering towers of boxes flew down streets crowded with vendors rushing for shelter. It was nearly impossible for Dare and Gil to walk in a straight line, let alone stay together.

"Wait up!" Dare called to Gil after she got caught behind a fisherwoman pushing a cart full of overripe goods. Gil patiently waited for her, but they kept getting separated as people scrambled for cover. Dare good and truly lost track of Gil when an automobile pulled right up onto the curb, nearly hitting her.

"Watch where you go!" she shouted at the driver.

"My apologies, miss," the driver said. "Was swerving to avoid a crash."

"Well, you nearly killed me in the doing," Dare snapped.

"Again, I'm very sorr—" He broke off when the rear passenger door flew open.

"Must I get my own door, Ernest!" the passenger scolded.

"It'll only be a moment, miss, and we'll be out of your way." The driver doffed his hat at Dare as he hurried to offer a hand to his demanding passenger.

Undaunted, Dare tried to shove her way past, but the auto's passenger alit onto the sidewalk at the same moment, further blocking her way. Dare had seen a fair number of ostentatious hats and dresses at the governor's mansion—her own mother had taken to wearing the most ridiculous clothes—but the hat that emerged from the auto was by far the most absurd. Covered with orange and pink feathers from brim to tip, the hat was wider than both the vehicle's door and the wearer's shoulders, forcing her to tip her head in a decidedly awkward manner to clear the doorframe.

"That's the most ridiculous thing I've ever seen," Dare muttered under her breath—or so she thought until the woman turned and looked down at her. Apparently, Dare's thoughts had been too loud to contain.

"Move on, urchin, you'll find no handouts here." The woman had a voice like a foghorn, low and loud and hard on the ears.

"I'm not an urchin, you frilly shrew!" Dare shot back, but the prime insult went to waste—the woman had already entered a nearby shop.

The chauffeur shut the car door and stepped out of the way, leaving Dare clear passage. "Apologies for the inconvenience, miss. Please, take this for your troubles." He slipped a shiny new quarter piece into Dare's hand.

Dare recoiled as if the coin were made of lava. "I don't need your money."

"Then pass it on to someone who does." He gave her a friendly wave before slipping into the driver's seat and steering the auto back into the mayhem of traffic.

Dare considered the coin. If that woman had given it to her, she'd have winged it after the automobile, hoping to shatter glass. But the driver clearly meant no insult, and it could come in handy the next time Madam needed medicine.

Dare slipped the coin into her coat pocket next to her other new treasure and took off to find Gil. She found him waiting for her at the next corner.

"Where'd you go?" he asked.

"I got held up by traffic," she quipped.

"If we hurry, I think we can still beat the storm."

"It's only rain," Dare said. "We won't melt."

"You might not, but these streets turn to pools of mud."

The edge of the Must opened onto a wide avenue with a trolley line running down the center of the street. There were a few other buildings scattered along the block, but the centerpiece was a single massive structure, a gleaming circular palace of pink marble and gold with a giant sign that read

Padgett's Palace of Wonders and Delights

"There it is, we found it!" Dare exclaimed. "Let's go!"

"Madam is waiting for the powder," Gil countered.

He was right, but she was so close.

"I'll have a quick look, then right home," Dare vowed.

She raced across to the theater, past banners printed in a brilliant rainbow of colors hanging from every lamppost.

Chills & Thrills!
Action & Adventure!

But it was a banner hanging from the palace marquee that she'd come looking for.

Spectacles, Marvels & Monsters!

"It's true. They really do have monsters." She whispered that last word, having been so chastened by Fortune for speaking it.

"They're not the kind you're thinking of," Gil replied.

"What other kind are there?"

"It's a spectacle, a show—" Gil broke off when a loud crack of thunder shook the street and unleashed great windswept sheets of rain. Quickly soaked, they raced under the marquee, joining a growing crowd of pedestrians also seeking shelter.

Dare hated crowds more than anything; they had a beastly quality—even cheerful gatherings pulsed with an unpredictable edge, as if they could explode at any moment. And this crowd was no different. People elbowed for room and growled with impatience—that is, until the front door of the theater swung open, and a broad-chested man with ruddy cheeks and a thick sweeping mustache strode out.

"What a storm!" he proclaimed, as if it were of his own making.

At the sound of his voice, the crowd immediately parted, creating a kind of makeshift stage for him.

"Come, my friends, come in from the damp! Have some hot drinking chocolate and delight in a few songs while we wait for the deluge to pass!"

The crowd erupted with an excited buzz. Dour expressions turned positively mirthful as people lined up neatly and entered the theater as if renewed, their annoyance at the storm suddenly lifted.

Eager for an up close look, Dare stepped forward to retrieve a ticket for herself. Now she'd get to see exactly what kind of monsters they had. But before she made it to the front of the line, Gil snapped, "Leave that!"

"Why? They're free. I want to see their monsters."

"Nothing's free, and I already told you, it's not real.

Besides, you have to get the medicine home to Madam. I'll get you a hansom cab. I'll be right back." Gil stepped out into the storm, leaving no room for debate.

He wasn't wrong. But was he fully right?

Dare wanted to see for herself.

Still, the crowd was too thick for her taste, so she stuck to the edges. She pulled the chinchilla out of her pocket and stroked his silky fur as she watched Gil out in the rain. "Look at him, getting drenched like that. Why's he helping me? What do you think he really wants?"

The critter gave a little shiver.

"I agree, he is very strange." Dare popped her pet back into her pocket to keep him warm. She was pulling up her own collar to stave off a chill when the ticket man tapped her on the shoulder.

"Come now, don't you want some hot chocolate?" His voice was loud and buoyant like a bright bouncing ball. "And a free show, to boot! It's a rare thing to be invited inside Padgett's Palace free of charge." He swept an arm toward one of the large posters displayed behind glass. "We'll treat you to some songs from *The Tragedy of Our Louise*—it's our most popular production."

Dare's tongue fell flat as her eyes landed on the poster, a full-color drawing of a tall, hairy beast with sharp claws and a crowlike beak poised to pounce on a girl with blond ringlets.

"Is that supposed to be the garbinol and Louise?" Dare did

nothing to contain her disgust.

"Why, yes. It's not too frightening for you, is it?"

"Frightening?" Dare balked. "That is the most ridiculous picture I've ever seen. If you knew anything about garbinols, you'd never, ever, ever have let that out in the light of day!"

Now it was the man's turn to balk. "My audiences love it."

"You're not supposed to *love* a garbinol! Monsters aren't entertainment, they're real and they're terrifying. I know, I've see—" Dare regained control of her tongue. She'd said enough. Fortune would be livid. "Your poster makes it look silly, and monsters are the furthest things from silly."

Rather than storming off in an offended huff, the man leaned in closer. "Tell me, how does someone so young come to know so much about monsters? They stopped teaching about them in schools some years ago, didn't they?"

"That was an absurd decision." And one that constantly got Dare in trouble at school.

"I agree with you!" The man laughed heartily. "So then, who taught you?"

"My father." Dare couldn't speak of him without a proud tilt of her head.

"Your father?" The man's chin nearly disappeared into his neck as his eyes widened and his mustached upper lip curled with joy. "Stars above! And here I brag all the time that I never forget a face. Though under the circumstances, it's understandable—grief is a terrible stressor. You're Dare,

Captain Coates's daughter, are you not?"

Dare froze. The mention of her father's name from a stranger's mouth hit her with an unexpected rush. "How do you know that?"

"I saw you at the funeral. I wanted to offer you my condolences, but you'd left the parlor before I could reach you. Forgive me—TR Padgett, at your service." As the man offered a bow, a bitter taste collected on Dare's tongue.

"Why would you travel all that way for a funeral? There to please Governor Kingston, were you?"

Padgett looked as if he'd been struck between the eyes. "I came to pay my respects to an old friend."

"Friend?" The word sounded foreign. Like herself, she'd never thought of her father as someone who had any friends.

"For many years. In fact, I had just written to ask his advice on the monsters for my show when I heard of his . . . passing."

For a man who spoke with such confidence, that was a very long pause. What word was he searching for? Or maybe trying to avoid?

"It was a terrible thing. He was as good a man as they come. I only wish he had known how highly I regarded him. That's not something trinkets and tokens of appreciation can express." He paused yet again, taking a moment to remove his hat and smooth his hair back. "Once I heard the news, I knew I had to make the journey. My first time back at sea in many years. You see, I'm terribly prone to seasickness. But nausea be hung—I set out for the Island as soon as I could. I lost my father at an early age, too. It's not something that's easy to carry, especially when, as you know, there are still so many questions."

Dare suddenly wasn't sure what to do with her hands. What did he mean by "so many questions"? If he was at the funeral, then he'd heard her outburst along with everyone else. Was it possible he'd been the only one there who didn't think her addled by grief, who thought the same thing about her father's death that she did?

But before she could get a word out, an usher in a tidy uniform stepped out of the theater and handed Padgett a note.

"That's my cue. Time to start the entertainment for these poor drenched souls. But what a lucky accident that you should find your way here to my theater! What say you come back tomorrow? I'll give you a tour, show you how the magic gets made, and we'll speak of monsters and . . . other things, too."

There was that pause again. This one unmistakably pregnant as a sow in midsummer, and broken only when he reached into his pocket and handed his calling card to Dare.

Like the man himself, it was showy and bold. His name—TR PADGETT—was engraved in gold letters and framed by an elaborate border. "You show that at the stage door and they'll call for me right away. Will you come?"

There wasn't a single doubt about it. The entire exchange

had left far more question than answers. "All right, yes." Dare nodded. "Tomorrow."

"Splendid! Make it one thirty. Until then!" Padgett tipped his hat and strode off into the theater just as Gil shouted for her.

"Dare! Over here!" He'd somehow managed to get a hansom cab to stop—the horse rearing up as it did—and was waving wildly for her to climb in.

Dare slipped Padgett's calling card into her pocket along with the coin and the packet of powder, then dashed out from underneath the protection of the marquee and into the cab.

As hard as it was to believe, good things, interesting things, were suddenly piling up.

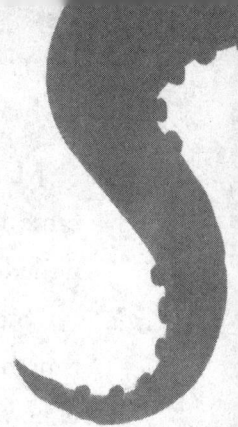

CHAPTER FIFTEEN
Presents from the Past

Dare had barely stepped through the front door when Mary was on her.

"What took you so long?" the maid demanded, one hand wringing the other pale. "Where's the medicine?"

Dare handed the packet over like the hard-won prize it was. But Mary quickly soured.

"What is this?" She held the brown paper packet between two fingers like a dirty rag. "This isn't from Crosby's."

"No, it's not," Dare conceded. "I don't know the name of the shop, it was somewhere on the edge of the Must. The shopkeeper said Madam could have as much credit as she wanted. It was the only place that agreed to extend—"

"Shh!" Mary aggressively mimed buttoning up her lips. "All this noise is likely to turn Madam's headache into a fevered fit."

Mary reached for Dare's coat, ready to remove it with the same lightning speed she'd put it on with earlier, but Dare pulled back.

"Stop!" she snapped, her awful peeking out for the first time here at Nesbitt House. She'd intended to keep that side of herself hidden from both Madam and Mary—consign it to her past. But she couldn't let Mary take the coat, not with the chinchilla in her pocket. "You take care of Madam. I'll do it myself."

Mary looked all too happy to be relieved of the work, although Dare did hear her cluck "Strange child" as she darted away up the stairs.

Dare waited until she heard a door upstairs open and shut before whispering to her pocket, "You must be starving, poor thing. Let's find you some food."

Dare gathered a small bowl of grapes, a few walnuts, a piece of bread—anything she thought a chinchilla might eat—then returned to her room. She knew she was breaking the rules, risking being caught out, but how could she not? The critter was so little, so dear. So dependent.

Unlike the other girls on Barrow's Bay, Dare never played house with dolls or volunteered to mind younger children. She detested the other girls' relentless focus on growing up only to devote the entirety of their lives to tending to others. What was the point of being a grown-up if you were still tied to the household?

But feeding and caring for the critter was different; it felt more like an exchange of caring. She offered food and a home, and it gave her comfort and companionship in return. A collaboration.

The rest of the day passed in focused pursuits. Dare's first chore was creating a well-hidden corner for her pet to sleep in the back of the wardrobe, somewhere Mary would never look. When that was accomplished, Dare turned to trying to find the right name for him.

"Lucian? No. Furry? Definitely not. Pretty Two? No, too sad." Dare was so intent on making her list that she barely heard the knock on her door.

"Your aunt is asking to see you before supper," Mary called through the door. "Change out of your day clothes and put something proper on. I saw a lovely green velvet dress in your wardrobe. The one with the white ribbons. She'll like it."

Dare grimaced. She hated that dress with a passion. It was one that Mrs. Malcolm had trussed up with ribbons and frills. But if it would please her great-aunt, Dare would wear it.

Emily Nesbitt sat in a chair in the parlor dressed as if she were going to a ball.

"My dear niece! Look at you, a vision in green velvet." The great actress's voice was deep and resonant, and Dare could almost feel the vibrations coursing through her veins. "I have been so eager to get to know you. Your father was so dear to me, even as we . . . well, didn't see each other for many years. I'm grateful to have a small piece of him with you. Now, I want to hear everything about you."

Dare had no idea how to respond. No one had ever asked her about herself. She didn't know where to begin.

"Begin with what you like, what you find interesting, then quickly get to what you despise." Madam's eyes flickered with a playful kind of mischief. "I always learn so much about a person by what they revile."

Dare began hesitantly, careful not to come off as awful or crass, but the more she told Madam about her life on Barrow's Bay, the more Madam encouraged her, and soon Dare was acting out imitations of some of the Island's greatest bores and snobs.

Madam laughed and clapped with delight at everything Dare said. Dare had forgotten what it felt like to have someone listen to her, laugh with her. Like her. She didn't want the evening to end, but after a while, Madam's energy began to flag, and soon she looked pale and tired.

"I think I need a rest now, dear," she said. "We'll visit more tomorrow. Is that all right? Mary can bring your supper to your room. You pretend you're in a fancy hotel having room service. How does that sound?" She looked as if her very happiness hinged on Dare forgiving her. And of course, Dare did, for even this short time with Madam had made her almost feel like she could be the new person she hoped to become, without having to give up all of her old self.

Back in her room, Dare started to change out of the terrible dress but caught sight of herself in the mirror and stopped. Suddenly she was seeing it, and herself, anew, as if through Madam's eyes.

Maybe the dress wasn't as terrible as Dare had thought. And neither was she.

Mary arrived a short while later with Dare's dinner on a tray.

"You can bring this back down with you in the morning. I'll have enough dishes to wash tonight." Mary was in a fluster, but as she turned to go, she paused, her nose seeming to have found a hint of something in the air. Dare tried to put herself between Mary and the wardrobe—but she wasn't fast enough. Mary threw the closet open and in a flash was riffling through the clothes like a dog on the hunt.

Dare had to forcibly push back the instinct to shove Mary out of the wardrobe, but letting her awful out now would only make things worse.

"What are you looking for?" Dare put on her most innocent voice, the one she'd used with her teacher on days she wasn't up for trouble.

Mary didn't answer.

Dare was a breath away from confessing when Mary whipped Dare's coat out of the closet.

"Damp!" she exclaimed, holding up the offending garment

like a rat from the trash. "You can't put it away like this. The fibers will mold, then rot. I'll take it downstairs and air it out properly. And please, change out of that dress. Ironing wrinkles out of velvet is a terrible chore."

"Yes, of course!" Dare exclaimed with far more enthusiasm than was needed. Yet no sooner did she think she was in the clear than Mary pivoted and stuck her head back into the wardrobe.

"What are you thinking, Dare!" she cried from within the cavern. "What's this doing back here?"

A lump the size of a fist lodged itself in Dare's throat. She was used to walking the edge of trouble, courting a reaction from people; she wasn't used to caring about not doing so.

"I . . . I'm sorry, I found it and I—"

"You found it?" Mary exclaimed as she extricated herself from the closet.

Which was worse: fabricating a lie, or admitting she'd willfully ignored Mary's orders about bringing anything into the house? Before Dare could try to choose, Mary emerged, a wrapped box tied up with grosgrain ribbon clutched in her hands.

"I set it aside when I unpacked your bag, assuming it was a gift for Madam," Mary said. "Your mother had mentioned the governor would be sending . . . something. I assumed you'd give it to Madam in your own time. It never occurred to me this might not be yours to give!"

"Oh, the present!" Relief ran down Dare's back. "No, it is mine. It's from my mother. I forgot about it."

"A gift from your mother to you. Not for Madam?" Mary reluctantly set the box down next to Dare. "I see. Then I'll leave you to open it."

Dare kept a thin smile plastered on her face until Mary, damp coat in hand, had gone.

Dare had lied.

She hadn't forgotten about it, she'd simply hoped it got left behind on the Island. Ever since the governor had given Mother unfettered access to his charging privileges at the shops, she'd been relentless. There was hardly a day she didn't come home with a new dress, hat, or pair of gloves. And on occasion, she also saw fit to buy Dare a useless bit or bob—worst among them that horrible, unspeakable hat.

Judging from the shape of the box, another awful hat was probably lurking inside. Dare wanted to leave it in the back of the closet, but that would only invite more questions from Mary.

Dare pulled at the ribbon, releasing a waft of the new perfume Mother had taken to wearing. Was it possible to both despise and miss something at the same time?

The note written in Mother's flourishing hand simply read *For you.*

Fully prepared to be irritated, Dare opened the present.

It wasn't a hat, nor another frivolous bit or bob.

It was another box, this one carved from eldolon wood—a tree native to Barrow's Bay.

Father's box.

Dare had never really noted the carving on the lid, until now. But it was curious: a line beginning at the outer edge that turned in on itself one sharp angle at a time until at last it ended at a three-pronged, trident-like design at the center. She traced the lines with her finger—forestalling the moment she'd open it, wondering what she'd find inside.

His needle and thread? Paper dolls? A chocolate?

What if there wasn't anything in there? Absence magnified would crater her.

So would not knowing.

Dare girded herself, preparing for a rush of feelings as she eased the lid open. Hints of Father's beard oil and morning coffee escaped, as if his very essence had been trapped inside.

But that's all there was, aside from the nub of a pencil, one of his little looping-line doodles, and a broken button. Hardly enough for an entire life to have left behind.

But it was enough for her. It would have to be.

Dare shut the box, hoping to trap the scent of him inside, then she set it on the highest shelf in the wardrobe, knowing that if she allowed herself to succumb to the waves of sadness cresting inside her, she might never return to shore.

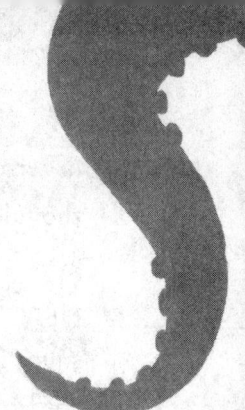

CHAPTER SIXTEEN
The Trick to the Tale

The monsters returned to her dreams that night. There were only two of them this time, not that that made them any less terrifying. There was a lypek crouched by the window, sharp claws digging into the ledge, the moon illuminating its dull green scales and the eighteen talons sprouting from the beast's neck. One swipe of those razor-sharp blades could slice a person to ribbons.

But it was the skerbin slithering up her arm that sent Dare's heart racing for escape. If you didn't know what it was, it could easily have passed for a snake. But looks don't always tell the tale. As it began winding itself around her throat, tighter and tighter, round pods running down the devil's neck puffed out and began emitting a deadly oil that was said to melt bones.

Helpless to scream, all Dare could utter was a weak croak

of terror as the lypek sprung from its perch and dove at her, the talons ringing its neck aiming for her heart. She tried to get up to fight, to hide, to flee, but the other beast had her pinned flat. Certain she was about to meet her end, Dare squeezed her eyes shut, shaking to her bones, waiting to be cut from stem to stern.

But the attack never came.

The stench evaporated, the screeching stopped. All was silent.

Though her heart was still pounding in her throat, Dare slowly peeled her eyes open. The room was empty, the first hints of daylight dispelling the dream, scattering the monsters from whence they came.

She'd been stupid to think she'd left the nightmares behind on the Island. They were no different from the inescapable shadow of loss; always there, hovering over her shoulder.

At least the new day held the promise of a direction, the chance to find out what Padgett was hiding in those pauses of his. After breakfast, Dare retrieved her coat, then tucked her pet and Padgett's calling card in her pockets. She'd prepared an alibi for Mary, an explanation for why she'd be out for lunch, but Mary only replied with a vague "Be back before dark."

Easily freed, Dare was about to step out into the overcast day when she realized she wasn't sure how to get back to Padgett's Palace—the route there had been so circuitous, and she'd forgotten to pay attention during the cab ride home.

She poked her head back into the kitchen. "Mary, how do you get to Padgett's Palace?"

Mary stopped sweeping mid-swing. "You don't!"

"But Padgett's—"

Mary cut her off quick. "Is not anywhere you need to go. That theater of his, those crass entertainments he puts on, killed Madam's career and led to the shuttering of the Grand. Why, his very name is enough to send Madam to bed for days. No, we don't go there—he'll not get a single penny from this household." And with that warning in hand, Mary shooed Dare out into the misty morning.

But Dare didn't get any farther than the front stoop. If Padgett was responsible for the shuttering of the Nesbitt Grand, Dare should hate him, too. Yet there were all those unspoken words of Padgett's, so much he seemed to know about Father.

What had looked like easy luck was now an impossible choice.

The chinchilla peeked its head out of Dare's pocket and nudged her hand with its snout. She pulled him out and let him jump from hand to hand, his floppy ears bouncing comically with every leap.

"You're a funny little beast, aren't you?"

"He is," a voice teased at Dare's ear. "Though I'd keep him

out of sight—you never know when someone might be looking your way."

Dare turned to find Gil leaning in over her shoulder.

"Don't sneak up on me like that!" she scolded. "You nearly made me drop him."

"See? Put him away, it's safer."

"With you around, it is."

"I'm the least of your worries." Gil sat down on the stoop next to her. "What are you doing out here in the mist, anyway?"

Dare's first instinct was to tell him to shove off, to mind his own business. But he looked like he actually cared, and she could use an ear.

"Trying to make an impossible decision."

"What about?"

"I have to choose between doing what I should, and what I want."

"That is tricky." Gil paused to think for a moment, his thumb absentmindedly playing over the scar on his chin. "Lying is bad business, it will always come back to haunt you. Unless you have a good reason for doing it—omission isn't always the same thing as a lie. Sometimes deception is protection."

Dare pressed her lips together, suppressing a smile. His pretzel logic was appealing. "Then it wouldn't be awful of me to do the thing I want to do as long as no one finds out?"

"If knowing what you did would hurt someone more than if they didn't know, then no, it might not be awful."

The knot in Dare's stomach loosened. "Thank you, Gil." Dare got up, put her pet in her pocket and set off down the street, her conscience clear and her sights set on Padgett's Palace. But she hadn't gotten more than a few steps before she stopped.

"What's the matter?" Gil called. "Lose your nerve?"

"Never." Dare pulled back from a growl. "I . . . I don't know how to get back to Padgett's Palace. This city is so confusing."

"More than you know," Gil agreed. "Why do you want to go back there? I told you, their monsters are artifice."

"I want to go back, is all." Dare hoped to leave it at that, but Gil didn't move—he wanted a real answer.

"Fine." What did it matter if he knew, anyway? "Padgett knew my father, he said nice things about him. I want to hear more."

"Oh." Gil looked more surprised than Dare thought he ought to. "All right, then yes, I'll show you the way."

As Dare followed Gil through the winding city streets, she couldn't help but notice how he strutted along as if he were the king of the row—plowing a straight line down the middle of the sidewalk, refusing to step aside for oncoming pedestrians. She kept waiting for the better-heeled folk to run him off course, challenge this street waif's refusal to step aside. Yet one by one, people did just that, leaving him a wide berth.

City-on-the-Pike—and Gil—were getting more interesting with every step.

"There it is." Gil gestured toward Padgett's Palace as they rounded a corner. "Want me to wait and walk you home?"

"No, I know the way now."

"Good luck, then!" Gil waved and set off the way they'd came.

Luck surely had nothing to do with it. Knowing that even just being here might upset Madam left Dare with the urge to wash her face, as if she could scrub off the stain of deception. But the thought of missing the chance to talk to Padgett about her father and explore all those unspoken words was even worse.

"This is only for now." Dare put her hand in her pocket, cupping her pet for courage, and headed down the stage door alley. She'd just reached the door when Padgett came bursting out.

"You came!" He threw his arms wide open as if she were his own long-lost daughter. "I'm so pleased! Come, come!"

Padgett was surprisingly nimble for such a big man—floating like a kite on high as he ushered her inside. "Welcome to my theater, a house built of pure magic!"

There was only one kind of magic Dare was interested in—the kind that could bring her father back—and she already knew it didn't exist. She was after something far more rare:

the truth of what had really happened the day her father died.

Backstage, Padgett's Palace was buzzing with people trundling costumes and set pieces about, climbing ladders and coiling ropes. Electric lights illuminated the simmering energy that hovered like a mist by the harbor. And in the middle of it all, Padgett planted himself and breathed in deeply.

"Not bad for a boy born to a seamstress driven blind from her work, eh?"

Dare set her jaw. Patience. Let him talk, warm up to her, before hitting him with a barrage of questions.

"I know what you're thinking," Padgett continued, leading the way deeper into the theater. "I had to have had help—my family wasn't really poor, or I had a rich uncle or some such. Well, you'd be wrong. Come, I want to show you something."

Padgett started up a narrow, twisting staircase. Up and up they climbed until finally the stairway let out onto a walkway suspended high over the stage. Dare swallowed for courage, although since her journey on the *Golden Slipper*, she'd learned there were far darker things to be afraid of than heights. Padgett stopped at the midway point and stepped onto a small platform placed in front of a large wooden star covered in thick black paint.

"What do you see?" He was gazing at the star as if it had fallen from the heavens.

Dare looked for the trick, but Padgett was the picture of earnest anticipation.

"A wooden star painted black?"

"That's what you think you see. Yet can you trust your own eyes?" Padgett cupped his hands around his mouth and shouted, "Give us some glow up here!"

Moments later, hot stage lights burst to life, transforming what had been a flat star-shaped piece of wood into a glittering wonder showering the stage below with brilliance and light.

"This is the magic I create, turning simple wooden cutouts into glistening stars. And this . . ."

Padgett clapped his hands and the very platform they were standing on began to slowly descend. Dare braced for another terrifying ride, but unlike the mizzenmast on the *Golden Slipper*, this platform's descent was slow, smooth, and controlled.

Padgett turned Dare to face out toward the audience. The view from on high was nothing short of astounding: three times larger than Madam's theater, rows of seats as far as she could see, five balconies, and an array of private boxes all topped by a ceiling painted like the night sky.

"Magnificent, isn't it?" Padgett waved an arm toward the highest balcony as the platform gently touched down on the stage. "Imagine thirty-five hundred pairs of eyes pinned to your every gesture, breathlessly waiting for your next move. The power of an assembly of strangers all feeling the same feelings, sighing the same sighs. And then, when the applause begins, it arrives like a wave, building and sweeping over you, a tide of pure adoration."

As practiced as she was at concealing her thoughts, Dare was getting lost in the spell he was weaving. She could practically hear the thunderous applause numbing her ears—her blood thrumming with what it must be like to be appreciated, lauded.

"Who doesn't want to be adored?" Padgett leaned in and whispered. "You can't tell me you have no desire for people to know how special you are."

The spell broke.

"What I want and what I get don't have anything to do with each other," Dare scoffed.

"Don't they?" Padgett didn't wait for an answer. "When I was young, people told me I was too much, too big, too messy. I did everything I could to tune them out, ignore them. I'd tell myself over and over, 'They know nothing.'"

He smoothed his mustache, a tiny adjustment turning his expression from serious to playful. "Then one day, I started listening, and I realized they were right. I was bursting the seams of my small life, leaving frayed edges everywhere I went."

His story was stepping uncomfortably close to Dare's; she needed him to back up several paces. "Being lonely doesn't make you special."

"No, it doesn't. What makes me special is that I left, made myself a new life, one where I could keep expanding. I have a keen eye to spot real talent, and the power to foster it. And now people flock here to bathe in the light of all I've built. You only think you can't be seen, Dare. I saw you from the first. You can go on trying to hide your talents, but your shine is far too bright."

Dare winced. Father was the only person who ever told her she shone, the only person she let her guard down with. Yet here she was. She'd been so busy watching for the tricks in Padgett's tale that she forgot to guard her own.

"Don't worry." Padgett leaned in conspiratorially. "Your secret is safe with me. For now. But warrant what I say: the time is coming when you'll be ready for your talents to be exposed."

Dare's first instinct was to shut the whole idea down. But there was that word again, the same one Tupper had used. "What do you mean by *talents*?"

"It's clear to me that you're not just any young girl. You're clever, decisive, and you seem to possess a rare ability to—" Before Padgett could get to the point, a loud, low voice that bore the most striking resemblance to a foghorn blared out his name.

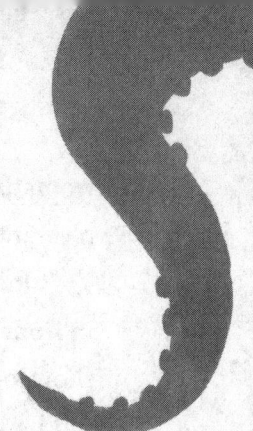

CHAPTER SEVENTEEN
In the Wings

"TR Padgett! Where are you!" That foghorn sounded hauntingly familiar, and when a perfectly coiffed woman pulling along a perfectly sullen girl stepped up to Padgett, Dare understood why.

It was *that* perfectly coiffed woman, the one whose car had nearly hit Dare in the Must.

"How many times do I need to tell them not to serve us cheese for lunch!" The woman grabbed the girl by the chin. "Show him your tongue!"

The girl glanced in Dare's direction for a hair of a second, then back at the woman. "Fan."

That's all she said. One barely audible word, yet it was enough to turn the woman's expression from stormy to sunny warmth.

"I didn't realize you'd taken to conducting tours, TR." The

woman's voice rose several decibels and even more levels of pleasantness.

"Only for the most special of guests." TR stationed Dare in front of him. "Dare, may I introduce the shining star of our show, our very own Louise, Nell Lawrence, and her beautiful mother, Mrs. Rose Lawrence."

"Oh, we've met." Dare made no attempt to sound remotely pleasant. "Don't you remember?"

"I'm afraid you're mistaken," the Foghorn blew. "Now, TR, about our lunch, you'll see to it—"

"It was only yesterday," Dare continued. "Your automobile, the sidewalk, my near death. How could you forget?"

Mrs. Lawrence's upper lip twitched as she tried to force a smile. "Oh dear, that was you? My driver is so careless. I really ought to fire that man."

"You're not firing Ernest." Nell barely spoke above a whisper, but her voice was firm.

"We'll not discuss it here, Nell." Mrs. Lawrence looked ready to break under the strain of trying to appear pleasant. "Come along, now, you'll gargle with salt water and pray you can hit your notes."

Mrs. Lawrence shuttled her daughter away—like a toddler from a flame—but the girl turned to watch Dare over her shoulder, a strange mix of fascination and curiosity in her gaze.

That woman wasn't worth a single moment of Dare's

attention, but the way Nell managed to chasten her mother without being awful or raising her voice made her someone worth watching.

"Let's continue our tour, shall we?" Padgett led Dare offstage and into the center of a bustling hive of cast and crew. Dare was primed to press him further on what he'd meant by "talent" and all the rest of his cryptic utterings when he sidled up to a balding man sporting a pencil-thin mustache and small, round, silver eyeglasses who was draping an actor on stilts in fur. "This is our brilliant costume designer, Leeds," Padgett announced. "And this is our garbinol. Far better than that picture, no?"

Dare couldn't contain her disdain if she tried, and she didn't try. "No, it's not."

Leeds peered over his glasses at Dare. "And who are you, exactly?"

"This young lady, Miss Dare Coates, knows a thing or two about monsters, Leeds. We'd do well to listen to her. Go on, please." Padgett leaned back against the wall. "Share your thoughts, theater is a collaborative art."

Leeds pursed his lips and raised a brow, a tacit—if surly—invitation for her continue.

"You're working so hard to try to make your monsters look real, and you'll never be able to do that," Dare began. "Monsters are terrifying because of how they make you feel, not necessarily what you see. My father said half of them didn't even look like monsters until they attacked."

"Like the skerbin?" Padgett asked.

The mention of the very beast she'd just dreamt about sent a chill through Dare strong enough to make the critter in her pocket stir. She plunged a hand in to comfort it, and herself.

"That's all fine and well," Leeds concluded, "but I'm a costumer not a magician."

"Aren't you, though?" Padgett laughed. "I have a brilliant idea! Dare, would you help Leeds here improve our monsters? I'll pay you the same money I offered your father in my . . . ill-timed letter. What was it you said, we must make the attack *feel* real?"

Absolutely not! She shouldn't have even been in the building in the first place, let alone helping the theater that led to Madam's downfall succeed in any way. But for the first time since Tupper, someone was asking her to talk about the monsters.

Fortune would be furious if he knew, but he wasn't here. And sitting and waiting for days and days until she'd see Tupper again was beyond tedious. Padgett was right here in front of her, right now. Plus, she had an opportunity to do some good by earning money to help pay for Madam's headache powder.

Deception as protection.

"All right," Dare agreed, then quickly added, "A day or two."

"Splendid!" Padgett clapped in joyful triumph, then moved a stool into the wings. "You sit here and watch the show, it's the best seat in the house!"

"Oh no, thank you." Dare backed away from the stool. "I know the story, I don't need to see it again."

Ever.

"Don't be silly! You must see what we do to know how to improve it."

This was not part of the plan. "I'd rather you tell me about it while we talk about my father, and what you meant by 'talent.'"

"There will be plenty of time for that," Padgett crowed. "For now, sit, enjoy the show, and see my monsters in action."

And just like that, Padgett slipped away, something or someone else capturing his attention.

The schoolmarm used to scold Dare all the time for being "too clever by half." She had never understood what that really meant, other than that it was the marm's way of humiliating her. Now it made sense. She'd thought herself so clever, agreeing to help Padgett with his monsters to find out what he knew, only to wind up exactly where she didn't want to be.

"I don't need to watch, really," Dare began explaining to Leeds, when an actor in full stage makeup came flying out of his dressing room door, hissing like a cat on fire. "LEEDS!"

Dare and her pet both jumped at the bellow, but Leeds kept at his work, calmly tying another actor's bonnet in place.

"What is it now, Frederick?"

"My belt isn't working. Again!" The actor thrust the costume piece at Leeds. "You said you'd fixed it the other day, yet it still won't close!"

Leeds finished with the bonnet, slowly wiped his hands on a linen rag he kept tucked in his back pocket, and only then took the belt from the actor.

"I did, and the week before, and three weeks ago, too . . ." Leeds paused as he tried to fasten the belt around the actor's middle. "I can only remake this so many times."

As the actor and costumer exchanged a round of barbs, Dare took the opportunity to sneak away, but before she got too far, Leeds turned on her.

"You." He motioned her close with a curling finger. "Can you make yourself useful?"

"I can." Dare left the "if I wanted to" unspoken, yet forcibly implied.

"Hold this. Easier to sew without the weight." Leeds tossed her the belt's buckle. He wasn't kidding—it must have weighed five pounds.

"Is this real gold?" she asked.

"Of course—authenticity is the key to my art." Now the actor preened like a cat on a sill.

Leeds lobbed another snipe at him, but Dare had stopped listening to everything except the beating of her own heart. The gold belt buckle was decorated with a squared-off spiral with a trident-like design at the center. Just like her father's box. It would have been easy to assume the symbol simply marked some connection between Bascombe Barrow and her father's position as Captain of the Guard—the trident being a symbol of Poseidon, the mythical defender of the seas. But she'd seen it somewhere else, too.

She pulled Padgett's calling card from her pocket. The border featured continuous repetitions of the very same design.

Two times might be a coincidence. Three was a pattern. And patterns led to answers.

"Hello?!" The pop of fingers snapping echoed in Dare's ear. "Is there something wrong with her, Leeds?"

Dare looked up from the buckle to find herself face-to-face with the actor's heavily pancaked mug.

"There's nothing wrong with me," she snipped. "Though you could do with some tooth powder."

The actor gasped as if he'd been slapped. "Did you hear that, Leeds?"

"I did, Frederick." Leeds retrieved the buckle from Dare and reattached it to the belt. "She's not wrong, is she?"

Frederick grumbled and grimaced as he snatched the belt from Leeds and stomped away to his dressing room.

Leeds removed his glasses and took another look at Dare. "You're handier to have around than I thought."

"And it's more interesting here than I thought. That design on the belt—" Dare broke off as the Foghorn blew.

"Leeds! Where's her shawl?" Mrs. Lawrence stormed right up to the costumer, dragging her poor daughter behind her. "We can't find it anywhere. Did you leave it out for someone to steal?"

"No, I have it here." Leeds met her near hysteria with a laconic reply. "I was repairing a snag."

"And you didn't tell us? The fright you gave me! I was certain another fanatic had snuck into her dressing room. TR will hear about this!"

"As he should—imagine, the gall of Leeds doing his job," Dare mocked.

Mrs. Lawrence looked down that thin nose of hers and sniffed as if she smelled something rotten. "And who are you?"

"I'm the one your driver nearly killed. Remember? We just talked about that not ten minutes ago."

Mrs. Lawrence waved a hand as if the effort to recognize Dare was exhausting. "You shouldn't have been in the way."

Dare licked her lips. This was going to be fun. She was about to wind up into a particularly colorful reply when Nell stepped in.

"Leave her be, Mama." Her voice was neither loud nor cold, but there was just enough frost there to quell her mother's fire. "I'll take the shawl, thank you, Leeds."

Nell wrapped the shawl around her shoulders—her expression as flat as the black paint on the unlit star—and stepped into the wings to wait for her first entrance. Moments later, the first notes of her music began, and her entire aspect lit up as if by the flip of a switch. Gone was the sullen girl, and in her place stood the star of the show, emitting a light all her own. And the audience must have felt it, too, for as soon as she stepped onstage, the entire mood shifted, and she was greeted by a swell of applause.

What must it feel like to have that kind of power over others?

"It's fleeting, you know," Leeds whispered over Dare's shoulder. "Fame is no realer than gold plating on a belt buckle."

"It looks real."

"That's the job of art—to tell stories." Leeds motioned for Dare to follow him out of the wings.

Her chance had landed at last. "And what story is the belt buckle telling?"

Leeds put a finger to his lips and whispered, "Don't tell Frederick it's only gold plating."

"Not that part." Dare pulled Padgett's calling card from her pocket. "The symbol etched into the buckle. Padgett's calling card has the same design. Why?"

Leeds looked over his spectacles to examine the card before handing it back to Dare. "Can't say I know. Looks like a crest."

"You mean like a coat of arms? Weren't those only for kings?"

"And men rich enough to pretend to be kings." Leeds nodded for Dare to follow him farther away from the stage. "All I know is that Frederick demanded a custom piece for his costume and TR wanted to make him happy. But he never spends if he doesn't have to. He probably already owned the buckle. I could easily see him having a crest made, then emblazoning it on all manner of things—his door knocker, his silver service. He probably even gives gifts embellished with it to signify his magnanimous generosity."

Gifts like wooden boxes, perhaps.

"So what does it mean? It has to mean something to him."

"Can't say I know, can't say I don't. Around here, it's all about trickery. Make one thing look like another, fool the eye, tease the mind. Nothing is as it seems here, Dare. At Padgett's Palace, it's all illusion."

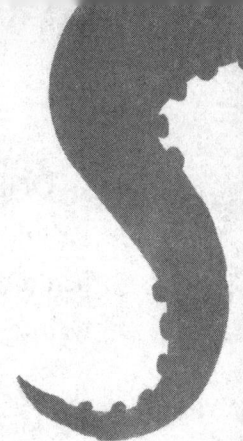

CHAPTER EIGHTEEN
Mirror, Mirror

Leeds's strange reply rang in Dare's head as she watched the rest of the play. Maybe he was right; sometimes a thing is just what it is, nothing more—and the design was simply Padgett's crest. But by the time the curtain came down, she knew one thing he'd said was most definitely right. The entire play was an illusion, and a bad one at that. Despite Nell's performance (for once, Louise wasn't portrayed as a complete ninny), the story was as ridiculous as ever, and the monsters were plain absurd. Especially the garbinol. That Nell was able to keep a straight face when that ragged collection of furs on stilts attacked and killed Louise was admirable. That was acting.

Dare left the theater irritated that she'd sat through that mess. But that wouldn't keep her from returning the next day to press Padgett to fill in those pauses he kept inserting when he spoke of her father's death.

Or if, as Leeds had said, discovering that it was all an illusion.

There was only one way to find out. She hated that she had to wait even another minute, but at least it was less than waiting on Tupper's return.

Since there were still a few hours of daylight left, she took the long way home through the park. It was so pleasant and peaceful, she perched her pet on her shoulder so he, too, could enjoy the day. They wandered past a duck pond, around a gazebo—the roof turned verdigris with time—and on toward a large fountain, where a boisterous crowd had gathered around a speaker standing atop a soapbox.

"We keep these engines running!" The speaker's voice was ragged from shouting. "Day and night, the factories don't run on coal or wood. They run on our backs!"

The crowd cheered him on.

"We deserve protections! We demand fair wages! Imagine what would happen if we walked off the lines—what then? The owners wouldn't take up the work, not ever! They need us, they need our labor to fuel their factories, their profits. And what do they do? Pay us starvation wages! We are the engines of industry!"

Dare had never witnessed anything like this; people on the Island never spoke of wages or fairness, let alone shouted about them in the streets. All she could do was stand and watch the scene unfold as if it were another play—this one full of actual, real tension.

"You know, a young girl like you shouldn't be out amid this mess. You never know when these rallies will turn."

Dare looked over to see a smartly dressed gentleman standing uncomfortably close. Though his coat was clearly of the finest cut—the fur trim at the collar a sure sign of his wealth—Dare got an immediate hit of something sour in the air. A kind of moldy irritation.

She moved to leave, but the man followed.

"That's a very cute pet you have there. What do you call it?"

None of your business was what Dare wanted to say, but if she was going to be someone new, then she had to be that person all the time. "He's a chinchilla, not an *it*. And he doesn't have a name yet."

"What about Fluffy?"

Dare fought the temptation to gag, or growl, and instead went with a tight-lipped "I'll find his name myself."

"I'm sure you will." The man reached out to pet the critter, and before Dare could swat his hand away, the chinchilla let out a noise Dare hadn't yet heard it make. This was no cute coo, or purr—it was a high-pitched bark.

"That's quite the beastly sound, isn't it?" The man chuckled as he withdrew his hand.

"He doesn't like strangers," Dare replied sharply.

"I understand. You stay safe out here, young lady." The man doffed his hat and offered Dare a sweeping bow before sauntering off.

The entire episode should have meant nothing. Another man offering her unsolicited advice. Except when he bowed, the folds of his cravat had fallen open, revealing an ornate tiepin.

Dare saw it for only the briefest moment, but she didn't have a singled doubt of what it was. As if by a secret handshake, the man had exposed his alliances, for his pin bore the now all-too-familiar insignia—Padgett's crest.

It could easily have been as Leeds said, a present from Padgett meant to signal wealth and connection. But if that were the case, why hide it under folds of silk and not flaunt it for all to see?

Dare was tempted to run after the man, ask why he wore the pin hidden. But liars lie. No, there was clearly more to Padgett and his crest than met the eye—and Dare was going to figure out what.

She did leave the park with one tangible thing, though: she now had the perfect name for her pet.

"What do you think about Beastie?" A sweet coo in response told her she'd hit it perfectly.

The minute Dare arrived back at Nesbitt House, Mary raced into the foyer in a flurry.

"No, no, no noise!" she buzzed, her words leading the way like a carpet sweeper trying to catch every crumb of noise. "Your aunt is finally sleeping. Go straight to your room, I'll bring your supper when it's ready."

"I'll be as quiet as a mouse," Dare vowed.

And she was. Until she landed on the second-floor hall and Beastie gave out a sharp bark.

Dare's insides nearly melted. Mary would blast her three times over; once for disturbing her aunt, and then twice more for having a pet in the house.

Dare slipped a hand into her pocket to quiet Beastie and made for the stairs to the third floor. She was nearly there when Madam's door swung open.

"Bijou, is that you?" Emily Nesbitt's voice was breathy and tight, until she spotted Dare, then it went tumbling down several octaves. "Oh. It's you, Dare. Did you hear that sound? I couldn't have been imagining it again, could I?"

Lying to get out of a mess was usually as easy as blinking, yet the thought of fibbing to Emily Nesbitt made Dare's stomach churn.

"Never you mind. It's just me, I'm sure." Madam extended her hand to Dare. "I am happy to see you. Come, sit with me."

Dare wanted nothing more than to take her great-aunt's delicate hand and follow her into her room. Yet such a simple action was racked with danger. Forget that Mary had expressly told her to not disturb Madam—Beastie could start barking again at any moment. It felt like she was being asked to climb to the roof and see if she could fly.

"I don't think I should. Mary said you weren't feeling—"

"I can't even think what I'd ever do without Mary, but she overworries. Come."

With no good choice, Dare placed a hand in her pocket, muttered something between a plea and a threat for Beastie to stay quiet, then followed Madam inside.

Emily Nesbitt's inner sanctum was very much like the actress herself. Draped in champagne-colored silks and sky-blue velvets, the room was elegance itself, and yet there was nothing too fussy or ornate about it. Even the late-afternoon sunshine streaming in through the large windows took on a softer glow, as if intent on pleasing her.

Even so, Madam looked more peaked than Dare remembered, more fragile as she lowered herself into one of two chairs in front of the fireplace.

"Sit, sit," Madam insisted, gesturing for Dare to take up the other chair.

There were so many reasons not to, but none could match the promise of being there with her great-aunt.

"It's been one thing after another since your arrival. We haven't had nearly enough time with one another." Madam sipped from a glass of water cloudy with undissolved headache powder. "I'm so sorry I've fallen under the weather. It's this smog, it never really clears anymore. Now, you tell me, dear girl, what do you think of City-on-the-Pike?"

"It's different here," Dare began. "It's loud, crowded, and dirty. It's cold and gray, and so are some of the people. I like it."

"Oh, you are funny!" Madam brightened. "I like your candor. It reminds me of your father. He was very witty, sharp as they come. Always ready with a smart remark—sometimes too ready."

Dare's bridge of stone and anger swayed at the comparison. She always knew she and her father shared some traits—but her aptitude for misplaced honesty was never one of them. "I didn't know that about him."

"Oh yes, at least back when he was your age." Madam leaned back in her chair and gazed at Dare. "You have his kindness in your eyes, though your face is the exact image of your mother's."

"No, it isn't." That came out harsher than Dare intended. No one had ever said she looked like her mother, for to say so would be to pay her a great compliment.

"It absolutely is." Madam rose and guided Dare to sit at her dressing table. "Now you look in this mirror and tell me you don't see your mother's face."

Dare knew she'd find none of her mother's beauty looking back at her. But what she saw in the glass was even stranger than her mother's face. For there, reflected in the mirror, hanging on the wall behind her, was a portrait of Emily Nesbitt, a small animal with floppy ears and a pug nose nestled in her arms.

An animal that—aside from the color of its fur, which was yellow flecked through with orange and brown stripes—

looked exactly like Dare's very own Beastie.

Dare's hand itched to pull Beastie out of her pocket. But caution must be taken.

"Who is that?" Dare asked, pointing to the mirror image of the painting.

"You silly girl," Madam replied, her complexion pinking up again. "It's you, beautiful you!"

"No." Dare whipped around to face the painting straight on. "That!"

"Don't you recognize me, darling? I know I've aged some, though I thought I still had my face."

"I'm sorry—yes, of course you do!" Dare was finding herself uncharacteristically short on words. "I meant in your arms."

"Oh." Madam felt for the locket hanging around her neck. "That's Bijou, my dear, sweet Bijou."

"That's who you thought you heard out in the hall." The pieces were coming together.

"It's foolish, I know." All the bright and cheerful joy drained from Emily Nesbitt's expression like water from a tap, leaving behind a wistful sadness. "Mary worries so when I have moments like this, my imagination taking over."

"What if you weren't imagining it?" Dare asked, testing the waters.

"Oh, that's impossible, dear, he was a marvel, a true one-of-a-kind marvel."

"I'm sure he was. My father felt the same way about his bird, Pretty."

"Did he?"

That Madam looked pleasantly surprised emboldened Dare. She dove in and pulled Beastie out of her pocket. "His name is Beastie. I found him. I've been keeping him hidden in my room. I know Mary doesn't want any pets. But if you wanted him, too, we could share him, then Mary would have to allow it." Dare held Beastie out to Madam, like an offering of water to the parched.

Madam started to reach for Beastie, then pulled back; she did this several times, until finally, she cupped her hands together and held them out toward Dare. "Will he even come to me?" she asked.

The reply came swiftly, as Beastie leaped from Dare's hands to Madam's.

She received him with a joyful gasp. "You found him?"

"He looks like Bijou, doesn't he? Except he's a different color."

Emily Nesbitt breathed deep, as if to inhale the nectar of an exotic blossom. "You're a very lucky girl."

Dare was beginning to think the same thing.

"He is perfect." Madam admired him from all angles, like a multifaceted jewel.

"We can keep him, then?"

"'We'?" Madam paled, the light fading from her eyes. "He

chose you, Dare, not me."

"We can share him—he can spend the day with you, though I'd like to keep him at night. I think he could protect me from monst—nightmares."

"That's not all he can protect you from, my dear. No, he is yours and you are his." Madam took another long, loving stroke of Beastie's coat, then handed him over to Dare. "Take care of each other."

"We will." Dare slid Beastie back into her pocket. "So will you tell Mary that I can keep him now?"

"Oh no." Madam shrank back. "You keep him to yourself."

"Why? She'll do whatever you say, you're her—" Dare broke off as Mary came bustling into the room, a large silver teapot in hand.

"I thought perhaps we could part with the tea service and—" Mary stopped at the sight of Dare. "What's this? You should be in your room."

"I called Dare in for a visit." Madam clung to her locket as if it were a tether that kept her from floating away. "Though I think I need time to myself now."

Mary helped Madam to her chair while scolding Dare over her shoulder. "Go, go to your room and don't come out until morning! And clean your ears while you're in there. You're not hearing very well."

Dare did go back to her room, and she even cleaned out her ears, not that there was any need for that, for she heard (and saw) everything all too clearly now, especially the stack of envelopes in Mary's apron pocket, all stamped *OVERDUE* in red ink.

Much like Padgett's Palace and the story of her father's death, things in Nesbitt House were not as they seemed. There were money woes piling up, and shadows only Madam could see. And like the monsters that haunted Dare's dreams, there was nothing anyone—not even Mary—could do to keep them at bay.

CHAPTER NINETEEN
Light of Day

Someone who was accustomed to being liked by others might not have noticed what was going on in the kitchen the next morning. But Dare immediately recognized the kind of cool disengagement Mary greeted her with at breakfast. Dare had been in the house no more than a week, and Mary had already decided she was irredeemably awful.

The old Dare would have railed at Mary. She'd have polished a nice pointy grudge, gone out of her way to rub her wrong, flung choice insults. But she saw the genuine love Mary had for Madam. Everything Mary did was for her. If only Dare could have protected her father with the same ferocity.

So instead of falling into her old ways, Dare decided to do something she'd never done before: she'd work to win Mary over. To that end, she made her own bed, braided her hair tight enough it would have even pleased Mrs. Malcolm, washed the breakfast dishes, and swept the kitchen. When the doorbell rang, Dare rushed to open it. She politely collected the envelope from the messenger, then dutifully brought it to Mary, taking great pains to make sure the maid knew she hadn't so much as peeked at the sender in the upper-left corner.

And right before Dare left the house for the day—Beastie carefully tucked into her pocket—she promised to return in time to help Mary with dinner. But it was the promise of the money Padgett was going to pay her that would be the real reason Mary would see her with new eyes—even if it meant Dare would have to lie about its source.

For now, Dare had Padgett's illusions to explore and one of her own to create.

"I'm here to see TR," Dare said, presenting his calling card to the backstage doorman at Padgett's Palace.

The doorman, a near giant of a fellow, didn't bother to look up from his newspaper. "He's not here. Said to send you down to see Leeds and he'd see you after."

All the anticipation she'd been holding, the practiced patience, crackled and snapped. "And when is 'after'?"

The doorman barely raised a shoulder to shrug. "Leeds's shop is down the stairs, end of the hall."

Dare grumbled and growled to herself. All the endless delays! She wanted answers now! But you can't get information from the air, so she reluctantly headed downstairs and into a long corridor. That there were no doors or signs anywhere raised an itch. Dare tried to quell it with reason: Padgett was her father's friend, who very well might have answers to her questions—she was perfectly safe here.

She was just beginning to believe it when an echo of footsteps began ringing out from behind her.

Heavy-footed, hard-soled boots.

Two sets.

Determined not to be spooked, Dare looked back over her shoulder.

It was the strangest thing. It made no sense.

The footsteps belonged to two men, both in dusty working clothes, maneuvering a large metal rack hung thick with ladies' coats out into the hall. One was directing the other, warning, "Go slow—we ruin these, and it'll be a year's salary." But when they caught sight of Dare, their eyes widened as if she were a ghost. Then, according to some silent agreement, they both moved to the back of the rack and pushed it in the opposite direction as fast as they could.

The strange part wasn't that two men were pushing a rack of costumes through the bowels of a theater. Or even that they'd acted so strangely when they spotted her. It was that Dare couldn't figure out where they'd come from. She hadn't passed a single door along the way.

Either she was imagining things, or there truly were illusions all around.

***

Dare was more relieved than she'd ever admit when she finally found Leeds's workshop at the very end of the corridor. Unlike the hallway, the costume shop was bright and colorful and buzzing with activity. Shelves filled with bolts of fabric and countless bins of buttons, ribbons, and lace trimmings lined the walls, and the center of the room was taken up by several sewing machines at which needleworkers sat stitching great lengths of silk together.

Dare found Leeds at the far end of the room, standing on a mirror-lined platform and chatting to the silhouette of someone on the other side of a tall changing screen.

"Beautiful clothes don't have to feel good," he was saying. "Come out when you're ready and have a look. I think you'll be pleased."

If Leeds was surprised to find Dare there when he turned around, he didn't show it. Instead, he was all business as he moved over to a headless mannequin draped in the garbinol costume. "So, your ideas to make our garbinol more frightening are . . . more fur? Higher stilts? Don't say a different color, it costs a fortune to dye furs."

"None of that," Dare said. "It doesn't matter how big or hairy you make it, nothing is scary when you know what it is. It's the things you don't know that frighten you."

"So your big idea is to send an actor out onstage dressed as the unknown?"

"No." Dare was used to her ideas being rejected out of

hand, but counter to the intention to shut her down, it fueled her. "I don't even know why it's onstage."

"Where else would it be? Up in the catwalk?" Leeds snipped.

"That's not a bad idea."

"I think TR and I read you wrong. You have no idea—" Leeds was about to wind up at Dare when Nell stepped out from behind the changing screen and planted herself in front of the mirrors. Draped in a purple dress trimmed with tiny pink feathers at the neck and wrists, she looked like she'd been back there sucking lemons, not trying on clothes.

"I hate it," she groused as she tugged at the neck, and itched at the cuffs. "Tell her I won't wear it."

"This is the fourth time I've remade it." Leeds sighed. "Do you really want to subject me to her again?"

"I'm sorry, Leeds, I refuse to wear this. What do you think?" she said, turning to Dare. "Would you wear this . . . I'm sorry, what's your name again?"

"Dare, and not on a bet. It's got all that . . . ridiculous frou-frou, and something of a funk."

Nell sniffed at her sleeve, then laughed. "I don't smell anything, but I do agree, it stinks. Sorry, Leeds."

"Nell, your mother said—"

"To make me a dress. So please, make me a dress I'll want to wear." Nell ended the conversation by marching back behind the screen.

Leeds pinched the bridge of his nose and sighed deeply before turning back to Dare. "Now, where were we? Oh yes, we were at you having lots of opinions about the garbinol costume and no good ideas."

"I never said that I said—" Dare cut off. She had it. The answer was right there in front of her, silhouetted against that screen. "Shadows."

"Pardon?" Leeds looked at her as if she were speaking gibberish.

Dare signaled him to be patient as she called out to Nell—or rather, to her shadow. "Are you almost done back there?"

"Yes." A few moments later, Nell stepped out wearing a lovely, yet simply adorned blue dress. "I couldn't get that feather-trimmed monstrosity off fast enough—no offense, Leeds."

"None taken, I suppose, though who knows what will be left of me when your mother hears about this."

"Tell her I broke out in hives or . . ." Nell paused and turned on Dare, who was busy throwing one of the garbinol skins over her head. "What are you doing?"

"Creating an illusion."

Dare stalked behind the screen, one leg slowly unfolding in front of the other. She splayed her fingers and curled them into claws as she raised her arms overhead and growled long and low.

"Now, imagine the actor up on stilts behind a screen or

curtain, something backlit like this is," Dare explained as she acted out the part. "That shadow slowly creeping up on the sleeping Louise. Claws bared, great tail slicing the air, fangs dripping with venom, and then it POUNCES and devours her whole!"

At "pounce," Beastie jumped in Dare's pocket, proof that her idea was good.

Or so she thought, but there was only the clatter of sewing machines in the room beyond the screen. "Well? What do you think?" Dare prodded, stepping out from behind it.

Both Nell and Leeds stood there, arms crossed, heads cocked to one side, saying nothing. That rush of excitement that always accompanies a great idea drained away. Their silence was worse than any nasty words.

Dare's awful was beginning to push toward the surface, readying to spew a few choice words, when Leeds broke out into a broad smile.

"Very clever!" he exclaimed. "I'll need to add more furs, make it shaggier, the claws and beak will need to be longer, and it needs more defined angles. But this is new, this is theatrical."

Relief pushed the awful back, though there couldn't be a full retreat, not until Dare knew what lay behind the inscrutable expression on Nell's face.

"And what did you think?" Dare tried with all her might to sound indifferent, but even she could hear the needy pinch in her voice.

Nell slowly unwound her arms, her grimace blooming into a grin. "I think it's brilliant."

"You do?" Dare couldn't have contained her shock if she'd tried.

"Yes! I work so hard every night not to laugh during the garbinol attack—it's ridiculous. But this is good, it's scary. I like it!"

The dam of tension burst, flooding Dare with something she hadn't felt in all too long: deep satisfaction and appreciation.

Leeds shifted into action mode. "We're going to have to show this to TR. I want to do it on the stage, it'll have more impact. I can lengthen the claws, and the beak is going to have to be fabricated to open and close. I need something sharp, with clear lines. Go check in the prop room, Dare. See what metal objects you can find. And Nell, you may go. I'm sure your mother is waiting on you. I'll come up with something to tell her about the dress."

"She doesn't run my every moment, you know," Nell said.

"I'm sure she doesn't," Leeds replied, his sarcasm as thick as the garbinol's furs.

Unlike the neat and orderly costume shop, there was no logic or order to how anything had been shelved in the prop room. Any attempts at organization had fallen victim to entropy. A bin marked *DAGGERS* was full of books, while the bin marked *BOOKS* was filled with ladies' fans.

Dare's excitement deflated. She'd be here all day.

Beastie must have felt it too, as he started scrabbling around in her pocket. "You can help me look. Just don't go getting lost."

Dare was about to set him down on a nearby shelf when the door flew open.

"I came to help you—" Nell broke off into a squeal. "Eww! What is that?"

"He's not an eww." Dare cradled Beastie closer. "He's my pet."

"I thought people only kept dogs and cats for pets."

Dare was about to tuck him back into her pocket, Madam's warning ringing in her ears, but showing him off to Nell made her feel special, shiny. "Boring people do. I have my Beastie."

"You named it Beastie?" Nell blinked in disbelief.

"It fits him. We both like it, don't we?" Dare held Beastie up and nuzzled his nose as he cooed in reply.

Nell laughed. But there was nothing cruel about it. "You're . . . strange."

Dare stood a bit straighter. "Thank you."

"People don't usually take that as a compliment."

"That's their loss, isn't it?"

Nell stared at Dare, her brow furrowed at first, but sunshine slowly filled her expression, melting the doubt away.

"Well, don't just stand there, we need to find the perfect thing to bring your idea to life. I don't want TR, or my mother, to have any excuses not to change the scene."

"You really liked it?" Dare wasn't fishing for flattery; it was hard to believe any idea of hers would actually get traction.

"I think it's brilliant," Nell said as she began picking through the shelves. "I'm glad you're here, Dare Coates. Life is about to get a lot more interesting."

CHAPTER TWENTY
Scars

Ideas are cheap. Everyone has them. Dare had had more than she could count. Some turned out well—like her idea to rescue Beastie from the Nesbitt Grand. Others ended up awful—like going to see the agicole on the ship after Tupper had strictly told her not to.

This was the first time other people had not only liked her idea, but also put it into action.

It was simple enough. Shadow plays in the night.

They used what was on hand: a few lights, a scrim, and a couple of musicians who weren't on break. And even though it had rough edges, it worked. The slow fade of the lights, the rumble of the timpani, and the trill of the piccolo at just the right moments made it feel so real. Immediate. Thrilling.

When the scene ended and the house lights came back up, it took a moment before anyone spoke. It was as if the members of the crew who'd been watching had been bound together in the same web, immobilized by dread.

Then the Foghorn began blaring and the spell was broken.

"It's absurd, is what it is!" Mrs. Lawrence crowed as she led Nell backstage. "It's so dark we can hardly see you!"

"You don't need to see me to feel Louise's fear," Nell replied.

"But your face, your beautiful face!" Mrs. Lawrence moaned.

"Is not the point of the play."

"Isn't it, though?" Mrs. Lawrence prattled on, until she was overpowered by Padgett bellowing "Dare, you clever, clever girl. Come!" from somewhere above.

Dare followed the sound of Padgett's voice to a small open window up above the top balcony, through which she could just make out his red cheeks and giant mustache. "My office. Hurry. The stairs are backstage."

Dare told herself she hardly cared if he'd liked what she did with the garbinol scene. She was only there to get close to him, to find out what was behind those pauses.

But having pleased him surely wouldn't hurt.

This had to be the moment. She'd make it the moment.

And as soon as she walked into Padgett's office he nearly burst at the sight of her.

"I knew you were something special! I told you so!" he thundered. "That swept me away, it felt as real as could be. It's truly imaginative and evocative! Here, let me take your coat." Padgett reached to help her out of it, but Dare pulled back, wrapping her arms around herself.

"No thank you. I'll keep it."

"As you like. Please, sit, sit." Padgett perched on the edge of his desk and gestured for Dare to take the leather chair across from him.

"I am very impressed by you. It's that shine, Dare, your inborn talent," he continued. "And I don't mean only for the theater. Yes, you have a gift for telling stories, but I believe it goes well beyond that. I've not met many people with such confidence, let alone anyone as young as you. It's incredibly admirable."

Dare snorted—"admirable" was the last word she'd ever heard used to describe her confidence.

"I'd like to show you something, if you don't mind. I believe you might understand it better than most, and it will help explain where I'm going with all this."

The only thing Dare minded was how long he was taking to get to his point.

"It's rather upsetting, so if you're squeamish—"

"Just show me!" Dare was close to bursting herself.

Padgett pulled up the right leg of his trousers, exposing his shin, which was marred by a long oval scar, the edges laced with the marks of hundreds of sharp, tiny teeth.

Dare forgot how to think for a moment.

This was no dog bite or snakebite.

Dare tried to assemble her thoughts, but all she could utter was "You were bitten by a monster."

"Yes. A maeder. It's one of the smallest of the beasts. Do you know of it? Their jaws are so strong, they are capable of biting straight through bone. A sting from their quills can freeze your blood. I was fortunate to have survived."

This was so much more than she'd expected. Dare scrabbled to make words. "You said you hadn't been to the Island before the funeral. So, when? How were you bitten?"

"It happened here, in the city, a few years ago. I know, I know—monsters never inhabited the mainland, Barrow's Bay is their habitat. Somehow, one of them landed on these shores. I'd left some friends after a lovely evening's entertainment. I wasn't paying attention to where I was going, turned up the wrong alleyway, and then . . . it pounced! Thanks to the fates, I have a loud voice, and some kind pedestrians came to my rescue. One got me to the doctor, while the other cornered the beast and killed it."

There were monsters in the city. Real ones. Dare could barely think through the pounding of her heart.

"Now, I don't want to upset you, opening up the wound of your devastating loss, but I'd be remiss if I didn't share something with you." Padgett leaned in close and lowered his voice to a whisper. "I heard the authorities said your father's death was a robbery. And I heard what you said at the funeral, and saw how everyone looked at you, shunned you. But you aren't the only one who thinks that. I too am certain your father's death was a monster attack."

Dare numbed from face to feet. Though it wasn't shock that stunned her. It was bitter anger. "Why didn't you say something then? Defend me? People would have listened to you!"

"I couldn't do that, Dare. Not without risking everything I've built here. There are those who are working against us. You never know where someone's allegiance truly lies unless you've gone into battle with them."

Us? Battle? Suddenly, Padgett was having a whole different conversation.

"My apologies. I've gotten ahead of myself." Padgett jumped up and began rummaging through a file cabinet. "I have something I think you would like very much. Now, where is it? Ah! Here it is!"

Padgett pulled a photograph from a file and handed it to Dare as if he were bestowing a great fortune upon her.

It was an older photograph, and so the faces were blurred due to the long exposure time. But nothing could blur the pang of knowing welling up inside of her. Though the beard was not yet flecked with gray and the brow not yet creased with time and worry, there was no mistaking that beautiful, warm face of Father's.

And there, in his hand, strung up upside down for all to see, hung a beast with five terrible horns sprouting from its head—a monster, as dead as could be.

"He *did* catch monsters." Dare had a hard time getting the words past the tears prickling the tip of her nose. "They're not all gone."

"Dwindled in numbers, but not all gone. And he did his work bravely," Padgett said. "Do you know what he has there?"

Dare examined the photograph more closely. "I think it's a brindled fexin. It looks like one, from his description of them. He told me they were said to move faster than the eye could see, and in addition to their horns, they had a jaw that unhinged, exposing eight rows of fangs. Father said they could swallow a rabbit in one bite. Or a man's foot."

"He taught you well. Very good." Padgett looked as proud as if he'd made her himself. "And the other man in the photo, do you know him?"

She knew the face on the right well enough—she'd seen it not too long ago.

"Yes! That's Tupper, the sailor who brought me here. We caught an agicole on the trip over. I didn't believe him at first then . . . he, well, he got hurt." Dare chose a half-truth over a full-on lie. She didn't want Padgett to think her awful. Not now.

"An agicole?" Padgett's voice rose, his surprise clear. "Now, those I thought were well and extinct. What did he do with the beast?"

"He put it in the hold. I asked him why he didn't kill it then and there, but his answer made no sense."

"He told you he was in the business of capturing, not killing monsters, didn't he?"

"Yes, exactly! I asked what that meant, but then the storm kicked up, and . . ." Dare trailed off as understanding set in.

Padgett tented his fingers and pressed them to his lips. "I

hate to be the bearer of bad news, Dare, but Tupper, Fortune, the entire crew of that ship, were not friends of your father's. Or should I say, he wasn't a friend of theirs. He'd been working on our behalf to entrap them, to make them think he'd turned and shared their twisted beliefs. Tupper didn't lie to you. They don't kill monsters. They set them free."

Dare might as well have been standing on the deck of that ship once again, she felt so tossed about. "No, that can't be. Tupper was teaching me, I helped him catch the agicole. He told me it was called droving. He said he'd help catch the one who killed my—"

Dare stopped. He never did say that. She'd only heard what she wanted to hear.

Padgett clucked his tongue. "It's disgusting, using a child like that. If not for that storm, he'd have filled your head with stories about how the monsters deserve to be preserved, saved. How your father came to see the light about them, too."

The heat of uncontainable anger spread up from Dare's stomach, turning her ears red and cranking her jaw too tight to speak. She'd been right about him at the first!

"Please, don't blame yourself, Dare." Padgett rested a warm hand on her shoulder. "It takes life experience to learn that everyone has a tell."

"A what?"

"A tell, a gesture, a tick, something they do when they're lying. I'm not the only showman in City-on-the-Pike. Know this: you're not alone. There are others like us."

Dare peeked out from behind the lifting haze of anger. "'*Us*'?"

"You, me. Your father. And others who know the monsters still live, and want to see them expunged, wiped out for good."

Others.

Things were beginning to fit. Dare pulled out Padgett's calling card. "Does this have something to do with it?"

Padgett smiled. "Why, Dare, you are as smart as I thought!"

Rare as it was to hear, she was in no mood for flattery. "Why this design? What does it mean?"

"It's an emblem, a kind of visual code those of us who share the same values and beliefs use to identify ourselves to each other."

"Like a secret society?"

"More like a guild, an intimate group of like-minded citizens dedicated to eradicating the monsters, and those who seek to protect them, once and for all."

"I don't understand. What about Governor Kingston? Why doesn't he know this? It's his responsibility to keep the Island safe from monsters. He refused to listen to me, but he'd listen to you. Or you should alert the mayor here, or the watch!"

"Lost causes. No one can afford a public panic; it would cost them their precious seats of power. They're content to withstand the occasional attack for the sake of keeping the public unaware that some monsters still live. No, they'll not be helping us. But you can."

Dare balked. "I thought it was you who'd help me."

"We can help each other. I believe you—"

A knock on the door interrupted them. "Mr. Weeks is here," someone announced from the other side.

"Oh, bother! If I could, I'd send him away, but investors won't be kept waiting." Padgett got up and extracted his billfold from his inside pocket. "Here, in the meantime, take this in payment for your fantastic work on the garbinol scene, and we will continue this conversation in depth later. I'd like a few of the others to meet you." Padgett counted out several bills and folded them into her hand.

Dare balled her fist around the bills. "Why is it always wait for tomorrow or ten days or never?"

Padgett laughed. "You and I truly have so much in common. I want everything now, too. Sadly, the world of adults is a tedious one made up of obligations and appointments. Let's say tomorrow, right here. How's noon?"

Dare wanted more answers now, but Padgett didn't wait for her reply. Instead, he hustled her out a door at the back of his office and onto the street, the small stack of bills in hand, and her entire understanding of the world of monsters spun upside down.

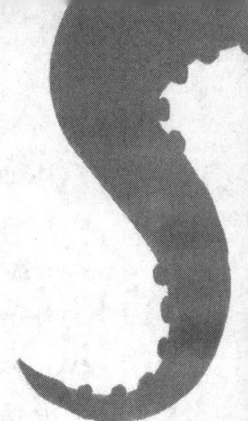

CHAPTER TWENTY-ONE
That Sinking Feeling

If Dare thought she had one true talent, it was her ability to judge the character of others, especially those with poor character. She could spot a bully or a liar at seven paces. But since her father's funeral, she'd been so desperate for someone to believe her, to help her, she'd wound up trusting the very people who told her not to trust anyone. Her skin crawled at the thought that she'd cared about Tupper even for a moment.

"I hope his wounds from the agicole are festering," she grumbled.

Beastie, who'd been sleeping soundly in her pocket, stirred and peeked his head out. With those large round eyes blinking against the light of day and the fur on the top of his head mussed, Dare couldn't help but be cheered by the sight of him.

"I'm glad you agree," she said.

Beastie made a kind of throaty yip. This was a new sound, and even though it was impossible, it sounded like he was saying "No!"

"Fine. It's not a nice thing to say, but he lied to me, and even worse, he thinks the monsters should be saved, and he tried to get me to help him! All that makes him as good as a murderer." Beastie shook out his fur and disappeared back into her pocket. "It doesn't make me a bad person—it makes me honest."

"But standing around with that much money in your hand kind of makes it look like you robbed a bank."

Dare barely startled at the voice that had snuck up from behind. She was getting used to Gil showing up when she wasn't paying attention. Still, it didn't matter what he said— only a practiced thief or a mime could be that stealthy.

"I earned it. It's called work, you might want to try it sometime. Padgett thought my idea was brilliant." Dare tossed her head like Frances Cooper, even though she knew it was a ridiculous sum for one idea.

"More the reason to keep it safe so no one tries to snatch it away," Gil warned.

"They won't have time. I'm going right now to pay off the debt at Crosby's and the other chemists."

"That's very kind of you."

"Don't sound so surprised." Dare put the money in her pocket and set off down the alley.

This plan had only just come to her, but it was perfect in more ways than one. It would make the waiting bearable, temper her anger at Tupper and Fortune, and help Madam without hurting her pride.

"I'll come along," Gil offered.

"Don't you have things to do? Pockets to—"

"I told you, I'm no pickpocket. Never was, never will be."

"Then what are you?" There were few things better for exercising a bad mood than starting an argument. "You keep showing up. First on the Island, then here. You always think you know everything, you're always here to help."

"Is there something wrong with that?"

"Yes, there is! I told you, it's weird. People don't just help."

A man in a motoring coat pushed past on the sidewalk, muttering, "Nor should they."

"Yes, they should!" Gil shouted after him before turning back to Dare. "We should all be helping however we can."

He wasn't wrong, but she was too surly to let him have that. "Fine, come or don't, I don't care."

"Well, with that kind of invitation, how could I say no?" Gil laughed as they set off.

Their first stop was Crosby's. While Gil waited outside, Dare went in and picked out the clerk who'd been so nasty. This would be fun.

"Good day," she said, putting on her best Barrow's Bay bite—a kind of accent that sounded as if one's jaw had been wired shut. "I've come to settle an account."

"Have you, now?" The clerk pulled out a ledger. To see him laboring to turn the pages, one might think they were carved out of stone. He was trying to intimidate her, make her feel small. Even dirty. It wasn't going to work today—not with all that money in her pocket. "Name?"

"Nesbitt." Dare articulated each syllable.

Now he looked at her. "That's a rather large account. Nine dollars and twenty-eight cents."

Dare peeled off two five-dollar bills and slid them across the counter toward him. Then she waited for those well-manicured fingers to reach for the bills before quickly pulling them back.

"I'll need a receipt stamped 'PAID IN FULL.'"

The clerk looked fit to eat nails as he settled the account, but a few minutes later Dare stepped out onto the street, receipt in hand. She was still fuming at Tupper and Fortune for taking her for a fool, but besting that clerk had helped improve her mood.

In short order, Dare had paid down the bills at all the chemists' shops except the last one in the Must. And though she'd never tell him so, she was glad to have Gil's company along the way. He knew everything there was to know about the city, the history of the buildings, how the streets got their names, what the waterfront of the Pike looked like before the factories were all built. With his help, Dare was beginning to see the run-down area for what it had once been: a thriving neighborhood unencumbered by smog and grime.

By the time they reached the chemist's shop in the Must another storm was gathering, and all the carts and shops had shuttered early. Including the chemist's.

"Nooooo!" Dare growled, as if she could intimidate the door into unlocking. "I wanted to go home with all the debts cleared."

"We can come back tomorrow."

"I can't, I have something to do."

"No offense, but what could you have to do?" Gil asked. "You already gave Padgett your brilliant idea. Don't tell me you've agreed to do more?"

Dare kicked at a loose paving stone. If she told Gil anything about her conversation with Padgett, she'd have to tell him about her father, and his death, and all of it. And then he'd look at her with those cow eyes and say something nice. She couldn't bear it.

It was while she was trying to look everywhere except at Gil that she saw it. She'd made no particular note of it last time she was here, but now it might as well have been screaming at her; the guild's emblem was etched around the building number of the chemist's shop.

She pulled out Padgett's calling card, just to make sure.

"What is it?" Gil peered over her shoulder. "That's odd. What do TR Padgett and this shop have to do with one another?"

Dare tried to shrug it off and change the subject. "The real question is, what time do they open in the morning?"

"That's not the real question, and it's not even a good fake question. You've got a secret." Gil paused before adding, "And so do I. You give yours up and I'll give mine."

"I knew you had a secret!" Dare tried to shove him, but he dodged the blow. "What is it? You're wanted by the watch, aren't you? What did you do? Who'd you hurt?"

"None of those things, and no one is looking for me. My secret has more to do with you than me, but since you made all those wrong guesses, you have to go first."

Dare grumbled, but fair was fair. The only question was, how much to tell him?

And so she settled on telling him enough, and not too much. She told him about her father's death and how the story of a robbery didn't make any sense. She only made a passing mention of Tupper without mentioning his or Captain Fortune's name, and when Gil pressed her about the emblem, all she really said was, "It's a symbol a group of people use to identify each other. People who share the same ideals, and ideas."

"About what?"

Dare pulled her lip; she'd hoped he'd leave it at that. She didn't want to have to hate him, but he'd no doubt laugh at her, or worse, tell her she was addled by grief. That left her to do what she did best: she told a half-truth (also known as a lie).

"Monsters. Everyone who's anyone on the Island is certain there are still some roaming."

"They are?" Gil sounded genuinely shocked.

"Yes, you know, special people."

"I see, like you?"

"Yes." Dare sighed as if he were a terrible bore. "Okay, what's your secret?"

"It's also about monsters."

That was unexpected. Dare stood up a bit taller. "What do you know about them?"

Gil gestured for her to sit with him on the shop's stoop before he began. "I don't know what they taught you in school, but I was taught monsters were scourges. Nature-made bloodthirsty devils. Deadly killers, vicious hunters who'll run a man through with their—"

"I know all this." His imagery was cutting too close. "Get to the point."

"The point is, they didn't teach us the whole story. Did you know they have powers? Not like magic, exactly, but abilities, gifts they can bestow. They're all different and . . . everything we've been told about monsters, all the way back to Bascombe Barrow, isn't true. It's all lies."

Dare backed off the stoop, putting distance between herself and Gil as if he carried the pox. "Why are you saying that? You don't really think that."

"We've had them wrong from the start. Yes, they're

animals, so if they're attacked, they attack. And they have some fearsome, terrifying defenses unknown anywhere else in the world." Gil paused here as if to gather momentum, or maybe courage. "They're not beasts, Dare. They're . . . well, they're marvels."

Dare's throat throbbed and her heart was racing so fast, she might as well have run the entire length of Barrow's Bay while holding her breath.

It all made sense now. It was all a web, a trap, intent on ripping her shattered heart from her very chest.

"You're one of them." It wasn't an accusation, more a tragic revelation. "You, Tupper, Fortune, the agicole. The reason you wouldn't tell me how you got back to the city from the Island so fast is because you *were* on the *Slipper*. What, were you hiding out, watching me the whole time?"

"You've got it all wrong," Gil insisted. "It's not like we're a cabal, Dare. We simply know the truth."

Dare had to fight not to take a swing at him. "You lousy liar! You set me up!"

"I did not. I couldn't just come out and tell you when I first met you, but it's important you know now. You have to fight for the right side."

"Oh, and that's your side, right? The monster-loving side?"

"That's not what I said," Gil shot back. "There's an awful lot of daylight between monsters and marvels."

The world blurred around Dare. Sound, light, movement,

all of it disappeared into a haze. Gil might as well have swung the blade that killed her father himself. When she'd imagined coming face-to-face with the beast that took her father from her, she'd envisioned herself as brave, fearless, taking its head as it had taken her father's. But now all she could do was try to keep the contents of her stomach from heaving.

Quaking inside and out, Dare slowly backed away. Then, with enough distance, she turned and ran as fast as she could, fragments of Gil's words chasing after her as he shouted, "Pretty! . . . your . . . pocket . . . It's true!"

Even if she'd had wings, Dare couldn't have gotten away from Gil fast enough! Legs pumping, feet pounding the cobbles, she raced through the Must until finally the foot traffic on the street was just too thick, forcing her to slow and catch her breath.

She'd done it again. What was wrong with her? How could she have made the same mistake again? Everything was simpler when she simply hated everyone.

Dare squeezed around a line of carts, pushed past peddlers with their wares in sacks heaved over their backs, and waded through groups of workmen standing around watching as the storm gathered. She'd almost made it through the crowds when she felt someone walking far too close to her.

Dare doubled her pace. So did they.

"Slow down, I only want to talk to you."

The words trickled up Dare's spine. For once, the voice at

her back wasn't Gil's, although she wished it was.

She put a protective hand in her pocket, cupping Beastie and the remaining money together. She spotted an open doorway and was about to duck inside when her shadow stepped up in front of her, cutting her off.

He wasn't a very tall man, but he was thick, and in possession of a patchy beard, thinning as if he'd caught the mange. His cheeks had been pocked by a fever, and his woolen cap was pulled down so low, she couldn't see his eyes, though she could feel them burning through her. Yet it was his hands—big as a pair of hams—that Dare was fixated on. The long and painful history of damage they'd done was written in every scar on his knuckles.

"Just want to know what you got in that pocket there." There was a hunger behind his words. Something wolfish and carnivorous.

She was cornered, couldn't go back or forward.

She ought to just surrender the rest of the money to him, but Dare was never very good at doing what she didn't want to do.

She cowered, easing back a step. "Please," she began, no need to force her voice to quaver, for both it and her Beastie were genuinely shaking. "Don't take it from me, it's all I have."

"It's too late for that." The brute stepped toward her, but Dare stepped forward quicker, and harder. She landed the heel of her boot on his foot with a lightning-fast strike. She was a flea compared to him, but the shock sent him reeling back just enough to give her room to push past.

She was free.

She took off at a run, and was just picking up speed when a hand grabbed hold of her coat.

No, this was not going to happen!

Pulling with all she had, Dare ripped herself free. Then, using the crowded street as a shield, she squeezed through gaps between people, buildings, and carts, until at last she was certain she'd lost him.

Breathless, terrified, and exhilarated all at once, Dare reached for Beastie.

"We did it!" she huffed in triumph.

But her hand came up empty, for neither her pocket nor Beastie were there.

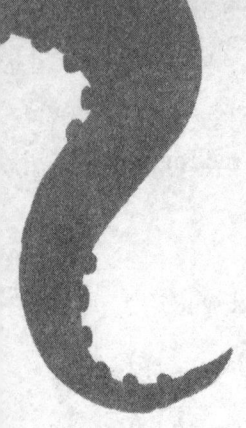

CHAPTER TWENTY-TWO
Lost, Found, Lost

Part of being awful meant being temperamental, judgmental, and willful. And while throwing fits and judging others as they judged her never served Dare, her refusal to give up was, at times like this, the only thing that kept her going. As tempting as it was to break at having lost dear Beastie, she refused to succumb. Sheer force of will would see them reunited.

Dare pushed her way back to the doorway where that creep had cornered her, her gaze sweeping every inch and crevice. The storm had begun dropping steely pellets of rain, sending people scurrying for cover and leaving her more room to search. But there were too many places Beastie could be. Behind those stairs, between those urns, underneath that call box on the corner. In the pocket of that brute.

No. Undaunted by the rain and that relentless pull toward panic, Dare searched, called, even used that whistle Father had used to summon Pretty: *Tweeewooo tweeewooo tweeewooo!*

"Please come out!" she called, peering into the spaces between buildings, the cracks in stairwells. What few pedestrians were left braving the downpour mostly ignored her, although there were several who stopped to chide her, calling her foolish, or muddle-headed for playing out in the rain.

If only she were playing. As she searched on, her whistles and calls and pleas became more frantic, until finally desperation took over and the temptation of tears grew too strong. Of course she'd lose the one thing that had brought her any real joy since her father had died.

She fell back onto a stoop and buried her face in her hands, letting tears pool in her palms. She tried to block out the comments and sneers from passersby, but one voice was too insistent. "What are you doing?"

Dare looked up, expecting to face another nosy pedestrian, but instead was met by surprise, for there, having emerged from a shiny automobile, a large umbrella unfolding above her, was Nell Lawrence.

Dare's defenses were soaked through, and all she could manage was a weepy "My Beastie, he got out of my pocket. I can't find him."

"Oh no." Nell held her umbrella high enough to cover both herself and Dare. "Let's look. I'll help you."

"Why? You'll get soaked," Dare said.

"No more than you already are."

"Miss Nell, your mother will have a fit!" The driver of the car stepped out, another large umbrella shielding him from the weather.

"She need never know!" Nell shouted over the storm. "Help us, please, Ernest. Dare's lost her pet."

"We meet again." Ernest tipped his cap at Dare with his free hand. "What's it look like?"

"He's got white fur, big green eyes, and a feathery tail, and he's adorable in an ugly kind of way," Nell explained.

Dare couldn't argue with that. And so, without another word, the two girls and Ernest fanned out, calling and whistling for Beastie to show himself.

And still the search remained futile. Dare was about to surrender to misery, to thank them for their help, when Ernest called them to join him a little way down the street.

Dare and Nell took off through pools of rain, no care for the mud staining their stockings, to join him as he pulled a shivering and soaked Beastie out from a narrow crevice between two tenements.

"Is this him?" Ernest asked, holding Beastie aloft.

Rivers of relief threatened to overrun their banks as Dare scooped Beastie into her arms. "Thank you, thank you!" she repeated over and over, nuzzling Beastie with her nose.

"Happy to help," Ernest replied. "We should be getting you home, miss."

"You're right." Nell held her umbrella higher to make room

for Dare. "Where can we drop you?"

"It's all right, I can walk," Dare said.

"You can. Though that would be silly. Come on."

Dare's first instinct was always to refuse help, but the offer was so open, so needed, she couldn't resist.

Inside, the auto was warm and dry, and the seat was far more comfortable than even the governor's carriage. Ernest handed back two warm hand towels, one for each of the girls, though Dare used hers to dry off Beastie first.

Nell dried her own hair then shifted on the seat to face Dare. "Can I hold him?" Her face suddenly, and for the first time, looked less adult and more like the girl she was.

"Didn't you say he was gross?"

"No, I said he was ugly," Nell corrected. "That's not the same thing. Can I please?"

"I guess, if he wants."

Dare set Beastie on her lap, leaving him free to choose for himself. He sniffed the air once, twice, then, calmly as you like, scooted into Nell's lap.

Nell touched him tentatively with one finger, then two, before quickly settling into long, gentle strokes. "Do you know how lucky you are?"

What could Dare possibly have that Nell Lawrence envied?

"Mother won't allow me a pet, or friends, or . . ." She let her voice drift off as she stroked Beastie's fur, listening to his coos.

"Where is the Foghor—" Dare scrambled to swallow back her words. "Your mother. Where is she?"

It was hard to tell if Nell looked horrified or amused. "Did you just call Mama 'the Foghorn'?"

Dare winced. She couldn't lie her way out of this one.

"The Foghorn," Nell repeated, rolling the phrase around in her mouth as if it were a particularly tasty piece of chocolate. "I like it!"

"You do?"

"It's perfect," Nell said. "What do you call me?"

"Uh . . . Nell."

"No, really. You must have a nasty little nickname for me."

"It's not like I walk around calling people names," Dare said.

"I bet you do, though." Nell laughed. It was a friendly invitation.

"Not for everyone. I don't have one for you. Honestly."

"Too bad." Nell sat back against the seat.

"If it means that much, I'll come up with one," Dare replied, then added, "So where is she? I thought you two were attached by a string."

"More like a thick hemp rope." Nell grimaced. "Except when she has engagements, dinner, parties, or the opportunity to go hobnobbing without me. Ernest, where's she gone tonight?"

"Can't say I know. All she said was to take you home, and

to tell the cook she'd be dining out tonight."

"What's she going to do when she finds out she gave me a ride home?" Dare asked.

"She won't. Earnest likes me a lot more than her. We're friends."

"No offense, but it's easy to like anyone over her."

"None taken," Nell said, before quickly changing the subject. "Now tell me what happened? Why were you out in the Must in the first place?"

Dare pulled back like a turtle into its shell.

"I'm sorry, I didn't mean to pry." Nell retreated to her side of the car seat. "I like to hear about other people's lives. Mine is so boring."

"I'm sorry, can you repeat that? I thought you said your life is boring."

"It's the worst. I do nothing except go between the theater and home. Occasionally Mama trots me out for a dinner, but that's worse than going home. The food is always dreadful, and the company is even worse. The only view of a real life I get is out of windows."

"You're on the stage, people adoring you every day," Dare said.

"Having people adore you when they don't even know you, it's very lonely. It's not all what it looks like. I—" Nell stopped, something out the window catching her attention.

The rain had since tapered off and people were out again,

including the paperboys, who were excitedly hawking the latest headline.

"Oh no, looks like another tragedy at sea." Nell sighed. "Ernest, can we stop and get a paper please?"

While Ernest pulled over and called a paperboy to his window, Nell continued. "I try to avoid the papers, especially the ones that are always writing about me—what I wore, where I went. I hate it. The one-sheets are different, though, they cover news as it happens."

"Here you go, miss." Ernest handed a newssheet back to Nell.

Dare had no interest in the news of the day, she had too many problems of her own to think about. But then she caught sight of the headline.

ANOTHER BOAT GONE!
THE *GOLDEN SLIPPER* LOST TO THE WINDS

The blows kept coming and making direct hits on Dare.

Not that she should care. They'd lied to her. Betrayed her and her father. They had his blood on their hands. And yet she couldn't muster the right kind of anger. This was a tragedy not even she could have wished on them.

"How did it happen?" Dare scoured the one-sheet for anything tangible.

"It doesn't say. The later edition should have more details," Nell explained.

Dare sat back, stunned, yes, and confused. How could the *Golden Slipper* have sunk? And in the winds no less. Fortune might have been a liar, but he knew how to slip the winds better than anyone.

And then it hit her. "The agicole."

Dare didn't even realize she'd spoken the word out loud until Nell asked, "What does that mean? That's the second time I've heard that word today."

That got Dare's attention. "You heard the word 'agicole' somewhere else?"

"Yes. I walked into my dressing room, and TR and Mother were in there. At first, I thought they said 'magical,' but then they said it again. It was clearly 'agicole.'"

"TR and your mother were talking about the agicole?"

"I guess so. What is it anyway?"

How was it possible for things to get even more twisted and strange? That Dare and Mrs. Lawrence should be on the same side of anything was nearly unbelievable. And if that were true, why bother trying to figure out who was what anymore? Dare surrendered.

"It's a kind of a monster, it lives in the sea along the Island's shoreline."

"I've never heard of it. But really, all I know about monsters, I learned in the show. They've been gone so long now, why would they be talking about one? Unless they're adding it to the show, maybe."

Dare could have left it at that, but it was too late to edit herself. "Well, you see, they aren't all gone."

Nell laughed. "That's ridiculous. If monsters still roamed your Island, we'd know. Every monster sighting would be screamed about on a one-sheet!"

"It's not like that," Dare explained. "They don't want people to know. Start a panic, I guess. I don't understand it. They should be protecting people, not hiding the truth from them. That's what my father did, even when people belittled him for it."

"Why would they do that?"

Dare shrugged and pulled into herself. She didn't want to have to recount it all again for the second time that day. It was too much, too sad, too tiring.

"I'm sorry. There I go again, prying and—"

"Excuse me, Miss Nell," Ernest interrupted. "Where are we taking the young miss?"

"Why don't you come home with me for a bit?" Nell offered. "We can talk freely there—Mama is out. Ernest can bring a message to your mother so she doesn't worry, then we'll bring you home later."

Home. Mother. Two words that had lost all meaning.

After all Dare had shared, it shouldn't have been a chore to tell Nell the rest, but it was too exhausting to explain that her mother was off honeymooning with a man who'd made his intentions toward her clear before Dare's father had even been buried. Or that she was living with Madam, who had descended into her own kind of despair after her life and career had been ruined by the likes of Nell and Padgett.

No, the only place Dare wanted to be was in her small, quiet room at Nesbitt House, safely cuddled up with Beastie, where she could disappear for a short time into the silence, joining her aunt in the land of the haunted.

CHAPTER TWENTY-THREE
Madam Knows Best

"Are you sure you don't want to come home with me?" Nell asked as they pulled up in front of Nesbitt House. "I could use the company, and I think you could, too."

"Thank you, no." Dare collected Beastie from Nell. "I appreciate what you did for me today."

"We were happy to, and I feel like I owed you. Your idea for the garbinol attack makes that dreary play so much more interesting."

"Then I guess we're even." Dare stepped out of the auto and was about to shut the door behind her when Nell stopped her.

"Wait! You live with Emily Nesbitt?" Nell suddenly looked like one of her gawking admirers. "I never saw her perform, but she's a legend. She was magnetic, they say."

"*Is* magnetic," Dare corrected.

Nell flushed, then turned coy, almost shy. "Do you think I could meet her? I don't mean right now."

"No," Dare said bluntly. "Mary says to not even mention Padgett's name in the house. You're the star of his show, it would probably send her into a fever. His theater is the reason she's fallen on—"

"Don't tell her that!" came a sharp whisper from up the street.

It was Gil, of course, hanging around the box office as always. Lucky for him, Dare was holding Beastie; otherwise, she would've picked something up and winged it at him. She had no intention of talking to or even looking at him ever again, but she did know he wasn't wrong.

Dare reset. "I'm sorry. But thank you for the ride."

"I understand," Nell said. "Please try to watch yourself on the streets, there are too many unsavory characters in the city."

"Oh, you mean him?" Dare tossed a thumb over her shoulder toward Gil. "He's the worst of the worst, but he's no mugger. Thanks again."

Dare closed the door of the auto and signaled for Ernest to drive off.

"Wait, who's—" Nell began, but the auto took off, carrying the rest of her sentence with it.

Dare pulled her shoulders back and lifted her chin in a somewhat worthy imitation of Mrs. Lawrence, then turned for the house, fully intending to ignore Gil altogether.

"I'm sorry about this," she said to Beastie, tucking him into her one remaining, and very wet, pocket. "We'll be warm and inside in a minute."

She'd nearly made it to the door, her tongue and fists under control, when Gil caught up to her.

"I know you think I'm wrong, but there are things you need to know." He paused for effect. "The *Golden Slipper* sank."

That was not news. Dare kept walking.

"I do think Tupper and maybe Captain Fortune and the crew might have escaped." Gil followed her up the front steps of Nesbitt House. "The details are still fuzzy, but I'm hopeful."

It would be a tremendous relief if they hadn't drowned—no one deserved a fate even close to that—not that it would change how Dare felt about them.

She was leaning in to pull the call bell when Gil stepped up, blocking her way. "You can do and think what you like—you'll do that anyway—but hear me out."

The unyielding look in his eyes sent an icy shudder of understanding through Dare. The final piece of the hideous puzzle snapping into place. "You were there when it happened, weren't you?"

"No, I wasn't anywhere near the sea or even the harbor. I was—"

"Not the sinking—my father's death." She shouldn't have been so calm, so collected, but sometimes that's how certainty lands—quietly. "Which were you—a witness? Or a willing participant?"

Gil winced, raking his hand through his hair like he was searching for the answer within his locks. "You've got it wrong. It wasn't any of us, not me, Tupper, or Captain Fortune."

The burn of acid climbed up from Dare's stomach into her throat.

"I don't know who it was, honest!" His eyes were wide and wild, and if she hadn't learned better, she might have believed him. "I need to know as badly as you do."

"No, you do not. No one does. Why would you say that?"

"Because it's true. I shouldn't even be here anymore. I'm supposed to be, well, somewhere else, far away from Barrow's Bay and even farther from City-on-the-Pike. But I won't go on until the truth about the marvels, and everything else, comes out."

"That's exactly what a liar would say." Dare yanked on the call bell. Let Mary yell at her, she didn't care. As long as it got her away from Gil.

"I am not the enemy, Dare, you have to believe that!" he said. "Be smarter. There are people who would kill to get hold of you and your little Beastie."

"Don't you ever speak of him again!" Dare set a protective hand over Beastie's head just as the door flew open, exposing Mary.

"Good days and nights!" she exclaimed as Dare rushed

past her, slamming the door behind her. "You're a fright! Your coat, your stockings. What happened to you?"

Everything.

"As if I didn't already have enough woes and work to keep me running ragged all—" Mary was winding up for a rant when Madam appeared at the top of the stairs.

"Dare, is that you? What happened, love?"

"I'm sorry, Madam. I didn't mean to wake you!" Dare felt so small and plain in her great-aunt's presence, even when Madam was wrapped in a simple robe and her hair was half down as it was now.

"Don't be silly." The once grande dame came sweeping down the stairs and put an arm around Dare, opening a crevice that left room for some of the truth to come pouring out.

"The ship that brought me here, the *Golden Slipper*, sank." Dare reported it with barely any emotion, for to do so would have opened the floodgates.

"Oh, those poor men!" Madam gasped. "That's the second sinking in as many months. You poor love, you're soaked through. The rains get worse every year. I think some warmed chocolate will do the trick. Bring us some, won't you, Mary?"

Mary offered an obedient nod and scurried off to the kitchen, but Dare caught the sadness in her eyes. She'd seemed so fond of Captain Fortune; the news had to cut deep for her as well.

"Let's get these off you before the leather seizes." Madam guided Dare onto the boot bench and had her boots off so quickly, Dare barely knew what had happened. "You get practiced at it with quick changes between scenes. And let's leave your coat here. You don't want Mary to come hunting for it. She has no compunction about rummaging through pockets."

Madam's not-so-veiled message came through loud and clear. Dare pulled Beastie out of her pocket and left the ruined coat behind on the coat rack, then padded up the stairs alongside her great-aunt and into the solar, that light- and plant-filled room. Madam pulled a white wicker chair with a great moon-shaped back closer to the fire for Dare, then draped a soft woolen shawl over her lap.

Nothing could make any of the awful, terrible things that had happened go away. Dare would never unlearn that Tupper, Fortune, and now Gil were as good as murderers. And she could never forget what it had felt like to lose Beastie, even for a short while. But being here with Madam, wrapped up and warm, was a start.

"This was my Bijou's favorite place." Madam ran her hand over one of the potted trees and plucked a small stone fruit from somewhere deep between the leaves.

"It might be mine, too," Dare said.

Madam took the chair next to Dare and offered the fruit to Beastie, who greedily took it in his front paws.

"And his," Madam added, gazing at Beastie as he ate. There was such love in her look, and there was also loss, sorrow, and the kind of longing nothing can sate—at least, nothing alive.

Dare knew what that felt like.

"Do you want to hold him?" Dare held Beastie out.

"I think it's best I don't." Madam reached for her locket, letting the small gold medallion play between her long fingers. "It looks like you've been taking good care of each other. His coat is nice and full, even damp as it is."

Dare winced. How could she tell Madam—of all people—that she'd been so awful as to almost lose her Beastie? Yet she also couldn't bear not to tell her.

"It wasn't my fault. Or maybe it was. I tried to get away, run, when he, I don't who he was, caught me, or caught my pocket, at least."

"I see." Madam tried to offer a calming smile, but there was a quiver of concern the great actress couldn't, or maybe didn't want to, hide. "You're a smart girl. You see and hear a great deal. You understand people, that's invaluable. Don't ever doubt that."

Madam's compliments had a way of filling Dare up with an unimaginable warmth.

"And like any inborn ability, you have to learn how to fine-tune those gifts. Find someone to teach you, guide you. Do you understand what I'm saying?"

Dare wanted to say she did, but she didn't.

Madam looked to the shut door, then back at Dare. "There are some terrible monsters out there, Dare. You must learn to spot them before they spot you."

Now Dare understood. She felt as if someone had come

along and lifted a fifty-pound sandbag off her neck. "You know about them, too? How long have you known? Did my father tell you?"

"No, dear, I told him." Madam paused. Dare was worried she was drifting away into her thoughts again when she returned. "Now, listen to me, they aren't always easy to spot. Most of the ones I've encountered have been clever as a fox, changeable as a chameleon."

Dare perched on the edge of her seat. "You've seen them? Here in the city?"

"Monsters are everywhere, Dare. They're shape-shifters—they look like one thing one minute, and another the next. You must learn how to keep them at bay, never let them get close."

"How do you do that?"

"Use your eyes to feel the truth."

Dare was hoping for something more tangible, actionable than that.

"Look for the people who know what they don't know," Madam explained, "who ask questions, who know everything is gray and ever-changeable. Do you understand?"

Dare sat back in the chair. She did now, in more ways than one.

The truth was, she and Madam weren't talking about the same kind of monsters.

CHAPTER TWENTY-FOUR
Not a Fox

Between all the terrible things Dare had occupying her thoughts about Tupper, Padgett, and Gil and the fright of losing Beastie, she completely forgot about all that money she'd lost until the next morning at breakfast. Things were getting tighter by the day. It was obvious by the thin bowl of porridge Mary served Dare and the pile of bills she was trying to hide in her apron pocket.

The chemist bills Dare had paid off were just a small portion of the household debts. And she still hadn't decided what lie, if any, to tell Mary about the cleared accounts, although she was leaning toward a mysterious benefactor. As for the money that had been stolen, Dare briefly considered telling Padgett she'd been robbed and asking him to replace the money—he certainly could afford it. But if it had felt wrong taking money from him once, twice would be even worse. No, there had to be another way to help the household stay afloat.

The answer—which was ridiculously obvious—came a short while later when Mary returned to the kitchen after collecting the post. She had several envelopes in hand, all of which sported those red-inked stamps.

"Are you certain Governor Kingston didn't send anything with you for Madam?"

"Nothing."

As always, any mention of that man made Dare's lip curl, but her disgust came with a side helping of inspiration. She had the answer she'd been looking for.

Dare cleaned her bowl and helped tidy the kitchen, then announced, "You needn't worry about me for lunch, Mary. That porridge filled me up."

Either she was too distracted, or truly didn't care, but Mary simply replied, "Back before dark."

Dare went to her room to collect Beastie, but the pull and tug of that creep's hand on her pocket pulled and tugged at her. She couldn't risk that happening again.

"You stay here. I'll be back soon." She tucked Beastie into the back of the wardrobe, grabbed the quarter Ernest had given her, and headed out the door, armed with some choice words perched on the tip of her tongue should Gil dare to show up.

That he was nowhere in sight was a promising omen that the day might just offer more good things to come.

Dare arrived at the telegraph office confident her little plan would work. Until the clerk told her the message she'd worked out would cost nearly three dollars.

It took her some time and some doing but Dare finally whittled it down to three words at a rate of twenty-two cents. *Dire. Send. Money.*

If anyone would understand a simple plea for funds, it was Dare's mother.

Certain she'd solved one problem, Dare turned to focus on the bigger issues at hand. She found a newsboy on the next corner and handed over her last three cents for a copy of the midday edition, certain there'd be an article with more details about the *Golden Slipper*.

But the headlines had moved on to screaming about something new.

NAIL FACTORY WORKERS STRIKE!
LAMPLIGHTERS DECLARE LIGHTS OUT!
UNIONS CRY FOUL!
BOSSES DEMAND
GO BACK TO WORK!!

She scoured every page of the newspaper, but not another word had been written about the sinking of the *Golden Slipper*. Just like the monsters everyone said no longer lived, it was as if the sinking had never happened.

Dare folded the paper, tucked it under her arm, and made for Padgett's Palace. There were questions to be answered, and she was determined not to let Padgett create any illusions.

* * *

It was easier said than done to hold the line with TR Padgett. He greeted Dare's arrival at the door to his office with even more ebullience than usual and looked ready to wind up into one of his patters before she'd even stepped inside. Until he noticed the newspaper tucked under her arm.

"I see you've read the news."

"Or not," Dare corrected. "Yesterday's one-sheets were all screaming about the sinking of the *Golden Slipper*, and today, not a word anywhere. Why?"

Padgett swept an arm to invite her inside where, to her surprise, two other men were already seated. "I told you, gentlemen," Padgett said. "Sharp as a tack. Misses nothing.

"Come, sit, we're all friends here, and we will explain." Padgett set a third chair between the two men for her. "Gentlemen, this is Dare Coates. Dare, please meet Roland Cummings and Dr. Endicott Hinckle."

Dare perched on the edge of the chair, trying to keep her impatience and her awful in check.

The first man, Cummings, a tidy fellow with hair parted neatly down the center and a pipe clenched between his teeth, met Dare with a rolling salutation of his hands. "I am at your service, Dare. I never had the honor of knowing your father, though I admire the work he did. You should be very proud."

"I always was." She didn't need anyone to tell her how to feel about her father.

Before Dare could let her irritation be fully known, the

second man, Hinckle, spoke up. "And I am equally proud to know you."

He wasn't nearly as lordly in his attitude, but how could he be when he looked exactly like a walrus, with those cheeky jowls, overlarge mustache, and great bushy eyebrows!

"Now that we're all friends, let's get to business." Padgett took his seat behind his desk and leaned back. "The ship did indeed sink, Dare. And while we owe the dead their due—no matter who they are—one of our good friends who owns several of the papers in town saw to it that the story was dropped."

Dare leaned in, quite certain she'd misheard. "Why would you do that?"

"You told TR about an agicole on board, yes?" Cummings wasn't really asking. "We believe that monster was responsible for the sinking. Now, reporters love nothing more than to go digging around, raising questions, and sending rumors flying around the city like soot from the smokestacks. No, it's best the story goes away. We need all such talk to remain in the margins, away from the public eye."

"The loss of any life is regrettable, especially to a monster," Hinckle said, picking up the narrative. "But the loss of that crew is especially worrisome."

"If they're working against you, why would you care if they survived or not?" Dare asked, although she didn't quite want to surrender the hope that they'd survived, either.

The three men exchanged glances as if to decide who

would speak first, with Hinckle apparently winning that silent drawing of straws. "Part of your father's legacy was that he made those people trust him. They thought of him as one of their own, and they divulged their secrets to him."

Dare sat up taller now. "What secrets?"

"How they operate, what they do with the beasts," Cummings said.

"If they told my father, what's the mystery?" Dare pressed.

"Well, unfortunately, he passed away before he could share that information with us. You see . . ." Hinckle paused, pulling at the ends of his walrus-stache before he finally continued. "He died the night he was to finally see their secrets for himself."

Dare's bones turned to ice. "Tell me. All of it."

Hinckle shifted uncomfortably.

"Go on, tell her, man!" Cummings chided.

"Very well. if you insist on knowing, I won't hold anything back." Hinckle pursed his lips, perhaps trying to find the right words before he began. "The coroner on the Island is a friend to us. He examined the bod—your father. And while the official report cites different facts, his truest assessment was that only an occisor could have assaulted your father when he went to meet Tupper and Fortune in the harbor that fateful night."

An occisor.

Acid filled Dare's throat.

The way Dare's father had described them, occisors were known to be one of the most lethal killers. A large, four-legged monster with thick leathery skin arranged in layers, forming a kind of articulated armor, they had the head of a bird and a long neck lined with countless ducts that could shoot a blinding poison. What made them so exceptionally lethal was their ability to camouflage themselves against any background, and their tail, a thin, whiplike appendage, was said to be so sharp, one wouldn't feel the cut of it until they'd nearly bled to death.

There wasn't enough water in the world to clear her throat. Dare reached for Beastie in her pocket for comfort before she remembered he was safely tucked away in her room at Nesbitt House.

She'd thought for so long that she wanted the details, the truth of her father's death. But the picture was too much to hold. She flashed from hot to cold and back to hot again as her stomach lurched and clutched. One of the men held a cup to her lips, insisting she take a sip of the sweetened water.

Eventually, she stopped shaking and her heart rate slowed, and she could make sense of the world around her once again.

". . . retribution, Dare," Padgett was saying. "We want to avenge your father. Tupper and Captain Fortune might be gone, but it's because of them that those beasts still live."

"Yes. Anything. Whatever it takes." Nothing else mattered more than seeing whatever had taken her father from her meeting a similar fate.

"That's the spirit!" Padgett cheered.

"If only spirit were enough to find that island," Cummings heaved in frustration.

"What island?" It was so hard for Dare to make sense of everything coming at her.

"The island where they're harboring the monsters," Padgett clarified.

"The poor girl was in shock, probably didn't hear you explain it, TR," Hinckle said.

"Of course. You've had a lot to take in." Padgett pulled a chair closer to Dare and started from the beginning, his voice quiet, calm for once.

"You father discovered that the *Golden Slipper* crew have an island somewhere out there, hidden by the trade winds, where they've released the beasts they've managed to capture. They refer to it as a refuge, as if these monsters deserve such a thing." Padgett's upper lip curled at the thought. "Anyway, as we understand, it has a climate, topography, and vegetation similar to that of Barrow's Bay. We've never been able to find it, but we know it's there. And every week that passes, those monsters are out there thriving. Reproducing. Their numbers doubling all the time. If we could find the island, we could end them all."

"And if we can't," Cummings said, picking up the narrative, "well, there's nothing to stop the airborne, or those that can swim, from finding their way to our shores, both here on the mainland and on Barrow's Bay."

Dare's worst nightmare wasn't a dream.

"We don't mean to frighten you, Dare. We want you to understand what we're up against. Most people don't want to believe the worst thing is coming. They cling to the stories they've been fed by the press and the politicians. They're afraid to ask the hard questions because they either don't want to be caught out not knowing, or don't want to hear the answers. We have no choice but to ask, and keep asking."

Look for the people who know what they don't know. Who ask questions, who know everything is gray and ever-changeable.

Madam's advice pealed in Dare's mind like bells in the morning. She could feel the truth and hear the questions. This was the right side to be on.

Dare kicked away the fear roiling inside her. "All right, what do we do?"

"We were hoping that you might have seen something among your father's effects, either before or after his . . . ? Anything that might have hinted where the island is. A list, a map, a nautical chart?"

"He had lots of maps and charts. He was often out on the water. But they're all gone. They burned everything, every paper of his. The only thing I have left is his box, the one you gave him, TR. And there's nothing in there, just a few doodles and a broken button. I have nothing left of him."

"That's criminal," Padgett clucked. "We were so hopeful you'd know something, had seen something that might hint at where this blasted island is hiding."

Disappointment fell over the room like a veil over a widow's brow.

This couldn't be the end. There was an answer out there, there had to—

It struck in an instant.

"Droving," Dare said.

"I'm sorry, what are you saying, dear?" Hinckle cupped his hand around his ear.

"Tupper said I had a talent for droving. Attracting the monsters. What if I—"

"Wipe any thoughts like that away, Dare," Padgett warned. "We'll not allow you to be in danger's path."

"But you have to!" Dare insisted. "I can do it. I can attract them. I can be the bait. I'll find them, they'll find me. Please. Let me do this."

Hinckle refused to hear another word, as did Padgett, but Cummings was intrigued. "How would that work, exactly?"

"I don't really know," Dare said. "We'd need a ship, countless sacks of marsh salt from Barrow's Bay, and a crew willing to cross the winds and face the beasts."

"That's a very brave proposal, Dare," Padgett said. "I think we need time to discuss it. I can't imagine we'd be willing to put you out front like that."

"If you won't help me, I'll find someone who will."

"Now, be reasonab—" Padgett broke off when the door to his office flew open, carrying the Foghorn in with it.

"TR! Nell won't cooperate. She rejects all the clothes we've chosen for the supper club—" Mrs. Lawrence stopped as she caught sight of Dare. But rather than curling her lips, she parted them over those long white teeth in what might have been an attempt at a smile. "I didn't realize you had company."

"Can this wait, Rose?" Padgett asked.

"Not for long."

"Very well. Dare, we'll take this as a timely break. We're going to have to consider this long and hard. Give us some time to think it over, won't you?"

"How long?" Dare would die on this hill if she had to.

The three men looked to each other, then Cummings spoke. "A day or two at most. And please, don't do anything drastic until we meet again. Can you agree to that?"

Waiting, waiting! All people knew how to do was tell her to wait. She never wanted to hear the blasted word again!

But the truth was, she couldn't do anything on her own—she needed them to make this happen.

"All right," she agreed. "Two days, no more. I will find another way if you won't."

"We believe you!" Padgett took Dare's hands in his. "We'll put an end to this, Dare. We promise."

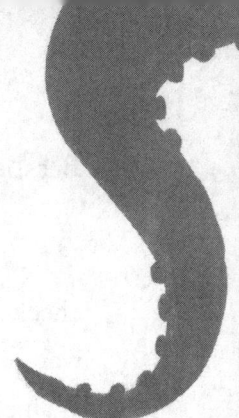

CHAPTER TWENTY-FIVE
The Itch of Knowing

Dare had long assumed that finding out exactly what had happened to her father would cure the itch. That the truth, as awful as it was, would allow her to accept what had happened and move forward. But knowing was almost worse. The answer only led to more questions: Why would anyone ever believe monsters deserved to be saved? Where was this island? Was it possible she could really find it using some talent she had but she knew nothing about? And was revenge really what she wanted?

No.

She wanted her father back—the very definition of an impossibility.

It was as Padgett had said: they'd thrown so much at her, she was exhausted by all the knowing. All she wanted as she left the theater was to go home and cuddle up with her

Beastie. Being with him was the closest she'd come to feeling the warm, unconditional glow of her father's love.

Wary that Gil might be lurking, waiting for her, Dare checked the alley before slipping out the stage door, but there were only a few stagehands out there stacking empty crates against the wall. Home free, Dare was turning onto the street when the door of an auto flew open and Nell popped out.

"There you are, I was worried I'd missed you! Can we give you a ride home?"

Dare would have loved a ride, but there had to be a hitch. Nell couldn't really want to be her friend. "Why?"

"Do I have to have a reason to be nice?" Nell asked.

"Most people do."

"All right, fine, I do have a reason, but I'd rather not say out here. Please?"

A ride did mean Dare would get home to Beastie that much faster. She climbed in.

As soon as the auto pulled away into traffic, Nell asked, "Can I hold Beastie again?"

"I left him at home, I didn't want to risk another mugging," Dare explained. "Is that why you offered the ride?"

"Not entirely," Nell confessed.

"Excuse me, Nell," Ernest called back from the front seat. "I'm meant to pick something up for your mother on the way. I hope that's all right with the young miss."

"Do you mind, Dare?" Nell asked.

How could she? She was lucky for the lift.

Nell told Ernest they were free to run the errand, then turned in the seat to face Dare. "I was sitting at luncheon earlier today with my mother and some of her friends. Her only friends, that is, aside from TR. Anyway, the conversation was boring as usual. All they ever talk about are clothes and dinner parties. This time, they were discussing some new supper club and how Mother had arranged for me to sing at the inaugural luncheon. Nothing new or interesting. Until I heard one of them mention the word 'agicole.'"

"Your mother and her friends were talking about the agicole?" Dare pressed. "Did they mention me?"

"No, should they have?"

"What are her friends' names?"

"Cornelia Cummings and Vera Hinckle. Why? Do you know them?"

She might as well have.

At this point, there was really no reason not to tell Nell everything, and several good reasons *to* tell her, especially now that Dare found herself in the awkward position of being on the same side as Mrs. Lawrence.

Dare poured out the entire story of her father's death. She told Nell all about the funeral, and the story about the murder being a robbery. She told her about the burning of Father's boxes, and about meeting Gil, and how he, Tupper, and Fortune had turned out to be the worst kind of people she could ever imagine.

She waited until Ernest parked the car and left to run into

a nearby shop before telling Nell the rest of it. About Padgett, and Mr. Cummings, and Dr. Hinckle. And what she'd now come to understand about Nell's own mother as well.

"Wait, so you think my mother, Padgett, Cummings, and all the rest are monster hunters? You have seen them, right? Picture Mother armed and tromping around in field boots. Or Padgett wrestling a monster." Nell cackled. "He couldn't run after his shadow."

"They wouldn't do the hunting. I would. And you're right about Padgett, he couldn't even run away from the monster that attacked him."

Nell blinked. "He was attacked? By what?"

"A maeder. I'd never heard of them. He said even though they're one of the smallest monsters, they're terrible, vicious creatures, with a bite that can melt skin. After seeing his scar, he's lucky to have a leg left."

Nell cocked her head and winced like she was trying to solve a particularly tricky riddle. "A scar? On his leg?"

"A great bite out of his shin. It happened right here in the city, two years ago, I think he said. It's healed a lot, but it's still awful to look at."

Nell scoffed. "We were on holiday with him not three months ago, Dare. I saw him in a bathing costume. I promise you—TR has no scar on his legs."

"You're wrong." Dare's awful reared its head and brought out her snarl. "I saw it myself. You must have missed it, not been looking."

"We sat in the sand making castles, burying our legs. I don't know what you saw. TR had no scars. I'm sorry, but whatever he showed you couldn't be real."

A storm began to gather deep inside Dare. How many versions of the so-called truth could she bear? No, there had to be a mistake.

"Why would he make that up?" Dare challenged as Ernest returned to the auto and handed a round hatbox to Nell.

"Your mother insisted we pick this up today," he said. "She had it made for you."

Nell received the box with a roll of her eyes before setting it on the seat between herself and Dare. "I don't mean to fight you. I know what I saw."

It would be so easy to hate Nell, assume she was being cruel, that she was no different from every other girl Dare had ever known. But unless Nell's entire life was a never-ending performance, Dare couldn't get herself to believe that.

She was about to say as much when her gaze landed on the hatbox.

MILLIE'S FINE MILLINERY was stamped on the top in gold—an ostentatious flourish, the kind expected from a high-end shop. What wasn't expected was what every letter *I* was dotted with.

The emblem; the same one on Padgett's calling card, that man's tiepin, and Father's box.

Dare grabbed hold of the box. "Does your mother shop here often?"

"I have no idea. I hate shopping, and all the clothes she's always trying to foist on me. No doubt there's some terrible hat in this box," Nell said. "Ernest, does Mother shop here often?"

"Very. I believe it's mostly custom orders here," he replied. "Hats, coats, gloves, special-occasion dresses."

"Thank you." Nell turned back to Dare. "Why did you ask?"

Dare told Nell about the emblem, and all the places she'd spotted it. "It's like a secret code for Padgett and his people."

"What could a milliner have to do with hunting monsters?" Nell gave words to the exact question that was banging inside Dare's head.

"Would you open the box?" Dare hardly got the question out before Nell was pulling off the lid and pushing aside the endless layers of tissue paper cosseting the contents.

"I can't believe it! She is relentless. I already told her I didn't want this pelt as a hat. Then she went and had it made over anyway," Nell exclaimed as she dislodged a brown fur muff. "She won't hear no!"

There should have been nothing remarkable about the muff; it was just a way to keep hands warm. They were common even among the women of Barrow's Bay, where the temperature never dipped below pleasant.

But it wasn't the fact of the item that set Dare's hands trembling; it was the coloring, the length, and the nap of the fur. A long, woolly coat covered over in black stripes rippling across a field of red. A brindled pattern, common to horses, to dogs, and to cats.

But there was only one thing Dare had ever heard of with brindled fur those colors, or that woolly and thick.

"Why would your mother have anything made of fexin fur?" Dare was truly hoping for a reasonable answer, even as she knew there wasn't anything reasonable about this.

"Is that what it is? Fexin? I've never heard of that," Nell replied. "Why wouldn't she, though?"

Dare chose her words carefully, spoke slowly. "Because fexin are monsters, Nell. Fox-shaped monsters with claws longer than an eagle's, and twice as deadly."

Nell dropped the muff as if it were poisoned. And it probably was. "Wearing animal skin is bad enough, why go beyond that to monsters?"

"That's the question, isn't it?" Dare raised a brow. "Do they know you in that shop?"

"No, but they'll know *of* me."

"That's even better. Can we go back there?" Dare posed it as a question, but she left little room for any answer other than yes.

"Absolutely—I was hoping you'd ask!"

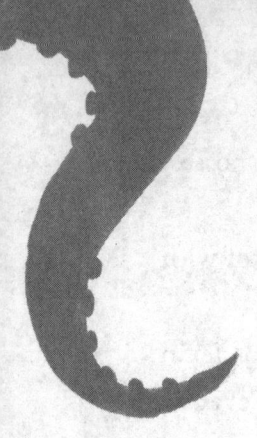

CHAPTER TWENTY-SIX
Grand Guignol

The exterior of Millie's Fine Millinery was as unremarkable as Mrs. Lawrence's motor car was ostentatious. The sign was hanging askew, and the window display of ladies' hats and gloves looked like it hadn't been changed out for twenty years. It took Dare a few moments to spot the emblem, but she finally found it etched into the glass on the door. Padgett's *small* guild seemed to be everywhere.

The girls agreed that Nell would do the talking, and Dare would do the listening. But there was a hitch; the door to the shop was locked, and the saleswoman, who they could see clearly through the glass panel in the door, was tacitly ignoring Nell's knock.

"Maybe there's a secret knock or password?" Dare asked.

"Could be. I have my own password." Nell took off her hat—letting her hair fall around her face—held the box up like a calling card, and knocked again.

The saleswoman's dour frown turned decidedly upright as her apparent case of myopia miraculously cleared. "Is that you, Miss Lawrence?" She opened the door only wide enough to peek her head out. "I'm so sorry. I didn't recognize you. Is there something wrong with the muff?"

"Not at all. I love it so much, and I was wondering if you might have a hat to match." Nell was shining her star power so brightly, some even dripped onto the saleswoman's waxen complexion.

"I think that's best discussed with your mother." The saleswoman's attitude teetered between snooty and fearful, no doubt caused by the thought of Mrs. Lawrence.

"You're right, and I'm sorry to show up this way, it's so impetuous of me. But as soon as I opened this box in the car, I knew I had to have a matching piece! Can you imagine how thrilled Mother would be to see me shopping on my own!"

At that, the saleswoman cut her eyes to Dare. She clearly didn't look like the daughter of a client. Nell was ready for that.

"I'm sorry, I apologize for my rudeness." Nell nodded toward Dare. "This is Kate, my understudy. In all ways, not just at the theater. When necessary, we send her out dressed like me—you know, as a decoy for the fans."

The saleswoman seemed to accept that explanation, but still wasn't convinced enough to admit them. She checked the watch hanging from a chain at her waist. "I'm afraid I have another appointment coming in twenty minutes; that's not nearly—"

Nell headed her off at the pass. "Fifteen is all I need! I'm very decisive."

Clearly outmatched, the saleswoman pulled the door open and admitted the girls. "Very well, I have a few pieces I can show you."

The shop was nearly as dreary and outdated as the window display, and twice as dusty. There was no way Mrs. Lawrence willingly shopped here. But then, like so much in the city, the trick was revealed as the saleswoman led the girls around the sales counter and through a heavy curtain. They emerged into a dim stockroom at the end of which sat a plain wooden door. The saleswoman bid them to follow her through the door, around tall wooden shelves, and then finally into a lushly decorated salon hung with gilded mirrors, a fitting screen, and silk-covered chairs.

This made more sense.

"If you'd like to take a seat, I can show you a few items I think might make a nice complement to the muff." The saleswoman disappeared behind a brocade curtain only to return a moment later with a long velvet-lined tray in hand. "As I'm sure your mother has explained to you, we feel it imperative that clientele who are new to our goods build their wardrobe slowly."

"Yes." Nell barely blinked.

"That fur muff you have is a wonderful enhancement. It's bound to increase your already infinite appeal. If you really want to add to it, I'd recommend you begin with some of these."

She set the tray down in front of the girls, revealing row upon row of ornately carved buttons. Some were made to look like flowers, others the sun or the moon, seashells or stars. Following Nell's lead, Dare looked but touched nothing. An easy enough task, because there was something about the buttons that was making Dare queasy.

"They're lovely, truly," Nell cooed, "but I'm hoping for something a bit . . . more."

"I understand. Buttons do carry power, Miss Lawrence. The effects of bone are understated, gentle. Honestly, I was surprised your mother insisted on the fexin. Our clientele tend to build up to pelts."

"Yes, well, we Lawrence women are impatient."

The saleswoman winced, clearly she'd been on the other side of that particular family trait with the Foghorn more than once. "I understand. I'll be right back."

Dare barely waited until the woman had gone before she was hissing in Nell's ear. "Bones? Enhancements? Nell, what is this?"

"I don't know, but we're not leaving until we find out."

The saleswoman returned next with a straw hat embellished with a pink grosgrain ribbon wrapped around the crown. There was nothing terribly gaudy or showy about it;

it was rather simple and made in surprisingly good taste.

"This is a lovely piece that will inspire fortitude in the face of difficulties. Don't be fooled that there are only three feathers—the verpid were known to be particularly powerful. We have a similar piece that has a few berlund feathers, which provide a most effective protection from those who seek to harm you. But truly, you're so beloved, I think this is a better choice."

As the saleswoman spoke, Dare flipped through the file cabinet of her mind, trying to place verpids and berlunds. She'd never heard of any of them, neither as common birds nor as monsters.

Then the saleswoman turned the hat to show off three small blue feathers with an iridescent green cast.

Nell sniffed indifferently.

And while Dare sat there also trying to look indifferent, bored even, her insides were churning. She knew the color of those feathers as well as her own hand.

Pretty's feathers were exactly that color.

No, it was impossible.

Pretty was a bird, one who'd fallen from the nest at a young age and gotten injured. That's all. A bird, not a monster.

All of this had to be wrong.

"It's lovely, but I'm looking for something with more impact," Nell said, making starbursts with her hands. "As you know, price is no object."

The clerk pressed her lips tight, offered a curt bow of her head, then disappeared behind the curtain again. "What is it?" Nell whispered. "You look like you've seen a ghost."

"I think I have." Dare tried to swallow, tried to tell Nell about the feathers, but before she could, the saleswoman returned with a small box in hand.

"This is the last item we have in our present inventory that I feel is appropriate for you today, Miss Lawrence. As you must know, supplies have dwindled over the years. We must follow very strict protocols."

"Yes, but the rarity adds to the value, no?" Dare had always thought herself a confident liar, but Nell was completely unflappable. "What do you have there for me?"

"The gifts this pelt offers are quite delicate, almost subtle. It does a lovely job of soothing, calming the nerves, inspiring confidence. I think these would provide a lovely complement to the muff, as the fexin's gifts are complicated. As you know, the fexin bestows a kind of magnetism, but can also leave the wearer a bit vulnerable to the ideas of others. It's a mixed gift." And with that, the saleswoman lifted the lid of the box and handed a pair of fur cuffs to Nell.

Dare already knew that life-shaking change doesn't happen slowly. It's sudden and jarring; it arrives with the slash of a blade, the strike of a match, the opening of a box. Those moments have a way of feeling like they last forever, as you hang suspended between life as it was before and as it can never be again. Until the truth is spoken aloud, and you have no choice but to know what you now know.

"The fur looks almost like feathers up close, doesn't it?" Nell noted as she inspected the pair of long-haired yellow fur cuffs flecked through with bands of orange and brown.

"Yes, it's quite unique to the maeder. They're rather rare, few were ever captured, so these do come at a dear cost." The saleswoman continued with a longer explanation, a dissertation on the gifts bestowed by the fur of a maeder, along with advice on how Nell ought to build up wearing the pelts, and in which situations to leave them at home. But most of that was lost to Dare, because there was only one fact that mattered.

Those cuffs were all that remained of Madam's beloved Bijou.

CHAPTER TWENTY-SEVEN
The Dawning

Were it not for Nell, Dare very well might have erupted with rage and started breaking things. Then again, she also might have fallen into a chasm of grief and never crawled out again. But Nell was quick on her feet and even quicker with a lie. She got Dare out of that shop and back to the auto without causing a scene or raising the saleswoman's suspicions. At least, they'd hoped so.

"It can't be. That pelt, the cuffs? I think it was Bijou. Madam's Bijou." Dare was having a hard time getting her thoughts out, the disbelief too hard to shake. "If Bijou was a maeder, then so is Beastie. How . . . ? And those feathers on that hat. They were the same exact color, length, everything, as Pretty's, my father's bird. He would never have kept a monster!"

"And would you or Madam?" Nell asked.

"No!" Dare declared. "Never! That's the thing. Beastie's so good. You held him. There's nothing cruel in him. Is there?

Am I wrong? Did I miss it? Am I a monster for not seeing it?"

"No." Nell was firm as rock. "Your Beastie is divine. When I held him, I felt so at ease in my own skin, comfortable for once."

"That's how he makes me feel, too." Dare could practically hear her heart cracking in half, for while that fact should have been all the comfort she needed, it was also exactly what the saleswoman had said the cuffs would elicit.

"Gil told me the monsters had gifts, abilities, strengths they can bestow," Dare confessed. "I hated him for saying that."

"And now?"

"I don't know . . . A monster killed my father. They killed stupid, helpless Louise. They killed most of Barrow's crew, and they kept killing until they were killed off. Or not, actually. They're relentless, evil creatures, and I should be glad to see every last one turned into a coat!"

"That's what we've been told, isn't it?"

Dare bristled at hearing Nell agreeing with Gil. But she wasn't saying anything Dare hadn't already thought.

"Just because a story gets told over and over and over again doesn't make it true. You know what you know about Beastie. No story can ever change those feelings."

Dare sank back in the seat. She felt so small, so frail, like her bones were made of paper, like nothing was real.

"How can you ever know anything for sure?" Her voice came out barely above a whisper.

"I don't think you really can," Nell replied. "Although I do know some things about my mother, and about Padgett, Cummings, and all the rest of that set, that are beyond true. They're ruthless, and nothing is beyond the pale if it helps them retain their wealth, their positions, and the impression that they exist above the rules. And it doesn't matter if they inherited it like Cummings, Hinckle, and so many others—the sons and daughters of the so-called Barrow Twenty—if they built it like Padgett, or if they married, then buried, the man who gave it to them, like my mother did."

"I didn't know you lost your father, too. I'm so sorry." Dare kicked herself for thinking she was the only one shadowed by loss.

"Thank you, but he wasn't my father. I barely knew him. My mother married Everett Lawrence when I was four. He died before I turned six. She got everything. And she's never told me who my real father is, so I can't really mourn him."

Talk of fathers gone pushed a new, even harder truth.

"My father was one of them. He helped *them*." The words tasted sour but Dare refused to swallow them back. "He was only pretending to work with Tupper and Fortune to find out the location of their refuge. That means he knew what they do with the monsters. Why they want them. But he had Pretty! And if she's a monster, why did he keep her? He loved her, or so I thought. Was he using her? I don't know how to know anything anymore! If everyone is on the wrong side of everything, who's right?"

Nell squeezed Dare's hand. "I'm pretty sure you're never going to stop until you figure that out."

Dare was completely turned inside out. And yes, she'd keep pushing until the truth came out. She didn't know how not to do that. But that also meant knowing her own father to be a kind of monster who had twisted the truth for his own gain.

It was him or Beastie.

How could she ever bear knowing which of them was what?

A hundred spiders might as well have been crawling under Dare's skin. "I need to get home. I need to see Beastie for myself. Maybe I'm wrong about him being the same as Bijou."

Dare looked out the window to see where they were, only to realize that while her entire world had been shifting under her feet, the auto had come to a complete standstill. "Why aren't we moving?"

"Ernest, can't you get us through this traffic?" Nell pressed.

"Wish I could," Ernest replied. "Strikers have taken over the avenue up ahead."

The girls rolled down their windows and stuck their heads out to see. The road was flooded with strikers marching, singing songs, and carrying signs that read *CANNERY WORKERS ON THE EDGE* and *WE WILL STRIKE FOR RIGHTS!*

"Looks like Cummings might have some new problems." Nell didn't sound very upset.

"Why him?"

"He owns the cannery. I'm sure he pays his workers less than nothing, keeps all the rest to himself. And now we know what he's buying." Nell grimaced as if she tasted copper on her tongue. "Dare, who's seen you with Beastie, besides me and Madam? Did Padgett, Cummings, or Hinckle?"

"No, not them, I don't think?" She pushed to calm herself, think clearly. "Gil, of course. And there was that man in the park, the one with the tiepin. When he tried to pet Beastie, Beastie let out the worst sound. And, Nell . . ." Dare paused, almost embarrassed she hadn't thought of it already. "That mugger. He wasn't after my money, was he?"

Nell pushed forward to lean on the back of the driver's seat. "Please, Ernest, you have to get us out of this traffic!"

"It's beginning to break up. I'll get us out as fast as I can," he replied.

"Dare, we have to move Beastie and find a safer place for him." Nell wasn't asking, she was telling.

Dare shut down. The day had been hard enough. "I can't do that," she insisted. "He has to stay with me."

"I understand. Still, think this through. Ernest could keep him for you. He's the soul of discretion, the most honest and kindest person I know. He'd never, ever tell anyone or betray you. And he's also as good as invisible to my mother and her friends. They'd never even think of him." Nell glanced out the window. "Ah! We're finally moving. Don't worry, Dare. You and Beastie will be back together in no time at all."

* * *

Nell wanted to come into the house to see Beastie for herself but Dare insisted she wait in the car. The last thing Dare needed was to raise Mary's suspicions.

There was only one problem. The front door was locked, and no one came to answer the bell.

Dare ran around through the alley to the back door, thinking Mary must be in the kitchen and not hearing the call. But the kitchen door was also locked, and there was no sign of Mary in her usual habitat.

Dare went back into the alley, ready to try ringing the front bell again when she heard from over her shoulder, "Try the back way in."

Dare was in no way ready to deal with Gil, to admit he'd been right. Not yet. She tried to ignore him. Yet he clung to her like a shadow, repeatedly insisting he knew of a way into the house until she broke.

"Why are you here again?" she snarled.

"Because I didn't like that you were mad at me, that you think of me as anything other than a friend to you, and the marvels. And because . . ." Gil stopped, understanding dawning. "What happened to your coat? Where is he, where is your Beastie?"

Dare tossed her head, fighting to exude the kind of confidence she wanted to believe she had. "He's upstairs. I left him at home. Why do you care?"

Gil's left eye twitched as his lips pressed into a thin line.

Dare's father used to get a look like that when he was trying not to get mad. At those times, she knew he was silently counting to ten, waiting for the initial flare of anger to subside.

"I told you to never let him out of your sight!" Gil snapped, not waiting for a count of ten, or even five. "Why didn't you listen?"

Dare had a thousand reasons, prime among them being who was he to tell her what to do? But none of them were good reasons.

"I can't believe you left him home alone." Gil stood there shaking his head, repeatedly clucking his tongue like a hen, until at last, he threw his hands up. "We'll talk about this later. For now, there's a back way into the house. I'll show you."

Dare had no more fight in her—all she wanted was her Beastie. She let Gil direct her into the dusty theater, then down a short hall to a door marked *JANITOR*.

"Why are you taking me to the janitor's closet?"

"It's not what it says it is. This was Madam's slip-away door," he explained. "It was designed to give her a hidden entrance back into her house. It leads to a stairway straight to the second floor. Perhaps you've seen the door next to Madam's room?"

"I have, yes. Well, thank you for, you know, showing this to me." Dare started into the passageway, assuming he'd stay back, but Gil followed on her heels.

"What are you doing? You can't come in the house. Mary will kill me," she insisted. "Wait here, I'll come back and tell you and Nell both that he's fine."

"Mary's not even home, I saw her go out," Gil said. "I am coming with you."

Dare didn't bother to argue, it wasn't worth it. Besides, she secretly wanted the company. Even as she told herself Beastie would be right where she'd left him, she wasn't sure she believed herself.

Back in the house, it was just as Gil had said. Mary was nowhere to be seen, and there was no sound coming from the solar—Madam must have been fast asleep.

Holding tight to the hope that she was moments from a reunion, Dare went straight to her room, threw open the wardrobe, and reached inside for Beastie, ready to give Gil a giant "I told you so."

But she couldn't.

Her hands came up empty.

Slowly, methodically at first, then with quickly mounting dread, she removed everything from the wardrobe. She searched in her empty suitcase, dress pockets, and up on the highest shelf. He wasn't there. Refusing to submit to panic, she looked under, behind, and on top of the wardrobe. By this time, Gil had joined the search, looking under her bed, in between the pillows, checking for any way the critter could have gotten out of the room.

Through it all, they didn't say a single word as they searched the rest of the house—high, low, in between, underneath. They checked every nook and cranny.

Still nothing.

Dare kept Madam's solar for last, certain she'd find him before she'd have to go in there. The risk of upsetting her great-aunt was too high. But with no choices left, she realized she'd been foolish; it made all the sense in the world for Beastie to be in there.

With her heart primed and ready to snap with relief, Dare eased into the room. Madam was asleep in a chair by the fire, her legs up, a light blanket warming her. Gil started to press into the room behind Dare, but she waved him back.

"You can't come in here!" she whispered.

Uncharacteristically, he listened to her, and stayed by the door.

Slowly and quietly, Dare crept toward Madam, certain she'd catch sight of Beastie's snowy fur. But there was nothing there, just Madam looking paler than she had the last time Dare had seen her.

Determined not to give in, Dare backed out of the room and took another three sweeps through the entire house. But no matter how much she and Gil called and whistled, or how much she begged the stars above and promised never to be awful again, they didn't find Beastie anywhere.

CHAPTER TWENTY-EIGHT
Pin Your Gaze and Keep Climbing

Dare sat on the bottom step of Madam's grand sweeping staircase, her head in her hands. She'd never felt more at sea. The familiar haze of grief compounded now by a shower of disgust with herself. She deserved whatever nasty words Gil threw at her. Loss was all she'd ever know, and ridicule all she'd ever deserve.

"Go ahead," she dared Gil. "I know you're dying to say it."

"I'm sorry he's gone," Gil replied. Just that, nothing more.

Dare peeled her head out of her hands. "That's not what I expected you to say."

"It's really all there is to say. I'm so sad for you, and for him."

His admission, so sincere, cracked her shell. "I thought I was doing the right thing leaving him at home. If I had known anything I know now, I never would have. . . ." There really wasn't anything she could say to defend herself. "You told me, and I didn't want to listen."

"It's hard to unlearn what you've been taught your whole life. We were all told that they were monsters. That's the lore, that's the story of Barrow's Bay. And maybe they are. But they're also marvels that have gifts to bestow. They're both things at once."

"If you knew they wear them to take their gifts, why didn't you tell me that? I might not have believed you, but I would have at least known—"

"They do what?" Gil turned gray.

"Wear them. They use their bones for buttons, their feathers to trim hats, their pelts as cuffs, and more. How do I know this and you don't?"

"You know many things I don't. But this, this makes no sense." Gil looked like he'd been stunned by an electric eel. "Their gifts are at their most powerful when they're alive, when they give them freely."

Dare scoffed. "Padgett and the rest of them could hardly keep a lypek or a garbinol around the house."

"You had a maeder, so did Madam. Sure, when provoked, their fur bristles and they can be as deadly as a skerb—"

"Stop, I don't want to hear it," Dare said, leaving no room for debate. "Beastie is gone, and I don't want to know what terrible thing he might have been capable of. I just want him back."

"I know. But you should know everything there is to know—" The sound of the kitchen door slamming shut cut Gil off.

Mary was home.

"You have to get out of here!" Dare whispered as she jumped to her feet. "Mary cannot see you."

"I wouldn't worry about that," Gil said.

"Don't tell me what to worry about. She'll have a fit if she finds you here. Go out the way we came in. I'm going out the front. I don't want her to know that I know about the passageway. I'll meet you back in the alley."

"It's probably best I clear out. I'll come find you later." Gil started up the stairs before turning back to add, "Don't worry, Dare, we'll find him. I know we will."

He might have only been saying that to make her feel better, but his certainty fueled her own.

Dare silently eased out the front door, taking great care to not let the latch make any noise as it reengaged. But her sigh of relief quickly turned into a strangled gasp when she turned and came face-to-face with Nell.

"Finally!" Nell grabbed Dare by the hand and pulled her down the street, away from the house. "I didn't want to ring the bell, but I was getting desperate waiting for you."

"Where are you taking me? And where is your automobile?" Dare protested, but Nell shushed her sharply and refused to say another thing until they were safely around the corner.

"He's gone!" Nell declared. "Beastie!"

"I know that." The reminder cut deep. "How do *you* know?"

"Because I saw him."

"What? Where? Did you try to catch him? Is he all right?" Dare became electric, wired to dart away in seven directions at once, until Nell took her by the shoulders.

"Listen," Nell commanded. "Ernest and I were sitting here waiting for you to come back when a watchman came and told Ernest he couldn't idle, and that's when I saw her."

"Him," Dare corrected. "Beastie's a him."

"No, *her*," Nell recorrected. "Your aunt's maid. I mean, I didn't know who she was until she came back here and went up the alley."

"What are you talking about? What does this have to do with Beastie?"

"I'm getting to it. After the watchman made us move, we drove around the block, which really meant having to drive three blocks out of the way on one-way streets so that we could come back this way. I wouldn't have even noticed it, but I know Padgett's auto. It's impossible to miss, it's the only one in the city with a bright pink top to match the Palace. I didn't want him to spot me, so I pulled the shade, but as I was doing that I caught sight of a woman handing something to the driver. A flash of white. White fur. Feathery tail. It could have been something else, but the driver handed her a pouch. A large one. Like the ones they use to make bank deposits. When the auto took off, Ernest followed it, and I followed the woman on foot. She made several stops, at shops and such, before coming back here."

Dare's jaw was clenched so tight, the cords in her neck threatened to snap. A flash of white. A feathery tail. Padgett's car. It all made such horrid sense—especially what Mary had done on the way home.

"Did Mary buy much at the shops?"

"Tons. I'm surprised she could carry all those packages."

A rush of awful raced up Dare's spine, rattling her bones, as if she were becoming a monster herself. Mary had sold her Beastie to Padgett!

"I'm going to scratch her—!"

"Stop, don't even think it," Nell counseled. "Revenge won't get you what you want."

"It could." Dare desperately wanted it to, but Nell was right, it wouldn't bring her Beastie back. "How could she do this? How did she even know I had him?" Dare searched her memory, looking for the moment, when it hit her. "The wardrobe. She was digging around in there the day I found him. I thought she hadn't seen him. But she knew all along and said nothing. Why? How could she do that?!"

"It was a large pouch," Nell said. "A lot of money."

"I knew Mary would do anything to save Madam, but this? This is lower than low."

This was the point at which Dare would normally have flown off into a rage, but something had switched inside her.

Instead of her anger propelling her toward spite, it did something different. It focused her, pushed her out of that drift of hopelessness. She didn't have to go under or surrender, not to loss, not to her awful, and most certainly not to Padgett, because she had something none of them did.

"We have to go get my Beastie!" Dare lunged to run off, but Nell pulled her up short.

"We have no idea where they took him, not until Ernest brings word."

"We don't have to wait for that!" Dare was too excited to speak. "I'm a drover, Nell! I helped find that agicole, and I found Beastie the first time. I can find him again!"

"This is a big city, Dare. You have no idea where to start."

"Yes, I do. At Padgett's."

"You can't go there. He knows you had a monster. What are you going to say?"

"Whatever I have to."

"You don't know what you're getting into. They're dangerous people, Dare!"

There was nothing funny about any of this, but Dare had to laugh. "You do know we're talking about your mother, too, right?"

"I do," Nell readily agreed. "That's why I say it. Please, can we wait for Ernest? At least then we'll know where to start, how to plan."

"There's no time for planning. Beastie could be a pair of

cuffs before the sun goes down!"

"Remember what the saleswoman said?" Nell prompted. "Maeder pelts are especially rare because they are slow to mature. I hate to put it this way, but Beastie is nowhere large enough yet."

Bijou did look to have been about twice Beastie's size in Madam's painting. Still, it was the coldest comfort. "I've tried patience—it only leaves time for more awful things to happen."

"But if you push, you might break our chances." Nell glanced at the watch she wore at her waist. "I have to get home before Mama gets there. If she sees me arrive in a cab, she'll never believe me, no matter what story I tell her. Go inside and see what you can get out of Mary."

"You mean like blood?"

"No," said Nell, ever the coolheaded one. "Information."

"I don't think I can trust myself not to throw a chair, or something even bigger."

Nell took Dare's hand and squeezed. "Then don't do anything until you hear from me. Promise?"

"Sure," Dare agreed.

Dare broke that promise as soon as Nell climbed into a hansom cab and headed for home.

The entire way back to Padgett's Palace, Dare thought her resolve was unshakeable, but once she was outside Padgett's office, a small quake washed over her. Her awful had a way of ruining things—once she was face-to-face with Padgett, chances were slim to nonexistent that she'd be able to contain the river of rage roaring inside her.

No, not this time. This time she'd lead, not react. All she had to do was pin her gaze and keep climbing.

Dare set her spine and knocked as if she were rapping on the gates of an ogre's den.

"Come!" Padgett commanded.

Dare walked into the office to find him head down in paperwork. "I told you not to bother . . ." He stopped mid-bark and his scowl quickly turned to a wide smile when he saw her.

"Dare! What a lovely surprise. I mistook you for someone else. Come, sit, sit! I have good news. We've discussed it, and while we intend to put your safety first, we do agree you should be part of the expedition. And that's not all. We've secured a ship certain to get us through the winds. We should be ready to sail soon."

"That's great news." Dare tried to exude the same kind of enthusiasm as she had the last time she'd sat in this very chair facing Padgett, who'd come to perch on the edge of his desk—just like last time. Everything looked and smelled the same in the crowded office: the pile of scripts on the desk, the empty coffee cups, the stale stink of cigars smoked long ago still hanging in the air. Yet everything was different.

Or perhaps it was Dare who was different.

She launched into her act. "I have something I have to tell you." She needed to use her words sparingly, lest the wrong ones—the cursing ones—fall out.

Padgett leaned in, intrigued.

"It's about a monster." Dare wanted to make the beginning of her story sound like a full-on confession, so she spoke in a halting manner, as if droving for each word. "It was in my house. I didn't know what it was when I brought it inside."

Padgett looked so surprised, Dare had to wonder if she'd gotten him wrong. Then she remembered where she was: a house of illusions, built out of one man's delusions.

"You see, I found it, and thought it was just a small animal, wounded, a chinchilla needing nursing."

"I see." Padgett leaned forward, pulling at the ends of his mustache.

"I'm too awful for words," Dare confessed, trying to mirror his sullen expression. "Then I happened to see some cuffs, uh, on a lady on the street, made from the same kind of fur. I sensed something was different, off. So I thought I'd bring it to you to see if I was right or not. You'd know what it was for sure. But when I got home, it was gone. I can't find it anywhere."

Dare let herself get carried off by what it might feel like if what she was saying had been true. Although enough of it was, so perhaps she wasn't acting after all. "I've let a monster loose in the city!"

Padgett smoothed his mustache—and his aspect—and leaned back, a man in control. "Now, let's stay calm. How big was it? What kind of monster do you think it was?"

Dare demonstrated the size with her hands. "I think, I think it was a maeder."

Padgett made an oof sound, as if the word pained him, before adding, "And you had it for how long?"

"Since the first day I was here in the city."

"And it was never aggressive? Never tried to bite or sting you?"

"No, sir." Finally, an answer that wasn't a lie.

"That's good, that's good." Padgett got up to pace the room, one hand stroking his chin, the fingers of the other idly rubbing together as if to conjure a brilliant idea. It wasn't the most convincing move, but Dare wasn't going to let on that his performance was tissue-paper thin.

After several more rounds, Padgett snapped his fingers as if seized by the perfect solution before returning to his perch on the desk. It was then that Dare finally realized what he reminded her of.

A catfish. A big, hairy-lipped bottom-feeder.

"I'm sorry this happened, Dare," he began. "Don't blame yourself. In fact, it's a testament to you. You're clearly a talented drover. Still so young, and a girl no less!"

Dare curled her toes inside her boots to keep from visibly reacting to that poisoned arrow, but there was a truth there that she needed to test. "So, do you mean, you think I can find it?"

Padgett nodded. "Yes, I do believe you can. With some help and coaching, of course."

"Of course." Dare inched up to the edge of her seat. "What do I do? Where do I start?"

"For now, go home and keep searching. They're small creatures and tend not to travel very far or fast. In the meantime, I will get word out to our friends that there's a beast loose. We'll listen for any reports of sightings, send out scouts. This is a big city, Dare, we must be methodical."

"That will take so long. Anything could happen!" Dare's agitation at this point was not an act.

"I have no doubt in your droving skills. You will find that creature. And once you do, we'll launch our expedition in search of that blasted refuge. Trust yourself, and please, trust me. I'll send word as soon as I have anything to share."

Padgett undoubtedly thought he was setting her up perfectly. He could even have been planning to plant Beastie somewhere she'd be certain to find him, either as a test, or as a way to boost her belief in her abilities.

But she'd beat him long before he could get that far.

"All right, I will." Dare slowly peeled herself from the seat as if she could barely tear herself away, and then—for added effect—stopped at the door to deliver an almost too earnest "Thank you, sir. Thank you," before marching out.

CHAPTER TWENTY-NINE
Droving

Dare left Padgett's certain of two things: Beastie was still alive. And she was going to find him.

It was everything in between and beyond that she didn't know, including where to start looking, and how to go droving. She hadn't done anything when she spotted the agicole, and she'd simply turned around and found Beastie. How was that a talent?

Dare took a turn around the theater, sniffing and looking, but Padgett would never be that obvious; he'd have some illusion at work.

How do you go looking for deception when the whole point is to mislead the mind?

Back out on the street, she found herself wishing Gil would turn up. But he was nowhere to be seen, and Nell was at home telling her own lies to her mother. As for Mary, Dare still couldn't trust herself not to do something truly regrettable to the maid. Dare was on her own.

"There has to be something to droving," she muttered as she walked down the street. "Something that happened to me, or that I did when I found the agicole and Beastie."

Still, she came up blank. There was no tingle in her blood, no voice in her head telling her *Look there!* There was nothing she'd done.

Could droving be less about doing, and more about receiving?

Dare was turning this question over in her mind when she reached the end of the block. She had to choose a direction, head either into the nicer part of town or into the Must.

The thought of walking those streets again gave her a chill—the memory of that mugger's mug so close to hers as he cornered her was too vivid for words. But the Must was where Millie's was, the one place she'd come closest to unveiling the illusions. She had to go back.

With her course clear, Dare came up with a story to tell the saleswoman about running an errand for Nell. Yet when she reached the shop, there was no use for a tale—it was buttoned up tight. Anyone who didn't know better might think it had been shuttered for years.

Another illusion.

The chemist's shop where she'd bought that headache powder was open, but if the clerk on duty—an old man she'd not seen before—had any stories to tell, they weren't the ones Dare was looking for.

The day was getting old, and Dare knew she should be heading home soon, but the thought of spending a single night without Beastie was too much to bear.

Just a few more blocks, a little while longer, soon turned into an entire circuit around the Must. Dare's feet were beginning to hurt almost as much as her heart, and her eyes were tearing, not from sadness—although she was bereft—but from the smog spewing out of a nearby factory. How the people of the Must lived every day with that stink was beyond—

That stink.

Dare's mind raced back to that first ride through the city with Captain Fortune, how she'd caught the waft of monsters that accompanied her dreams, and how quickly the captain had shut the shade.

"Where was that?" Dare tried to remember anything that would lead her back to that spot, but kept drawing a blank. Then the loud work whistle from a nearby factory started wailing overhead, making it even harder to think.

She was about to surrender to the inevitability of twilight when the gates of the factory flew open, expelling a flood of workers. Men, women, even some children her own age flowed out of the gates, their faces as drained as the empty lunch pails they carried. Dare had learned a few things about getting through crowds since her arrival in the city, first of which was that there's no point in fighting against the current. She set her back against a brick wall and waited for the flood to recede.

When the flow had slowed to a few stragglers, Dare pushed off to head home. And that's when she caught the scent.

That unmistakable vapor that haunted her nearly every night.

Dare tried to track it, but the harder she tried to smell it, the more she realized the scent wasn't in the air around her, exactly. It might not even have been something she could really smell; maybe it was more of a feeling, a memory. Whatever it was, she hadn't caught it until the workers had passed her by.

Dare joined the crowd, trying to locate the smell, recapture the tingle it sent up her spine. She stayed close enough to catch pieces of the workers' conversations, yet not so close as to seize anyone's suspicion. In and out she wove between small groups. Two men and a woman here. A man and a boy who was likely his son there.

The only odor she caught was the funk of a long day's work.

That is, until she caught up to two men wearing gray coveralls with heavy leather gloves clipped to their sleeves.

There it was again—unmistakable for anything else.

Dare followed as close as she could, straining to hear the men's hushed conversation over the sounds of the city. It wasn't until they reached the corner and the other workers dispersed in different directions that she could finally hear them clearly.

"I don't know," one was saying to the other. "It's rough work, but it's all I know."

He was a short man, with a blocky build that made him look like he could withstand any blow thrown his way. He cut a sharp contrast to his companion, who, while not much taller, was as thin and rickety as an old ladder. A summer's breeze looked enough to knock him over.

Yet the thin man was the one who spoke with more authority and power. "It's simple. They want us to keep going in there, they need to pay. You see that new one they brought through? Doesn't look like much, but I hear it can bite straight through bone."

The men kept talking, but Dare had heard everything she needed to. Beastie was somewhere in that factory.

She doubled back as fast as she could and managed to land back at the gates just as a guard was shutting them.

"My dad forgot his lunch pail!" She made her eyes wide with worry. "He told me not to come home without it!"

The guard looked as tired as the shift workers, and clearly didn't care much. He waved her through.

Dare was so relieved to have been let in that she almost missed the large sign over the entrance to the factory. *CUMMINGS'S CANNERY.*

There was no surprise in that at all. Padgett and his people were everywhere.

Dare entered the factory floor, fighting to look like she knew where she was going, but the factory was nothing like she'd expected. To hear the schoolmarm back on Barrow's Bay talk about them, you'd think they were warm and happy places where the workers labored like contented elves. This loud, echoing cavern filled with clanging machinery and endless conveyor belts was most definitely not that.

There were still some workers on the floor, mostly mopping or wiping equipment. Others were stacking large crates filled with tin cans onto dollies and moving them onto the loading dock. No one spoke or looked up from their work, and they certainly didn't pay any attention to the girl with the ripped coat and messy braids walking past them. Their misery gave Dare the cover she needed to go looking, searching. Droving.

Or at least she tried to, but nothing she did helped her catch that vapor again; the only things she smelled were fish, sweat, and dirty mop water. She'd walked the entire length of the factory floor all the way out to the loading dock and was about to turn back for another look when a door on the back wall of the loading dock creaked open. Determined not to get caught out, Dare slipped behind a stack of empty crates to watch as two workers slowly emerged through the doorway.

Dressed in the same gray coveralls as the men on the street, this pair was a man and a woman. Like the two men, they had heavy gloves clipped to their belts, and more important, they carried that certain stink on them.

Monster.

Dare's skin prickled and her ears began to buzz; she was so close. Close enough now to realize the man was carrying something—a small bundle cradled to his chest.

A white bundle.

The world stopped turning.

She'd found him!

Forcing herself to stay put, Dare strained to watch through the slats of a crate as the pair headed toward the factory floor, her mind spinning, trying to think of how to get her Beastie away from them.

As the pair were about to cross back into the factory, the man turned back to look over his shoulder at the door they'd come through. And in that moment, Dare saw that the bundle he carried was the man's own hand swaddled in a thick bandage, flecks of bright red blood seeping through the fabric.

"Come on, Jed," the woman said softly as they disappeared into the factory. "It's not following us, don't worry. Let's get you to the doctor, he'll sew your hand up like new."

Dare's heart, which had been pounding like the surf after a storm, nearly stopped.

There had to be another explanation. Beastie would never do anything like that, not even to his captors.

Right?

Dare swallowed twice for courage, then, after double-checking that the loading dock was empty, crept out from her hiding spot and made for the door the pair had come through.

But when she got to the wall, there was no door there, just solid brick.

Impossible. She hadn't imagined it.

Dare ran her hands up and down the wall looking for the trick. Nothing but rough brick.

It was there, it had to be.

As her dread mounted ever higher, Dare pushed herself to pause, to think slowly and clearly. Maybe it was like droving. Maybe the harder you looked, the less you saw. She tried to soften, to view the wall as an opportunity, not an obstacle. A puzzle.

It tried more than her patience as she pushed and prodded, until eventually she spotted something that looked like hope. It was a small divot in the brick, no thicker than a thumb. Yet it was so much more. With just enough pressure, the brick gave way and a gap eased open. Dare slipped through the opening without a second's thought into a wide corridor lined with gas lamps.

It wasn't the dim that hit Dare, nor even the knowledge that should someone come, she had nowhere to run. It was the stench that hit her hardest. Only now it wasn't just monster, or fish, or dirty mop. It was the stink of filth, of rotting food, of waste and misery.

Dare covered her mouth and nose with her hand and pressed down the hall, which was beginning to take on a slope. The farther she went, the stronger the smell became. She was fighting to keep her stomach from lurching, to keep her feet from turning to flee, when she spotted the door at the bottom of the hall.

An obvious door, made of metal, with a sliding peephole at the top and a massive padlock fixed in place.

No.

A stupid piece of metal was not going to stop her now!

Dare's awful reared its head as she kicked at the lock, slamming it as hard as she could with her bootheel. It was foolish and useless and left her breathless and aching, but she had nothing else on which to take out her anger.

Yet it also turned out to be a stroke of pure brilliance, for if she hadn't kicked it, she wouldn't have noticed the lock wasn't fully engaged. One more kick and the lock fell open.

Soaring on the surprise of success, Dare raced through the door, certain she'd find her Beastie on the other side.

Never in seven lifetimes could she have imagined anything more awful, appalling, and wretched than what she found behind that door. For inside lay a cold brick cavern, the grated floor haphazardly covered with rotting marsh grass littered and dampened with waste. A single electric bulb hung overhead, casting a glare over the entire room.

Yet it was the iron cages that threatened to crack Dare in two.

There were large ones and small ones strewn all around

the dungeon, absolutely misery traps all. Dare expected the room to erupt into a clatter of barks and snarls, whistles and howls, at her arrival, but it was mostly silent, except for some soft whimpering and a low thrum of guttural growls.

Monsters, at least six or more different kinds, were shut into cages by type. No food, no water, barely any light, only the wretched hum of misery.

Dare slowly approached the closest cage, careful not to make any sudden movements, but the occupants of that terrible box barely registered her at all.

Jacklers—easily recognizable by their ducklike bodies, flat, protruding snouts, and the fleshy pink fingerlike appendages encircling their mouths. There were two adults (a mating pair) and five, perhaps six young clustered into the nest so close together it was hard to tell one from the other. Even if their mouths truly could excrete a poison that paralyzed their prey, the poor things were too sickly and weak to be a threat to anyone or anything.

The next cage was occupied by a pair of caltung, another beast Dare recognized easily from her father's descriptions. Their sharp antlers and impenetrable reptilian hide provided them with great defenses, but it was the caltung's muscular, jackrabbit-like back legs that made them deadly hunters. And yet this poor caged pair was shedding scales as they lay pressed against the corner of their prison, shaking.

A pair of speckled droben lay curled together atop a filthy

pile of grass. If droben truly were built like wild pigs, one would never know it by the looks of these two; they were so thin and weak, they could barely muster the energy to raise their long necks or flare their pincerlike mouths.

But it was the garbinol—sealed into a large cage all alone—that made Dare's knees buckle. Its coat was matted and thinning in patches, and its beak broken at the tip. The corners of its eyes were crusted with thick yellow pus, and its feet had been picked red.

Even as wretched as they all were, Dare longed to reach out and touch them. But the bandicots had started bristling, the razor-sharp spikes lining their backs standing on end.

Dare continued picking her way through the room, looking for Beastie. She had to fight with herself to stay clearheaded even though she was surrounded by cages full of actual living monsters.

Except for Beastie. He wasn't there.

He wasn't anywhere.

CHAPTER THIRTY

In the Solar

By the time Dare got back to Nesbitt House, the sun had nearly set, and with the lamplighters on strike, the city was falling into darkness. Torn between droving until she dropped, running home to tear into Mary, and flat-out giving up, Dare barely dragged herself home. There were too many should-haves for her to carry any longer.

She should've waited for Nell or Gil.

She should've released the monsters.

She should've realized that Padgett had far worse secrets than wearing the beasts' bones and pelts.

But she hadn't. And now she'd returned to a house that she could never again think of as home, not as long as Mary was there.

Still, Dare promised herself she'd remain calm, apologize for being late, then beg off dinner so she wouldn't have to see the treacherous maid one minute longer than necessary.

Yet all that stoic hardness Dare had prepared melted away the moment the door opened.

"At last! Mary told me you weren't home yet. I was getting worried!" Madam's relief came with a heavy sigh and a hungry hug as she pulled Dare inside. "It's so dark out there, and the city is, well, what it is. I'm so glad you're here! Are you all right?"

Dare tried to put on a brave face, but her lower lip broke ranks.

"Come, my love, we'll go sit together." Madam knitted her fingers with Dare's and led her up to the solar.

Even at night, there was a sunny warmth to the plant-filled room. It finally dawned on Dare what it was about the room that felt so familiar: it was like being on Barrow's Bay again. Only without all the awful people. But not even the scent of a breeze blowing through the salt marsh could have lifted Dare's veil of gloom.

Madam let them sit in silence for a while, giving Dare the room to settle, before she spoke.

"I thought I heard your father earlier today, out in the hallway," Madam began. "I was convinced it was him, although it wasn't the him you knew—it was the him I knew. When he was young. Dreams do funny things, don't they?"

Dare winced. She could lie to Padgett and Mary for the rest of her life and never have a regret. Not so to Madam.

"I think that was my friend you heard," Dare confessed. "I'm sorry, I told him not to come in. He—"

"It's fine, Dare. You need friends, we all do."

"He says he knows you, or his mother did. I think."

"It's nice to be remembered." Madam smiled, but not at Dare; it was a smile for something, or someone, a million miles away. She lingered there for a few moments, her eyes brightening and dimming with some memory she'd never share, until she landed back in the moment. "Are you ready to tell me what happened to you? And your Beastie?"

The question rang through Dare like a bell. Did Madam know what Mary had done? Dare's ears thrummed with the fear that Madam might be in on it. "How did you know he's gone?"

A pall fell over Madam and her fingers began playing through the chain that held her locket. "He took your shine with him, love." Madam picked up a hand mirror from the table at her right and handed it to Dare. "That look in your eyes; I see it every morning, too. Bijou has been gone for two years, and it might as well have been just a day."

How awful it is, knowing someone you love shares your deepest pain and is there like a tour guide, ready to show you around the new terrain.

"I feel like my insides have been hung on the outside," Dare said. "How do you go on?"

"The same way you've gone on since your dear father passed."

"I haven't done that, either!"

"Yes, you have," Madam said. "If you hadn't, you'd never

have found Beastie in the first place. Like all of nature, marvels need certain things to grow. Reciprocity with companionable familiars is part of that."

"I don't know what that means."

"It's like the relationship between trees and the fungi that grow on their roots. They help each other, tell each other things. Keep each other safe, fed, and thriving. Marvels are also clever enough to sense those who want them only for the gifts they offer. That's when they're monstrous—when they're threatened. But aren't we all?"

"So, you knew what Bijou was." Once again, things weren't as Dare thought. "Did my father know, too?"

"He did—in fact, he told *me*. And when I refused to surrender Bijou to him, that was the point of departure for us. It's also when I began my acquaintance with Captain Fortune. Your father stopped accepting my letters. Refused to come see me. Until, well, until the weeks before his passing. He'd sent word that he'd be in the city soon, and I was hopeful we were bound for a reunion."

Madam paused to clear her throat, or maybe to wait for a tremor of sadness to pass. "But understand, Dare, Bijou was no monster, and neither is Beastie. The only monsters are those who've used them, abused them, and seen them nearly killed off."

Dare pulled at a loose thread at the hem of her skirt. "Like my father."

"We do the best we can, Dare. He thought he was doing the right thing."

"But he didn't question it. Even after Tupper and Captain Fortune told him, he still worked against them!"

"I hope you never know what it is to make the wrong choice. It happens, even with the very best of intentions."

Dare's heart pinched. Madam wasn't only talking about Father. She'd known so much loss, Dare wasn't sure if she could bear any more. But how could she not tell Madam what she'd seen at the cannery? And that her most trusted maid was a traitor?

But just as Dare was funding the nerve to share the awful truth, Madam stood up, took Dare by the hand, and escorted her to the door. "Don't do what I did, Dare. Don't surrender to the loss. You are too young, too vibrant to let that happen."

"I won't, I'm not," Dare vowed, and she meant it, too. "But there's something you need to know. There are monsters—I mean, marvels—here in the city. I saw them. They're being kept in awful conditions, they're . . . waiting to be . . . well, you know. And your own B—"

"I know all of this, Dare." Madam was as curt as Dare had ever heard her. "I know what they do, all too well. I have no doubt what became of my Bijou. I'm only sorry you know, too. And now you need to leave it at that. They're too much to take on. They'll break you." And although she didn't say it, "like they broke me" rang in the background.

"No, they won't." Dare might not have completely believed it before, but she did now. "I won't let them. I will get him back."

"Hope is a lovely idea, but sometimes that's all it is. I'm sorry. The fight is over, the fighters are all gone. Be glad you had him for a time. That you knew the magic."

"You don't understand. I *can* get Beastie back. Padgett knows—"

Madam threw her hands over her ears, her entire body withering in pain. "Never say that name here, never!"

"I'm sorry! I'm sorry." Dare waited until Madam slowly uncoiled, but when she had, the circles under her aunt's eyes were darker, her lids heavier, and her hands shakier.

Still, Dare couldn't leave it there. "Just because they've always won doesn't mean they always will."

"That's very sweet, Dare. If only it were true." Madam opened the door and gently nudged Dare out. "I need to rest. I'll see you in the morning."

And just like that, poor Madam shut Dare out, her own monsters too fierce to keep battling.

As much as Dare wanted to rush back out into the night to keep droving, it was foolish at best, and incredibly dangerous at worst. Nell was right: they did need a plan. And while Dare still struggled to admit she might need anyone else, she wanted Nell's and Gil's help. So she lingered downstairs all evening, checking the windows, hoping to catch sight of Gil waiting for her outside, or for the bell to ring heralding the arrival of a note from Nell or more lies from Padgett.

By nine o'clock, nothing and no one had arrived, and Dare surrendered herself to her room for the night.

But Beastie's absence echoed louder there than a demon's scream. She could hardly bear to look as she opened the wardrobe to retrieve her nightgown. And that was when she saw what else was missing.

Her father's eldolon box.

Mary. She must have given it to Padgett along with Beastie.

Dare could search for the rest of her days, and she'd never find it, not unless they wanted her to. Like the agicole, she'd practically handed it to them herself.

But why did they want it? There was nothing of value in there, just a pencil nub, a broken button, and meaningless doodles.

As Madam said, they knew too much, they were too strong.

Well, at least for Madam, they were—she was too kind, too soft, too honest.

Dare was none of those things.

All those edges and angles that she'd been trying to smooth over were exactly what she'd need to save her Beastie.

CHAPTER THIRTY-ONE
Spiraling

She hadn't meant to fall asleep. She hadn't even thought she could; her mind was a tempest, trying to untangle the meaning of, well, everything. This was so much bigger than Beastie, or her, or the refuge, even. This was about Barrow's expedition and Louise. It was about Tupper, and Captain Fortune, and maybe even the strikers. And in the middle of it all was her father's box and whatever truth could be found among the stray pieces he'd left behind.

She remembered thinking she'd shut her eyes for just a moment, but moments became hours, and those hours could easily have become most of the next day, if not for the whistle. It folded neatly into her dreams at first. Her father's whistle, trilling over the salt marsh as they took their weekly wander together. Then it began to change, the notes getting higher, more urgent, loud enough to push her out of the solace of sleep and finally to understanding. It was coming from outside her window.

Tupper?! Nell?

Dare shook off what remained of her dream and threw the window open.

Neither, it was Gil.

"Any luck?" he whispered.

She shook her head. "You?"

"Not on finding Beastie, but I did hear something interesting."

"I'll be right down!"

She got all the way to the front door when she remembered—Mary. Dare never shied away from direct confrontations, especially with someone who'd betrayed her as Mary had. But if she wanted to keep up the ruse with Padgett, she had to with Mary as well. Besides, there were bigger fish to fry, uglier monsters to catch. Dare changed course and took the back way out of the house and into the alley.

But as soon as she arrived, she was caught short by how tired Gil looked. His normally rosy cheeks were pale; even his cowlick seemed to be drooping.

"Are you all right?"

"I'm fine, exactly as I should be." Gil shrugged off her worry. "I heard something, Dare. Something awful. At the cannery. They've got—"

"I know. Monsters, I mean, marvels, held there," Dare

finished his thought. "I saw them myself."

She caught Gil up with the shortest version she could of all that had happened—her conversation with Padgett, what she'd seen in the cannery, and all she'd come to know since she last saw him. She expected him to scold her for going off on her own, for being out close to dark. He didn't say any of that. All he did was shake his head and comb his fingers through his hair as if it might help him to understand the darkness humans were capable of.

"Now what?" he asked.

The hard part.

"I don't know. My father's box has to be part of the answer. I wish I could figure out why Padgett wanted it. What value is there for them in a nubby pencil, a broken button, and some doodles?"

"Doodles?" Gil repeated.

"Pictures—well, more like random lines. Squiggles on a piece of paper, some intersecting, others off in the margins. When I asked him what it was, he said he was trying to find a direction."

Hearing the words come out of her own mouth suddenly gave them meaning.

They weren't aimless scribblings.

"He was trying to map out the route to the refuge." The taste of bile stung Dare's throat. "He truly was working with Padgett."

"I don't know. It doesn't make sense. If that's what it was, wouldn't he have noted longitude, latitude, made it easy for them to find? But he didn't. He obscured it." Gil looked even more ashen, or was it queasy? "I think he was making it for someone else."

"Who? Tupper and Fortune wouldn't need it."

"That's right, they wouldn't." Gil waited, his look telegraphing that she was getting closer to the answer.

Dare saw it then, not that she believed it. "For me?"

"Yes, in case he—well, in case what happened . . . happened."

"What could he want me to do with it? I'm twelve, why would he want me to drove monsters for Padgett?"

"I don't think it was Padgett he was thinking about."

Dare laughed. "You're saying he wasn't really—that he meant for me to save the . . ." Dare couldn't even say it.

"Think about it. He had Pretty. Anyone in his position as Captain of the Guard would have known what she was. But he kept her, and according to you, he loved her. And he knew you loved her. I think he was on Tupper and Fortune's side. I don't know when or how he landed there, but it's the only thing that makes sense."

It did—it made complete sense, it sewed up all the seams that had been ripped open since his death. Pretty, his behavior, even his letter to Madam asking to see her again.

And it also left Dare with one giant problem.

"How am I supposed to do that? Even as weak as they are,

those monsters at the cannery could kill me with one swipe."

"I wish I knew." Gil's attention wandered just for a moment before he snapped back. "I'll go down to the docks, look around, see what I can find or hear. Can we meet back here in a bit?"

"No, I'll come with you," Dare insisted.

"It's faster if I go alone. I won't be long. I promise."

Dare didn't even have time to reply before Gil took off down the street.

Of course, she could have followed him, demanded he take her along. After all, she knew nothing about him: where he came from, where he lived, or where he meant to go. He could easily be as big a liar as Padgett. Yet he'd been exactly who he was from the start—that had to mean something.

Dare started to make another sweep through the alley for Beastie—she could imagine Padgett planting him somewhere easy for her to find, then testing her resolve by taking him away again.

She'd only begun looking when Nell's auto pulled up to the mouth of the alley. Ernest rolled down his window and called Dare over.

"Did you find him?" Dare asked, her heart not daring to soar yet.

"Sorry, I didn't. And I've got all of two seconds to idle here," he replied. "Nell was detained by her mother, but she asked me to take you to her. Can you get in?"

Dare climbed into the auto before he could even finish

asking and began peppering him with questions. Yet Ernest had startlingly few answers.

He'd lost sight of Padgett's automobile the night before after a hansom cab collided with a dray wagon right in front of him. "Then Mrs. Lawrence kept Nell in her room all night," he explained. "She hired a cab this morning to take them somewhere and sent me off to the outskirts on errands for the cook. But Nell and I've got a system. She got word to me by stuffing a note into an uneaten biscuit on her breakfast tray."

As they pulled into the most downtrodden part of the most wretched section of the Must, Ernest took care to assure Dare that Nell knew what she was doing by having them meet here. "I'm going to let you off on the next corner. There's a butcher shop in the middle of the next block. Go in and ask for corner-cut lamb chops. Act like you belong. Oh, and take this with you." Ernest handed Dare a small stack of bills, mostly fives and tens. "Understand?"

"No, but that's nothing new." Dare climbed out of the auto. "Thank you, Ernest."

"Always. Good luck." Ernest offered a sly salute and drove off.

Out on the street, Dare tried to summon her awful to help her feel big and capable, but being alone in the Must once again with money in her (one remaining) pocket raised the shadow of that mugger who'd cornered her. If he'd even been a mugger at all.

She kept looking over her shoulder as she crossed the

street—a task that was no mean feat in the Must—until she spotted the sign for the butcher shop, Charnel's Butchery. It was as dingy and covered with soot as all the other shop signs. Unless you knew what to look for—then it stood out, because in place of the apostrophe was the small square insignia.

Dare gathered her coat tighter around her, but not even a feather duvet could have warmed her now. The chill came from deep inside, the kind born from bad experiences.

"I really wish Gil was here." She muttered it aloud, so when she heard his voice mixed in with the noise of the city, she was sure she'd conjured it in her imagination.

Then he called again, and again, and soon Dare spotted him as he dodged and ducked through the flock of pedestrians. "Wait up!"

The sweet balm of relief chased the chill away. "I'm so glad you came," Dare said. "I thought you were on your way to the docks. How did you know where I was?"

"I, uh, saw you drive by." He was fighting to catch his breath, so every word came out separately. "Wasn't sure if you were in trouble or not."

"Oh, I am in trouble, deeper than I know how to get out of. But that was Ernest. Nell sent him to bring me here."

"Did she say why?" Gil was settling, looking less ragged, though still pale.

"No. Guess we have no choice but to go order some lamb chops."

Gil squinted at her, confusion curling his lip.

"It's what Ernest told me to do. You coming?"

"Absolutely," Gil said. "Let's go find your marvel."

Dare walked into the narrow meat shop as if she were a regular customer fully accustomed to the slanted and dirty floors, the bare shelves, and the clutter of dirty knives and cleavers littering the counter.

"Good evening," she chirped.

The butcher, a very short man with a very large and hairy mole on his very ruddy left cheek, eyed Dare and Gil with a look resting somewhere between confusion and derision. "Help you?"

Dare smoothed the collar of her coat and blithely replied, "We've come for some lamb chops. Corner-cut, please."

The butcher folded his arms. "We don't have any more."

Now Dare understood what the money was for.

"I think you should look again." She handed the butcher a crisp new ten-dollar bill, and like magic—the kind only a hefty bribe can conjure—he lifted up the end of the counter, creating a gateway.

Still, Dare hesitated. She couldn't kick back the fear she was walking straight into a trap, but she could feel Gil there, right behind her, a comfort that came as close to the touch of Beastie's coat as anything could.

The temperature dropped several degrees as Dare and Gil followed the butcher down a steep staircase and into a long corridor that smelled of ice and earth with a heady hit of something about to take a sour turn. He led them past several meat lockers all secured with heavy padlocks and on toward a benign-looking door with a simple keyhole lock. The butcher opened it, then stood back and waved the duo through.

"You'll find your corner-cut lamb chops down there."

Dare looked over her shoulder to make certain Gil was still close behind as she crossed the threshold.

"Don't worry. I'm right here," Gil said, then added in a whisper, "If you've got any more money, now would be a good time to share it."

Dare found another bill in her pocket, this one a fiver, and tucked it into the butcher's hand. "We've planned something of a surprise. We'd appreciate it if you kept this between us."

"I don't care what any of you do or say, as long as I get paid." The butcher shut the door, leaving Dare and Gil to find the rest of the way on their own.

"All right, Nell had a reason to send us here—let's find out what it is." Dare set her chin and headed down the hall. Unlike the corridor they'd just left, this hall was well-lit and tiled with black and white squares. Dare didn't realize it had a slight downward slope until they took a tight turn to the right and another right a short time later. The pattern repeated twice more, and each time the angle of the slope dipped a bit deeper than before.

They'd just taken yet another turn when the floor ahead of

them fell straight off into a deep, dark hole.

A web of dread laced Dare's neck as she and Gil stood on the edge, peering into the abyss. "It was all a trap, wasn't it?"

"I don't know. Was it?" Gil laughed, and before Dare could stop him, he took a leap straight into the chasm.

As a cry unwound itself from deep inside her belly, the oddest thing happened, or rather, didn't happen, for Gil was still standing right there on solid ground.

"It's an illusion." He jumped up and down to drive the point home.

Fright quickly annealed into irritation; at herself, not Gil. Dare was embarrassed at her own stupidity. "Of course it is! This is Padgett—I bet this entire place is an illusion. We should have been looking for it all along. Wait a minute—this whole time it's been like we've been walking down, down, down a square spiral."

"And . . . ?" Gil impatiently waved at Dare to get to the point.

"Where else have we seen a square spiral?" she prompted.

Signs of searching his mind were etched into the furrow between Gil's brows, until at last, he got it. "The emblem."

"Exactly!" Dare declared as she tromped over the nonexistent chasm. "I'm not really sure what the trident at the center could mean, though. Maybe it's a symbol of the sea, or Barrow's Bay?"

"Or fishing, maybe?" Gil added.

"Whatever it is, we have to stop looking for what we think we know and begin questioning everything we don't."

Bolstered by finally having a sense of direction, they hurried down the hall, stopping to test the walls, jump on the floor, anything to find the trick. Yet it wasn't until the stale air took on that chemical romance of rosemary, thyme, garlic, and butter marrying to create sauces, stews, and soups that Dare finally understood where they were heading.

The answer was so obvious, she was ashamed she hadn't thought of it before. It was also so nauseating, so awful, so unthinkable, her mind probably couldn't even conceive of it.

Until it had no choice.

"I know what it is." Dare nearly gagged on the very words. "A supper club. Their supper club!"

It wasn't a trident at the center of the insignia. It was a fork.

CHAPTER THIRTY-TWO
True Story

"You don't mean they . . . ?" Gil looked as sick as Dare felt.

"Do not say it!" Dare blocked her ears. "If you say it, it becomes real, and that's not to happen! We're simply going to find where they took Beastie and then get out of here, fast!"

They followed their noses, trying to trace the scents of a dinner, hoping the smells would lead them on, testing every surface to find a way out of the never-ending hall. But the farther they spiraled down, the more the scent of cooking faded, and soon they were left with nothing except damp and mold filling their noses.

When the hall made yet another turn, Dare stopped, letting her back slide down against the wall until her chin hit her knees. The trail had run dry. "I don't get it. Why did Nell send us here if there's no way out?"

"There is. We're just not seeing it yet." Gil sank down next to Dare. "Maybe it's like seeing pigeons."

Maybe he was short on air. "What?"

"Think about it. There are plenty of things you miss every day until you know to look for them. Like pigeons. You never notice how many there are until for some reason you start thinking about them. Then suddenly, you see they're everywhere. They were there all along—you just didn't notice them."

"You never noticed pigeons until you did?" Dare mocked.

"I'm using it as an example." Gil almost looked hurt. "Okay, better example: Maybe it's like droving for marvels."

Dare couldn't restrain a snarl. "How is this at all like that?"

"You tell me. What do you do when you go droving?"

"I wish I knew. Nothing. I just look in the right places."

"Well, that's the answer. Look in the right places."

"Obviously!" Dare's fingers itched to gather into a fist. "You're either entertaining yourself at my expense or you're seriously trying to undermine me."

"Neither. I mean it, Dare. Think about it. Illusions are nothing more than suggestions. Look here, not there. Listen to what I tell you, not what you see, not what you know. It works all the time, in the theaters, in the newspapers, and in everyday life. It's what keeps those factories spewing and the workers working. They've been told this is how it is. Factory work is hard and dangerous, but it's steady work, and the benefits of manufacturing for everyone are so great, people accept it. This is how life is now. Until you realize it's all a trick, it's all manipulation."

"What am I supposed to with that? There's no action there."

"I think it's the opposite of an action. I think your real talent is in your ability to shut out the shoulds, to ignore the voices that tell you something's improper, or impossible, or ridiculous, when you know what you know is true."

Dare scoffed. "That's hardly a talent. And it still doesn't mean I know how to get us out of this corner . . ." Like a light snapping on in the middle of the night, she got it! "Spiders and snakes! *Corner*-cut lamb chops. It's the corners!"

Dare leaped to her feet and urged Gil to help her as she began tapping on the corners at the turn of the hall. Between the two of them, it didn't take long for the trick to reveal itself. There was an impression in the brickwork, another thumb-size divot, just like on the loading dock. Dare pressed it, and the wall became a door.

She was about to barrel through the opening when Gil stepped in the way. "Look first."

"I'll learn to be prudent another time." Dare pushed past, charging forward into what turned out to be nothing more than an overstuffed storeroom filled with dishes, crystal stemware, and precariously stacked tables and chairs.

"Come on." Dare impatiently waved for Gil to follow. But he stepped back instead.

"You see what's in there. I'm going to check the other corners. See where they lead."

Dare hated the idea of him leaving her alone, but they

needed to cover more ground. "Just hurry back."

The storeroom was dimly lit, and there wasn't a single path forward that might not end in the toppling of crates and the shattering of crystal. As Dare began picking her way through the gauntlet, sweat broke out on her neck. She didn't have enough patience for this kind of challenge right now—or really ever!

Then that sweet sound reached her ears. A song being sung, high and sweet, the voice of an angel.

Nell.

Gauntlet or not, forward was the only way. Dare carefully made her way around each obstacle until she caught sight of the prize waiting for her at the other end of the room: a closed wooden door with a transom window at the top. And there was a bonus prize as well: large boxes stacked nearby, the perfect perch for her to stand on to watch the events unfolding on the other side of the door.

The transom afforded her a view of a room so ostentatious, it could only have come from Padgett's imagination. Gleaming with the light of five enormous chandeliers, the room was edged with gold, draped in voluminous green velvet, and filled with countless enormous flower arrangements. But the clear star of the room was a larger-than-life portrait of Bascombe Barrow, draped from head to toe in furs and festooned in feathers.

Nell was standing at the front of the room by a gilded piano, singing, her hands lodged in that vile fexin muff.

Anyone who didn't know her might think she was lost in her performance, but Dare heard the edge in her voice, saw the look of disgust behind the smile on her friend's face.

The gathering didn't look very different from those awful parties at the governor's. Except Dare understood so much more. These men in finely tailored suits adorned with carved buttons and sleek leather trim and women weighed down by hats plugged full of plumage, furs, and glittering jewels weren't simply leaders of industry.

They were the monsters. All of them.

As the last notes of her song faded and the applause crested, Nell curtsied and tried to make a quick exit, but Padgett rushed in from the side.

"Isn't she perfection?" Louder applause provided the reply. "We will be seeing a lot more of this talent here, a lot more. Won't we, Nell?"

Nell delivered her brightest smile, proof that she was every inch the consummate actress, for it was at that moment her gaze skimmed past Dare. It happened in a snap, but Dare saw the flash of recognition, followed by the subtlest look that made it clear that Dare should stay where she was.

After the second round of applause faded, Padgett finally let Nell leave, but not without first whispering something in her ear. She made another curtsy and waved to the crowd before finally exiting out a side door, while Frederick, the actor who played Barrow in Padgett's awful production, took possession of the stage. After milking as much applause as he could from the audience, he launched into a dramatic reading of excerpts from Barrow's memoir. It was dreadful, although not nearly as horrible as when Padgett returned and wound up into a speech all about how he had imagined and built the supper club, diving into tedious detail about the architecture and design before assembling the entire group for a photograph.

And while all this nonsense went on, every moment loomed like a mountain for Dare as she waited for Nell.

She had begun to question her reading of Nell's look when she heard hinges sigh and felt a rush of air that ushered in Nell's arrival.

"I'm so glad you figured it out. I knew you would!" Nell threw her arms around Dare, and Dare not only let her—she welcomed the hug. "I nearly yelped when I saw you back here. I'm so sorry I couldn't tell you more in a note or anything. I barely made it here myself."

"What happened to you? Ernest said your mother—"

"*She's* what happened to me." The gleam in Nell's eyes dimmed as she tossed the muff away as if it had teeth. "She locked me in my room all night long, cut me off from Ernest, and shouted until she turned blue. Still, Mama's only part of the problem. You should listen to this next bit of TR's speech."

"It's going to be horrid, isn't it?" Dare winced as they climbed back up onto the box, taking care to keep out of sight as they peered through the window.

"... and so here we are, gathered for the first of what will be countless meals together. Let us not forget that we've survived these very lean years largely thanks to the ingenuity of many of you. Elias Daniels, our master tailor, without whose genius we—nay, the city—would have been lost. For without his ingenious way to keep us fortified, there would be no industry, no prosperity, and no order."

A man at one of the tables stood to soak in the admiration, turning to wave at all in the room.

Dare nearly toppled from her perch. It was the man from the park with the tiepin, the one Beastie had barked at.

The little maeder should have stung him instead!

"Mayor Beatty, as always, we appreciate all that you and the good members of the watch do to protect our endeavors. We also owe all gratitude to Roland Cummings," Padgett continued. "He too has seen to it that our needs have been sated with his ingenuity and his 'uncanny' innovations." Cummings stood to absorb the outbreak of laughter and applause.

Dare looked to Nell, hoping to see something on her face that explained what was happening, but Nell only gestured for Dare to keep listening as Padgett continued.

"We've had to learn the hard way that our valuable resources must not be squandered. We never want to find ourselves so at risk again. While Daniels's designs have kept us going, and Cummings's clever cans have helped to make the waning supply last, we have now got all we need and, more important, *who* we need to ensure that we will never go hungry again!"

Padgett waited for applause, and while there was some,

there were also some grumblings. "We thought that before, didn't we?" someone called out.

"Yes!" Padgett emphatically replied. "Except it's different this time. She's young and, mark my words, angry as the day is long. She will make a rare and loyal drover, exactly what we need to keep cultivating a never-ending supply!"

That was enough to turn the grumbles into cheers that ricocheted off the coffered ceiling and right into Dare.

He was talking about her. They were cheering for her, for this plan to use her to their revolting ends.

"No longer will we have to rely on leathers and pelts, or make do with lesser quality provisions, raised in subpar conditions—no offense, Cummings, you've done the best you could. But the days of canned and paltry parceled-out portions are over. With our young drover's help, we will at last find that blasted island, make it ours, and have an endless supply of wild-caught provisions and all the gifts the beasts have to offer. With our talents and power returned to the strengths we once knew, all this unrest and talk of unions will be easily quelled. And we begin tonight!" Padgett clapped three times, summoning a waiter pushing a gilded serving cart atop which sat an enormous covered platter.

"Wild-caught and cooked to perfection—it is my pleasure to present our main course!"

Every nerve in Dare's body ignited as Padgett removed the silver dome exposing the awful, harrowing truth. For there, surrounded by a garnish of parsley and potatoes, its gray skin mottled with purple blotches, lay the lifeless agicole.

Her agicole.

The monster she'd gone droving for.

The beast that had attacked Tupper.

A natural-born marvel.

She'd been so horribly right about Padgett and his lot—they were monstrous. And she'd also been so naive about the depths to which they'd go to get what they wanted, a fact her poor father likely hadn't learned until it was too late.

Pushed far past rage, it was too much for Dare to contain now. She lashed out, sending her fist slamming into a stack of crates that was teetering nearby. Nell lunged to stop her, but she was too late to prevent the crash. The sound of shattering crystal and splintering wood joined the clamor of whistles and cheers out in the other room, bringing Dare back to her senses.

"Maybe no one heard it over the noise out there," Nell whispered, trying to sound hopeful. But after Dare climbed back up to peek through the window, she saw that at least one person might have heard something.

She didn't need to wait until he turned around to know who he was. She knew him by the way those long fingers smoothed his perfectly coiffed hair before he turned to look up at the transom window.

They stood there, the two of them, Dare and Governor Randolph Kingston, suspended in time—she peering out the corner of the transom, he searching for something behind it.

She couldn't tell if he saw her, but since when did the governor need proof to do anything?

Then it came—a simple gesture, just a nod, that summoned someone to his side.

Dare couldn't see the man's face as the governor pointed him toward her hiding place. But she knew the walk, the lurching stalk, those greedy hands. The mugger.

Before he could even turn, Dare went tearing for the exit, pulling Nell behind her as if there was a band of garbinol on their heels, for truly, what's the difference between a monster and a man who eats them to attain power over others?

Plates crashed in their wake, crystal shattered, and still Dare ran, Nell close behind. Out the door and down the hallway for no reason other than that was where Dare's feet took her. Blood was pounding so loud in her ears she almost missed it—a whisper from around the corner. "Dare! Over here!"

It was Gil! Thank the stars!

The girls rounded the corner, and there he was, waving them into an opened portal.

"Go, go!" Gil hissed.

So down they raced, Dare leading, their lungs lurching and their bodies nearly flying.

Dare knew she might not ever be able to outrun these newfound awful, terrible truths—her Beastie was still gone, and the world was more horrid than she could have imagined—but in that moment, she thought maybe, just maybe, they could escape before they were caught.

CHAPTER THIRTY-THREE
Canned Goods

They ran until they couldn't run anymore, until the stairs dead-ended at a solid brick wall. Dare felt at the corners, looking for the trick, and found it straight off. Gil started to remind her to look before going through, but the odors filtering out through the opening told her exactly where they were.

"We're below the cannery, and right through that door is where they've got the monst—the marvels." Dare pointed out the metal door at the end of the hall.

"They're right through there?" Nell shrank back into the stairway. "How many? Can they get out? Can we?"

"There's maybe twelve, twenty? I'm not sure. And no, they definitely can't get out. They're all caged up. They're sickly and miserable. Besides, it's not the poor beasts we have to worry about getting past," Dare explained, "it's the workers up on the loading dock."

"And we can't go back the way we came, either," Nell added.

"Then we look for a third way. Pull that lever, would you?" Gil pointed to an air vent halfway up one wall.

Dare gave him a funny look but wasn't about to argue. She reached up, standing on the tips of her toes, and grabbed the wooden handle that opened and closed the vent. But rather than control airflow into the hall, the lever engaged a door.

Nell, who Dare had come to think of as unflappable, looked stunned. "How did you know about that?"

"There are tricks everywhere." But Dare's hopes for an exit out of the cannery were quickly dashed. "It's just another hallway, and a dank one too."

The corridor was dim and narrow. The walls were nothing more than vertical wooden planks clapped together.

"I think you should go back up, Nell," Dare said. "We have no idea where this leads. If you hurry, your mother will never know you left."

"I don't care if she does. She chose this life for me, and I doubt she'd ever endanger the feed bag. The worst that can happen is . . . well, the worst."

"She's not wrong," Gil said. "Why don't you two go that way and I'll see what's happening on the loading dock."

Dare hesitated—there was strength in numbers. But speed mattered, too.

"All right, then, if you're sure. Let's go!" Dare declared.

Gil nodded and ran off as Dare led Nell in the opposite direction. She held her chin high, exuding confidence. But inside, Dare's thoughts churned. Everything had gotten so much bigger than her, bigger than her father's death, bigger than poor missing Beastie.

"I should have known that ragged worm Governor Kingston was in on this!" She spat out his name like a mouthful of dirt.

"I think at this point we assume everyone is. Padgett, my mother and all their friends, your father somehow, Mary—who knows who else."

Dare stopped. She knew who else.

"Oh, Nell, my mother." The words stuck like glue in her mouth. "I hadn't even thought about her, after my telegram, which she just ignored. All those clothes she's bought since Father's . . . the hats. The . . . my hat, that awful hat! That's why the agicole went for it!" Dare replayed that terrible scene in her mind. "It must have been made of—" She stopped, not wanting to finish the thought.

She couldn't do this. They truly were everywhere. She and Gil and Nell were nothing against Padgett, the governor, and the rest of that heartless lot. They had the mayor on their side and half the watch too. Her insides began to crumble and doubts began to spiral, but that's also exactly when the whistling began.

It was soft, muffled yet insistent.

Tweeeewooo tweeewooo tweeeewooo!

"That's your whistle, isn't it?" Nell asked.

Sort of. It was really her father's, and Tupper's.

"Do you think it's a trap?" Nell whispered.

"Even if it is, we can't be any more trapped than we already are."

The girls tried to track the sound, following it slowly, carefully, until at last it sounded like it was coming out from the very wall next to them. A wall with no chinks, no cracks, and no air vent levers to pull.

It was all too much, Dare's awful came spewing out and she pounded the wall as hard as she could.

She thought at first she'd broken the wall, as those vertical slats of wood began to shift and move. But they weren't falling, they were rotating like venetian blinds opening in the morning, turning from flat faces to edges, revealing the slats to be bars.

Prison bars.

"What in Thalia's name?" Nell whispered as the whistling stopped.

Dare leaned in toward the bars and sent a whistle into the void—not a loud one, not even a very assured one; a tentative, quiet whistle.

"Maybe this is a bad idea," Nell warned.

But it was too late for caution—Dare's whistle had already summoned a response.

The voice was scratchy and rough from disuse, the words it uttered hard to decipher. But it also carried the unmistakable salt of the sea, a scowl and shuffle that could belong to only one person.

"Is it really you?" Dare whispered, as a hand with skin as thin as paper and fingers as strong as steel wrapped itself around one of the bars.

"Is it really *you*?" the voice returned.

"Really who?" Nell asked, as a face emerged from the dark.

He was thinner than before, his face marred by lacerations and his hair thinned out in patches. But it was him! That nasty scowl of his staring Dare right in the face.

"Tupper!" Dare declared. "Are you all right? I can't believe you're alive! Where's the rest of the crew?"

"I was hoping you'd know that." Tupper leaned against the bars for support. "Only thing I know is after that agicole got me, I was knocked out. When I woke up next, my crew and Captain Fortune weren't there, but a gang of murderers was. They brought me here. Tried to make me make a deal. Fools. Told them ain't no one on the *Slipper* that'll deal with them. So they locked me here. Figured I was gonna die in my grave. When I heard you, I was sure I'd gone delirious."

"I can't believe it." Dare's voice went soft as she wrapped her hand around his. "You're alive. Gil said he thought you were."

"I won't be much longer if I have to stay in here."

"Right." Dare shook off the sentiment and examined the lock keeping the slats in place. "Do you think we can break it?"

"Gimme a hairpin, would you?" Tupper asked. "Lemme see what I can do."

Nell pulled a long pin from her hair and handed it to Tupper. He didn't take it at first, just looked her over, his suspicion clear.

"This is Nell," Dare said. "She's my . . ." The word stuck.

But it came easily for Nell. "Friend."

"Well, *friend*"—Tupper hit the word hard—"thanks for the pin. Soon as I open this and get back to the *Slipper*, all will be fine again."

Dare grimaced; she hated to have to tell him, but he'd hate not knowing more.

"It's gone," Dare said. "Sank."

Tupper cackled like a crow. "That's the stupidest thing I ever heard. That ship is unsinkable. How'd you think it makes it through the winds any time of year?"

"You told me how—Captain Fortune," Dare replied.

"He's a fine captain, but it ain't really him," Tupper grumbled. "You think that rapacious pack of fur-wearing murderers are the only ones using marvels' gifts? No, ma'am. Except we don't steal them. Only take what's offered."

Dare's head was beginning to spin. "You're saying the *Slipper* is protected by marvels?"

"A few. The whisk-wolf that keeps her afloat. Then there are a couple others that live on board. A pair of mynart birds that are always good for getting a wind in the sails when we hit the doldrums."

"Mynarts," Dare repeated, as her first visions of the *Slipper* played through her mind. "I thought they were vultures. I didn't see the spots on their feathers, or the humps on their backs."

"They know when to make themselves scarce," Tupper replied. "The point is, that ship might be lost, her crew dead or missing, but it ain't sunk."

Dare should have been relieved, but there was something awful lurking in that truth. "What would happen if someone else took control of the ship? Would those marvels still protect it?"

"As long as there's a drover on board, probably."

There it was—the awful. "Padgett told me they got a ship, one that was guaranteed to get through the winds."

Tupper stopped plying the lock. "Gotta admit I never thought it was possible. Fortune is the toughest son of the sea you could ever meet. Never thought the day would come when they'd get to him. That's a loss that hurts." Tupper sucked his teeth, or maybe he was trying to swallow the emotion seeping out of him. "Still, they're gonna need a drover, else they're not getting to that island."

He turned back to picking the lock, leaving Dare cringing at what she had to tell him next. "They do have one. Me."

Dare launched into recounting everything that had happened from the moment the agicole escaped all the way through what they'd witnessed at the supper club. She told

Tupper about the doodles in Father's box, the ones she was almost sure were a map. She told him about Beastie, and then she laid out her plan to make Padgett and his cohort think she was on their side.

"It's not a half-bad plan," Tupper said when she'd finished. "Told you you're like your daddy. He'd be proud."

"Hardly—I basically handed them the map, the agicole, and the *Slipper*!"

Tupper huffed, he wasn't impressed. "We can only do what we think is right, unless we intend to do what we know is wrong. He made his mistakes, you made yours. See, he thought what he'd been told and what he'd seen out in the field when he was an apprentice was true. Then he found that bird, and he come to see for himself the wonder of the marvels."

"You mean Pretty?"

"That's the one. It's a shame what happened. We tried to save her, but they got to her first."

"Wait." Dare was going to need a diagram to keep up. "Were you there at the governor's the day they burned his boxes?"

"I'm the one what pulled you out of the fire. Knew then you were a fighter."

"That was you? I bit you, didn't I? Why didn't you tell me that on the boat?"

"Like I said, you're a fighter," Tupper repeated, as if that were the obvious answer. "Wasn't looking to get bit again. You think you'd have believed me if I told you the story of the monsters was made up just 'cause there's them that would do anything for a fix of marvel marrow?"

Nell cringed. "It's the marrow?"

"That's where it starts. It spreads into the entire beast—meat, fur, bones, feathers. Wearing them is powerful, eating them is more so, makes others believe you got something they don't. A kind of shine. But you wanna keep it, you gotta keep eating. And those greedy fools nearly hunted the marvels into extinction."

"And that's why they want that island, your refuge," Nell said. "How did they even find out about it?"

Tupper sucked his teeth; clearly, he didn't want to answer.

So Dare did. "It was my father, wasn't it? He did start out spying on you for them, didn't he?"

"Like I said, truth comes hard sometimes. He worried himself ragged, for what—two years?—trying to undo what he did. And it landed him . . . well, you know where it got him." Tupper suddenly got very interested in picking his nails clean, taking a moment to let his emotions pass, until he was ready to continue. "The whole truth is sticky pudding. It's not all lies. Some of them marvels are nasty. When Barrow and his crew landed on that Island of yours, they weren't the only ferocious beasts out for blood."

"What do you mean?" Nell asked. "They came to rescue the *Paragon*."

"Funny idea of a rescue." Tupper was working the pin in the lock like a master thief, but the lock wouldn't give. "Way my grandpa told it, Barrow knew the *Paragon* was after something special. He followed 'em, was planning on firing on 'em as soon as the Island came into sight. Then a storm kicked up, sank the *Paragon*, sent Barrow off course. By the time Barrow found the Island, he was sure he'd have it and all of them marvels all to himself. I'da paid to see his face when he found that little girl sleeping in a cave, that garbinol and a whole passel of other beasts protecting her as if she was their own cub."

"Louise was a drover." Nell smiled at the idea.

But Dare bristled. With every new fact, things only got muddier. "If your grandpa knew that, why didn't he make sure the truth came out? Tell everyone Barrow was lying?"

"The truth isn't always what's best. What would happen if people knew what the marvels can do?"

"They'd know that they're special." Obviously.

"And what do people do with things that are special?" Tupper pressed. "If everyone knew what eating them poor marvels could do for them, you think they wouldn't want a piece, too? That's the nature of the human beast. Then what? We'd still be where we are, marvels hunted nearly to extinction. Blow it down!" Tupper threw the snapped hairpin to the floor by the girls' feet. "I'm gonna crack this lock and get that ship back if it takes every pin in your heads."

CHAPTER THIRTY-FOUR
Visitors

Seven bent and broken hairpins later, Tupper was still locked in.

"You're gonna have to get a hold of a key or a set of picks, otherwise, we're never gonna get that ship back." Though he'd never admit it, Dare could see his energy was flagging, and so was his confidence.

The thought of leaving him there, in that cold dark cell hidden behind a wall, was more than wrong. It also felt like the end of hope. Yet Dare and Nell had no choice now, as voices and the sound of keys clanking began filtering down the hall.

With a solemn vow to return quickly with some way to get him out, the girls turned the slats flat, shuttering Tupper back in.

"Come on." Dare grabbed Nell's hand and made to flee in

the direction they'd come, but Nell resisted.

"They'll hear us running," Nell whispered as the voices grew nearer. "Let me do the talking, I'll get us past whoever they are."

"Are you sure you can—" Dare cut off at the sight of three members of the watch racing toward them, their billy clubs out and swinging.

"Where'd you two come from?" one of the watchmen demanded. His left eye had a cut over it, and his knuckles were red and raw. Either he was a boxer in his off time, or he wasn't exactly the picture of a public servant devoted to keeping the peace.

Dare's throat ran dry and her mind ran out of lies, but Nell was as calm as a summer day.

"At last!" She fanned herself as if she were about to faint. "We have been wandering trying to find our way out of here! Do you know that the walls move and turn to doors? We've been so scared!"

The members of the watch looked at one another, then back to the girls, then Raw Knuckles squinted at Nell. "Miss Lawrence, that you?"

"Oh, how nice of you to recognize me! I'm so embarrassed. I thought I had listened carefully to Mr. Padgett's directions on how to get out of the supper club." Nell's voice had risen several octaves. "I have no memory for anything that's not a song or lines in a script. Please, can you help us find our way out? I must get back to the theater. My public needs me!"

Nell was pouring it on so thick, Dare could hardly stop her eyes from rolling, but the members of the watch were loving it.

"Of course, Miss Lawrence. Right this way. And we'll make sure to let Mr. Padgett know what happened to you in there."

"Don't be silly!" Nell cooed. "Don't you worry about it. It's probably best if my mother handles it."

"Understood, miss." The way Raw Knuckles nodded, it was clear he'd been on the wrong side of the Foghorn at least once.

The watchmen ushered the girls the rest of the way out of the hall and onto the wharf. They insisted on driving Nell to the theater, but she had another story ready for them about getting nauseated in horse-drawn wagons. "I'll only ride in autos now. Thank you for the offer."

Arm in arm, the girls walked away from the wharf and up to the street as calmly as they could—until they rounded the corner and were out of the watchmen's sight.

"I can't believe they believed you!" Dare nearly exploded.

"It's not me really. It's the fame. I could declare the seas are made of cheese and people would believe it. It's tragic."

"One more tragedy of many," Dare grumbled. "Poor Fortune and his crew."

"Maybe, like Tupper, they're not all lost?"

"I don't know anything anymore except we have to get him

out of there." Dare blew out a deep sigh. "I bet Gil will know how to break that lock. I hope he got out all right."

"Out? Where was he?" Nell asked.

"What do you mean? You were there when he—" Dare jumped back from the curb as an auto came careening to a stop next to them.

"There you are!" It was Ernest, and he was not his usual calm self. "I've been looking for you. We've got to get you home before your mother gets there."

"Ugh." Nell grimaced at the mention of her mother. "I suppose you're right, though. Come on, Dare, we'll drop you." Nell climbed into the back seat.

"I'm afraid we can't do that today." Ernest was all business. "She made it clear that you're to be home before her, or we'll both be in deeper than we can dig. Time's up."

"Fine. I suppose today's not the day to fight her." Nell handed some coins out the window to Dare. "Take a hansom and lie low until tomorrow. We'll meet at the theater at eleven. If we're going to get Tupper out, find Beastie, and make sure they never find their way to that island refuge, we're going to have to be just as devious, and as well prepared, as they are."

Dare spent the ride back to Nesbitt House with her awful on boil. At least Padgett had gotten one thing right about her: she was angry. It's just that the object of her ire had shifted along with the sands of truth.

By the time she'd arrived back at Madam's house, all Dare wanted to do was wash her face, eat something, then head right back out to find Gil. But she hadn't even reached for the bell when the door flew open.

"Dare! There you are!" Dare's mother stood with her arms open, waiting to swallow Dare in a hug.

Dare stuck to her spot. "What are you doing here? You finally decided to answer my telegram?"

Mother winced. "You're mad. I knew it. And you have every right. Please, give me the chance to speak, I have so much to tell you."

Dare's upper lip twitched and twinged. "About what, your honeymoon? How busy you are, socializing? Your new wardrobe, or perhaps your latest meal?"

"I deserve that, and more. But we cannot have this conversation standing in the doorway like this." Mother looked up and down the street and then offered Dare her hand.

Dare intended to stay mad, and get madder still, but there was something different about Mother. She was still trussed up in a fine silken gown, her hair tortured into an immovable coif. Yet there wasn't a feather, a bone button, or a stitch of fur anywhere on her clothing. And that hungry look she'd always had about her—the searching eyes ravenous for attention and approval—was gone now, replaced by something sadder and even lonelier.

Dare declined her hand but followed her mother into the parlor.

"Madam is resting upstairs, and Mary is out. We're alone, aside from my maid, who's in the kitchen."

"Ruthann's here?" Dare started for the kitchen.

"No, this is a new maid. Someone Randolph, the governor, hired for me." Mother's voice sounded as breezy as if she were playing a hand of bridge, but there was a tightness in the creases of her mouth, a strain around her eyes. "Come sit."

She patted the cushion next to her, but Dare chose to sit across from her, a safer distance away.

"I understand now why you're angry with me." Mother's fingers nervously played with the lace trim on her skirt. How many times had she scolded Dare, told her that fidgeting was unladylike?

"I have made some awful mistakes," Mother continued slowly, and so quietly that Dare had to lean forward to catch every word. "I've been asking Randolph to come get you since you left. It was wrong of me, Dare. It was all wrong. I should have been listening better, and not let him convince me to . . . I'm sorry. I wish I could undo it all. I don't know how to. I'm trapped in a web of my own making."

Dare shifted in her chair. Her mother had never spoken so openly before, not even in the days following Father's death. Part of Dare yearned to tell her everything—about the marvels, about Beastie, and about Father's real work. But Mother had married a monster. How could she be trusted?

"What was it your teacher used to say? 'You're too clever by half'? Well, I wasn't nearly clever enough. I didn't know what

I'd gotten us into." Mother checked the door to make sure no one was coming, then pulled a tightly folded square of paper out from the sleeve of her dress. "Not until I got this—it's the telegram you sent to me."

"That you ignored," Dare corrected.

Mother cast a glance toward the door again, passing a finger across her lips. "I know it looked that way. I only saw it for the first time yesterday when Mrs. Malcolm tucked it under a plate on my breakfast tray. I'd have rowed here myself if I'd seen that telegram when it arrived!" Mother smoothed her already wrinkle-free skirt. "There are a great many things I didn't understand about your father, or Randolph, or Barrow's Bay until . . . well, until it was too late."

"You mean like the m—"

Mother put a gentle hand over Dare's mouth and tipped her head toward the kitchen and the new maid before continuing in a whisper. "Randolph has spared me nothing, except the opportunity to make informed choices about my own daughter. When I finally saw your telegram, I put my foot down and told him I was coming to get you."

"You did?" Dare blinked, unable to hide her surprise.

"And that's when he tried to leave Barrow's Bay without me. Thankfully, Mrs. Malcolm isn't as fully devoted to the governor as one might think—she has her moments."

Dare smiled. "I saw that in her, too."

Mother brightened for a moment before she leaned in

closer to Dare, her voice even softer now. "I told him I'd come around to seeing things his way, though I certainly have not. It was hard enough allowing you to travel through the winds to come here, but this plan of his to send you off on some expedition goes too far. I will not allow him to ship you around like a crate of oranges. I've already lost your father. Enough is enough."

"No! I want to go, I need to. You have to let me! They want to—"

Mother didn't let Dare finish. "It's preposterous. I won't have it!" She set her chin, as resolute as Dare had ever seen her.

Dare could easily outmatch her, but this was no time for being awful. This moment required something Dare was only recently learning how to employ—patience.

"Father would want me to go." There was no snarl, no anger in Dare's voice, just the simple truth.

"You're right." Brief flashes of a smile licked over Mother's face, a flame fighting to stay lit in the wind. "I'd forgotten how much you look like him."

"I haven't," Dare said.

"I'm glad." Mother started to push a stray lock of Dare's hair behind her ear, but then pulled back, letting it fall where it wanted.

With that simple gesture, Dare came within an inch of telling her mother everything, until Mother glanced at the grandfather clock in the corner of the room. Her posture went rigid, taking her tone along with it. "We're going to have to continue this conversation another time. For now, run upstairs and get changed for supper. Randolph will be here any minute."

Any warm feelings circulating through Dare frosted over. "He's coming here? Why?"

"He wants to meet Madam. It's only for dinner, and afterward you and I will have more time to talk about what comes next."

"No! He can't come here, he might have seen—" Dare was about to spill everything, but the doorbell rang, and the next thing she knew, Governor Kingston had arrived at Nesbitt House.

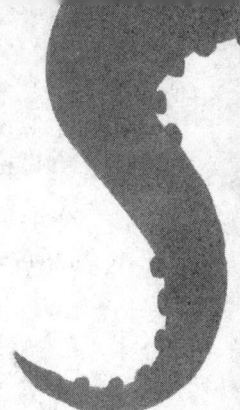

CHAPTER THIRTY-FIVE
Plot and Pitches

The governor's presence at Nesbitt House changed everything. As soon as the bell rang, Mother reached behind the settee and placed a hat festooned with pink and gold feathers on her head as if it had been there all along.

Dare bristled at the sight of that atrocity, but Mother leaned in close and issued a strained warning. "Before you say anything, Dare, don't. I know what I'm doing. The berlund feathers on this hat protect me in more ways than one."

So Mother did know about the marvels. Still, Dare couldn't bear the idea of her wearing them. "Father would despise this."

"Sometimes doing whatever it takes takes doing something you thought you never would. Now, put on a sweet smile." Mother checked herself in the mirror, then opened the door to greet her husband.

Dare was ready to combust, but she kept her awful at a low simmer. Maybe it was Nell's influence bringing out the actress in her, but Dare somehow found it in herself to greet the governor with something close to courtesy.

"Darvlah!" he declared. "Look at you! How we've missed you!"

A cordial smile was all Dare could chance—words felt too risky as she stood there watching her mother fawn over her husband, smoothing his lapels, cooing about how she couldn't believe Mrs. Malcolm still hadn't repaired something on his vest. Unbearable. But if Dare thought this was the hard part, she was wrong.

Governor Randolph Kingston hadn't been inside more than five minutes before he came up with the "brilliant" suggestion that they spend the night as a family together at Nesbitt House.

"So much friendlier than a hotel, don't you think, dear?" There was no question that it wasn't a question. It had also obviously been prearranged with Mary—she already had the guest room set up with clean wash water and fresh flowers.

The better to keep a hawkish eye on Dare, no doubt.

Madam did come down to greet the governor, but when he announced that he'd like to invite a few friends to join them for dinner, she excused herself, complaining of a headache. Dare tried that, too, but Mother quietly insisted she strive to keep up appearances.

So Dare remained, and kept her tongue tightly clamped between her teeth while the governor held court at Madam's dinner table. And while she made certain not to call attention to herself, Dare refused to eat any of that meal except the potatoes. By the time dessert arrived, the governor was crowing about how many new homes were to be built near the marshlands on Barrow's Bay, and had presumably lost all interest in "family" time.

When at long last the adults went to the parlor for coffee, Dare practically flew up the stairs to her room. She figured she had an hour or so before the governor would even think about her again. It wasn't long, but it might be enough time to find Gil and get him to help her free Tupper.

She quickly changed out of the suffocating dress her mother had made her wear and was easing back out of her room, certain she was in the clear, when someone sprung out at her.

Dare yelped from sheer surprise before realizing who it was. She tried to cover it over with a cough as Gil waved her back into her room.

"I'm sorry to scare you," he said as she shut the door. "I'm so glad I caught you before you tried to leave. Do you know there's a thug out patrolling the front door, and two more out in the alley? All built like rhinos, been there for hours guarding the house."

Dare cast a look out the window down into the alley. There they were, exactly as Gil described them: a pair of thugs with broad shoulders, thick legs, and heads like boulders. Human rhinos.

"The governor's idea of family, no doubt," she grumbled, pulling down the shade.

"I'm sorry I didn't come back to find you at the cannery," Gil said. "Things got very interesting, very fast."

"For us, too."

"You go first," Gil said.

Dare told him all about finding Tupper and not being able to break the lock, about the watchmen with the keys, then about the governor and her mother.

"She said she regretted marrying him?" Gil looked stunned.

"Not those exact words, but yes. I thought she'd found heaven on earth with him. I think she and I both underestimated her." Dare blew out a big breath to try to shake loose all the feelings swirling through her. "What did you find?"

Gil grinned and waggled his brows. "The *Golden Slipper*."

So much for keeping anything contained—Dare nearly exploded. "Tupper was right! He said it's unsinkable, that marvels protect it. Where was it? I thought for sure Padgett had it. What about Fortune and the crew? Were they there, too?"

"That's a lot of questions; I don't have answers for all of them," Gil admitted. "I'm guessing you're right about Padgett. It's been painted and renamed the *Mighty Way*, which is the worst name for a ship ever. I saw no crew anywhere. But I know that mast—it's the *Slipper* for sure."

"Where is it?" Dare pressed.

"Docked right at the cannery. I think they're getting ready to move, Dare."

This wasn't really news—Dare had already known the moment was coming—but hearing it from Gil made it real enough to know she wasn't ready.

"Tupper wants to pirate it back, except he's locked up. We have to get him out. I can't go with them to that island and simply hope for the best. I could wind up like Louise, or . . ." Dare dreaded saying it.

"That's not going to happen." Gil was emphatic. "Not again, not to you."

Dare blinked as her bridge lost yet another few stones, it's hard to remain bricked up with loyal friends like Gil and Nell.

Still, she knew what they were up against. "You're barely any bigger than me, you can't protect me from them."

"I can. I have. And I will continue to," Gil said. "And to that end, I'm telling you not to try to leave here. Not tonight."

"No. We have to go free Tupper and find my Beastie!"

"You cannot leave. Not with Kingston in the house. He could check on you at any moment. Besides, you have no way of getting past that pair down in the alley."

"Then what do we do? We can't just sit here and wait."

"We're not going to. I'll go and get Tupper out of there. Once he's free, I'm sure he'll have ideas of how to find your

Beastie. And before you say anything, I got through the loading dock unseen. I can do this, too."

Gil had truly proven himself to be reliable and loyal to a fault. But still, something stuck.

"Why can you get past that pair of rhinos in the alley and I can't?"

"I told you, people don't see me." His confidence might have been completely irrational, but it was also contagious. Or maybe it was simply that it was all Dare had now.

"Let's say you can, and you get Tupper out—where will you bring him, and how will you let me know?"

Gil thought for a moment. "If I can, I'll get him to come to the theater. Though he may have his own ideas of where to go. If that happens, I'll leave word for you in the theater. Even if the rhinos are on patrol, you can get in there and back into the house safely through Madam's passageway, so check in the morning."

Dare hated not going herself, but it was a stupid risk to take. "You promise on everything you have?"

Gil put a hand over his heart and bowed his head. "On my very being."

Minutes later, Dare stood watching out a corner of her window for Gil's exit through the alley. But she never saw him go, because just as he should have been trying to sneak past the governor's thugs, the gas lamps in the alley went out.

Poof!

All was dark out there.

Dare could hear the rhinos snorting and scrambling for a match, and by the time they had gotten the lamps relit, Gil was gone.

Dare fought the temptation of sleep but it finally won; then it called on her dreams to keep her pinned down until late the next morning.

These weren't dreams filled with monsters stalking her, or the fear of being ripped to shreds. They were quiet and comforting visions of walking with Beastie and her father by the marshlands. It was a scene she never wanted to leave, but like all sweet things, it came to an end. And with that end came the crush of reality. She was late, she needed to get into the theater!

While there was only one Rhino out in the alley now—the bigger of the pair—she'd still have to use the back way in.

Dare tried to take the stairs to the second floor as quietly as she could, but as soon as she hit the landing, Madam called out from behind her closed door. "Who's out there?"

"It's me, Madam," Dare said. "I'm sorry to wake you."

"Oh! Not at all, Dare. Come see me."

Even though she was anxious to see if Tupper had made it, or if Gil had left any news for her, she couldn't ignore her great-aunt.

The room was darkened by the closed curtains, yet even in the dim, Dare could see how tired and wan Madam looked.

"I could have sworn I heard Virgil again last night," Madam

said. "Now, don't worry. I knew I was imagining hearing your father. . . . Oh, you must think me a silly old woman, hearing loved ones who are long gone."

Dare sat on the edge of Madam's bed. "No sillier than the dream I had of Father last night. We weren't doing anything. Walking. It was perfect. I didn't want to wake up and remember how awful everything really is."

Madam laid her hand on Dare's. It was cool and felt more brittle than before. "I'm glad he comes to see you. He'll always help you through the awful, Dare. Next time, send him my love, won't you?"

"I will," Dare vowed.

Dare waited for Madam to drift back to sleep before creeping out of the room, feeling sturdier, better prepared to face all that the day held.

Until her mother's maid appeared at the top of the stairs.

"I was coming to fetch you for breakfast. Mary's gone to do the shopping," the maid explained, "and your mother and father have gone out."

It took every ounce of Dare's strength not to snap at hearing that worm referred to as her father.

"The governor said to tell you that they'll be back for tea this afternoon and he expects you to join them. For now, it's downstairs with you for breakfast."

"I'm not hungry, thanks." Dare started for the stairs back to her room.

"The governor wanted to make sure you ate." Of slight build, the maid could have been no more than ten years older than Dare, and she had that look about her that all the servants in the governor's mansion did—abject fear. But she also had a feral air of someone eager to snitch. "He was worried you'd only eaten some potato last night."

As if he was so concerned. Fine, two could play his game.

"Wonderful. Breakfast sounds grand." Dare dropped a curtsy at the maid—which was a ridiculous thing to do—and went down to the kitchen.

She sat at her place and regarded the meal. The toast and jam looked safe enough, as did the fruit cup and glass of juice. But she'd sooner eat seashells and sand for a year than risk the eggs, lest they'd not come from chickens. After eating what she could, she went to put her dish in the sink, and that's when she spotted the newspaper on the counter.

She'd never seen a paper in Nesbitt House before, so it struck her as especially odd. But it was the headline that nearly knocked her off her feet.

FINAL PERFORMANCE TODAY
PADGETT'S BLOCKBUSTER
OUR LOUISE
STAR, LAWRENCE, TO TAKE IT ON THREE-YEAR TOUR!

The worst thing that could happen was happening.

CHAPTER THIRTY-SIX
A New Story

Dare dropped the paper as if it had fangs. She needed to find Nell immediately, but there were two guards out in the garden in addition to the one in the alley. They were multiplying like mold on wet wood.

"You fed the men their breakfast already, didn't you?" Dare turned her inner Foghorn on the maid.

"What men?" her mother's maid asked.

"The ones outside, in the front, in the alley. They work so hard for the governor. My mother promised me she'd have you bring them in for proper meals. Didn't you?"

"I . . . she didn't say anything—"

"Are you saying she lied?" Dare challenged, watching with glee as the maid shrank into herself. "I won't tell her if you go get them now. They must be starving!"

The maid looked so confused and scared as she went out to fetch the men, Dare almost felt bad. Almost. There were too many others who were more deserving of pity.

Dare waited until she saw the maid leading the herd of rhinos into the kitchen before running upstairs to slip out the back stairs and into the theater. She'd briefly considered taking one of her mother's feather-filled hats as a shield against harm, but the thought of hiding behind poached protections made her gag.

Dare passed into the theater holding tight to the hope that Gil and Tupper would be waiting there for her. When she found the theater empty, a stitch of worry took hold of her stomach, imaginings of what could have become of them running through her head. It was only as she was on the verge of tipping over into the abyss of dread that she spotted it.

Not an envelope. Not even a proper note. Just a single word scratched in shaky letters into the dust on the floor of the theater.

Canne, with an *r* and a *y* nearly rubbed out.

Cannery.

Dare's throat ran dry with one thought: the rhinos had caught Gil.

She needed Nell, and she needed her now!

Dare had just rounded the corner into the stage door alley of Padgett's Palace when she spotted a rhino on patrol. Of course they were here, too. And just like the ones at Madam's, he was broad-shouldered, with a face scarred from fights both won and lost. Except this one had an additional feature all his own, one she knew only too well—a pair of hands as big as hams.

The mugger was guarding the door.

As Dare backed out of the alley to figure out another way in, a cool breeze wafted past her neck. It wasn't exactly a chill, more like a frosty tickle. She brushed it off, yet moments later it happened again.

Imagination working overtime.

She'd begun to backtrack up the street when she heard a crash. More like a smash. A small crowd of passersby immediately gathered at the mouth of the alleyway to see what had happened. It was exactly those rubberneckers who afforded Dare the perfect cover to try to sneak past her mugger. But as soon as she pushed her way to the front of the pile of gawkers, she saw there was no need. Ham Hands had been laid out flat in the alley, left groaning in pain, a large packing crate smashed to pieces by his head.

A few good Samaritans rushed to his aid, while the rest of the crowd stayed to gawk or walked on. The show was over. It wasn't Dare's brand of awful to ignore a person in trouble, but his pain was her chance. She pushed past the few people left gathered around him, and in through the stage door.

Dare made it all the way to Nell's dressing room without being seen by anyone, but stopped short of going in—the Foghorn was blowing hard inside.

". . . risking everything I've built! I won't have it. Your behavior will dictate how long this tour runs. Toe the line, and you could be back in six months. Continue as you've been, and you'll be out there until you've played every backwater town in the farthest reaches of the territories. As for today, you *will* give your greatest performance ever, leaving the audience without a single doubt about you, Louise, and the truth of the monsters."

Dare couldn't hear Nell's response, though she knew what it looked like: a searing gaze fit to ignite stone.

The doorknob clicked and Dare quickly pulled back, pressing herself behind a piece of scenery leaning against the wall. The Foghorn blew again, and though Dare couldn't make out her words this time, she did hear the door open, then slam, followed by the pounding of footfalls receding into the distance, a thunderstorm moving off.

Uncertain if it was safe to come out of hiding quite yet, Dare gave a soft whistle: *Tweeewooo tweeewooo tweeewooo.*

The door squeaked open, and the signal was returned: *Tweeewooo tweeewooo tweeewooo!*

Dare slowly leaned out from her hiding spot and found Nell, her head barely peeking out of her dressing room door. "Quickly," Nell whispered as she grabbed Dare by the wrist and pulled her inside.

"How did you get in?" Nell's voice was barely audible. "They've got an army of watchmen and random thugs stationed throughout the theater just waiting for you to arrive."

"That mugger was stationed at the stage door, but he had an accident," Dare explained, sparing no pity for the brute.

"Some of the empty crates stacked out there fell on him and knocked him out cold."

"Poor man." Nell clearly was neither sorry nor sad. "Mother has been hovering over me like a bad dream. I have too much to tell you."

"I saw the headline. I'm so sorry. I didn't want anything to happen to you."

"It was bound to happen anyway. Hats off to her for finding a way to make me miserable and keep earning off me. I can take it, Dare. There are bigger problems. They're planning on sailing tonight. Ernest heard Mother and Cummings talking. They said the governor has you locked up."

"That's what he thinks." Dare smirked as she told Nell about the repainted *Slipper*, her mother, and Governor Kingston. She saved the worst of the news for last. ". . . but I have no idea if Gil got Tupper out, or if the rhinos got Gil first."

Nell tore off her wig and threw it on the dressing table. "You know what? Forget this last show. My mother has already done her worst, anything more will be icing. I'll go with you, we'll stop that ship on our own, and find Tupper, Gil, and your—" Nell stopped. A thunder of footfalls were approaching out in the hall, accompanied by a clatter of chatter, with the loudest of the voices overpowering all the rest—the braying of someone holding court.

Padgett.

Nell looked the way Dare felt, wild-eyed and ready. She threw herself into her chair at the makeup table and began powdering her nose, while gesturing wildly for Dare to hide behind the dressing screen. Dare had just made it when a quick rap sounded on the door, followed by the squeak of hinges as it opened.

"Some friends wanted to say hello before the show," Padgett announced without waiting for an invitation to enter. "I believe you know many of these gentlemen. Cummings, the good doctor, Clarke, Madsen. Though I don't believe you know Governor Kingston of Barrow's Bay, or his lovely bride."

Dare had to clap a hand over her own mouth to keep from screaming.

"We're looking forward to having your mother in residence on the Island." The governor was sparing none of his slimy charm. "Although I understand you'll not be joining her, at least not for quite a while."

Dare hoped Nell was slicing him open with her eyes.

"We've got a packed house for your farewell performance, Nell," Padgett continued. "Many important people along with members of the press will be out there watching and listening. Do break a leg."

And with that not-so-veiled threat leveled, Padgett and his retinue of monsters retreated from the room.

Dare waited until there was silence in the hall before exploding out from hiding.

"Please tell me my mother looked horrified!" Dare begged.

"Honestly, I could barely see her behind that hat." Nell

picked up her wig and smoothed it out. "Dare, do you think you can go without me?"

"Of course. Sure. You changed your mind. It makes sense." Dare tried to hide her disappointment. Really, why should Nell put her entire life on the line for Dare? "I understand, I do, I—"

"No, you don't." Nell sat at her mirror and fixed her wig in place. "If I stay here, I can change the story and expose them all!"

"How would you—" Like cylinders engaging inside a lock, it all clicked into place. "Can you really do that? What about the rest of the cast? The crew? Won't they shut you down?"

"I have a ten-minute solo in the second act. Most of the cast and backstage crew—including the riggers manning the curtains—go outside during it, have a smoke, gossip. Including Frederick. Leeds never leaves, though I have a feeling about him. And I hate to say it this way, but the ushers would do backflips on ice for me. All I have to do is ask, and they'll make sure I have a captive audience and let only the press out until the curtain comes down two and a half hours later."

"That's all very devious. But what will you say? Like Tupper said, we can't tell people about the marvels."

"Oh, people can go right on thinking they've all been wiped out. Except now they'll know the truth of how first Barrow, and now Padgett and all the rest of them, used the marvels up. That their power and wealth weren't ever gained by bravery, ability, wisdom, or talent. That they stole them.

And I'm going to tell the story of Louise, the *true* story. All three thousand five hundred audience members will hear she was strong and brave, sensitive, and smart, not some frail and helpless girl. Knowing the press as I do, the streets will be flooded with one-sheets before the curtain comes down."

Dare broke out into a chill. "This is brilliant!"

"It was your idea—you're the one who said we needed to retell the story." Nell started to tie her bonnet on, then stopped. "What if you can't find Gil and Tupper? That leaves you alone to stop the ship. You can't get on that boat and pretend to drove for them. It's too dangerous. You could get hurt or . . ."

"Wind up like my father? I could. Or I could finish what he died trying to do." Nell did not look convinced, so Dare continued. "They've already taken my father, Pretty, and my Beastie from me. Now they're trying to take what little magic still exists in this world, along with my mother and my best friend. I can't let them have any more."

Nell met Dare's gaze in the mirror, her nose crinkling with joy. "Your best friend?"

"Well, one of my two friends." Dare couldn't help but crack a smile.

"You actually have three," Nell corrected. "Don't forget Ernest. Half of what we've done so far is thanks to him."

"You're right, but I can't bring him into this any further. I've already endangered his job enough."

"That's not an issue. He'll be quitting as soon as I get

shipped off. He's only ever stayed for me. It's almost like he's been waiting for this moment. He's already been spreading word with his friends in the unions and at the papers about the factory owners, the bankers, the mayor, and the rest of the dirty lot using up the marvels to secure their power." Nell jotted a quick note and stepped out into the hall, where she hailed a stagehand. "I left my wrap at home, would you be so kind as to get this note to Ernest, please?"

"Yes, Miss Lawrence," came the reply.

Nell waited for the footsteps to recede before continuing.

"I told him about the *Slipper* and asked him to get a crew together as fast as he could and get them to the cannery. If anyone can do this, it's Ernest."

"What about your mother? Won't she be looking for him?"

"She told him to park out front today—she wants me to make some grand exit, sign autographs and whatnot after the show. He and I will both be more than happy to disappoint her."

Dare was truly lost for words. It was one thing to finally have people who believed her, but to have someone who believed *in* her left her grasping.

"I . . . it's too much to ask."

"You're not asking, and I'm not offering, I'm telling you." Nell stepped behind the changing screen to put on her costume. "Now go. It's showtime, Dare. Go find Gil and Tupper, and break a leg!"

CHAPTER THIRTY-SEVEN

Stuck

Dare slipped out of Nell's dressing room and made for the stage door, determined to let nothing, not even a human rhino, stand in her way. But tenacity wasn't going to be enough to stand up to the large unit of watchmen out in the alley, who were literally standing in Dare's way. Knowing what she did about some of their number now, Dare shrank back behind the door to listen as three of them talked.

". . . he says to tell her that her mother's worried about her," one of the watchmen was explaining to the others. "And don't mention Kingston to her. They say she's mouthy, got opinions up to here. She might even bite."

"I'll just let this do the talking," another replied, accompanied by the *thwack, thwack* of a billy club smacking his palm.

"I don't care what happens to her as long as we catch her and collect that reward," the third one added.

Dare growled silently. Of course they'd offered a reward

for catching her. That's all these people understood.

Undeterred, Dare went to find another way out. But there were members of the watch out in the lobby, trolling the aisles as the audience filtered in, and even posted at the bottom of the stairs up to Padgett's office. Dare tucked herself in a dark corner behind the stairway up to the catwalk to try to figure out her options. It was a fine place to hide out, or so she thought, until a watchman spotted her from above.

"Hey!" he shouted. "It's you, isn't it?"

Dare dashed out from her hiding spot and raced through the backstage, jumping over rigging and weaving through costumed cast members and crew getting ready for the show as two more watchmen joined the chase.

"Clear out!" they shouted, their whistles blaring, boots stomping.

Dare was certain she'd lose the watchmen in the crowded backstage area, but rather than make a pathway for her, the cast and crew started closing in around her.

"Let me through!" she cried. But like a school of fish encircling their prey, the theater people boxed her in. She pushed and shoved but gained no ground until at last they shuttled her through an open door.

Finally free, Dare moved to sprint back out of the room, but the door slammed shut and wouldn't budge.

"Let me out, you rotten fakes!" Dare spat as she pounded on the door.

"Is that how you say thank you?" a voice from behind asked.

Fists ready to fly, Dare spun around, primed to fight, until she saw where she was, and with whom.

It was Leeds, standing there with an inscrutable smile on his face in a room crowded with shelves and old furniture.

Dare remained still, wired to flee or fight, as he clucked his tongue.

"Now, those uniformed gentlemen out there are most decidedly not illusions," Leeds said. "And you're going to need one to get past them. Let's see what we can do."

Dare's knees buckled. "You mean, you're helping me?"

"We all are. Ernest has been filling us all in on the goings-on. I knew there was something off with those buttons and furs they kept insisting I add to Nell's costumes. They were like nothing I know. Still, I never would have guessed what they were." Leeds gave a little shiver as he went rummaging through the shelves. "If we had time, I'd give you a full change of clothes, too. This will have to do."

Leeds produced a curly brown wig. "I had it made for Nell. I'd been digging around, researching the real Louise, and learned she wasn't the ivory-skinned maiden she's portrayed as. Padgett wouldn't hear it. He made me box this up and make her as blond as could be. Ridiculous. What good is telling a true story without the truth?"

Leeds fit the wig onto Dare, then stood back to regard his work. "This will help. They're looking for a girl with long stringy plaits—their description, not mine. Let's add something else to throw them off. Here, how about this?" He pulled a straw basket filled with painted plaster-cast rolls and biscuits off a shelf and handed it to Dare. "Better. Don't let anyone too close to that basket and you'll pass as a bakery girl, I think. Now, to get you out, go straight through the alley. Hopefully most of them are still chasing after you through the bowels of the theater."

Leeds opened the door, checked the hall as casually as he could, then signaled for her to go. It seemed the proper thing to do would be to promise to somehow return the favor, but Leeds had already shut the door behind her.

Saved.

Dare made for the exit as calmly as she could, fighting the urge to run or to scratch under the wig. It was itchy and smelled of must and mildew, but it was working—she waltzed right past the two watchmen remaining in the alley. Still, she was far from home free. There were plenty more watchmen fanned out all up and down the avenue.

Dare fixed her hold on the basket and her composure—she even tried to imagine her Beastie was there in her pocket, purring and cooing as always. But there were so many of them, and they were eyeing everyone who walked past. Even the bakery girl with the curly hair. Crossing the street was out of the question; there were so many carriages and autos pulling up in front of the theater, she was certain she'd get crushed. So, head down, she plowed on.

"Hey!" one of the watchmen called. "Sell us a bun, won't you?"

Dare ignored him and kept walking, but he grabbed her arm and pulled her back.

"I said, sell us a sweet bun!" The watchman set his face inches from hers.

Maybe it was his breath, sour as rotten milk, or his thick gums and mossy teeth that looked too small for his head, but in that moment, he was every nasty person on Barrow's Bay, every single one of Padgett and the governor's evil club, the embodiment of everything awful in the world.

Whatever it was, something snapped, and Dare's awful came roaring out. She swung the basket filled with those plaster-cast buns right at his face.

She knew she'd made contact when she heard the crunch, the nauseating sound of bone snapping. With her arm free of his grip, Dare took off running faster than she knew she could. As she fled, she heard the whine of wheels slipping, felt the reverberation of wood crashing and smashing as it hit the pavement behind her.

She didn't chance turning to see what had happened until the crackle of laughter echoing all around filled her ears.

Her chest heaving, Dare snuck a quick glance behind her. That one look was enough to know she could slow down; she was in no danger now. Not while the sidewalk was covered in smashed barrels oozing molasses that had tumbled off a passing wagon, the great sticky mess pinning the watchmen where they stood.

It was a glorious scene of destruction, one Dare wished Nell and Gil were there to see, too, but there was no time to relish the mess. Her path to the cannery was clear.

Dare knew there was something amiss as soon as she hit the wharf.

It was too quiet for midday. There should have been ships piled on either side of the *Slipper*—nay, the *Mighty Way*—workers trundling cases and crates here and there, the endless whir and hum of machinery buzzing in the air, smokestacks spewing. But the repainted *Slipper* sat silently bobbing on its moorings, and there was only a smattering of workers on the cannery loading dock.

Dare found a stack of barrels that afforded her cover and an unfettered view of the loading dock. Even with that silly wig on, she couldn't risk being seen.

All remained quiet; nothing happened for the longest time, and Dare began to wonder if they really were planning on shipping out that evening. Then something shifted. The workers who had been lazily stacking empty crates all walked off into the factory as if by command.

If they were closing for the day, this might be her chance, assuming she could get down to the marvels and drove them onto the ship all by herself.

But it was complete folly. Even if she could get them out of those cages and onto the *Slipper*, then what? She could no more sail that ship than turn into a mushroom—she'd just be doing Padgett and Kingston's work for them.

The inevitability of defeat was beginning to take hold when something new happened: the door down to the marvels' hold opened and a line of people all dressed in gray jumpers with heavy leather gloves clipped to their belts filed out.

The keepers. The human ghouls who kept the marvels in such horrid conditions started lining up a series of wooden crates on the loading dock.

Fueled by pure awful, Dare rocketed from her hiding spot. Screaming like a banshee, she raced toward them without a single thought to how she'd actually fight them off. But before she could reach even one of those gray-clad demons, someone grabbed her from behind, pinning her arms to her sides, robbing her of any chance of escape.

CHAPTER THIRTY-EIGHT
Drovers Droving

"What were you thinking?" a voice snarled in Dare's ear as she fought to get her arms and legs free. But their hold was too tight.

That left her with only one defense.

Dare strained and craned her neck, trying to get close enough to clamp her teeth down on one of the arms. She was in striking distance to bite when she saw them. Tattoos, thirty or more monsters of all shapes and sizes etched into skin.

Feelings, too many to count, flooded Dare as she was gently set back on her feet and that nasty, beautiful laugh echoed through her bones.

Tupper!

"You haven't learned very much, have you?" Tupper clucked. "Now, imagine if it weren't me who caught you about to do something stupid. And what's this you got on your head?"

Dare pulled the wig off and threw her arms around the crusty old sailor. "I was so scared you were still locked up!"

Seeing him there, free and whole, sent more stones from that bridge in her heart crumbling—it was barely a footbridge at this point. Although Dare still wasn't entirely sure how to be herself without it.

She pulled back, trying to pretend the hug hadn't happened. "I knew Gil could get you out."

From Tupper's expression, he apparently hadn't been so certain. "It was one of the oddest things . . . but we ain't got time for reminiscing, we got beasts to load and a ship to take back."

"What about Padgett's crew? And these keepers, they work for Cummings."

"We got our own crew, they were here waiting on me, had already dispatched the ones Padgett hired. Ernest did good."

"Wait, you know him?"

"Padgett and Kingston have their *associates*, and we've got ours."

The thought that Ernest had been spying on the Foghorn all these years, feeding information back to Tupper and Captain Fortune, filled Dare with a special kind of glee.

"As for these folk"—Tupper nodded toward the keepers—"soon as they heard there was a chance to release them beasts and put Cummings in a corner, they jumped. A different kind of strike than they'd been planning. Even that one over there with the half-chewed hand jumped to help."

Dare spotted the man with the bandage she'd seen the day she found the marvels. While she was glad it hadn't been Beastie who'd wounded the keeper, seeing the man sent a pang through her, a painful reminder that her poor maeder was still lost to her.

Dare tried to push back the pull of sadness and focus on the moment. "How did they know to come now?"

"They'd already been ordered to move the beasts to the ship. All that's changed is who they're doing it for. Seems rumors about monsters—the human kind—and their tastes in clothes and food been swirling all over the city since yesterday, riling people up. I was lying low in a boarding house last night when the talk reached me."

"Ernest again?"

"Yup. He's been waiting a long time to get this information out to folks. Anyway, now we got work to do. You get droving them beasts into these crates and I'll see them loaded onto the *Slipper*."

"Me?" Dare teetered between exploding with laughter and dissolving into a puddle. "I can't do that. There's bandicots down there. A garbinol! I don't even know what to do!"

"Sure you do. Start easy with the jacklers—use the whistle, it keeps them calm. Get them out of the cages, up the hall, and into the crates, repeat and repeat until they're all out."

"Oh, is that all?" Dare mocked.

"And work fast, time and tide ain't your friend. You're ready for this—go on, get droving." Tupper patted her on the shoulder with a rare touch of affection before he hustled off to the *Slipper*.

Dare was not ready for this at all. How could she ever be? The marvels might not be the monsters they'd been portrayed as, but they still possessed dangerous defenses. Jacklers were a perfect example. They might be the smallest and meekest of the marvels down there, but their primary defense was an acid-like liquid they could expel like a skunk, and their long snouts looked sharp enough to run her through. The idea of walking alongside them was terrifying at best.

Yet not doing it meant leaving the marvels—and herself— at the mercy of Padgett and his cadre of rhinos, an even more terrifying thought.

This would be a great time for Gil to arrive, to have Nell there standing by her side. But Dare couldn't afford to think about what might have happened to Gil, or what Nell might face if their plan went awry. So she did what she could do: she buckled up her nerve and marched herself down into that awful dungeon to get to work.

She was expecting the same miserable scene she'd seen the other day. But while the cold, dark dungeon was still terrible beyond words, the filthy hay had been raked up, and the marvels had fresh food, water, and bedding. They were more alert now, heads turning as Dare walked in—some were growling or mewling, or, like the caltung, were outright hissing.

But not the garbinol. It was slumped in the corner of its cage, beak agape, barely able to lift its head.

The keepers had already unlocked the cage doors, so all Dare had to do was muster the nerve to open them. There was no amount of deep breathing or any other kind of preparation she could do to meet this moment. She simply had to do it.

She wet her lips to raise a whistle, but her mouth was so dry, the notes came out broken and breathy, shaded with a combination of fear and fascination.

She tried again, this time imagining Gil and Nell and Beastie were there with her. It helped, and the whistle, though still a bit stilted, came. She started off softly, gently repeating the tune over and over again as she slowly pulled the door to the jacklers' cage open.

Carefully, and very slowly, Dare began backing away toward the door, whistling all the way.

The jacklers didn't follow. They barely bristled or squawked or even seemed to notice the cage had been opened.

They'd probably been in there since they hatched—what did they know of leaving that prison?

Dare eased down to a crouch, and while she avoided making eye contact, she changed the whistle from a sharp, staccato call to something softer, more melodic. As she did so, a gentle stillness quieted her thoughts. Something yielded in her; that knot of fear loosened, leaving room for wonder and tenderness to unspool. And soon, something similar began to happen to the jacklers. They stood up, splaying their stubby webbed feet, cocking their heads as if trying to place a sound from long ago.

It took time, but slowly the mature jacklers moved to the opening, sniffing and pecking with those long beaks, testing the ground, stepping out, then hopping back in. Maybe they, too, were looking for the illusion.

When at last the pair of adults left the cage, followed by four hatchlings stumbling on wobbly legs, Dare had to fight to keep her tune going and her heart open to the miracle of these marvels.

One backward step at a time, she led them out of the den, through the hall, and out to the loading dock where a pair of keepers—both women—were waiting for her next to an open crate.

"Well done," one said. "Now take three large steps to the right. If this works, the jacklers will walk right into the crate, and we'll shut them in."

If this works were the only words Dare really heard.

Three side steps to the right later, and all the jacklers marched into the crate, diving onto the pile of ripe peaches and grass waiting for them inside.

Seeing them safely contained, then lifted to be loaded onto the *Slipper*, filled Dare with the strangest combination of joy and relief. But this was no time to let down.

"Now the droben, then the caltung," one of the keepers instructed.

Dare felt relatively safe with the droben trailing behind her; one had to be close to the creature to be hit by their quills, should they shed them. And while the caltung's high leaps made her nervous, their shorter front arms flapped about in such a silly manner, she couldn't help being cheered by them. It was the bandicots that tested her resolve and ability to remain quiet, focused.

Known to be especially erratic, a bandicot could be calm one moment, then attack the next. The way they stalked, so low to the ground, spines raised, and those fangs of theirs glistening like knives, raised a sweat on Dare's back. But if anyone knew the value of honing one's sharp edges it was Dare.

When at last all but one of the cages had been emptied, Dare went to look for Tupper. No matter how confident she'd become in her abilities, she wasn't going to drove that garbinol on her own. Not on a bet. But she couldn't find Tupper anywhere.

"He'll come help with the garbinol, after we've gotten all the others loaded," the keeper with the wounded hand explained.

"They're all out already," Dare countered.

"No, they're not." The keeper showed his clipboard to Dare. "Last cage to the left. I can understand why you thought it was empty—that creature's got a chameleonlike ability to change color. It spends most of its time the color of concrete."

An occisor.

Even as she knew Padgett must have been lying when he'd blamed her father's death on that specific marvel, the thought of facing one left her feeling like her tongue was suddenly too large for her mouth.

"Don't just stand there. We've got less time every minute." Using his one good hand, the keeper spun Dare about and gave her a gentle shove back down the hall. "Go!"

The last cage on the left. He was right; she'd assumed it was empty, but now that she knew what to look for, she saw it, plain as day. The occisor lay in the corner, its four long, hoofed legs folded underneath it, only those diamond-shaped eyes with their vertical pupils moving as they tracked her every move. It was indeed the same color as its dreary surroundings, proof of its extraordinary ability to practically disappear. That's what had made Padgett's tale so believable—how could anyone protect themselves from that which they can't see?

But standing this close to it now, Dare easily found the lie in Padgett's tale, right there in the occisor's tail. For while it was indeed as long and thin as a whip, it was covered over in softest downy feathers. Unless that plumage was concealing ten thousand tiny barbs, there was no way it could have killed her father, not with its tail. No, the actual murderer was clearly something, someone else.

Once Dare got the occisor moved and crated, she was ready to face the garbinol. But Tupper had another plan in place.

"I'm sure that poor fella can't hardly walk," Tupper said. "We'll push that cage out, and you be by to help keep him soothed once we get him up here. Till then, go have a sit. I'll call you when we get it all in place."

Grateful for a break, and even more grateful that the garbinol would remain caged, Dare wandered out to the wharf to take in some air. She sat down, legs dangling over the edge, leaned back on her arms, and closed her eyes.

Of all the things she'd seen and learned in the past many months, the one she still had the hardest time accepting was that her father was really and truly gone. Even after more than half a year had passed, one small part of her kept thinking he'd come back at any minute, that she'd find out it was all a great mistake. A fever dream.

"You look so comfortable." A voice broke the silence. No surprise this time that it was Gil, only relief and, yes, real joy. Dare scooted over to make room for him to sit next to her.

"You did it, Dare, you really did." Gil was shining her with a smile as wide as his face, but he looked thinner than he had the night before. Worn-out.

"*We* did it—you, me, Nell, Tupper, and Ernest. Well, we almost did it. We still have to load the garbinol," Dare corrected.

"That poor devil is so beaten down, he won't give you any trouble."

"I hope not." But Dare's concerns weren't for herself anymore. "I know that once they find out what we've done, Nell's mother and the governor will do their worst to us, but we're both used to that in different ways. I'm more worried about you. You look awful."

"Why, thank you," Gil quipped. "No, if you're safe, I'll be more than fine, too. I am going to have to leave, though. As soon as the marvels are safely on their way. This trip of mine has already been delayed. It's time."

"No! You can't do that. Cancel the stupid trip," Dare insisted. "Where do you even have to go so badly? No, you need to stay here. We need to get you better, strong."

"I'm stronger now than I ever was. I'll come back from time to time, I'll always find you. I'm just so sorry we couldn't find your Beastie. I still believe he's—"

"Time's up!" Tupper called, his voice full and robust. "Let's get this monster loaded!"

"That's our cue." Gil got up and followed Tupper.

As much as he might try to cover it over, she knew Gil needed a rest, a long rest. His trip would wait. Dare resolved to insist that Madam take him in when this was all over.

When it was over.

The idea was rather stunning, how far she'd come, how her world had turned over, then over again since that awful day her father died. No matter what she felt, she'd never get him back, and she'd never stop missing him, but at least now she could help finish his story, and maybe begin one of her own.

Dare had just taken a deep breath, necessary fuel for moving the garbinol, when the strangest odor overwhelmed her senses. Sweet yet pungent, it hit the back of her throat like an iron-fisted punch. She barely had time to react before the entire world went black around her.

CHAPTER THIRTY-NINE
A Terrible Tale

Dare's ears were still buzzing with the silence of an unnatural sleep, her vision was still too blurry to see, but she didn't need to see or hear to know where she was. She could feel the rattle and hum of the factory machines through the floor. And she knew the voices she heard, though still muffled, belonged to the truest kinds of monsters—Padgett and Governor Kingston.

There was one sound she couldn't place yet, a constantly repeating kind of metallic twang. Dare tried to see through the blur.

"Here you are, back with us at last. That ether certainly knocked you out." The drip of the governor's nasal tones made Dare want to retch. "What a time you've had, Darvlah. I had really hoped the change of location would have helped excise your grief, cure your overactive imagination. Yet you've only gotten worse."

"I don't know about that, Randolph." This was Padgett, sounding all too pleased with himself as usual. "I found their little trick at the theater clever. It's something I might even have thought of, though I'd never have missed so many of the fine details. It was sloppy work. You didn't even consider Nell's exit, did you?"

Dare's stomach sank. They really hadn't.

"She'll be returning to the original script for her tour." Dare wasn't expecting this voice, though it shouldn't have been a surprise that Mrs. Lawrence was there, too. "She's so easily influenced. The artistic temperament is fragile, she'll find herself again soon enough."

Dare's vision was clearing now, bringing the ghoulish trio before her into focus. They were, of course, fully decked out in all their devilish attire. Padgett and Kingston both wore suits trimmed with what Dare now knew to be some poor marvel's hide, and finely carved buttons, while Mrs. Lawrence was as ridiculously outfitted as ever, from her hat to her shoes to the fur muff cosseting her hands.

"You needn't worry about Nell," the governor advised. "It's time to think only about yourself. And your mother."

The mention of Mother swiftly cleared whatever fog still lingered in Dare's head. And that's when she saw a fourth face—that mug she'd come to know too well. Clearly recovered from the crates he'd taken to the head, Ham Hands, the rhino who'd cornered her and ripped off her pocket, was standing in the corner, snapping a thin length of wire with small wooden handles attached to each end. That chilling twang echoed through the office over and over as the wire went taut, then slack, taut, then slack.

Dare's throat ran dry.

It was a simple device, one that could be mistaken for a cheese cutter, or a broken piano wire. But in the mugger's hands, Dare knew exactly what it was, and what it had done. Choosing to pin her Father's murder on the occisor was the one truly clever thing Padgett had ever done.

"I see." Dare nodded sagely, a ploy to hide the very real fear twisting her insides. "You mean to kill me, and possibly my mother, the same way you did my father."

"This is what we're talking about, Darvlah. You're unwell. Prone to flights of fancy and delusions." The governor clucked his tongue in imitation of someone who cared, then motioned for Ham Hands to leave the office. Clearly his part had been played.

The governor continued. "We've had countless reports of you muttering to yourself as you wander the streets of the city chasing after imaginary problems." A breeze blew in from somewhere (even though all the windows in the office were sealed shut) and ruffled the governor's cleanly parted hair. Having to smooth his silvery waves back added a sullen edge to his voice. "It's all gone far enough. I should never have allowed you near your father's aunt. Her illness is clearly contagious."

"You leave Madam out of it!" Dare tried to jump to her

feet, but she was still woozy.

"We're happy to leave everyone out of this as long as you—" The breeze kicked up again, this time sending the longer locks Kingston kept so artfully combed over the top of his head flopping into his eyes. His irritation mounting, he moved to the opposite corner of the office, all the while trying to reset his coif. But either the breeze had followed him, or his hair had developed a will of its own, for it refused to stay put.

"Looks like Cummings's office has its own trade winds," Dare quipped.

The governor was not amused as he fought to reclaim his unflappable facade. Dare was about to dig in deeper to humiliate him further when she caught sight of two truths.

She'd already figured the governor wore the emblem somewhere on his person. That she hadn't figured out where until now chafed at her. But there it was, on his cufflinks, fully exposed by his upstretched arms. She'd watched him twisting and turning them countless times, fastidiously making certain they sat straight as soldiers awaiting inspection. They'd been so obvious.

Less obvious, and more stunning, was the second truth.

Mother had tried to tell her, in her own way, but Dare didn't see it until now. Yet it had been there all along, right there, where the thin gold bar and chain that kept Kingston's pocket watch tethered to his person attached to his vest. A button that was broken clean in half—a button that had long been in need of repair.

As the governor smoothed the last of his stray hairs, the entire story fell into place in Dare's mind. It was all so ghastly, so awful, she knew to react would be to break. So instead she gritted her teeth and shoved her feelings down and away, one last time.

"As I was saying, this matter need not involve anyone else as long as you come to understand things as they truly are," the governor continued. "Whoever's been filling your head with falsities is no better than a murderer. There are facts and there are lies. Truth tellers and liars. It's high time you knew which is which."

Dare blinked several times. "I think I understand now," she began slowly. "So, the people who are lying are the ones responsible for my father's murder? Is that what you mean?"

"Exactly, and they want to use you and the very special gifts you inherited from him for their own twisted benefit."

"Right." Dare took her time, selling her transformation with every breath. "I see it now, I do."

Kingston buttoned his jacket, his composure reclaimed. "We should have had this conversation earlier, before you came and caused all this trouble for Padgett and Mrs. Lawrence."

"I agree, sir." Dare sat up straighter, a posture for reciting a poem for the schoolmarm. "There are no more monsters, and my father was killed by a common ruffian."

"You're getting it at last," Mrs. Lawrence huffed, her right hand continuously stroking that fur muff of hers. "There might be a chance yet for you in decent society."

"See, I told you both, she's a gem." Padgett gestured for Dare to continue.

"And because both of those things are true, I need to go droving and help you move the monsters that have been raised in captivity here, in Cummings's Cannery, to the refuge island so that you can . . . ?" Dare left the end of her sentence dangling in case any of them wanted to finish it for her. When they didn't, she continued, picking up speed as she spoke. "So that you can continue to eat them and steal their gifts to enhance your own positions and wealth. Does that cover everything? Oh no, it doesn't. One question: Were all of you there when my father was killed, or just the governor and that friend of yours who just left the office?"

"That's beyond enough. I should never have listened to you, Padgett! She's exactly as I said she'd be!" Kingston yanked Dare up from the chair by the arm. "There are schools for girls like you, places where you *will* unlearn the idea of having ideas!"

"That might be, though I'll never unlearn the truth of what you did to my father!" Dare spat as she fought to wrest herself free. But Kingston had her like a hawk on its supper as he dragged her out of the office, down the stairs, and onto the factory floor, with Padgett and the Foghorn following in their wake.

And that's when Dare stopped struggling.

From everything they'd said, it didn't sound like they knew what was happening out on the loading dock, that the keepers were working against them, or that Tupper had escaped. If she could just stall a bit longer, Tupper might have enough time to get the last of the marvels loaded and out to sea.

But they were mere steps from reaching the swinging double doors out to the loading dock. It was all about to come crashing to a halt.

"Wait! Please." Dare turned her best cow-eyed look on Padgett. She knew better than to try to reason with the Foghorn or the governor. The showman was malleable. "I'll cooperate with you, do whatever you want, but I want Beastie, my marvel, back first."

"Absolutely not!" Mrs. Lawrence clutched her fur muff to her chest. "We're not negotiating with you. Tell her, Randolph!"

Yet before the governor could reply, Padgett stepped up. "I don't see why we can't reach an agreement. She's got what we need, and we've got what she wants."

The governor joined the argument then, sputtering on about discipline and how Dare was too much like her father.

That she'd gotten them to tacitly admit the truth twice filled Dare with the kind of confidence she used to only pretend to have. The longer they stood there arguing among themselves, the more time she bought for Tupper.

But events were swirling too quickly for an argument to slow, for just then, a watchman burst through the street-side doors with a fighting and snarling Nell in tow.

"Caught this one and her driver prowling around outside," he announced proudly.

"Nice to see you here, Nell." Dare tipped her head.

"You too, Dare."

"I warned you not to cross me, Nell!" the Foghorn bellowed, followed by an impressive string of curses.

"If that's how members of *decent* society speak, I'm ready to join right now!" Dare quipped.

"Sign me up, too, please!" Nell cackled in delight.

"Think you're a funny pair, do you?" The governor tightened his grip on Dare and motioned for the watchman to follow him as he kicked the double doors open, warning Padgett and the Foghorn to stay where they were.

The girls both fought with all they had, but there was no way to stop the inevitable now. And inevitable it was, for just as they burst onto the dock, the door leading to the dungeon flew open and out came Tupper, whistling the call of the marvels, followed by a line of keepers pushing an enormous cage.

The garbinol hadn't been loaded yet!

Everything that happened next happened in an instant. The watchman blew his whistle, summoning a flood of other members of the watch onto the loading dock. Dare tried to use the confusion to break free, but the governor's hold was too tight. Even stomping on his foot only made him flinch as a swarm of watchmen surrounded Tupper, the keepers, and the caged garbinol. Shouts, cries, and angry curses filled the air, yet above it all rose a howl that ached with primal fury. Sharper than any dagger, the roar ran straight through Dare, threatening to crack her wide open.

"Stop that noise!" the watchmen bellowed, hitting the garbinol's cage with their clubs. But the garbinol's wail reached higher and higher as the beast repeatedly slammed the full measure of its weight against the cage door. Metal bent, without quite yielding.

Until, in an instant, it snapped.

Deep dread and terrible hope filled Dare as the cage door flew open and that great ragged creature, claws bared, fanged beak snapping, came crashing out onto the loading dock.

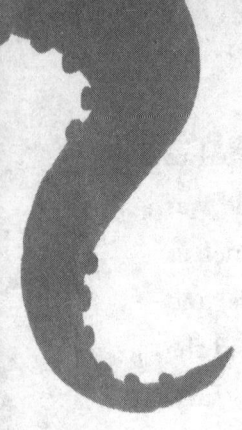

CHAPTER FORTY
Another Tale to Tell

Panic erupted all around. Watchmen dropped their tough facades along with their captives and went scrambling to get away from the garbinol. Some fled into the cannery, others onto the wharf, then straight into the Pike with a splash.

"What the devil is happening out here?" Padgett's voice thundered with bravado as he burst onto the loading dock. But the great showman took one look at the unfolding scene, turned gray as a ghost, and raced back behind the swinging doors.

The only person who'd not flown into a panic (aside from Dare) was Governor Kingston. He barely flinched, as he shifted his grip to twist Dare's arm up and behind her back.

"Get droving," he hissed in her ear. "Get it back in that cage."

Dare was about to reply with some of those curses she'd just learned from the Foghorn when Nell sprinted past.

"Yes, Nell! Run!" Dare shouted at her. "Find Gil!" But Kingston whipped his other arm out and easily grabbed Nell.

"Do it, or I'll feed her to the beast," Kingston snarled, twisting Dare's wrist harder still.

For Nell, and only for her, Dare fought to settle her mind, to ignore the pain ricocheting up her arm, and to raise a whistle on her bone-dry lips.

Twee— twoo, tweeee . . . twoooo! The call came out broken, and weak. But it was there, and it was enough to make the garbinol turn its gnashing beak in their direction.

"Now send it back into the cage," the governor ordered as the garbinol began to slowly stalk toward them.

Dare's whistle grew stronger, and when Nell joined in it became louder still, each sound of the call drawing the garbinol one stumbling step closer.

As the beast kept coming, Dare's resolve grew stronger, her connection to it deeper.

"Into the cage, not toward us!" Governor Kingston cried, his calm finally cracked, as he quickly backtracked, dragging the girls toward the double doors. With one decisive blow he kicked at the doors to open them, but they didn't budge.

If she were not facing down a very large, very hurt, and very angry garbinol, Dare would have laughed. Padgett had locked the governor out!

"Hang you all! Let us in!" Desperate to escape, the governor dropped his grip on both girls and pounded on the door.

Reason should have dictated that the girls also try to flee. But, hands clasped, they stood their ground together and whistled on.

As their tune grew louder, the garbinol's approach began to slow, the screaming ceased, and soon the marvel stopped in its tracks. Head tilting, beak open, it looked as if it were hearing its own name for the first time. Blinded by the pus encrusting the corners of its deep-set yellow eyes, it kept turning its head, looking for the source of the calls, until finally it found them.

Dare saw recognition pass over the creature's face, understanding beginning to retract those terrible claws, smooth the spikes lining its arms.

They were doing it! They were soothing the beast.

Except at that very moment, Mrs. Lawrence came bursting through the swinging doors, knocking the governor back as she cried, "My baby, my beauty!"

That's all it took.

The garbinol bucked and blindly lunged at Mrs. Lawrence. One swipe from that spike-studded arm and the Foghorn landed in a pile on the ground, sending her hat flying off in one direction, her fur muff in the other.

"Mama!" Nell cried as she broke away from Dare and went racing directly past the garbinol to her mother's side.

Dare tried to reignite her connection with the marvel as the governor, in a complete panic, went racing across the loading dock. But the garbinol was on the attack. All it took was one smack of the garbinol's mighty tail to send Kingston flying into the air. He landed with a thud against a barrel of salt, sending it spreading across the floor.

Still, Dare fought to calm the marvel, whistling over and over again as she followed its every movement, hoping to catch its gaze with hers.

She'd never know for sure if it was her whistling or the garbinol's truest nature that finally made it stop. But once it looked directly at her, it stopped, then gently swept her, along with Nell and the wounded Foghorn, toward the wall with the soft side of its tail.

Cloistered there behind the beast with Nell and her unconscious mother, Dare knew she should have been terrified, her heart ought to have been ready to explode. But there was a quiet and a peace to the garbinol's movements as it positioned itself between the wall and the door to the factory floor at the exact moment it burst open.

A new band of watchmen, too many to count, flooded in as Padgett screamed commands at them. "Attack the beast!" Yet neither their numbers nor their spiked batons nor even the few pistols the commanders carried could protect them from the garbinol. One by one, the marvel batted them back until all were either splayed out on the ground or had retreated.

As a deathly silence filled the air, Dare left Nell at the Foghorn's side and cautiously stepped out from behind the marvel's shadow, whistling all the way.

Tweeewooo tweeewooo tweeewooo.

It might have been the salt littering the loading dock, or simple exhaustion, but the garbinol seemed to bow its head in Dare's direction before it teetered on its feet and slumped against the wall into a half-dazed sleep.

Dare slowly sidled up to the marvel's side and lay a gentle hand on its filthy, matted coat. She longed to see it as it should be, its fur long and thick, its eyes clear, a healthy beast at home in the wild. But for now, there was only one thing to do.

"Thank you," she whispered. "I promise you'll be safe soon."

"And so will you," a voice cracked behind Dare. She spun around to find Tupper there, completely untouched, a giant sack of marsh salt in his hands.

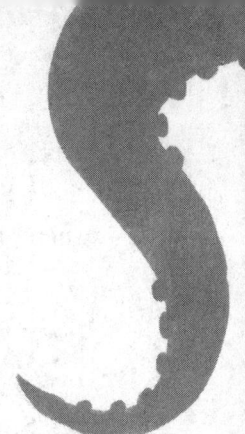

CHAPTER FORTY-ONE
There, Then Gone

"Guess we know that part of the Louise story is true," Tupper clucked. "Darned thing was ready to die for you. Me and them keepers will get our friend here loaded up. You might want to check on this lot, though." Tupper nodded at the bodies littering the loading dock.

Members of the watch, the governor, and a few keepers were writhing in pain, suffering from deep and nasty lacerations on their faces, legs, and arms. Though they would all surely be riddled by scars, they, like Mrs. Lawrence, would live to tell the tale.

But Dare had a different, more urgent matter to attend to. Finding Gil.

She had just stepped out onto the wharf to look for him when she heard the creak of steps behind her.

"Gil?" Dare called as she spun about.

It wasn't Gil.

It was Padgett. And he wasn't alone. Ham Hands was there, the wire pulled taut in his hands.

"What do you want from me?" Dare challenged, her entire body primed like an arrow ready to fly. "It's over—you're over."

"So bold of you!" Padgett laughed. "You must be eager for a command performance of how your father met his end."

The mugger gave the wire a decisive snap. One twist, and she'd be gone.

Dare stepped back, palms up, a gesture of peace. "Fine, you win. What do you want? Say it and I'll do it. No tricks, no illusions."

"I want my reputation back, but you two broke it." Padgett launched into a soliloquy about his career, all he'd done for Nell, and for Dare. How all he wanted was to make people happy.

But all Dare heard was the faint sound of Gil's voice echoing in her mind. *The occisor. It's there on the dock behind you. Call it.*

Once upon a time, Dare would have snarled at the idea of heeding a voice in her head, but she'd since learned that friends have a funny way of taking care of you even when they're not there with you.

She dropped her gaze, hoping to look like someone being duly rebuked, when really, she was hoping to catch sight of the camouflaged beast out of the corner of her eye. When that proved fruitless, she wet her lips. One whistle was all she had. Either it would summon the marvel, or ignite Padgett's ire and let loose that wire-wielding thug.

Tweeewooo tweeewooo tweeewooo!

"Stop her!" Padgett commanded as he motioned to Ham Hands. Dare was certain she was about to be ended. Then she saw it. A flash of yellow, a ripple of thick, leathery hide, only for an instant, before it disappeared again.

The occisor.

Padgett lunged at Dare. Yet at that very same moment, he lost control of his feet and went flying off to the side. Propelled by an invisible force, he crashed into a pile on the wharf. He unleashed a painful yowl as he tried to get up, to escape. He'd barely made it back onto his feet when he let loose a cry fit to curdle blood. Dare thought he was being dramatic, until she saw the legs of his trousers—they'd been neatly split open, exposing thick, weeping gashes across both of his shins.

The symmetry of the occisor's attack on Padgett's legs was an act of revenge fit for one of the showman's own spectacles. But that was real blood, and he was in real pain.

Dare started to race to his side, but then she heard a crash, the sound of wood splintering, and an anguished cry from up the dock. She quickly pivoted and was running toward the noise when a thunderous geyser erupted, spraying water up and over the dock, drenching her in its wake.

Once the water had receded, Dare pushed her soaking-wet hair out of her face and tried hard to suppress a laugh. The top mast of a small fishing boat anchored at the dock had been broken clean in half. That explained the crash. As for the splash, the cause of it was floundering out in the bay, arms waving, raspy voice calling for help from the army of keepers that had begun flooding the dock. A few keepers dove into the bay to haul Ham Hands back to shore, while others stopped to tend to Padgett.

And yet as chaos swirled around her, all Dare could do was stand in wonder as the occisor, who'd padded over to her side, dropped its camouflage. First its yellow head appeared, followed by the rainbow of colored feathers adorning its neck, and then, finally, its sweeping white tail.

The creature cocked its head, turning one golden eye on Dare. "Thank—" she began, but as soon as the word started to form on her lips, the marvel bowed its head, then ambled up the gangway and straight onto the deck of the *Slipper*.

The occisor was right—no words were necessary.

"You're just making friends all over the place, aren't you?" Tupper arrived on the dock, a wry comment ready as always, and a sackcloth in hand, which he wrapped around Dare.

"Strange, isn't it?" she said, gathering the cloth around her. "It's like it knew I needed its help."

"You helped it. It'll help you. That's how it works with them, just not always with people." Tupper sucked his teeth, the conversation apparently veering too close to emotions for him. "I'm gonna get that one into a crate, no telling what that tail could do next. You go on inside, dry off. We got everyone accounted for."

Tupper followed the occisor onto the ship, leaving Dare alone on the dock. But he was wrong. Not everyone had been accounted for. Despite hearing his voice so clearly in her mind, Dare still hadn't seen Gil since they'd been together right at this spot earlier.

She knew better than to imagine him dead or in custody. He was too resourceful for that. And while she refused to believe he'd leave without saying goodbye, it would be like him to do exactly that.

Still, Dare searched everywhere she could think of—on the factory floor, down in the now empty dungeon, and finally back on the loading dock. She asked everyone she saw, but no one had an answer. She was just about to ask Nell, who was still tending to her mother, to help her look when the cooing she'd been aching to hear once again filled her ears.

"Beastie?" The sound of his name delicious on her tongue.

A quiet coo echoed in return as sweet, beautiful Beastie crawled out of the Foghorn's dreadful muff and raced straight to Dare.

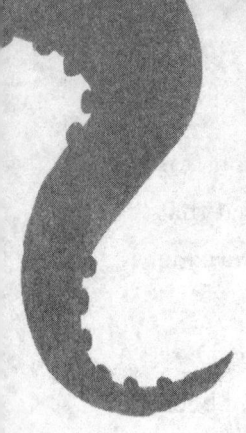

CHAPTER FORTY-TWO
Curtain Calling

The tide was high, and the time had come. The *Slipper* was loaded with marvels and ready to set sail. Everything that could be done had been done, and most everything that could be said had been said.

Most everything, except for the hardest thing.

Dare had always thought walking away from other people was easy—turn your back and be rid of them. Yet standing in the entry hall of Nesbitt House, she could no more face parting from Nell and Madam than ever let Beastie out of her sight again.

"Are you sure you won't come, Thalia?" Dare shifted Beastie from one shoulder to the other, hoping for the answer she wanted to hear.

Nell laughed at she always did at the nickname Dare had come up for her. "I am truly not worthy of being named after the goddess of theater," Nell said. "As for coming with you, I'd only be taking up space, and would be of little help."

"And she will be of immeasurable help to me," Madam said consolingly. "In the time you're gone, we'll have the Grand cleaned up and ready for rehearsals to begin. We'll all be so busy the time will fly, and then you'll be back!"

Madam was right. Dare was being silly. She'd be gone no more than a few weeks, and she truly was thrilled that Nell and Madam had bonded so quickly and completely. There was an immediate understanding between the two actresses, as if they both spoke a language no one else could understand. And now with Nell's support—emotional and financial—the Nesbitt Grand and Madam's career would be resurrected and infused with new energy. Nell would be exactly where she wanted to be, doing what she wanted to do. And Madam's best days could no longer be said to be behind her.

Dare couldn't wish for more for either of them.

"There's still one thing you need to do before you leave," Madam reminded her.

Dare grimaced. "No time, I'll do it when we get back."

But Madam wasn't having it. A raised brow was all it took for Dare to capitulate.

"Fine."

She'd rehearsed this conversation enough times to know it by heart, but as she trudged to the back of the house, she still couldn't trust her awful not to take over.

"You've come, thank you." Mary greeted Dare's arrival in the kitchen with a shy smile, and an offering of a basket filled with baked treats. "There's something in here for everyone's tastes, even Tupper's and Beastie's. And I left something on the bottom just for you. It took some doing to get it back, I hope it brings you some joy."

As predicted, Dare's awful was itching to be set loose—especially since Mary was looking for extra points just for baking. Still, she stuck to the script she'd written for herself. "Madam's explained it all to me. I know everything you do is for her. You were scared, didn't want to see her lose even more than she had, and you—"

"Broke your heart to try to save hers." Mary could hardly look at Dare. "Fear drove me beyond reason, as it does to some folks. And when that Dr. Hinckle came to see me, offering all that money, I . . . well, all I can say is I am deeply sorry, Dare."

Mary could apologize every day from here to eternity, and still Dare would never fully trust her again. But Dare also couldn't afford to carry all that anger along with her. Like the basket, it was too heavy.

Dare returned to the foyer as a car horn blared outside.

"Ernest is here, let's not keep him waiting." Nell helped Dare on with her coat. "After he drops you at the dock, he's going to take me to the hospital to see Mama. Her doctors said she'll be well enough to set sail for Barrow's Bay in a few days to settle into her new home there. They say the sunshine will help her heal."

"I hope it goes more than skin deep," Dare said.

Nell laughed and pulled Dare into a hug.

Madam waited until the girls broke their embrace, then took Dare into her own arms. "Safe travels, dear Dare." She then reached under her collar, pulled her necklace off, and slipped it over Dare's head.

"Your locket?" Dare gasped, cradling the treasure in both hands. "You can't give this to me! This is yours, you always wear it."

"I've been wearing it since your father left home, and while you'll most certainly be back here soon, it seems only fitting that it should be yours now. Come, give me another hug and be on your way."

Dare didn't want to let go, but she could practically hear Tupper grumbling at the dock all the way from here. Madam gave Beastie a loving pet, then she and Nell followed Dare out to the curb.

"We're all ready, Ernest," Nell said as she opened the front passenger-side door and waited for Dare to climb in.

"Speak for yourself," Dare quipped.

"You're more than ready, Dare! We'll see you soon!" Nell shut the door and gave Ernest the signal to drive on.

As Ernest slowly maneuvered the car into the street, Nell called after them. "Hey, if Gil does show up, tell him I want to finally meet him!"

"What do you mean, 'meet him'?" Dare shouted back, but the auto was moving faster now, and Nell and Madam were quickly becoming small dots in the distance.

Dare shrugged it off; she must have misheard. Still, the reminder that she hadn't seen Gil since they'd sat together on the dock stung. She'd been so certain he'd pop up as he always had. But in the days since they'd liberated the marvels and seen Padgett, the governor, and many other club members brought to justice, her certainty had dwindled to close to nothing. And yet, while the Dare she used to be would have expected disappointment, the Dare she'd become knew to keep a window open. Hope might still fly in.

"I've got all the day's papers for you," Ernest said. "More articles and pictures to add to your scrapbook."

Dare didn't really need to read the articles to know what they said. Ernest had been impeccable in spreading the version of the truth they wanted told about the monsters—how they were truly marvels used up to feed the ambitions of fools.

Even if word about the refuge and that some marvels still lived did leak out, change doesn't come for people overnight. Unlearning a lie requires an unraveling of stories that have been stitched in so tightly, they must be removed one by one. It was enough for people to understand the depths of deception and manipulation Padgett, Kingston, and the rest had sunk to. To see how the abuse of the marvels' gifts had led to their own, very real woes. And while the only island Kingston would ever see again was the prison atoll where he'd be serving a life sentence, Cummings saw his cannery was seized and shuttered, and Padgett would never again preside over his Palace, there were still some club members who hadn't suffered any sanctions, legal or social.

At least not yet.

For now, the fortunes of the mayor, city leaders, and many of the factory owners would rise or fall depending on their own natural abilities, unaided by the power of the marvels.

"We're here," Ernest announced, as he pulled up to the dock. He started to get out of the car to open the door for Dare, but she stopped him with a hug.

"I've got it, you've done more than enough for all of us."

"I'd been waiting years to see some justice here. Now, you be safe and come back quickly."

"We will." Dare lugged the basket out of the car and went to meet Mother, who was waiting for her at the bottom of the *Slipper*'s gangway. She met Dare with a smile and a warm embrace. "Finally! Tupper's beyond impatient, his language is getting saltier by the moment."

Dare was still adjusting to the new Mother. Though there were traces of the woman she used to be, there was a lightness and peace about her now. Gone was the hungry look, as if she were always searching for something outside herself. After shedding all those awful clothes—along with the governor— she had quickly settled into a kind of relaxed contentment with herself. It was an air Dare one day hoped to acquire herself.

Mother took the basket of baked goods from Dare and started to lead the way up the gangway. "What did Mary pack in here? It's so heavy."

"I don't know. She said there was something for everyone."

Mother pulled back the linen covering the baked goods, exposing muffins (for the humans), birdseed cookies (for the mynarts), toasted walnuts (for Beastie), and, underneath it all, something hard and made of wood.

"I think that's for you." Mother broke out into a wide smile. She held the basket in two hands as Dare reached in to lift it out.

"Father's box." The words nearly choked her as she opened the cover, releasing a whiff of beard oil, salt, and pure love.

"It took Mary the last many days to get this back from the inspector's office. They'd been holding it and the contents as evidence. You'll still have to wait for the drawings until after the trials are over," Mother explained. "I believe the promise of a pair of tickets for him and his wife to the reopening of the Nesbitt Grand was the only thing that worked to get it back."

Dare laughed. Of course, bribery. Some things were never going to change in City-on-the-Pike. This gesture, as kind as it was, wasn't really going to earn Mary any more points, but it wouldn't cost her any, either.

Tupper rang the bell on the deck, his impatience clear from the quality of the clanging.

"Come on, love," Mother said. "We need to go."

"I want to wait, just five more minutes, please," Dare said. "If he hasn't left town already, he'll come. Please, he's always late."

Mother cast a look at Dare that teetered dangerously close to pity. "I think he's already left, Dare. You told me he said he was leaving."

"I know, but that wasn't a proper goodbye."

"Not everyone likes a goodbye. Your father despised them. He said knowing it's the last time you might ever see each other is too hard, that it's best to leave room in your thoughts for the possibility of someday again." Mother's attention drifted away, likely to the past, before Tupper rang that blasted bell again, snapping her back to the present.

"Not a minute more. Neither the marvels nor Tupper can take much longer. I know it's hard to leave, but we'll be back very soon." As Mother leaned in to kiss Dare on the forehead, Madam's locket caught her eye. "What's this?" She balanced the delicate locket in her hand.

"Madam gave it to me. I told her it was too special, that she shouldn't have. She wears it in every one of her paintings. I can't believe she'd part with it."

"I can. Your father meant the world to her, and you do as well," Mother said. "What's inside?"

"I don't know." With Beastie and her mother looking on, Dare pulled the locket up and unhinged the small clasp, leaving the locket to spring open. She'd long assumed Madam carried a picture of Bijou or perhaps a few strands of his fur close to her heart. Knowing Madam, it might also have been a picture of herself.

But never would Dare have thought it would be a photograph of Gil.

"How incredibly thoughtful." Mother sighed.

"You think so? It's a bit strange, isn't it? How . . . why would she give me this? When did she even have the photograph taken?"

Mother took the locket in hand to inspect it more closely. "I don't think there's anything strange about it at all. I assume she had the photograph made before he left."

"How was there time?" Dare pressed.

Tupper's relentless ringing of the bell drowned out Mother's reply.

"Tide ain't waiting on you, and neither am I!" Tupper shouted down from the deck.

"Yes, yes, we're coming!" Mother called back as she shut the locket and left it to dangle on the chain. "It's a wonderful picture of your father, Dare. Wear it well."

"My father?" Her hearing must have been worse than she thought. "This is Gil."

There was no doubt of that. There was that funny way his hair hung, and that scar on his chin.

"Yes, that's right. He couldn't have been much older than you when it was taken. He grew a beard as soon as he could to cover over that scar on his chin. I was never sure what happened. I think it had something to do with his early training on the island. But he said he preferred to leave it behind with his childhood, like his old nickname. I'm surprised he told you that he used to be called Gil, not Virgil." The bell clanged louder now. "I'm afraid Tupper might truly cast off without us, and that wouldn't do at all." Mother gathered her skirts and hurried up the gangway.

But Dare couldn't follow. She remained stuck, quite uncertain how, or what, to think as she stared at the photo.

Had she fallen into some trick world where blue was red, and left was up? She had to have misheard.

"No. Now *that's* an active imagination at work!" Dare laughed and tried to shake the thought away.

But it held fast.

Still, how was it even possible? She'd walked down the street with Gil, watched as people stepped out of his way on the sidewalk. . . .

No one can see me.

She'd never questioned how he knew the things he knew, or how he got around the rhinos, or freed Tupper when she couldn't. Why the lamps in the alley went out when they did. But it was what Nell had said that set her back on her heels.

If Gil does show up, tell him I want to finally meet him.

They'd been together, fleeing the supper club, looking for a way out.

Or had they?

Dare tried to reason with herself, find something close to an explanation. She couldn't.

And also, maybe she didn't want to.

Did it really matter what, or who, Gil was? She knew who he'd been to her. He'd been her friend, someone who believed in her, helped her, pushed her to do what she wasn't sure she could do.

Maybe whether he'd been real or some lingering part of her Father didn't matter nearly as much as the way she felt about him.

"Hey! Up here, real person talking to you," Tupper called down, his hands gripping the gangway, ready to pull it in. "You either board now, or you're gonna swim for it!"

It was one thing to not be sure what to think about Gil, but Dare would never doubt Tupper would leave her to swim.

She reluctantly boarded the *Slipper*, trying to convince herself that there was a perfectly good explanation, one that Gil would laugh at her for not thinking of herself.

That had to be it. Didn't it?

"About time," Tupper grumbled as he yanked the gangway in. "I'm going below to make sure your mother understands what it means to tie everything down better than you did. You can stay here till we get close to the winds."

Tupper stalked away muttering to himself about all he had to do—although there was no question that he was happier than he'd ever been.

As the ship slowly pulled away from the dock, Dare perched Beastie on her shoulder and looked out at the receding shoreline. The wharf was busy as usual, as was the city beyond it. By the next day, the newspapers and one-sheets would be screaming about a new scandal, a new tale for City-on-the-Pike to chew over. And the story of the monsters, and how they had come to be known forever more as marvels, would soon be nothing more than a cautionary tale.

As for Dare's own story, for now she'd have to live with the unknowable. There was every chance it would come to be told that Gil just happened to look exactly like her father.

Or perhaps her imagination really was . . .

Dare stopped and squinted at the dock.

Someone was standing there waving at her.

She'd been staring at the same spot the entire time and hadn't seen anyone walk up.

And yet there he was, cowlick and all, that divot on his chin turned into a dimple by a smile, his arm raised and waving like a flag in the breeze.

"Gil?" she shouted. "Gil!"

She waited for him to call back, to prove he was as real as she. Yet no sooner had his name escaped her lips than he began to fade, growing paler and thinner, until at last he was nothing more than a wisp of a memory.

Gone.

Nothing but air.

Nothing left of him but a story to carry on.

Acknowledgments

Monsters in the real world might not have claws or fangs, but they do exist. Some are beasts that appear out of the mist and disrupt our lives in ways we could never have imagined. Others are hiding in plain sight, draped in sickness, anger, or fear. And when they emerge, writing around, through, and past them can be incredibly hard. But marvels are also real, and they're far stronger and more powerful than the monsters could ever be.

To all the marvels who held me up and helped me as I wrote this book, I am eternally grateful.

Amalia, Emilia, and Sylas are the very best beta readers. You're not allowed to outgrow reading middle grade books, please and thank you.

I am a lucky one to have brilliant writer friends in Alyssa Colman, Heather Kassner, Kaela Noel, Rebecca Ansari, and

Sylvia Liu: thank you for listening to my endless thinking, occasional whining (maybe not occasional?), and most especially for wading through clunky drafts for me.

Kate Albus and Yvette Clarke did all that and more for me, and I thank the fates for bringing them into my life.

Maia Rossini is a fantastic friend and story guru, and is always my first reader. She's also my favorite lunch date.

To Ann, Fox, Kelly, Lesa, Nancy, Stephanie, and Virginia: thank you for your brilliance and wisdom. You can't know how much it means to me.

My traveling buddies in Authorcade are an endless source of inspiration and support, and they make this writing life so rich and fun.

The middle grade book community is the warmest, kindest, and most inspiring collection of people I know. Thank you to the teachers, librarians, booksellers, and readers who are out there every day battling the monsters trying to take stories away from us.

Thank you to Linda and Chris for countless dinners, for teaching me awful card games, and for weekends with the ever-divine Claire and her wonder dock.

Matt, I love you. You're one amazing monster fighter.

Kate, I'd never not thank you!

Thank you, Victoria Marini, for believing in my tales and for seeing that we land well. V has amazing taste and you all should go read her entire client list stat!

Infinite thanks and apologies to my copy editors, Ivy McFadden and Erin DeSalvatore, for whom I did not make it easy. And boundless gratitude to Delany Heisterkamp, Patty Rosati, Mimi Rankin, and Lauren Levite for helping to usher Dare's story out into the world.

There are no truer magicians than the artists who created the stunning cover for this book. I am in awe of illustrator George Eros, who channeled Dare and her world so beautifully. And designer Joel Tippie brought it all together with a magnificently delicious edge of creepy.

Erika DiPasquale is a champion not only for stories, but for all that's right. Thank you for your passion for this book and for tirelessly fighting the good fight!

It is a gift to work with the brilliant Megan Ilnitzki. She is a wise and deeply insightful word witch. She is also incredibly kind, which makes the work a great joy. Thank you for loving our Dare and steering her out into the world.

Writing might not be brain surgery, but brain surgery is. Infinite gratitude to the actual brain surgeons at Vassar and Columbia Presbyterian who work miracles every single day. And finally, to the truest of marvels: Dan, Owen, and Oona. Thank you, my loves, for all that you are and all that you inspire me to be.